# About the Author

Like the heroine of *Brown Girl, Brownstones,* Paule Marshall, whose parents emigrated from Barbados during World War I, grew up in Brooklyn during the Depression. After graduating Phi Beta Kappa from Brooklyn College in 1953, she worked as a magazine writer and researcher with assignments in Brazil and the West Indies. Much of *Brown Girl, Brownstones* was written on trips to Barbados in the late fifties. Two years after its publication, in 1961, Marshall dealt with the problems of aging in her collection of short stories, *Soul Clap Hands and Sing.* In 1969 she published her most ambitious novel, *The Chosen Place, The Timeless People,* the story of a black woman who wrestles with the corruption of history to find her place within the hemisphere, not just within the family. Marshall's forthcoming novel, *Praisesong for the Widow,* continues her obsession with the need for black people to make the psychological and spiritual journey back through their past.

MARY HELEN WASHINGTON, Associate Professor of English at the University of Massachusetts, Boston, is the editor of two collections of stories by black women, *Black-Eyed Susans* and *Midnight Birds.*

Other books by Paule Marshall

*The Chosen Place, The Timeless People*

*Soul Clap Hands and Sing*

# Brown Girl, Brownstones

## *Paule Marshall*

With an afterword by
Mary Helen Washington

THE FEMINIST PRESS
at The City University of New York
New York

**To My Mother**

First Feminist Press edition, fourteenth printing
This publication is made possible, in part, by public funds from the
 New York State Council on the Arts.
Manufactured in the United States of America
ISBN 0-912670-96-7

## Acknowledgments

The author is indebted to the following for permission to reprint
excerpts:

"Romance in the Dark," words and music by Lil Green. Copyright ©
MCMXL, MCMLVIII, by Duchess Music Corporation, 322 West 48th
Street, New York, N.Y. All rights reserved. Reprinted by permission.

"Small Island," words and music by S. C. Patterson. Copyright © 1957, by
Ludlow Music, Inc., New York, N.Y. Reprinted by permission.

"Pam Palam" and "Don't Stop the Carnival," lyrics by Cecil Anderson, Duke
of Iron, based on traditional themes. Used by permission.

Cover: Untitled painting by Ernest Crichlow

# Contents

# BOOK

## 1

*A Long Day and a Long Night*

# 1

In the somnolent July afternoon the unbroken line of brownstone houses down the long Brooklyn street resembled an army massed at attention. They were all one uniform red-brown stone. All with high massive stone stoops and black iron-grille fences staving off the sun. All draped in ivy as though mourning. Their somber façades, indifferent to the summer's heat and passion, faced a park while their backs reared dark against the sky. They were only three or four stories tall—squat—yet they gave the impression of formidable height.

Glancing down the interminable Brooklyn street you thought of those joined brownstones as one house reflected through a train of mirrors, with no walls between the houses but only vast rooms yawning endlessly one into the other. Yet, looking close, you saw that under the thick ivy each house had something distinctively its own. Some touch that was Gothic, Romanesque, baroque or Greek triumphed amid the Victorian clutter. Here, Ionic columns framed the windows while next door gargoyles scowled up at the sun. There, the cornices were hung with carved foliage while Gorgon heads decorated others. Many houses had bay windows or Gothic stonework; a few boasted turrets raised high above the other roofs. Yet they all shared the same brown monotony. All seemed doomed by the confusion in their design.

Behind those grim façades, in those high rooms, life soared and ebbed. Bodies crouched in the postures of love at night,

3

children burst from the womb's thick shell, and death, when it was time, shuffled through the halls. First, there had been the Dutch-English and Scotch-Irish who had built the houses. There had been tea in the afternoon then and skirts rustling across the parquet floors and mild voices. For a long time it had been only the whites, each generation unraveling in a quiet skein of years behind the green shades.

But now in 1939 the last of them were discreetly dying behind those shades or selling the houses and moving away. And as they left, the West Indians slowly edged their way in. Like a dark sea nudging its way onto a white beach and staining the sand, they came. The West Indians, especially the Barbadians who had never owned anything perhaps but a few poor acres in a poor land, loved the houses with the same fierce idolatry as they had the land on their obscure islands. But, with their coming, there was no longer tea in the afternoon, and their odd speech clashed in the hushed rooms, while underneath the ivy the old houses remained as indifferent to them as to the whites, as aloof . . .

Her house was alive to Selina. She sat this summer afternoon on the upper landing on the top floor, listening to its shallow breathing—a ten-year-old girl with scuffed legs and a body as straggly as the clothes she wore. A haze of sunlight seeping down from the skylight through the dust and dimness of the hall caught her wide full mouth, the small but strong nose, the eyes set deep in the darkness of her face. They were not the eyes of a child. Something too old lurked in their centers. They were weighted, it seemed, with scenes of a long life. She might have been old once and now, miraculously, young again—but with the memory of that other life intact. She seemed to know the world down there in the dark hall and beyond for what it was. Yet knowing, she still longed to leave this safe, sunlit place at the top of the house for the challenge there.

Suddenly the child, Selina, leaped boldly to the edge of the step, her lean body quivering. At the moment she hurled herself forward, her hand reached back to grasp the bannister, and the contradiction of her movement flung her back on the step. She huddled there, rubbing her injured elbow and hating her cowardice. Slowly she raised her arm, thin and dark in the sun-haze, circled by two heavy silver bangles which had come from "home" and which every Barbadian-American girl wore from birth. Glaring down, she shook her fist, and the bangles sounded her defiance with a thin clangor. When her arm dropped, the house, stunned by the noise, ceased breathing and a pure silence fell.

She smiled, for this was the silence she loved. It came when the old white servant upstairs slept amid her soiled sheets, when her father read and napped in the sun parlor, her sister slept in their basement bedroom and the new tenant Suggie was out. Above all, it was a silence which came when the mother was at work.

She rose, her arms lifted in welcome, and quickly the white family who had lived here before, whom the old woman upstairs always spoke of, glided with pale footfalls up the stairs. Their white hands trailed the bannister; their mild voices implored her to give them a little life. And as they crowded around, fusing with her, she was no longer a dark girl alone and dreaming at the top of an old house, but one of them, invested with their beauty and gentility. She threw her head back until it trembled proudly on the stalk of her neck and, holding up her imaginary gown, she swept downstairs to the parlor floor.

At the bottom step she paused in the entrance hall, which was a room in itself with its carpet, wallpaper and hushed dimness. Opening off the hall was the parlor, full of ponderous furniture and potted ferns which the whites had left, with an aged and inviolate silence. It was the museum of all the lives that had ever lived here. The floor-to-ceiling mirror retained their faces as the silence did their voices.

As Selina entered, the chandelier which held the sunlight frozen in its prisms rushed at her, and the mirror flung her back at herself. The mood was broken. The gown dropped from her limp hands. The illusory figures fled and she was only herself again. A truculent face and eyes too large and old, a flat body perched on legs that were too long. A torn middy blouse, dirty shorts, and socks that always worked down into the heel of her sneakers. That was all she was. She did not belong here. She was something vulgar in a holy place. The room was theirs, she knew, glancing up at the frieze of cherubs and angels on the ceiling; it belonged to the ghost shapes hovering in the shadows. But not to her. As she left, her shorts, bagging around her narrow behind, defined her sadness.

She made only a cursory tour of the master bedroom next door, opening the drawers to smell the lavender amid the seldom-used things, running a finger along the fluted edges of the high bed in which she had been born—the only piece of furniture they had brought with them. Whenever she was sick enough to have the doctor she slept there. Then the mother put on sheets that smelled of lavender and her father brought her up through the hall and laid her gently down. And it was always like falling out of herself into its soft depth . . .

Going downstairs to the basement she leaned against one of the high-back chairs ranged solemnly around the table in the dining room. Her eyes reflected the stained-glass wisteria lamp, the special crystal in the china closet and the family photograph, which did not include her, on the buffet. She wanted suddenly to send up a loud importunate cry to declare herself, to bring someone running. With the impulse strong in her she burst into the bedroom she shared with her sister.

Her sister, Ina, lay under the sheet, her body limp in sleep and her tight-clustered curls glistening. Watching her, Selina felt an inexplicable resentment. It flowed out from her, across the room, finally penetrating Ina's sleep. Ina opened her eyes, suddenly, apprehensively, awake.

"Whaddya want?" she cried. "Go away."

Selina bared her teeth and drew closer.

Ina scrambled up, gathering the sheet around her. "You heard what Mother said. You're not to bother me today. I'm sick," she cried from behind the sheet, shying away from Selina as though she embodied all that was rough and loud and undisciplined in the world.

Selina, remembering the mother's admonition, stopped, rubbed her sneaker on her leg and glared.

Ina was thin but soft, passing gracefully through adolescence, being spared its awkwardness. But she seemed somehow defenseless because of this—as though she would never really be fit for the roughness of life. Sensing this softness, Selina said, "You were sure ugly as a baby. Didja ever take a good look at yourself in that picture on the buffet? You were sure ugly."

The fear eased from Ina's face at the frailty of her attack. "Go away, pestilence, you're not to bother me when I have my pains." She was deeply involved with the changes taking place in her body and loved giving herself up to them, matching the summer heat with the blood-heat of her body. She had no patience with Selina and her boy's shape. Her voice stiffened with sarcasm now. "Look who's talking about somebody being ugly as a baby! You were ugly then, you're uglier now and you'll get worse. There!" And laughing, she rolled over and burrowed her face in the pillow.

Outrage clogged Selina's throat. She wanted to leap on Ina, pin her to the bed and then ground her fists and knees in that softness until the tears came and the whimpers and the apologies, until her own anger drained from her. But behind the blur of her tears she knew there was nothing she could do—for Ina was sick with some mysterious thing that made her unassailable.

Outside in the dining room she tried to swallow the impotence that was like hardened phlegm in her throat, and the room, like a dark, fragrant mother tried to soothe her. But she would not be comforted. She snatched up the family photograph from the buffet and stared at it bitterly in the scant light.

It was her father, mother, Ina and the brother she had never known. The picture of a neat, young family and she did not believe it. The small girl under the drooping bow did not re-

7

semble her sister. The young woman in the 1920's dress with a headband around her forehead could not be the mother. This mother had a shy beauty, there was a girlish expectancy in her smile. Then there was the baby on her lap, who stared out at Selina with round blank eyes. His hair capped his head like fur and his tiny fists held tightly onto nothing.

"He's like a girl with all that hair," she muttered contemptuously. He had been frail and dying with a bad heart while she had been stirring into life. She had lain curled in the mother's stomach, waiting for his dying to be complete, she knew, peering through the pores as the box containing his body was lowered into the ground. Then she had come, strong and well-made, to take his place. But they had taken no photographs . . .

Her father was the only one she believed in the picture. Despite the old-fashioned suit and the spats, it was her father. The angle at which he held the cane, his detached air, the teasing smile proclaimed him. For her, he was the one constant in the flux and unreality of life. The day was suddenly bright with the thought of him upstairs in the sun parlor, and slamming down the photograph she bounded from the room, taking the steps two at a time.

They were very proud of the sun parlor. Not many of the old brownstones had them. It was the one room in the house given over to the sun. Sunlight came spilling through the glass walls, swayed like a dancer in the air and lay in a yellow rug on the floor.

Her father was there, stretched dark and limp on a narrow cot like someone drunk with sun. He had lain there since the mother left, studying a correspondence course in accounting that he had just started, reading the newspapers and letters, listening to the radio. Selina sat on the floor facing him, waiting, watching his lids move as his eyes moved under them.

Deighton Boyce's face was like his eyelids—a closed blind over the man beneath. He was well-hidden behind the high slanted facial bones, flared nose and thin lips, within the lean taut body, and his dark skin, burnished to a high fine gloss, completed the mystery.

"How the lady-folks?" he called finally, his eyes reaching over the letter he was reading. They were a deeper brown than his skin with the sun in their centers.

His tone was the signal that they had stepped into an intimate circle and were joined together in the pause and beat of life. Selina scratched where the elastic of her sock made ridges in her flesh. "I couldn't go to the movies today because old Ina has her pains. I don't see why I can't go with my girl friend, but Mother says not without Ina."

"You got to heed yuh mother."

"I know, but I still don't understand why. Ina doesn't look after me."

"Yuh mother know best."

He returned to his letter and she closed her eyes. The sun on her lids created an orange void inside her and she wanted to remain like this always with the sun on her eyes and bound with her father in their circle.

"I don know what wunna New York children does find in a movie," he said after a time. "Sitting up in a dark place when the sun shining bright-bright outside."

"There's nothing else to do on Saturday."

"We had Sat'day home too and found plenty to do when we was boys coming up."

She opened her eyes and there was a halo of bluish orange around his head. She blinked. "I don't see what you could do that's better than the movies."

"How you mean? You think people din make sport before there was movie? Come Sat'day, when we was boys coming up, we would get piece of stick and a lime and a big stone and play cricket. If we had little change in we pocket we would pick up weself and go up Kensington Field to football . . ."

"What else?"

"How you mean? I's a person live in town and always had

9

plenty to do. I not like yuh mother and the 'mounts of these Bajan that come from down some gully or up some hill behind God back and ain use to nothing. 'Pon a Sat'day I would walk 'bout town like I was a full-full man. All up Broad Street and Swan Street like I did own the damn place."

"What else?"

"How you mean?"

"Didja play any games?"

"Game? How you mean? Tha's all we did. Rolling the roller and cork-sticking . . ."

"What's that?"

"But how many times I must tell you, nuh? It some rough-up something. Throwing a tennis ball hard-hard at each other and you had to move fast, if not it would stun you good . . ."

"What else?"

"Plenty else!" he cried, angered that she remained unimpressed. "We would pick up weself and go sea-bathing all down Christ Church where the rich white people live. Stay in the water all day shooting the waves, mahn, playing cricket on the sand, playing lick-cork . . ." Anticipating her, he lifted his hand. "Don ask, I gon tell you just-now. Lick-cork is just play-fighting in the sea after a cork."

He paused, lifting his head, and the sunlight lanced his eyes. "And when a tourist ship come into Carlisle Bay we would swim out to it and the rich white people from America would throw money in the water just to see we dive for it. Some them would throw a shilling and all. I tell you, those people had so much of money it did turn them foolish." He smiled, his teeth a dry white against his darkness, and abruptly returned to his letter.

Selina closed her eyes again and in the orange void tried to see him diving after the coins. But thoughts of the mother intruded. What had she and the others who lived down in the gullies and up on the hills behind God's back done on Saturdays? She could never think of the mother alone. It was always the mother and the others, for they were alike—those watchful, wrathful women whose eyes seared and searched and laid bare, whose tongues lashed the world in unremitting distrust. Each morning they took the train to Flatbush and Sheepshead Bay to scrub floors. The lucky ones had their steady madams while the others wandered those neat blocks or waited on corners—each with her apron and working shoes in a bag under her arm until someone offered her a day's work. Sometimes the white children on their way to school laughed at their blackness and shouted "nigger," but the Barbadian women sucked their teeth, dismissing them. Their only thought was of the "few raw-mout' pennies" at the end of the day which would eventually "buy house."

They returned home laden with throw-offs: the old clothes which the Jews had given them. Whenever the mother forced her to wear them, Selina spent the day hating the unknown child to whom they belonged. Anger flashed now within the orange depth and it was only her father's voice which restored her.

"Yes, lady-folks, we did make plenty sport when we was boys coming up . . ." he was saying, his eyes pierced with memories.

"What is it like—home?"

"What I must say, nuh? Barbados is poor-poor but sweet enough. That's why I going back."

"When?"

"Soon as I catch my hand here. You see this?" He held up the accounting manual. "This gon do it. I gon breeze through this course 'cause I was always good in figures. I ain even gon bother my head with all this preliminary work they sending now." He tossed aside the manual. "I gon wait till they send the real facts and study them. Then a job making decent money and we gone."

"Taking me?"

"How you mean! And we gon live in style, mahn. No little board and shingle house with a shed roof to cook in. We gon have the best now." He waved the letter he had been reading, then as quickly dropped it, turning suspiciously to the door. "Where yuh sister?"

11

"Downstairs, I think."

"You sure? 'Cause I thought I did hear somebody outside . . . You know how she does sneak 'bout listening to what we say and then lick she mouth to your mother."

"She's supposed to be sick and sleeping."

Reassured, he held up the letter again. "You see this? Don't broadcast it to the Sammy-cow-and-Duppy but my sister that just dead leave me piece of ground. Now how's that for news?" His teeth flashed in a strong smile. "Now let these bad-minded Bajan here talk my name 'cause I only leasing this house while they buying theirs. One thing I got good land home!"

For a moment she did not understand. From his smile and the way his eyes glowed she knew that it was important. She should have leaped up and pirouetted and joined his happiness. But a strange uneasiness kept her seated with her knees drawn tight against her chest. She asked cautiously, "You mean we're rich?"

"We ain rich but we got land."

"Is it a lot?"

"Two acres almost. I know the piece of ground good. You could throw down I-don-know-what on it and it would grow. And we gon have a house there—just like the white people own. A house to end all house!"

"Are you gonna tell Mother?"

His smile faltered and failed; his eyes closed in a kind of weariness. "How you mean! I got to tell she, nuh."

"Whaddya think she's gonna say?"

"How I could know? Years back I could tell but not any more." She turned away from the pain darkening his eyes.

"Ah come nuh!" he cried after a long pause. "What I frighten for? It my piece of ground, ain it? And I can do what I please with it. So come, lady-folks, let we celebrate with something from the candy store . . ."

"Hootons!"

He brought the coins from his pocket. "I tell you, this Hooton

12

is the one thing you children here have that I wish we did have when we was boys coming up."

She laughed and shoved the coins around in his palm until she found a nickel. With her hand still in his, she suddenly sat on the bed and, leaning close, whispered, "Look, I know you told me not to tell the Sammy-cow-and-Duppy about the land, but might I tell Beryl since she's my best friend? I'll make her swear and hope to die not to tell anyone . . ."

"Tell she," he said tenderly and closed his fist tight around her hand. "Your mother will know soon and then the world and it wife gon know." He freed her and swiftly she was gone, through the master bedroom, hurtling through the hall, her arms pumping, stopping only on the stoop to pull her socks out of the backs of her sneakers.

Chauncey Street languished in the afternoon heat, and across from it Fulton Park rose in a cool green wall. After the house, Selina loved the park. The thick trees, the grass—shrill-green in the sun—the statue of Robert Fulton and the pavilion where the lovers met and murmured at night formed, for her, the perfect boundary for her world; the park was the fitting buffer between Chauncey Street's gentility and Fulton Street's raucousness.

The sun was always loud on Fulton Street. It hung low and dead to the pavement, searing the trolley tracks and store windows, bearing down until the street spun helplessly in an eddy of cars, voices, neon signs and trolleys. Selina responded to the turbulence, rushing and leaping in a dark streak through the crowd. Passing the beauty parlor she saw the new tenant Suggie and turned in.

Suggie Skeete's full-fleshed legs and arms, her languorous pose, all the liquid roundness of her body under the sheer summer dress hinted that love, its rituals and its passion, was her domain. As Selina's shadow slanted across her she looked up, greeting her with a laugh murmurous as water. "Wha'lah, wha'-lah, Selina? But where you always running to with yuh head down like a goat when it ready to butt? Look the clothes in strings like you belong to some string band society. The eyes wild like a tearcat. The hair like it curse comb, damn oil and blast the hairdresser. Come, let Miss Thompson slap the hot comb in it."

"Not me, Miss Suggie. I'd never get my hair done in this heat."

"Well you best put a comb to it before your mother come and put that mouth of hers 'pon you."

"Selina?" A voice hurdled above the tangled voices and the angry clicking of the hot curling tongs inside the shop.

"Yes, Miss Thompson, it's me."

A tall drawn woman—a faded brown in color and no longer young—came from behind the partition, whirling a smoking curling tong in one thin hand and flicking perspiration from her face with the other. The soiled nurse's uniform fell straight down her fleshless body, hiding the bones jutting under the skin. Her long lean shadow cut into the sunlight and brought a sudden darkness into the waiting room. Amidst the noise, she and Selina shared a quiet tender smile.

"I'm on my way to the candy store," she said softly. "You want me to bring you a Pepsi?"

"No thanks, honey. Just had one. That damn Pepsi don't do nothing but fill me with gas anyways. What I needs . . ." She thought a moment, her sunken eyes with the circles of age and weariness under them turned toward the sun in the doorway. "What I needs is to be sitting out in the park with them cool breezes blowing over me. That's what I needs. One of them c-o-o-l breezes. Then I'd feel human instead of like some old mule. That's all I needs," she repeated, sighing and turning away, "and it don't cost nothing and don't gimme no gas . . ."

On her way back through the park, Selina heard her name rising in a strident chant behind. Turning, she saw the girls waving their bright movie handbills and recognized her best friend Beryl. She was suddenly jealous of the others for the hours

14

they had spent with her in the dark theater. She gave them a disinterested wave and hurried on.

"You missed the best Tarzan chapter today, Selina," one shouted. "Tarzan was captured and he . . ."

"I'm bored with Tarzan," she cried and wanted to shout that she would be leaving them soon to live in a big house in a sweet land and that they would miss her. She walked faster.

At the park gate Beryl caught up with her. "I knew you'd be mad. I was gonna come and ask your mother if you could go but I knew she'd of said no. And I knew you'd be mad."

Something in Beryl always soothed her and destroyed her anger. Perhaps it was the way Beryl's thick braids rested quietly on her shoulders or the way her tiny breasts nudged her middy blouse. They made Selina shy, those breasts, and ashamed of her own shapelessness. "I'm not mad."

"Yes you are. But I didn't have any fun today without you. And Tarzan *is* boring because he always escapes. Today he . . ."

As she talked Selina watched the shifting pattern of sun and shade on her face. She wished suddenly that her eyes could pierce Beryl's skin and roam inside her. What would Beryl be like inside? Like a small well-lighted room with the furniture neatly arranged around it.

"You're not listening."

"I was too. Look, I gotta give my father these Hootons. You want one?"

"No, it's too hot for chocolate. Can you come out later?"

"Maybe, if you come ask my mother. Oh, do come, I've got something to tell you." She grabbed her arm, remembering, and felt Beryl's warmth rush into her. "Something very, very special. Come later and ask," she shouted, running up the stoop.

She found her father asleep, seduced like her sister and the old woman upstairs by the siren call of the afternoon. He still held the letter, and she slipped it away and placed it on the pillow beside his face. Downstairs she put his share of the candy in the icebox, then went up to the parlor and sat in the window seat behind the curtains. She ate slowly, melting the chocolate between her hands and then carefully licking it up from each palm and finger. As it slipped warmly down, her mind filled with warm thoughts of the secret she would share with Beryl. When she finished she watched a train of ants move along the ledge and wondered whether to kill them and make it rain . . .

She had decided to kill them when she sensed the mother, and her hand paused mid-air. It was strange how Selina always sensed her. Even before she looked up and over to the park she knew that she would see the mother there striding home under the trees.

Silla Boyce brought the theme of winter into the park with her dark dress amid the summer green and the bright-figured house-dresses of the women lounging on the benches there. Not only that, every line of her strong-made body seemed to reprimand the women for their idleness and the park for its senseless summer display. Her lips, set in a permanent protest against life, implied that there was no time for gaiety. And the park, the women, the sun even gave way to her dark force; the flushed summer colors ran together and faded as she passed.

There was something else today in the angle of her head that added to Selina's uneasiness. It was as though the mother knew all that had transpired in the house since morning—her father's idleness, her quarrel with Ina, the news of the land—and was coming to chastise them all. Selina's eyes dropped to the mother's legs, and with drawn breath she sought the meaning in that purposeful stride. Suddenly in one swift pure movement she was in front of the mirror, struggling out of her shorts and tugging at her matted braids.

# 2

*"That concubine don know shame. Here it tis she just come to this man country and every time you look she got a different man ringing down the bell . . ."*

SILLA

As the late summer sunset flamed above the brownstones Suggie Skeete prepared her meal of cuckoo. In the solemn pose of a priest preparing the sacrament, she stood at the stove in the cramped kitchen, slowly pouring yellow corn meal into a pot of simmering okra and water. Then with a wooden spatula she blended the meal and okra water, adding more water as the meal thickened. Soon steam flew up in little puffs from the turning meal, and her stroke quickened until perspiration broke in bright nodes on her brow and the flesh under her arm shuddered. When the corn meal was done she lopped it into a bowl lined with butter and slapped the bowl between her hands until the cuckoo—smooth and glistening with butter, studded pink and green from the okra, with steam rising from its dome—resembled a small speckled sun. Over this she poured a thin gravy of flaked, salt codfish.

She ate sitting on the edge of the bed, and from the way she held the bowl in her palm and solemnly scooped up the food she might have been home in Barbados, eating in the doorway of the

17

small house perched like a forlorn bird on the hillside. She could see the yam patch from there and the mango tree with its long leaves weighted down by the dusk, and beyond, all down the soft-sloping hills, a susurrant sea of sugar cane. As she ate, lizards sidled under the dry leaves and her goat knocked its dainty legs against the paling. When she finished, something openly voluptuous crept into her pose. With a languorous gaze she watched the darkness race over the cane; her hands rested on the inside of her open thighs. Her pose was so natural that it was innocent. In those moments she became more than just a peasant girl on an obscure island but every woman who gives herself without guile and with a full free passion . . .

The empty bowl in her hand, she stared now at the harsh enamel blue walls of her crowded room—and there was no repose in her face or figure, only wistfulness. Sighing, she cleaned the dishes and dressed, then sat at a vanity table, her wide red skirt falling like red-glazed water from her hips. Dozens of perfume bottles covered the entire vanity—all shapes and sizes of bottles waited there, cool glass without, warm amber perfumes within. Their contents had never been sampled. Suggie's hands would flit reverently over them and occasionally she would pick one up, unscrew the top a little and pass it slowly under her nose, repeating this until her eyelids drooped and the earrings under her thick hair flashed with amber tints as her body swayed.

Every Saturday, her day off, she waited this way for a lover, knowing that she could not endure the next week without having someone tonight on the noisy bed. Tomorrow, early, she would return to the country, to the sleeping-in job and the insolence of white children, to the lonely room under the high roof . . .

The bell rang and she rose, the dress swishing around her knees as she crossed the room. In the hall, her perfumes joined the smell of the house, that aged odor of carpets and dust, and flowers pressed for years in a book. As she stepped onto the landing she almost stumbled over Selina.

"Hey-hey! Selina, why you always draw up in this hall frightening people?"

Selina, with fresh braids and in a dress with a matching hair ribbon, drew up her legs and leaned away from her, disturbed by the pagan theme of her red dress and glinting earrings.

"I'm waiting for Beryl to come ask my mother if I can go out."

"Well, I hope to God she come 'cause you's like some duppy out here. You know what people gon say when they see you always draw up in some dark place . . ."

"I don't care what they say."

". . . they gon say you love darkness 'cause your deeds is evil!"

Slowly Selina lifted her head, and when her eyes met Suggie's they were wide with knowing. Pointing downstairs she said, "I bet you and him be in the dark."

"C'dear, but look at my crosses!" Suggie's laugh rippled the air and she bent, brushing her lips across Selina's cheek. "You's a wicked something, in truth." Laughing, she continued downstairs and opened the thick door with its stained-glass panels. She greeted the man with a light laugh and led him up the stairs, past Selina, into the enameled blue room . . .

> *"But look at she! She's nothing but a living dead. She been down here since they said 'Come let us make woman.' She might of pass on and pass away and make room in the world for somebody else."*
>
> SILLA

As Suggie's door closed, the last remnant of the sunset faded and dusk, in a dark swollen cloud, moved across the sky. Yet, next door in Miss Mary's rooms, the light remained a tarnished dust-yellow. It was always like this. For time, in these rooms, and the seasons had long been crowded out by furniture piled under gray sheets and cracked paintings stacked on the floor, by boxes of old clothes and delft and the drawn green shades of the past.

In the midst of this dust and clutter Miss Mary's bed reared like a grim rock. She lay there, surrounded by her legacies, and holding firm to the thin rotted thread of her life. Her face was as yellowed with age as the air, her eyes smeared with the same stale light. She raised up, painfully trying to pull the sheet over her legs with their broken veins, over her sere body, and fell back, unsuccessful, and her hands, warped with arthritis, struck the air. After a time, her gaze traveled the room, lingering on each relic, and the old dream began. Today, out of the heaped memories, she selected the days of dying: the master lying in state in the parlor . . . the letter announcing her lover's death in the 1904 war even as his child swelled her stomach . . . her shame as she faced the mistress . . . the great war and the young master dying . . . the joyless years afterward and the mistress slowly wasting . . . and after her death the daughters fleeing the house as though they hated it, leaving behind the rooms of furniture downstairs, and leaving her behind with her daughter . . .

Suddenly her daughter, a woman now, entered, and her voice sounded high and querulous in the room. "I wish they'd keep that brat downstairs where she belongs. She's enough to scare you silly sitting out there on the landing."

The woman, Maritze, stood at the door, her dull eyes and slack body in keeping with the room. "You sleeping, Ma?"

The comforting past was gone and the old woman cried irritably, "And did you ever see anybody sleeping with their eyes open excepting they was dead? I was thinking, that's what, thinking of the times I could get about and look after meself and not have to depend on the likes of you."

Maritze did not respond. Indeed, there seemed to be nothing inside her to respond. She was drained, it seemed, of all emotion. "I went to mass after work," she said listlessly, unpinning her hat. "It's so cool in church."

"You and mass. Oh Blessed Mother, as if that was going to help her!" she said to a statue of the Virgin on the mantel, its head shrouded in dust and the arms extended in mute invitation.

"I'll fix something light as it's Saturday and so hot."

"Didja say it was Saturday now?" Miss Mary suddenly brightened. "I always cooked light on a Saturday too in the summer. For the mistress and the girls, that is. Not for the master though. Oh no! He'd say Mary . . ." Slowly her eyes clouded over as once again she dredged up the memories. Her voice trailed Maritze while she changed and began preparing dinner.

". . . after dinner they'd sit out under them pear trees in back watching the sun go down . . ." Her voice filled the kitchen, cracked and strangled and relentless. Gradually a little angry color slid under Maritze's pallor and her hands trembled as she turned on the faucet. There was a rusty cough and the water stopped as somewhere downstairs someone also turned on a faucet.

"Aye, there it goes again . . ." the old woman called gaily. "Turn it off till they finish. The master always said we needed new pipes. It's like only the other day he said . . ."

Suddenly Maritze opened the tap wider and the pipes protested with a loud and ominous vibration that shook the sink. Still she pressed, her body heaving strangely, her hair clinging in damp strands to her forehead, the blood beating visibly at her temples. As the noise rose, her mother pursued the past in an even louder voice and Maritze whispered savagely, bearing down on the tap, "I don't want to hear about those people . . . I don't want to hear . . ."

> *"But look at he. Tha's one man don know his own mind. He's always looking for something big and praying hard not to find it."*
>
> SILLA

Downstairs in the master bedroom, Deighton heard the rasping complaint of the pipes and muttered, "These old houses is more trouble than profit."

He was alone, dressing by the fragile light of a pink-shaded lamp on the dresser while the shadows loomed like silent on-lookers around him. His hands, very thin but strong and very dark, caressed a new silk undershirt which he had just taken from its wrapping. Deighton loved the feel of silk next to his skin, and he smiled now as he slipped on the new shirt and the silk passed in a cool caress over his face and neck.

Dressing for him was always a pleasurable ritual. Tonight, as usual, he carefully inspected the crease in his trousers, brushed his coarse hair till it lay flat, and puzzled over the many pairs of shoes in his closet before he chose a new pair of white and brown spectators. Occasionally he paused and cocked his head, smiling as though he heard an imperceptible song welling out of the shadows. He was through finally, and standing for that last moment in front of the mirror, he looked very young and irresponsible with his shirt opened at the neck and the triangle of dark flesh showing.

Outside, in the hall, the smell of Suggie's codfish hung in a dead weight, and he hurried downstairs, afraid that the smell would insinuate itself into his clothes and he would carry it with him all night as the undisputable sign that he was Barbadian and a foreigner. In the basement he paused uneasily at the kitchen door, shaken as always by the stark light there, the antiseptic white furniture and enameled white walls. The room seemed a strange unfeeling world which continually challenged him to deal with it, to impose himself somehow on its whiteness.

His wife stood easily amid the whiteness, at the sink, in the relaxed, unself-conscious pose of someone alone. He glimpsed her face in the mirror above the sink: the resolute mouth, the broad nose, the bold yet well-molded contours of the bones under her deeply browned skin—and wished that there was not this angularity about her. Then he thought of how cool her skin would be despite the heat and his fingers suddenly ached for that touch. He thought of the narrow void between her legs which was still like a young girl's even after the three children, and desire quickly surged in him. Perhaps, tonight, with the heat and the thick night it would be right again. He would open the door between their bedroom and the sun parlor so that they could see the sky with its low stars from the bed. He might find the words tonight to bring trust again to her eyes; his hands might arouse that full and awesome passion they once had . . .

"I tell yuh, that girl got the house stink down with codfish," he said.

He saw her now as she was whenever he was near, with her clenched back and wary eyes warding him off. Yet, when she answered her voice was friendly. "Like codfish does smell that sweet! She got to let the world and it wife know she ain long off the boat. Some these Bajan does come to this man country and get on worse than they did home. And now the so-called boy friend just gone up and the bed gon be sounding bruggadung-bruggadung all night through the whole house."

He drew nearer, laughing. "Remember that indifferent woman next door years back in South Brooklyn who ate codfish for breakfast, lunch and supper?"

Her laughter joined his as she flung her head back in a lovely free gesture. "And had 'nough money up in a bank. That's a Bajan for you."

Feeling this softness in her tonight he wanted to tell her of the land. He hesitated and his indecision charged the room. She turned, questioning, and saw the shirt opened casually at his throat, the dapper spectator shoes—and as her eyes slowly traveled up to his face again they revealed a tangle of emotions. A helpless admiration. A burst of passion stronger than his even. A possessiveness that reached out to claim him despite all. But at the same time her resentment shaded all this from him, and he saw only her eyes hardening and her face shutting like a door slammed on him.

He buttoned the shirt to the top. "I thought I'd catch little air on the avenue," and the words sounded lame and incriminating in the room's hostile whiteness. He breathed deep, "Silla . . ." and her name rushed out with his exhaled breath. This time her reply was to plunge her hand into the chicken she was cleaning and with one savage wrench lay the viscid clay-yellow entrails into the sink.

"Silla . . . where Selina?"

"Out playing with Beryl Challenor," she flung at him irritably.

"I might of think that when Ina's sick you could let her go to the movies with Beryl."

"Not two foot without Ina. Who know what to happen to she out there and she like a tearcat. You does think she's a boy" —she turned accusingly—"always filling her head with foolishness and her guts with Hooton. You like you does forget the boy dead and she ain he."

"Oh Christ-Jesus, woman, why reef up that?" He flung up his hand and turned from the room.

"Wait!" Her voice impaled him. "You put aside anything this week toward the down payment on the house?"

"Not penny one!" he cried and wanted to wind his arms tight around his head to shut out her voice, wanted suddenly to strike her into silence.

Silla's wrath broke and she whirled from the sink, her voice flailing across the kitchen. "You mean it all gone on fancy silk shirt and shoes and caterwauling with your concubine."

He shrugged at the old accusation. "You's God; you must know."

Suddenly her anger was tempered by bewilderment. "But be-Jesus-Christ, what kind of man is you, nuh?" She jerked her head away and seemed to address someone else in the room, "But what kind of man he is, nuh? Here every Bajan is saving if it's only a dollar a week and buying house and he wun save a penny. He ain got nothing and ain looking to get nothing . . ."

"How you mean I ain got nothing," he flared, "I got plenty. I ain like wunna Bajan that come here hungry from down some gully or up some hill behind God back and desperate now . . . I got plenty!"

"You ain got a pot to piss in."

"I got land."

"Land?"

"Land."

"What you talking 'bout?"

"Piece of ground home."

"You lie."

"I hear today self. Piece of ground muh sister that dead left me."

"You lie."

"I lie then." He turned to leave.

"Wait, nuh. Land, in truth?" she whispered.

"The letter in my pocket." And in the awed silence he slowly took it out and ceremoniously spread it on the table. "Come," he beckoned her, smiling. "Come look Silla-gal, since you's such a doubting Thomas."

She drew near, treading cautiously, chicken feathers clenched in her hand. She did not come up to the table but leaned in and read it from a distance.

As she read Deighton expounded, "Yes, a good piece of ground that you can throw down I-don-know-what and it would grow . . ."

"How much ground?" She lifted incredulous eyes to him.

"Two acres almost. A lot in a place that's only 166 square miles—and a lot for a colored man to own in a place where the white man own everything."

"What it worth?"

"What I care—I ain selling. Eight hundred, I guess."

"Eight hundred . . . ?" Her voice was a choked whisper, her mouth parted in bewilderment. "It can't be true. Eight hundred . . ."

"Land, Silla-gal, not money, and mine to do what I please with," he shouted and rapped his chest.

Still she remained dazed and disbelieving. "It can't be true. This is all some forge up something."

"All right, I lying then," he cried, suddenly angry, and

snatched up the letter, shouting over his shoulder as he left her stunned and open-mouthed in the glaring white kitchen, "You's God; you must know."

After he had slammed the heavy iron-grille door he stood there, breathing angrily, his elation gone, his triumph undermined. She had ruined it all with her doubting. For what was the land, what did it mean if she did not believe him? He wanted to return and, gripping her arm, force her to read it until she believed . . .

Then, as though to mock him further, he heard Ina and her friends laughing from the stoop above, and he turned, peering through the stone balusters. "Miss Ina, what you getting on so foolish for?" he cried.

The laughter ceased and Ina started. Quickly she drew apart from the other girls and smoothed her dress down over her knees. She said nothing but hurt filmed her eyes.

He looked off, ashamed, disturbed too by something he always sensed in his daughter but could not define. She had been conceived in love, coming swiftly in the first year of their marriage, and she seemed to reflect the love they had lost. It had endowed her with a graceful body and quiet eyes and a mild manner. She was lovely as it had been lovely, and fragile as it had been found to be fragile. And there was something else in her that puzzled him. In those eyes that were so quick to widen with hurt, in the submissive drop of her head he could trace his mother. She had passed on that look through him to Ina to remind him of what he had done to her. How often had he stood before her, the Singer sewing machine between them and the golden word "Singer" gleaming in the small dark house, and seen that same wide hurt in her eyes, seen her head bow in that same quiet willingness to suffer. Peering at Ina through the stone balusters he remembered his mother and guilt almost choked him, then Silla and love lost over the years and regret dried his mouth.

"Come, Miss Ina, here's some change for candy. And vuh best

get off the cold stone before it give you more cold," he said tenderly.

"It's summer and the stone isn't cold," she said, taking a nickel. "Besides, I wasn't sick with a cold."

She did not laugh but the others did, and the girlish laughter rose like a shrill coda in the dusk, driving him toward Fulton Street . . .

> *"Poor Thompson. Somebody mussa put she so that she does break down work to support somebody else's wild-dog puppies, instead of taking care of that life-sore 'pon she foot."*
>
> SILLA

Through the smoke-blurred windows of the beauty shop, Miss Thompson glimpsed him passing and noted, "There goes Selina's daddy," and remembered Selina standing in the doorway that afternoon with the sun skimming her uncombed hair. Her last customer was gone and she sat on a high stool in her booth, painting her nails an almost fulgent red and watching the street above the low partition, her hollowed face serene beneath her graying hair, her sere, elongated body poised solemnly on the stool like an ancient wood statue. Around her the talk and laughter spiraled up with the smoke, water gushed in the basins, the electric driers rasped loud—and these sounds along with the smell of singed hair set the rhythm and tone of the shop. Finished, Miss Thompson blew dry her nails, admiring them coquettishly. She eased down from the stool, and as she put her frail weight on her legs, the left one buckled and she crashed against the table.

"Who you fighting in there, Miss Thompson?" someone called.

"Ain't no fight, honey," she said, her pale brown skin suddenly gray with pain. "Just this old foot. I gotta go see about this old foot soon . . ." She fussed as she walked, dragging the foot slightly, through the tumult and smoke to the bathroom.

It was no more than a closet, and ducking down, Miss Thompson squeezed her lean frame between the basin and toilet and sat on the covered bowl, propping her long left leg against the door. Very carefully she eased off her stocking and then the bandage. There was an ugly unhealed ulcer, yawning like a small crater on the instep of her foot, with a hard crust, pale center and slightly fetid odor. She sighed as she dressed it. This done, she leaned back and, for the first time in the twenty-four hours since she had been up, permitted herself to feel tired. Fatigue suddenly hummed in her ears and seeped like a narcotic through her blood.

Her work day had begun at nine o'clock last night in the office building where she worked as a cleaning woman. At dawn she had eaten in an all-night diner, dozing over her coffee; then, as the morning cleared, she had come to the beauty parlor. Time, there, was measured by the customers filing in and out the booth who, shielded in its semi-privacy, confessed their troubles. Miss Thompson's gaunt face would become almost distorted with compassion as they spoke; she murmured always: "It's the truth, honey . . . ," "You telling me . . . ," and all the while her deft hands wielded the smoking comb, transforming their coarse hair into shiny-black limpness. Time was the fried-fish sandwiches and Pepsi-Colas throughout the day, the number runner sauntering in:

"What's good today, Long John?"

"Everything's good, Miss Thompson," and the white salesmen with their battered suitcases and wet eyes who always paused as they entered, momentarily overcome by the smoke and noise and gleaming dark faces. Every Saturday Miss Thompson bought something for the three small girls of the woman with whom she had roomed for years, her dull eyes becoming luminous as she chose the skirt or dress.

Now that the day was almost over it seemed unreal—as though not she but someone with more endurance had lived it. Only her total tiredness convinced her. Slowly she struggled up and changed from the soiled uniform into a dark shapeless dress that fell to her ankles.

"Going home already, Miss Thompson?" one of the beauticians called as she passed.

"Yes indeed, honey," she nodded absently, "I done worked round the clock, did more work in twenty-four hours than these good-timing niggers out here on Fulton Street done for the year, and I'm headed for my bed . . ."

> *"Of all things upon the earth that bleed and grow, a herb most bruised is woman."*

As Miss Thompson trudged down Fulton Street looking, in her severe black dress, like one of the saved sisters who gathered in the store-front churches each night sobbing and shouting for Jesus, Silla sat in the grave house beyond the park, her stunned eyes encountering nothing, her hands still clutching the chicken feathers.

"But look how trouble does come," she whispered, straining forward as though addressing some specter-shape. "Look how it does come . . . What is it," she demanded with sudden fierceness, "that does give what little luck there is to fools . . . ? Not a soul ever give me nothing a-tall, a-tall. I always had to make my own luck. And look at he! Somebody dead so and he got ground so. Got land now!" She broke off and slowly lapsed into a dull bewilderment. Her entire body gave way to it so that she seemed either drunk or drugged or so tired that she had fallen into a sodden sleep. After a long time, the chicken feathers slowly wafted from her limp hand, and the silence when they settled was like the kitchen, sterile and rigid and splintered with white light.

She remained like this until a voice blustered through the hall and a round, almost white face emerged from the darkness there like a moon from behind a rack of dark clouds. Virgie Farnum entered the kitchen, bearing her swollen stomach with a slightly startled expression—as though it was an enormous ball which someone had shoved in her hands and left her holding.

"Silla-gal, you still cleaning chicken and night near falling?" her voice boomed in the quietness. "How?"

"I here, soul," Silla said listlessly. "Sitting and thinking hard-hard." She surveyed Virgie with amusement and concern, "But how, Virgie?"

"Suffering."

"No doubt. You like you gon bring the child before the night out. But look at you," she said with tender disapproval. "You's a disgrace to come tumbling big so soon after the last one."

"C'dear, what I must do? It's the Lord will."

"What Lord will?" Silla sucked her teeth in disgust. "Woman, you might go hide yourself. These ain ancient days. This ain home that you got to be always breeding like a sow. Go to some doctor and get something 'cause these Bajan men will wear you out making children and the blasted children ain nothing but a keepback. You don see the white people having no lot."

"I know, soul." Virgie's pale skin flushed. "And this one's the worse. The little demon does get on inside me like it got nettle."

"It's a girl-child. They does do so. Both these I got did kick like horses inside me. But the boy, God rest him in his grave, did lay easy-easy inside me. Y'know," she said wistfully, her hand groping for Virgie's as the memory of him softened her face, "he was a child who look like he never knew a sick day. But the heart wasn't good." Her hand trailed from Virgie's. "The heart wasn't good."

"I know, soul. A boy-child is a hard thing to raise."

"And then the wuthless father had to take him out in a piece of old car and shake up his insides so it near kill him . . ."

"Silla, hush. It don do no good to reef up."

"Reef up? Virgie, I has never forgot," she said solemnly. Virgie's gray eyes flitted uneasily over Silla's numb face. A pain struck and she clutched her stomach, the blood draining from her thin lips and the broad nose spread across her face as the one sign of her scant Negro blood. "Oh there it go, the little whelp lan'ing me hell inside and gon land me more outside."

There was no response from Silla, but although her eyes remained abstracted she took up a newspaper from the table and carefully fashioned two fans and handed one to Virgie. Slowly the blood filtered back to Virgie's skin as she fanned. She tucked the dress under her stomach and called loudly, "Where he is?"

"Who?" Silla lifted remote eyes.

"The beautiful-ugly Deighton. Upstairs?"

"Upstairs, what! You know every Sat'day he does run bird-speed to the concubine to lick out what's left from his pay."

"But Deighton oughta stop." Virgie roared her disapproval. "Nobody din say he can't have the hot-ass woman but, c'dear, his own got to come first."

"Ah Virgie, you does talk sense. Who in the bloody hell care how many women he got. Those women ain got nothing but a man using them. But his own got to come first." And then remembering the land, she added bitterly, "Yes, they gon be spree-ing tonight over the land."

"Wha'? Wha' land?" Virgie's body slumped over her huge stomach, straightened with interest. "Wha' land?"

"He got piece of ground home, soul."

"Deighton? Who give he?"

"The schoolteacher sister that dead left him."

"How much ground?"

"Near two acres. A good piece of ground, he say."

"But hey-hey!" Amazement struck Virgie's broad features. "That Deighton is a lucky something, nuh?"

"In truth." The same amazement scored Silla's voice. "That's what I was thinking when you came. How there don seem to be no plan a-tall, a-tall to this life. How things just happen and don happen for no good reason. I tell you, it's like God is sleeping."

"What he gon do with it?"

"Soul, I don know."

"You don know?" Virgie struggled up, incredulous, the blood surging to her face. "You don know . . . Don be a blasted idiot woman," she roared. "Make him sell it!"

"He already say he not selling."

"Don mind he!" She dismissed him with a violent gesture. "Make him! The money would be the down payment on this house."

"How I could make him?" Silla cried despairingly. "For years now I been trying to put little ambition in that man but he ain interested in making a head-way. He's always half-studying some foolishness that don pan out. Years back it was the car. He was gon be all this mechanic till he lose interest. Then it was radio repairing and radio guts spill all over the house and he still cun fix one. Now he start up with figures . . . I tell you I getting so I can't bear the sight of him. I does get a bad feel when he come muching me up 'pon a night. Virgie," she whispered, her eyes narrowing menacingly, "I feel I could do cruel things to the man."

Her words hung solid and foreboding in the air and for a moment they both paused, uneasy, and then Virgie said softly, "No soul, it don does make good living like that. But you can't tell me nothing 'bout Deighton Boyce. Don forget I raise near that man. My mother and his was like so!" She held up two fingers twisted around each other. "And he used to land it to the mother even worse. And Ianthe Boyce was a refine somebody. A seam-stress, if you please. Never a curse word cross that woman mouth. But she was foolish 'cause she did think the sun rise and set 'pon Deighton one, 'cause he was the last and the only boy. That woman raise him and the two girls without a father—'cause the father did run off to Cuba the week before Deighton born. That boy had some of everything coming up. Always with shoe 'pon his foot and white shirt. Ianthe spend money she din have send-ing him to big Harrison College so he could be a schoolmaster like the two sisters. She used to say that if she had the money she would send him to England-self to be some big doctor and thing . . ." Her voice soared, staining the kitchen with its violent color; her fan rattled the air, and each time the child kicked her skin blanched.

"And what she get for it? I know he land she in she grave with the lot of worry and aggravation. She cun do nothing with him. If he din had every hot-ass girl 'bout the place he din have one. He was always putting himself up in the face of the big white people in town asking for some big job—and they would chuck him out fast enough. He was always dressing up like white people. Then after the mother die he pick up and went to Cuba—just like the fatha before him—and then jump ship into this country. And now he got land." The fan fell silent at this and she gazed across at Silla, awed again. "But Silla, what you gon do?"

"I don know, soul. I don know. But mark muh words, I ain gon rest good till I do something."

They were silent after this, but her words remained, tumescent and threatening, between them.

3

*"In the dark, it's just you and me,*
*Not a sound, there's not one sigh;*
*Just the beat of my poor heart*
*In the dark . . ."*
ROMANCE IN THE DARK—A BLUES

The summer night, starless and without a moon, was a dark cloak flung wide over Chauncey Street. Under its weight the trees met overhead to form an endless echoing arcade, and the tall lamps hidden in the leaves cast a restless design of light on the sidewalk. Under the enveloping night the brownstones reared like a fortress wall guarding a city, and the lighted windows were like flares set into its side.

Behind one of those lighted windows Suggie and the man sat drinking rum and talking. "C'dear, there's nothing like good Bajan rum," she said, filling their glasses again.

"How yuh mean!" the man said, and they drank, tilting their heads and throwing the rum over their tongues in a deft motion. As it seared their throats and coiled hot in their stomachs, they fell silent. The man, dull-black and stocky with slow gestures and a hesitant look that declared he had not long come from "home," thoughtfully turned the glass in his strong stiff hands and finally said, his eyes abstracted, "I wus just thinking how different drinking here is to home. Here people does mostly take a drink 'pon an evening. But home anytime is a good time to fire one. Drinking while the sun hot-hot now!" He glanced up, smiling. "I tell yuh, sometime yuh wun know whether it was the sun or the rum or both that had yuh feeling so sweet."

She smiled, understanding. Her eyes wistfully sought the bottle of rum on the low table between them, seeing in it a cane field at night with the canes rising and plunging in the wind, hearing again the ecstatic moan of the lover inside her. Suddenly her eyes held the man's in a look which confessed that they had passed beyond the talk and drinking, that it was night now and her body was warm and impatient under the red dress . . .

They met in the narrow space between their chairs and Suggie lifted her face for his kiss with the trust of a child. They kissed deeply for a long time, searchingly, as though sounding the depth of passion in each other. Then, their mouths together still, the man carefully undid her buttons and the dress slid to a red pool at her feet. With her help, he removed the other things and his work-roughed hands closed over her breasts and wandered in a slow controlled caress over her hips and thighs. She

34

moaned then and with a fierce shake of her head tore her mouth away and stepped out of the circle of clothes. They strolled across the room, their arms joined and leaning together like new lovers. As they passed under the dangling light, Suggie momentarily scanned the garish walls and sagging bed, the high black wall of night outside the window. Imperceptibly she shuddered; remorse flitted across her face and she quickly pulled the light cord.

She lay on the bed, listening to the soft sounds of his clothes dropping to the floor as he undressed in the dark. Then he was groping for her. She found his hand and pressed it hard on her breasts. A tremor passed from his hand into her and like a flare bursting in the dark room their full passion broke. With a joyous cry Suggie pulled him down between her insistent thighs, striking him gently with her fists, begging him for those first measured thrusts which would nullify the long week of general housework and the lonely room in a stranger's house.

"Hear them? Hear the bed? They're at it again." Maritze almost screamed, her quivering finger pointed at Suggie's wall. Her slack body stiffened with rage, her skin bled white. She had reached the crest of her anger by now, goaded on all during the meal, all during the evening's slow descent into night by her mother's unceasing recountal of the past.

"Every Saturday night it's the same. But what do you care?" She whirled accusingly to her mother. "You lay there all day thinking nothing's changed. Talking about those dead people as if they ever cared about you. They'd never have left you at the mercy of that black foreign scum downstairs or that evil woman in front if they had . . ."

All during her shrill outburst, Miss Mary had lain unperturbed on the high bed. Now she regarded her daughter with wizened contempt as Maritze's voice dropped to a despairing whine. "Every decent white person's moving away, getting out. Except us. And they're so many nice places where we could live. I . . ·

I saw one in the paper the other day . . ." Hope tinged her eyes suddenly and she hurried to her room, returning with her pocketbook, and nervously drew out a newspaper clipping. "It . . . it says they're building inexpensive houses on Long Island. Nice little houses . . ." With a pleading look she held the clipping close to her mother's face.

The old woman's gaze was elsewhere. Pointing to a canary huddled in its cage like another relic of the past, she said fretfully, "That canary doesn't even sing. It's not like the ones we had years ago . . . They sang the whole living day . . ."

Maritze's eyes were almost demented now, her hand twitched. "It says anybody can afford one. I could get a loan and with what I have saved . . ."

Miss Mary's high cackle suddenly swept aside her voice. "A nice little house on Long Island, is it now?" And as quickly the laugh died, her eyes hardened, "Be-Jees, you just try moving me from this house. You just try! Always bothering my old head with wild talk of moving . . ." Again her mood changed and her eyes gleamed maliciously. "Girls your age should be thinking of a young man, that's what—thinking of a ring and a fine wedding and a picture of yourself in a white gown with a young man beside you . . ." Her derisive laugh shook the motionless dust. "When you're past thirty that's all you should be thinking of . . ."

The frail hope died in Maritze's eyes and she was a wan and broken thing again, as empty of life as the room with its dust-yellow fog. Slowly she folded the clipping and put it back in her pocketbook with the rosary and the book of prayers she read on the subway going to work. Slowly she raised her head. "Think of it? Think of it?" she whispered, choked. "And did you think of it when you had me? Do you have a picture of *him* and you in your fine wedding gown? Weren't you just like them in there . . . sneaking in the dark . . . dirty . . ." she screamed and then caught herself, the scream tapering into a whimper. "Oh forgive me, forgive me, Blessed Virgin . . . forgive me . . ." she repeated in a penitent obligato to her mother's cracked laughter.

36

Unlike Chauncey Street, Fulton Street this summer Saturday night was a whirling spectrum of neon signs, movie marquees, bright-lit store windows and sweeping yellow streamers of light from the cars. It was canorous voices, hooted laughter and curses ripping the night's warm cloak; a welter of dark faces and gold-etched teeth; children crying high among the fire escapes of the tenements; the subway rumbling below; the unrelenting wail of a blues spilling from a bar; greasy counters and fish sandwiches and barbecue and hot sauce; trays of chitterlings and hog maws and fat back in the meat stores; the trolleys' insistent clangor; a man and woman in a hallway bedroom, sleeping like children now that the wildness had passed; a drunken woman pitching along the street; the sustained shriek of a police car and its red light stabbing nervously at faces and windows. Fulton Street on Saturday night was all beauty and desperation and sadness.

Deighton walked slowly, loving it. The thought of his frustrating talk with Silla, the memories evoked by Ina's silent hurt sloughed off like so much dead tissue, and another self emerged —one that was carefree and uncaring, that loved the tumult and glitter around him. He opened his collar again so that the triangle of flesh showed and a bit of the new silk undershirt. With a light step, he sauntered past the stores, beauty shops and theaters, past the ubiquitous dim-lit bars with the little islands of men standing outside as though waiting to enter and drink when those inside were finished. They grappled and boxed in rough playfulness, knocking off each other's broad-brimmed hats, cursing tenderly, "Dirty bastard . . . sonovabitch . . ." Laughter boomed from deep in their chests, blending with the noise of the street.

Occasionally Deighton paused and watched them at a distance, jarred always by the violence in their coarse play, yet strangely envious and respectful. For somehow, even though they were sporting like boys, there was no question that they were truly men; they could so easily prove it by flashing a knife or smashing out with their fists or tumbling one of the whores in the bar onto a bed. But what of those, then, to whom these proofs of manhood were alien? Who must find other, more sanctioned, ways? It was harder, that was all . . . None of this ever crystallized for Deighton as he stood watching them, and he would turn away thinking only that they were somehow more fortunate.

As he passed a store marked "Yearwood's Women's Apparel," a spare dry man with swift eyes darted out from its dim interior and hailed him. "Boyce, what the hurry?" Seifert Yearwood's voice flicked out like a lasso, snaring him. "What you know good?"

"Nothing much, mahn, just taking little air." Deighton paused, uncomfortable suddenly. "No business tonight, Yearwood?"

Seifert Yearwood shrugged his narrow shoulders. "It does ease off come this time. They gone now to lick out their money in the bars and whiskey stores. I tell you, these people from down South does work for the Jew all week and give the money right back to he on Sat'day night like it does burn their hand to keep it."

"Wha'lah, Yearwood, you like you faulting the Jew. You ain no better."

"Who say I faulting the Jew? I lift my hat to him. He know how to make a dollar. He own all New York! Talking 'bout owning, you start buying the house yet?"

Deighton looked longingly down the street. "Not yet."

"But, Boyce, what you waiting for? You might not get the chance again to own such a swell house—with all those good furnitures the white people left. Remember," he began, his restive eyes stilled for a moment, "when we first came here in 1920 we was all living in those cold-water dumps in South Brooklyn with the cockroaches lifting us up?" He gave a high wheezing laugh but his eyes burned with outrage. "The white people thought they was gon keep us there but they din know what a Bajan does give. We here now and when they run we

38

gon be right behind them. That's why, mahn, you got to start buying. Go to the loan shark if you ain got the money."

"Yearwood, what the rush?" Deighton laughed, for his land was a high wall against Seifert's rebuke. "I don owe tiger nothing that I got to break loose my inside buying these old houses."

Seifert Yearwood stared unbelievingly at him and asked quietly, "How else a man your color gon get ahead?"

"You got to get training and get out here with them!" Deighton said, but somehow his voice was too loud, too strained. "Like I starting up this course in accounting. When I finish I can qualify for a job making good money."

Seifert Yearwood fixed him with a look of tragic concern and shook his arm as if to rouse him. "Boyce, mahn," he began softly, "you can know all the accounting there is, these people still not gon have you up in their fancy office and pulling down the same money as them . . ."

Seifert's hand might have penetrated Deighton's shirt to rest hot and offensive on his flesh, for acute physical distaste gripped him. That touch recalled things thrust deep into forgottenness: those white English faces mottled red by the sun in the big stores in Bridgetown and himself as a young man, facing them in his first pair of long pants and his coarse hair brushed flat, asking them for a job as a clerk—the incredulity, the disdain and indignation that flushed their faces as they said no . . . He broke from Seifert Yearwood's hold and before Seifert could recover he was hurrying away, calling back, "I gone."

He almost ran now, desperation in each step, his eyes blind to everything. Turning off Fulton Street he walked southeast, into mean streets of tenement houses with fire escapes scrawled across their ravaged fronts. He entered one, unlocked the front door and climbed through the dimness and smell of stale urine and garbage to the top floor. The room he entered was cluttered but comfortable. An old-fashioned Victrola stood in one corner with a record on the turntable, but the machine needed winding so that the sound was indistinguishable. Quickly Deighton went and gently turned the handle until the song took shape. Then he knelt and pressed his ear against the speaker.

"Is that you, baby?" a woman called and entered. She was as careless and comfortable as the room, with tan skin and thick features and big gold cartwheel earrings that swung dangerously each time she moved. "How come you so late?" When he did not answer she came and stood over him. "Aincha even got no hello for me tonight?"

He did not look up or answer. The woman said, "I thought you'd go for that record. I know you like your music sweet like your women. Huh, baby?" She laughed and lifted his face between her ringed hands. "Honey, you looks beat," she said quietly. "C'mon, what you need is a drink."

When she returned with the whiskey he drank it with closed eyes. Then, still kneeling, he reached up. His fingers spread over her breasts, tearing at their softness, and slowly slid down her body. With a deep moan he flung his arms around her hips, kneading her buttocks, burrowing his face into the warm oblivion of her stomach.

Three blocks away in a similar tenement apartment Miss Thompson stood laughing in the kitchen as three small girls, their bodies sweaty from play and dried tears on their dark faces, rushed her. "Big Momma. Big Momma," they squealed, hooking their knees into her bones, their small hands caressing her. "Big Momma, what you brought?"

"Hush it. I ain't been gone a year," she said, straining them close and examining their soiled and sleepy faces. "Where's your momma?"

They hung back, not answering, then reached for her again.

She held them off. "Ain't nobody talking, ain't nobody hugging. Ain't no presents sharing either."

"She's gone out, since yesterday," one said timidly.

"Since yesterday! Where?"

"She din say where."

Suddenly her anger burst. "Gone good-timing with the rest of them loud, good-timing fools out there on Fulton Street, that's where. Gone to sit up in some low-down bar like some damn bar-fly. Gone screwing. . . . I know it ain't none of my business but it ain't right. If she keeps on doin like she's doin I'm gonna get me a room someplace else. I'm gonna move . . ." The familiar complaints, her rage soared unbounded, until after a time they seemed to encompass not only the woman but the accumulated abuse of her long day, the pain that occasionally blazed up from her foot; they reached out to all of life. The children hovered near, quietly submitting to her bitter outpouring. Their resignation was frightening. It was as if, even before they had begun to live, they were defeated by life and knew it.

At the sight of their bowed heads the words tangled in Miss Thompson's throat and she ceased. Slowly the seizure passed and her anger cleared. Love, suddenly, was a warmth flowing from her wasted body and the children stirred, touched by it, and shyly lifted their faces. They smiled.

"All right now," she clapped, and they scattered laughing. "Big Momma's here and the holiday's over. Everybody in the tub . . ." She bathed and fed them and then distributed the presents. Finally the only sound in the darkened apartment was the complaint of the bedsprings as she settled her body. Lights from the passing cars careened across the room, and as they swept over her face it resembled an African wood carving: mysterious, omniscient, the features elongated by compassion, the eyes shrouded with a profound sadness . . .

Suddenly the door of her small room opened, bare feet scurried across the floor and three small bodies clasped hers.

"Big Momma . . ."

"Hush it," she said sleepily, gathering them into her arms, "you all done come in here, now go on to sleep."

"Get home safe, soul. Send one the children when your time come 'pon you," Silla called and watched Virgie Farnum merge with the darkness. She remained at the gate, her strong full arms folded, a little of the tenseness gone from her back. Slowly, as she stood there, she was drawn into the calm center of the night, which nested in the trees and stirred with each warm stirring of the wind. Her eyes lifted to the glow of Fulton Street above the dark rise of trees, and she forgot the land and all that she and Virgie Farnum had talked of. For that nebula of lights sprinkled like iridescent dust on the night sky held the meaning of Saturday night—its abandonment and gaiety, love in dark rooms. She could not stave off the thought of the women in the bars with their warm eyes and bright mouths and the men hovering over them. She gazed up at Suggie's darkened windows and the scene there rushed over her mind. Her thoughts reached out to Deighton and the faceless woman together somewhere. Suddenly she felt old and barren, deprived, outside the circle of life. But she only succumbed briefly to this feeling, then her back was stiff again, her face resolute, and she sucked her teeth, dismissing them all.

"Ma, can I have a nickel to get a soda?" Ina, strolling with her friends, saw her and called.

"Not penny one. That cold soda just gon give you more cramps."

"But it's so hot," she said, coming up to the gate. "Well, can I just go with them to the candy store then?"

Silla studied her mild face, her graceful pose at the gate, and glanced at the breasts rising softly under her blouse. "Not two foot! You does just be going there to meet boys. That's all this drinking soda is. But lemme tell you, soul, if I ever see you with any boy I gon break your neck out in the streets 'cause I not tolerating no concubines and I ain supporting no wild-dog puppies . . ."

Distress filmed Ina's eyes, her head slowly bowed under the familiar threats. Then suddenly she leaned close and said pointedly, "I saw Daddy going down Fulton Street."

Silla broke off. She feigned indifference, but after a time she asked, "Which way?"

"Down. He never goes up—not on Saturday night anyway." She glided into the yard. "Gosh, it's hot." Then she whispered, "Is it true we've got property home?"

"He tell you so?"

"No. They were talking."

"Who they?"

"Him and Selina. They were talking this afternoon in the sun parlor and I heard him telling her about it. Does it mean we're rich?"

"Rich what!" she cried scornfully. "How rich, when people in this country does own thousand upon thousand of acres."

"Does it mean we're going to have to live there?"

"Live where! Barbados is someplace to live too?"

"Well, he was talking about building a house there."

"Yes? Yes! What else he had to say?"

"Not much else but . . ." Ina whispered all that she had overheard, and the thick night, the brownstones looming around them joined their conspiracy.

"So they making their plans," Silla said grimly when Ina finished. Her head snapped up suddenly; she whispered between clenched teeth, "Call she here for me."

Ina rushed out and Selina's name echoed hollow under the trees. She darted back. "She's coming. Can I go to the candy store for just a little while, please? Just ten minutes . . . ?"

"Oh, g'long," she said absently, her eyes fixed on the street behind her.

As Ina slipped soundlessly into the darkness, Selina's bangles clamorously announced her coming. Before Silla could prepare herself Selina was there, her dress shooting in a white puff under the trees, her form wheeling out of the darkness. And then abruptly, in the midst of all that flurry, she halted and lifted her eyes, clear and bold and questioning, to the mother.

43

"Get in the house."

Again she was all movement and sound, racing in a white streak past Silla, her bangles singing their dissonant tune.

They were in the kitchen now, immured within its white walls, and although they were motionless they seemed to be warily circling each other, feinting, probing for an opening. The mother's voice swung wildly across to her, "What you two was talking today?"

Selina's gaze did not shift, neither did her head drop from its high, obstinate angle, yet inside she tensed. For she knew how those eyes could pierce and prize out her thoughts. "Who two?" she said quietly.

"You and your beautiful-ugly father."

"When today?"

Silla's arm whipped out, the hand ready to sting Selina's face. "Oh, you's playing smart."

"I'm not. I'm just asking when, that's all."

"When?" she cried. "You know full well when. When the two of you was out in the sun parlor this afternoon making your plans."

"What plans?"

This time she lunged but even then Selina did not move. Not that she didn't cringe inside. Not that a kind of terror didn't spur her heart. But she could not move. For if she did, her defeat was certain. The mother would pounce, and under the stinging slaps she would confess all.

"I just asked what plans," she said evenly.

Again Silla retreated, disarmed. "Don play ignorant," she hissed. "The plans 'bout the piece of ground."

"Oh that," she said casually and for the first time shifted her weight. "It was about us having some land home."

"Yes, yes, but the plans."

"What plans?"

"Somethin' 'bout a house and thing."

"No . . ." She tilted her head thoughtfully. "Somebody must of been sneaking around hearing things nobody said."

The mother's hand quivered just inches from her face now. "Oh, your womanishness gon do for you, soul."

"But I don't even know what you mean by plans."

"Well then, what he said he's gon do with it?"

"He didn't say nothing but that he got this letter about us having some land." Softly she added, "I think I'd like it."

"Like what?"

"Going there to live."

"What you know 'bout Bimshire?"

"Nothing, but it must be a nice place."

This, strangely, infuriated Silla more than Selina's evasiveness and she swung away, rage congesting her face, words choking her. "Nice? Bimshire nice?" She swung back. "Lemme tell you how nice it is. You know what I was doing when I was your age?"

Selina shook her head.

"I was in the Third Class. You know what that is?"

Again she shook her head, but as the mother continued to glare down, demanding a fuller response, she said, "No . . . unless it's got something to do with school."

"School, ha!" Her sardonic laugh twisted the air. "Yes, you might call it a school, but it ain the kind you thinking of, soul. The Third Class is a set of little children picking grass in a cane field from the time God sun rise in his heaven till it set. With some woman called a Driver to wash yuh tail in licks if yuh dare look up. Yes, working harder than a man at the age of ten . . ." Her eyes narrowed as she traveled back to that time and was that child again, feeling the sun on her back and the whip cutting her legs. More than that, she became the collective voice of all the Bajan women, the vehicle through which their former suffering found utterance.

"And when it was hard times," she was saying now, "I would put a basket of mangoes 'pon muh head and go selling early-

early 'pon a morning. Frighten bad enough for duppy and thing cause I was still only a child . . ."

Selina listened. For always the mother's voice was a net flung wide, ensnaring all within its reach. She swayed helpless now within its hold, loving its rich color, loving and hating the mother for the pain of her childhood. The image of her father swaggering through the town as a boy and bounding on the waves in some rough game slanted across that of the small girl hurrying from the dawn ghosts with the basket on her head. It seemed to Selina that her father carried those gay days in his irresponsible smile, while the mother's formidable aspect was the culmination of all that she had suffered. This was no more than an impression, quickly lost in the haze of impressions that was her mind at ten. But it was there, fixed forever.

"No," the mother was almost shouting now. "No, I wun let my mother know peace till she borrow the money and send me here. But what"—her voice dropped tragically—"I come here and pick up with a piece of man and from then on I has read hell by heart and called every generation blessed."

The silence was pale after the rhapsodic fury of her voice. She squinted down at Selina, seeing her only dimly through the vision that still crowded her eyes.

Selina had not moved. Outwardly she was unyielding still, still uninvolved. But inside she was frightened by the thought of those memories always clashing within the mother. She was afraid that they would rend the mother soon and kill her finally, and she would be left without her. The world would collapse then, for wasn't the mother, despite all, its only prop?

"Yuh still think Bimshire is so nice now?" Silla cried.

"I still think I'd like it."

Oddly, instead of angering, Silla regarded her with a kind of enraged love. "But look at you," she muttered, appraising the wide-set eyes which filled the small adamant face. "Look the dress. Full of chocolate. Look the knees. Like they never touch water." She thought of the heart leaping inside the narrow chest.

"Always tearing 'bout like a holy gig with yuh heart beating like a band of music inside. Look how yuh brother . . ."

Suddenly Selina sprang forward and leaning close into the mother shouted, "I keep telling you I'm not him. I'm me. Selina. And there's nothing wrong with my heart." For a moment the words hung between them, then Selina darted around her and strode from the kitchen.

Stunned, Silla could only stare at the thin swift legs below the puffed skirt, at the frail neck bravely supporting the head and the small back as unassailable as her own. "But look at my crosses," she whispered, awed, as Selina disappeared. "Look how I has gone and brought something into this world to whip me."

# BOOK

## 2

*Pastorale*

# 1

For long months the question of the land draped itself in a thin gauze throughout the house and they were all caught within its mesh. At night the children were often awakened by muffled arguments from the master bedroom; savage words sparked in the darkness: "Sell it, sell it . . ." and always the same reply, growing more weary each night but persisting, "It's mine to do as I please . . ."

Listening to those voices raging in the dark, Selina often thought of the family who had lived there before them. The nights had been safe and quiet then with the children asleep in the nursery upstairs, the pale mother and father lying in each other's arms below and the heavy door locked against the chaos outside. As those voices soared, Selina, the sheet wrapped tight around her head, imagined that she was one of those children, secure in sleep. During the day there was no escape, for no matter what was said it was as if they were all speaking of the land. It loomed behind each word; each look contained it.

It was summer again now and Sunday, and Selina had been wandering the house since dawn. When Maritze was at mass she sat with Miss Mary in the dust-yellow room while she wheezed and gasped her dirge of memories. Afterward she stopped at Suggie's and found her sprawled amid her rumpled sheets, sluggish from the rough pleasures of her night. She laughed a good deal, a lovely sensual sound, and Selina gazing shyly at her from the foot of the bed said, "You're a summer woman, Miss Suggie."

The laugh became more wanton; Suggie struggled up, wrapped her naked body in the sheet and trailing it behind her, sauntered into the kitchen. She returned with a small glass of rum. "Come," she beckoned, "I gon make you a summer woman too, just for your womanishness."

Despite Selina's struggles she forced open her lips and the rum bit into her tongue and spurted hot down her throat. They stood quietly afterward, Selina rubbing her chest and frowning.

"Y'know, it feels kinda good," she said after a time.

"'Deed it does, faith!"

On her way downstairs, the rum coiling hot in her stomach, she felt that she, like Suggie, carried the sun inside her. Passing the parlor she glimpsed her sister at the piano and gave her a shout, receiving only an exasperated sigh in answer. Ina's body was bent in the same exasperated pose, her head bowed as if pressed down by the heat. Selina peered at her through the parlor's embalmed gloom, wondering at her strangeness, wincing at the wrong notes that punctuated her playing.

"Hey, cut out that noise," she called, passing on. "Daddy's in by now and trying to sleep."

He had come while she was upstairs and was asleep in the sun parlor with his clothes on. One arm shielded his eyes from the sun; his body seemed sapped like Suggie's from his night with the woman. For a long time Selina sat on the bed, gazing down at his face, innocent in sleep, at his chest moving lightly under the shirt. He was a dark god, she dreamed, tiptoeing away, who had fallen from his heaven and lay stunned on earth . . .

The mother was the only one who had not succumbed to the day's torpor, and as Selina entered the kitchen she helplessly admired her. She sat cool, alert, caged in sunlight from the barred window, holding the newspaper a little away from her as though the news of the war in Europe might contaminate her.

Selina said, "Let's have some lemonade."

The mother gave her a look that was shifting and complex. On one hand it dismissed her and the offer of the lemonade; on the other, it beckoned her close as though to embrace her. She said, "The best thing in heat like this is a hot-hot cup of tea."

"I'll make tea then."

"What kind of tea you could make?"

"I can make it."

The mother was silent and Selina made the tea and brought it to the table. Silla put down the newspaper and, without looking at her but frowning scornfully, took a quick sip. "Lord-God, tea strong enough to choke a horse," she complained but drank it, and they sat within the cage of sunlight, drinking the hot tea, reading and sweating, an ease and intimacy between them. Selina grew bold as the rum and hot tea fired her blood and asked after a time, "Can I go to Prospect Park with Beryl?"

"Pestilence," Silla said without annoyance, "here it tis the world is almost in war and all you thinking 'bout is patrolling the streets."

"Can I go?"

"You must gon hoof it there 'cause I'm not giving you penny one."

"But can I go without Ina? Just this once, please."

"What you need Ina for any more? You's more woman now than she'll ever be, soul. G'long."

Selina folded the funnies and placed them on the table. She did not hurry, afraid that if she did the mother might renege. But once outside the kitchen she ran, fleeing the house and its tumid silence, racing down Chauncey Street, which dozed in the Sunday torpor. The brownstones leaned against the soft sky, the ones owned or leased by the West Indians looking almost new with their neat yards, new shades and fresh painted black iron fences, while the others where the whites still lived looked more faded in the hard sunlight.

Selina thought of the white people behind those drawn green shades as having wasted faces and worn hands, as sitting all day in bare rooms. She was annoyed, for they seemed to disdain her by never showing themselves. She picked up a stick and ran, rasping it on their fences, hoping to startle them out of their dusty silence and bring them to the window . . .

There were new cream-colored shades with fringes at every window of the Challenor house and behind them filmy curtains waving in the warm wind. The Challenors had started buying the house two years ago. The wife, Gert Challenor, despised by the Bajan women because of her docility, did day's work. The husband, Percy, worked in the same mattress factory with Selina's father and sold stockings at night to meet the two mortgages. Silla always said with grudging respect, "But look at Percy. He's nothing but a work horse."

Selina stood in the dining room now, looking at him where he sat at the head of his table with his six children arrayed around him and his plump anxious wife facing him. To Selina he was a pagan deity of wrath, his children the subjects cowering before the fire flaring from his nostrils, his wife the priestess ministering to his needs. A thought cringed in the corner of her mind as she greeted him: he was too big to live among ordinary people . . .

"Selina getting big," he said, and it was like the pronouncement of an oracle.

"In truth," Gert Challenor agreed hurriedly, "these New York children does shoot up fast enough. How old you is, girl?"

"Eleven."

"How things at the house?" he commanded.

"All right."

"Silla and yuh fatha?"

"Fine."

"And Ina there? I guess she's a half a woman by now."

"She's okay."

"Yuh fatha still studying figures?"

"It's accounting. Yes."

"These white people ain gon hire him."

"Selina mussa get she smartness from Deighton," Gert Challenor added quickly.

He excluded this with a blunt gesture. "How his piece of ground home?"

"All right, I guess," she murmured and her stomach tightened.

"He done anything about it?"

"Like what?"

"Sell it?"

"No."

"Percy . . ."

He silenced his wife with a hard look. "He ain renting it either?"

"I dunno."

"But c'dear, how the child could know that?" his wife said.

"How yuh mean? Selina know full-well everybody in Brooklyn talking 'bout she fatha and his piece of ground. I tell you those men from Bridgetown home is all the same. They don know a thing 'bout handling money and property and thing so. They's spree boys. Every last one them . . . There ain nothing wrong with wanting piece of ground home but only when you got a sufficient back-prop here. I tell you, he's a disgrace!"

And for Selina, listening with lowered eyes, Percy Challenor had established irrevocably that her father was a disgrace. She felt the hate uncoil and tears prick her eyes. She waited eagerly for his next question, ready to meet his eyes with venom.

But Beryl rose between them, asking, "Can I go to Prospect Park with Selina, Daddy?" and his eyes swept across to her.

"Where wunna getting the money?"

"We've been saving what people gave us . . ."

Even the smaller children stopped eating while he deliberated. Finally he declared, "All right then. But make haste back here."

Outside, under the poised sun, they stood apart, suddenly shy. Then glancing up, they smiled secretly, and Selina hooted loud and began to spin. Beryl, laughing, rushed around her, snatching at her dress to stop her. Their hands met and Selina separated Beryl's fingers and meshed them with hers. Together, their hands closed into one fist, their bodies joined in a single rhythm, they skipped the three blocks to the Tompkins Avenue trolley.

They took separate window seats on the trolley so that they could watch the panorama of Sunday in Brooklyn strung out under the sun. To Selina the colors, the people seemed to run together. Dark, lovely little girls in straw bonnets flowed into little boys with their rough hair parted neatly on the side; into women in sheer dresses which whipped around their brown legs; into a bevy of church sisters swathed in black as though mourning their own imminent deaths; into the vacant, sun-grazed windows of the closed stores; into endless colonnades of trees down the side streets; into a blue sweep of sky; into dark little girls in straw bonnets . . . Life suddenly was nothing but this change and return . . .

Those colors, those changing forms were the shape of her freedom, Selina knew. She had finally passed the narrow boundary of herself and her world. She could no longer be measured by Chauncey Street or the park or the nearby school. "Lord," she whispered behind her hand, "I'm free."

In Prospect Park, with her hand in Beryl's and the sun shimmering before her eyes, she was drunk with freedom. She swaggered, Beryl in tow, into the zoo; she breathed deep the rank animal smells even as Beryl held her nose; she stopped at every vendor stand and bought ices, popcorn and peanuts and scattered the wrappers and shells behind her. At the seals' pond she leaped as they leaped into the sun and cried loud with them as they crashed sobbing into the water. Holding Beryl's waist she watched a lioness with her cubs sucking savagely at her teats.

"It looks just like Virgie Farnum," she said.

Beryl nodded. "It does a little. I'm only having two children when I get married. A boy and a girl. The boy first."

"I'm not having any. I'd never let them chop loose my stomach."

"Whaddya talking about—chop loose your stomach?"

"Don't you know yet that's what they do when you have a baby?"

"That's not so. They don't chop anything. It just pops out."

"Pops out?" she laughed. "Pops outta where?"

"Underneath," Beryl cried, angering.

"Underneath, where? Who told you that lie?"

"A girl in school. And it's not a lie." Beryl pushed Selina's arm from around her waist.

"Ya see. Somebody in school. A kid. When I heard Virgie Farnum telling my mother how they chopped loose her stomach and took out the baby. Grown-up people now who have children and should know."

Beryl glowered across at her, "I'm a year older than you, Selina Boyce, and I know too. You might be smart in school but you don't know anything else. You're a kid, a silly little kid still. Besides, I saw my mother naked once and she didn't have any scars on her stomach."

"They had healed."

Beryl turned away in disgust. "You think you know everything."

Silent, not touching, they walked out of the zoo into the picnic grounds, where families ate a Sunday dinner of potato salad and fried chicken out of paper plates and small children screamed and raced across the scarred grass. On the slopes, amid the rocks and trees there, lovers lay in each other's arms, their faces close and murmuring. Selina gazed at them and slowly her lips parted, blindly her hand groped for Beryl as she was shaken by something she sensed in them. It seemed that they—those laughing girls with grass in their hair, those bold boys with daring hands—had attained the fullest freedom. Back on the trolley she had had the merest glimpse of it; it had charged her blood like a stimulant when she was walking in the zoo. But their freedom was richer, fuller and denied her.

"Look, two of them are kissing," Beryl said, clinging to her arm.

It was more than just kissing, Selina wanted to say, watching their mouths open into each other and their bodies slowly sink into the grass. They were pouring themselves into each other. Suddenly she could not look any more. Tears stung her eyes. Pushing Beryl away she raced into a small wood near by and bounded up a low ridge there. Yelping, she plunged up and down the rise, the shrubbery cracking loud and the twigs whipping her legs, while Beryl stared open-mouthed below. Finally she paused on the crest, her wild shouts died and she stared, rapt, down onto a field where boys were playing baseball. From this height, she felt a profound detachment from them, from everyone, even Beryl. She was no longer human, she told herself, but a bit of pollen floating over the field and circling the world on a wind.

"Wait till your mother sees your dress," Beryl said when she climbed down.

"I don't give one damn."

"You're mad again," Beryl said helplessly. "Well come on let's get outta this sun. My mother says I'm getting black running around with you in the sun."

They searched until they found a shaded place within the shadow of a high rock. Beryl sat on her handkerchief and modestly tucked her dress under her knees while Selina sprawled flat on the ground, her face pressed to the earth, which was fecund with the oncoming summer; her lips brushed the grass, which was still cool and a little damp from the dew.

"I'm sorry I cursed," she said gently, touching Beryl's silver bangles. "You got new bangles?"

"Uh-huh. My grandmother sent them from home."

"I've still got the ones I wore as a baby."

"Me too. In a drawer someplace."

"Mine turn black when I'm sick."

"So do mine. My father says they know what goes on inside your body."

"It's funny," she began musingly, thinking of Percy Challenor presiding at the table. "I can't imagine your father ever being small. Or my mother either . . ."

"Well they were and my father was smart in school too. Maybe that's why he beats us so when we get bad marks."

"My father only beat me once. Long ago. I can't even remember why now." What she could remember was that after the first blow she had been strangely numb to the others. Instead she had been aware only of his body against hers, his muscles moving smoothly under his skin as he flailed her, and his heaving chest crushed against hers. She had been fused with him; not only had he breathed for her but his heart had beaten for them both.

She slapped at a fly on her leg and killed it.

"My mother never beats me," Beryl was saying.

"See, I killed it." Selina showed her the squashed fly and then wiped her hand on the grass. "Ugh, they've got blood like people." Then in the ample silence of rock and sky she said, "I imagine sometimes that I don't belong to them."

"Them who?"

"My family."

"What makes you imagine that?"

"I dunno. I saw a dead girl once. Ina took me." She ran her hand hard over the grass, still cleaning it.

"What'd she die from?"

"I dunno, but she was pretty. I think of her a lot and think of me instead of her in the box and everybody crying."

"Those aren't good thoughts, Selina."

"I know. And then maybe being dead is like before you was born, not knowing what's going on and not being able to see. Then I wouldn't know who was crying and who wasn't."

"My father wants me to be a lawyer since I'm the oldest. He told me the other day," Beryl said brightly after a long silence. "My father says you can always make money at that among your own people. What does your father want you to be?"

Selina still wiped her hand on the grass.

"Selina!"

"What?"

"What does your father want you to be?"

"He never said I had to be anything."

"Doesn't he care?"

"Of course he cares," she shouted.

"Maybe he'll let you be a poet."

"A poetess."

"If I get good marks this term I'm getting ice skates."

"Doris has some."

"Doris, I can't stand her!" Beryl said venomously. "She thinks she's cute because she's light and has good hair and all the boys like her. D'ya know she's got boys coming to see her already?"

"I hate boys," Selina cried.

After a hesitant silence, Beryl said, "So do I."

They lay in the ample silence of rock and trees, staring into the enormous blue expanse of sky and at the rock shutting out the sun. They heard a sharp crack and shouts from the baseball field and Beryl said, her eyes averted, "Remember what we were talking about in the zoo when you got so mad?"

"You got mad, not me."

"Okay. Well anyway what I was saying is true. I can prove it. I bleed sometimes," she said quietly.

"What?"

"I bleed sometimes."

"So what. Everybody does."

"Not from a cut or anything but from below. Where the baby pops out. Ina does too. That's why she gets pains every once in a while. I'll tell you, if you want to hear . . ."

"Tell me." And beneath her eagerness there was dread.

Beryl raised up, gathering her dress neatly under her. Her eyes flitted nervously across Selina's intense face. Then, with her head bowed and a squeamish look she explained it all. "That's why I'm getting these things," she concluded, jabbing her small breasts. "It happens to all girls."

Selina stared very quietly at her and, for that moment, she was quiet inside, her whole self suspended in disbelief. Then an inexplicable revulsion gripped her and her face screwed with disgust. "It's never gonna happen to me," she said proudly.

"If it doesn't happen by the time you're twenty you die."

"Well then I'll just die."

"It'll happen. It hurts sometimes and it makes you miserable in the summer and you can't jump rope when you have it but it gives you a nice figure after a time."

Her eyes searched Beryl's face. "How come?"

"I dunno. It just does. Look what's happening to Ina."

"Well if it ever happens to me nobody'll ever know. They'll see me change and think it's magic."

"Besides, it makes you feel important."

"How could anyone walking around dripping blood feel important?"

"It's funny but you do. Almost as if you were grown-up. It's like . . . oh, it's hard to explain to a kid . . ."

"Who's a kid?"

"You, because you haven't started yet."

"I'll never start!" And beneath her violent denial there was despair.

"Oh yes, you'll start." Beryl nodded wisely. "Wait, lemme try to explain how it makes you feel. The first time I was scared. Then I began to feel different. That's it. Even though nothing's changed and I still play kid games and go around with kids, even though my best friend's a kid"—she bowed to Selina—"I feel different. Like I'm carrying something secret and special inside . . . Oh, you can't really explain it to a kid . . ."

"Who's a kid? I was drinking rum today with Miss Suggie and I didn't bat an eye."

"Oh, Selina, nothing will help till you start."

Selina drew aside in a sullen despairing anger. A bit of the sun edged around the rock as though it had been hiding there listening and was coming now to upbraid them. As she squinted

61

through her tears at the sun's bright fringe, the promise of the day was lost. The mother had deceived her, saying that she was more of a woman than Ina yet never telling her the one important condition. She had deceived herself on the trolley and on the rise in the park. She was not free but still trapped within a hard flat body. She closed her eyes to hide the tears and was safe momentarily from Beryl and Ina and all the others joined against her in their cult of blood and breasts.

After a time Beryl came and lay close to her. She placed her arm comfortingly around her. "What was that poem you wrote about the sky?" she asked. And always her voice calmed Selina. Her disappointment, her anguish tapered slowly until finally her tears were gone and she turned to Beryl and held her so that they were like the lovers on the slope. "It wasn't about this kind of sky," she said and began to recite, her thin voice striking the rock and veering off into the sky, her eyes closed. When she finished and opened her eyes Beryl's were closed, her face serene in sleep. Whispering, Selina recited then to the rock, to the dome of sky, to the light wind, all the poems she had scribbled in class, that came bright and vivid at night.

Beryl stirred in her sleep and pressed Selina closer. Just then the sun rose above the rock. The strong light seemed to smooth the grass, to set the earth steaming richly. They were all joined it seemed: Beryl with the blood bursting each month inside her, the sun, the seared grass and earth—even she, though barren of breasts, was part of the mosaic. With a cry she buried her face between Beryl's small breasts, and suddenly her happiness was like pain and a long leap into space.

On their way home a summer rain fell even as the sun shone. Holding each other close, they laughed and, pointing to the sun-lit rain, chanted softly, "The devil's beating his wife. The devil's beating his wife . . ."

# BOOK
## 3

*The War*

# 1

*If I wus a grasshopper*
*I woulda hop about in de grass*
*And when Adolf Hitler pass along*
*I would dash a lash in his . . .*
  *as' no question.*

*Yuh come fuh to kill muh*
*Yuh come fuh to kill muh*
*Yuh come fuh to kill muh*
*I would dash a lash in yuh . . .*
  *as' no question.*
    BARBADIAN FOLK SONG

The war came later that year. On the cold December afternoon
Selina, Ina and the mother made a stunned tableau as the an-
nouncer—a leashed hysteria running swiftly under his urgent
voice—shattered Sunday's tedium with news of the bombing.
Each word built a picture of disaster and added new tension to
the still unresolved tension over the land. When he finished the
children turned to Silla, waiting for her to define this in some
way, to fit the war somehow into their lives. She stared at them
with a kind of hopelessness for a moment, then burst out, "Nineteen fourteen again. Thank God I ain got neither one to send to
die in another white-man war."

Moments later Selina burst into the sun parlor, where her
father lay on the cot bundled in a heavy sweater and socks. He

65

was napping, his breath coming in white wisps in the cold and the latest accounting manual lying neglected on his chest.

"We're in the war," she shouted.

"Yes," he said, his eyes closed, and it was as though he were still sleeping. "If it din come today it would of come tomorrow. How it happen?"

As she told him she sensed him shrinking from the news as from some ugly sight. "Are they gonna draft you?"

"Draft what? I's something to draft too?" He laughed bitterly. "As far as the record goes I ain even in this country since I did enter illegally. Y'know that's a funny thing when you think of it. I don even exist as far as these people here go."

"Howdya mean?" she asked, uneasy, wishing that he would open his eyes.

"I mean if they don have some kind of record or something so on you, you don exist. You can be walking 'bout like other men, breathing like everybody else but not existing fuh true. That's a funny thing, nuh?"

"Yes," she said, not understanding, and then remembering the war, said, "Lordy, I hope they don't bomb Barbados."

His eyes opened and he laughed and pulled her down beside him. "Le's hope they don't, lady-folks. Let's hope they don't." And still laughing, but ruefully now, he got up and dressed, putting on new gray suede shoes and a matching hat, and went out.

For a long time she did not really believe in the war, even with the air-raid drills in school, and Chauncey Street occasionally plunged in blackness, and Fulton Street chastened by the brown-out. Not until later that winter when the war seemed to reach out and claim her. For her body was in sudden upheaval —her dark blood flowing as it flowed in the war, the pain at each shudder of her womb as sharp as the thrust of a bayonet. Remembering all that Beryl had said she did not complain. Each morning for a month she felt her chest, sitting up in bed in the chilly room while Ina slept beside her. And each morning she sadly pulled down the shirt over her flatness. Then bathing one night she felt a barely perceptible swelling under the washcloth, and splashed up, staring down at it and then over to the other, her long limp arms hanging, water dripping from her lean frame. Suddenly she smiled, shyly at first, then triumphantly. There was hope.

But sometimes she was frightened by the war and herself, and those times she would wander into the kitchen and sit at a small table in the corner, out of the mother's way yet near her. She would sit for hours, her feet hooked on the chair rung, her chin in her hands, staring out the window at the pear trees in the back yard, at the nude branches clacking in mournful chorus against the somber sky.

On Saturdays the kitchen was filled with fragrances, for Silla made and sold Barbadian delicacies: black pudding, which is the intestines of the pig stuffed with grated sweet potato, beets, animal blood and spices until it is a thick sausage, then tied at the ends and boiled; also souse, which she made by pickling parts of the pig; and coconut or sweet bread, a heavy bread with coconut running in a rich vein through the center.

From early one Saturday Selina and Ina had been grating until, by noon, their fingers were torn and their blood mixed with the shreds. The bell rang, relieving them, and a shaft of wind brought voices and a feel of the snow crusted hard along the curbs.

"Dear-heart, the pudding and souse smell too sweet! How?" Iris Hurley entered, her wide nostrils stiff with cold. She was tall and big-boned like Silla, with smooth black skin, high hard facial bones, evasive eyes.

"Iris, I still here," Silla said and turned to the other woman. "Florrie, how?"

"Suffering, soul!" Florrie Trotman's short legs carried her chunky body as if it was an unfair burden. She had dull yellow skin, oblique eyes, an innocent mouth and huge breasts that swelled over her brassière so that it appeared that she had four breasts instead of two. Sometimes Silla affectionately called her "Bubby-Island."

"Come soul, sit, do." She motioned her to a chair. "You's blowing like a whale."

Florrie Trotman sat heavily; her bosom heaved. "We ain staying Silla-soul. We just stop to see if you was still living or dead. Wha'lah I din see the children." She twisted around to them. "C'dear, I never see girl-children so features their father as these two, Silla."

"They's his all right—frighten for work just like he."

Florrie struggled out of her coat and swung her pocketbook high on her arm. "But in truth these New York children don like work. They soft. Look that half a man I got there. All day his head does be up in a radio listening to jazz like he's some jazz fiend or the other. Only yesterday I had to up hand and give a cuff that near kill him."

"You best watch that heavy hand," Silla said, "'cause this is New York and these is New York children and the authorities will dash you in jail for them."

"Never mind that! They want licks!" Florrie shouted. "You got to wash their tail in licks. You remember what the old people home did tell us: hard ears you wun hear, own-ways you'll feel."

Iris Hurley spoke for the first time. "But c'dear, I don does have no trouble with mine. Maybe if you two would of send the children to church . . ."

"But Iris, who ask you?" Silla flared. "You always bringing up the church in everything. Don you think I sent the little beasts to Barrow's Church and they was up there reciting the 'Little Lord Jesus lay down his sweet head' and thing so! You think that change them?"

"As for you! It's years since you darken the door-mouth of a church," Iris said.

"And years to come!" Silla added, "And you know why, Iris? It's not that I's some heathen or the other, but that my mind turn from the church. I see too many hypocrites prostrating themself before the cross each Sunday. The same ones buying house by devious means. Lemme tell you, Iris, you don see God any better by being sanctified and climbing the walls of a church and tearing off your clothes when you's in the spirit, or even when you's up in the so-called High Church, choking on the lot of incense and bowing and kneeling for hours and singing in various tongues. Not everyone who cry 'Lord, Lord' gon enter in . . ."

"I gon pray for you, Dear-heart."

"Don waste breath, Iris. Each man got to see God for himself."

Florrie Trotman sucked her teeth, annoyed. "But why wunna two hard-back women always arguing 'bout the church. . . . Silla, those new curtains?"

"Woman, who can be buying anything new with all this war and foolishness going on?"

Iris Hurley sent a blast through her wide nostrils. "But do you read how many thousand upon thousand they killing out each day? But c'dear, these white people getting on too bad. They say that Hitler put all the Jews in a gas chamber. But you know, somebody oughta take up a gun so and shoot down that man so, 'cause he's nothing but the devil-incarnate."

"In truth," Silla said with bowed head and her face drawn with sadness. Suddenly she cried, her voice tremulous with anger, "It's these politicians. They's the ones always starting up all this lot of war. And what they care? It's the poor people got to suffer and mothers with their sons."

"Oh Jesus-Christ-God, Silla!" Florrie shuddered. "Don speak do. Livingston's due to go, y'know. He ain no good but he's my only son."

"They'd never get a child of mine in no army," Iris said. "I'd make him eat soap each day to make the heart beat fast first. Wait, no . . ." She paused. "I might if he was gon fight direct for England and the crown."

"But Iris you's one ignorant black woman!" Silla said softly. "What John Bull ever did for you that you's so grateful? You

69

think 'cause they does call Barbados 'Little England' that you is somebody? What the king know 'bout you—or care? You best stop calling the man name like you and he does speak. You think the king did care when you was home heading canes? Or when the drought come and not a pot stir 'pon the stove for days . . . ?"

"Dear-heart," Iris said placidly, "you like you come to read the burial service over me."

"You deserve to dead," Silla cried, her face working and her eyes boring into Iris, who remained unmoved and unimpressed. Silla leaned across the table to her, whispering, "Iris, you know what it is to work hard and still never make a head-way? That's Bimshire. One crop. People having to work for next skin to nothing. The white people treating we like slaves still and we taking it. The rum shop and the church join together to keep we pacify and in ignorance. That's Barbados. It's a terrible thing to know that you gon be poor all yuh life, no matter how hard you work. You does stop trying after a time. People does see you so and call you lazy. But it ain laziness. It just that you does give up. You does kind of die inside . . ."

"It's the God truth," Florrie whispered.

"I ain saying that we don catch *H* in this country what with the discrimination and thing and how hard we does have to scrub the Jew floor to make a penny, but my Christ, at least you can make a head-way. Look how Roosevelt come and give relief and jobs. Who was one the first Bajan bought a house? You, Iris. When they pass this law to hire colored in defense plants who was the first up in the people face applying? Your husband, Iris. Even I gon apply for one those jobs. So c'dear, give credit where it due, nuh," she pleaded softly, then as Iris still ignored her, she lashed out, "You's an ungrateful whelp."

"Dear-heart," Iris laughed, "I ain able for you to kill me with words!"

Florrie had listened rapt, respectful to Silla, and now she said solemnly, "Talk yuh talk, Silla! Be-Jees, in this white-man world you got to take yuh mouth and make a gun."

70

During the long lull Silla served the black pudding, souse coconut bread and ginger beer. The children watched from their corner: Ina with the pained look of someone caught in a world she couldn't understand and didn't like, Selina leaning forward excitedly, the grater lying idle in her lap. The words were living things to her. She sensed them bestriding the air and charging the room with strong colors. She wondered at the mother's power with words. It was never like this with Selina. In school she could sense the veil dropping over the other children's eyes when she recited, and other thoughts crowding out her voice in their minds. Only afterward, when it was too late, would her mind be flooded with eloquence . . .

A door closed upstairs and Florrie Trotman's small eyes darted up. "Who that, Silla?"

"The old white woman daughter, a religious fanatic and a walking-dead. She and the mother does fight like tearcats."

"But why you don get them and that free-bee Suggie out the place and rent those rooms for good money?" Iris Hurley asked.

"I only leasing the house."

"You could still do it."

"It's Silla's fault." Florrie sucked her teeth in disgust. "I told she to put down something to make them move."

"How you mean—put down something?" Iris glared suspiciously.

"I mean, if I must explain my explanatories, that Silla should go to a spiritualist and get something and put down outside their door and *make* them move!"

"What you pretending for?" Silla turned to Iris. "You know Florrie does still believe in obeah and does walk 'bout with piece of coal tie round she waist and carrying finny and goat foot for luck."

Florrie rose, bristling. "Oh, wunna laughing cause I got sense enough to protect muhself against all the evil people does try to do yuh. But I know what I doing. When I was a girl home I did see obeah work on somebody and the person is dead-dead today . . . You did know Affie Cumberbatch?" Her slit eyes swept them, reaching out to include Selina and Ina in her question. "A good-looking clear-skin girl from Cane Garden with hair down she back? You know who I talking 'bout?"

They nodded reluctantly.

"That girl die when she was only twenty and in perfect health. Now tell me what she die from?" She pointed to Silla.

"Woman, how I could remember and that thing happen donkey years?"

"Then, lemme tell you and listen and believe. This Affie was running with my wuthless uncle. Now his wife, my dear-aunt Do-Da, was always a thoroughfare, and when she found out she swear she was gon kill Affie. She took me with her to the obeah man. I hear she tell him she want to work obeah on Affie and she pay him good-good money. And I see the bag of the obeah man . . ."

"Florrie, yuh lying now!" Iris gasped with fear.

Her outcry halted the tightening mesh of Florrie's voice. In that moment Ina sprang up and dashed from the room, her face stiff with terror. No one noticed her; they all waited for Florrie, including Selina, who was crouched low in her chair.

"Who tell you I lying? I see the bag! It had in some rusty nails and feathers and broken glass and thing so. He took some out and put in a bottle and bury it, and all the time he chanting. He give muh dear-aunt Do-Da duppy dust to put in muh uncle food so that he would pass it on to Affie when he was in the bed with she. He told muh dear-aunt not to worry, that Affie Cumberbatch was as good as dead. And I kiss muh right hand to God." Florrie kissed both sides of her right hand and raised it. "When you hear the shout, Affie Cumberbatch took in sick. Her people throw 'way money enough on doctors and still cun find what was wrong with the girl. They even boil lizard soup and give she, but it din do no good. Affie said she felt like a crawling under she skin and she continue cry for a pain. She said she heard the duppies walking 'pon the roof at night and a hand cold as death 'pon she body. And be-Jees, before the year out Affie Cumberbatch was in she grave. Now tell me that's some game-cock bring ram-goat story!" She glared at them triumphantly.

Silla said, "Florrie, I gon tell you like the old people home did say. What you believe in you die in. If you believe there's a duppy walking 'pon the roof, then one is there."

Winded, Florrie sat down. Her eyes gradually lost their wildness, her face settled into its broad calm again. In the silence that followed, they heard the faltering sound of Ina's piano.

"Guess who I butt up on in De Kalb Market looking like Laddy-da and buying up all the half-rotten fruit?" Iris Hurley started their talk again.

"The great 'Gatha Steed," Silla said.

"C'dear, the very one."

"But look at she! She favor dog. How many house she got now?" Silla said.

"Three. And I hear she looking now to marry off the daughter so she can have a big wedding. But the longface girl is liking some boy from down South, and they almost had to tie 'Gatha down with wet sheets when she found out. She want the girl to marry a Bajan boy who's here on the immigration scheme."

"Ah, you see," Silla said, "the woman is nothing but a blackguard. I don say that she should let the girl marry no boy from the South but she don have to get on like she never christened."

Iris Hurley dismissed this and said, "You hear Ena Roacheford finally buying the house she been leasing since the year one?"

"Who Ena Roacheford?" Silla's head snapped up.

"A red woman from Rock Hall home. Look Eulise Bourne. She buying another one despite the wuthless husband . . ."

"Where?" Silla asked her sharply.

Iris ignored her. "I butt up on Vi Dash on Fulton Street crying poor but she buying the second house, best-proof."

"But how she does do it, and the husband is nothing but a he-whore?" Florrie asked.

"How yuh mean? She does beat he and take 'way the money,

nuh. Dear-heart"—Iris turned to Silla who was standing behind her now, listening with suppressed fury—"you did know a girl name Eloise Gittens?"

"Yes . . ." Her voice was choked.

"Well, soul, she and all buying house."

"She's nothing a-tall," Silla said hoarsely.

Iris shrugged and turned away. "I know she still buying. I don know how some them doing it."

Florrie laughed, unaware of the tension. "They doing it some of every kind of way. Some working morning, noon and night for this big war money. Some going to the loan shark out there on Fulton Street. Some hitting the number for good money. Some working strong-strong obeah. Some even picking fares . . ."

Selina muffled her laugh. The mother seemed not to hear while Iris gave Florrie a cold smile and droned inexorably, "Ena Sobers just bought one in Crown Heights. Up with the white people, if you please . . ."

She continued listing the names in a colorless, unrelenting voice, never once turning to Silla, yet addressing only her. Silla stood silent and seething behind her. At each name she winced and envy darkened her eyes. After a time, her big frame began to buckle, it seemed, under Iris' unceasing assault, until suddenly her head snapped up. Another voice, heard only by her, might have sounded, for her eyes narrowed and probed the air as if seeking the face. Her own face became taut, her heavy breathing stilled. Suddenly her body convulsed and her voice clashed loud and exultant into Iris' monotonous recital. "Oh God, I can get the money!"

"What, Dear-heart?" Iris asked calmly, glancing over her shoulder. "What money?"

"From the land."

"But Dear-heart, why you continue persecuting yourself 'bout that piece of ground?" she chided, turning away. "You can't make the man sell it."

"*I* gon sell it . . ." Silla lunged, halting just behind Iris' chair. Selina and Florrie Trotman shied at her violent movement, but Iris did not move.

"How she can make Deighton sell?" she asked Florrie. "He's keeping his land to build house and thing so."

"His mouth look like a house," Florrie whispered, her apprehensive eyes on Silla.

"I gon do it." Silla's voice wedged between theirs. "Some kind of way I gon do it."

"How?" Iris snapped, still not turning to her.

"How . . . ?" She paused, confused.

"Yes, how?" Sarcasm edged Iris' voice. "You must gon work obeah. That's the only way you could make him sell—and there ain no obeah that strong. You best forget the piece of ground and save what you make selling pudding and souse and scrubbing floors to make the down payment. Deighton ain gon sell!"

"Be-Jesus-Christ, I gon do that for him then. Even if I got to see my soul fall howling into hell I gon do it." Her words hung portent in the white silence. The air sagged with them. From her table in the corner, Selina visualized them as ominous birds, poised, beaks ready to rip her father. She knew, even as the dread seeped her blood, that this was not just another one of the mother's threats about the land. The way her body had heaved as she spoke proved this. Fear for her father sounded in a wild alarm throughout her. It clamored even louder as she looked up again at the mother.

Silla stood calm, confident, almost smiling in their midst. Her eyes had clouded over and she had forgotten them. Now she sought the presence who always listened and sympathized. "It's strange," she mused aloud to him, "how you can try to figure out how to do a thing for years and then suddenly it's clear in your mind. For months now I has sat at this same table, lain in that bed up there 'pon a night figuring for this thing till I thought I would go mad so. Two years racking my brains. And now, in a minute so, it's clear-clear what I must do. Clear like somebody draw a picture so and show me." Then her eyes, hard with her resolve, reached out to them. "As God is my witness I know how to sell it for him."

Only Iris spoke. "How, I ask? Neither name of yours in on the papers for it."

"I don need that."

"Then you must gon work obeah."

"Silla-soul, don do nothing you'll regret," Florrie Trotman whispered. "Maybe you best forget it . . . This obeah don does always work."

"Forget it?" Silla's laugh drowned her warning. "I just now start to think 'bout it. Everybody buying and I still leasing? Oh no, Florrie. I gon fix he and fix he good. I gon show the world that Silla ain nice!"

With that she raised her arms, her body reared, and as she stood there pledging her whole self while the others sat struck silent, the day changed. The early winter sunset stained the sky beyond the pear trees with harsh yet lovely threads of mauve, wine rose, brassy yellow, and the last light reached in long attenuated strips into the kitchen. Shadows were there also, spreading their dark tentacles as the sun thinned. Silla, the barred sunlight and shade on her face, was imprisoned within this contradiction of dark and light. Indeed, like all men, she embodied it. Yet somehow it was more marked in her. Perhaps because the struggle was nearer the surface and more intense.

"Selina," Florrie Trotman whispered nervously, "get yuh mother some water."

Selina hesitated, then as Florrie motioned again, she drew the water and, with it slopping over her shaking hand, approached the mother. Silla did not shift from her threatening pose but simply glared down at her. Then quickly she swooped, her hand struck, knocking the glass from Selina's hand, and grasping her close, she whispered between closed teeth, "If I was to hear one word outta you 'bout what I said here today I gon kill you. You hear? I gon kill you even though you's my child and I suffered plenty pain to bring you . . ."

76

Selina said nothing; neither did she struggle. Behind the fear in her eyes, behind the welling tears there was the old resistance that so infuriated the mother. Seeing it now, Silla pushed her away, saying bitterly, "Oh I know. I know I isn't to do a thing against your beautiful-ugly father. He's Christ to you. But wait. Wait till I finish with him. He gon be Christ crucified."

"Silla!" Florrie sprang up, shouting. "Stop frightening the child. What she could say anyway?"

"The Lord make peace," Iris intoned.

Florrie slowly approached Silla and touched her compassionately. "Silla-gal, I know it's hard. That man had led you a dusty road. But forget the piece of ground. Forget it!"

Under Florrie's soothing touch, the harshness faded in Silla's eyes, but she still whispered, "Mark my words, Florrie, I gon do it."

Florrie shook her head and turned solicitously to Selina. She bent over her and with the same compassion placed her hand on her shoulder. "Come, girl," she said, shaking her gently. "What you crying for? Tell your mother that you's no more little girl, but near a full woman like us now that you's filling out—and that you can hold your tongue like a woman . . ." And as she spoke and laughed tenderly, her hand passed from Selina's shoulder through the wide neck of her middy blouse and, with a casual fleeting gesture, brushed one of her small breasts.

Selina sprang away too late; her hand struck out at Florrie Trotman's hand too late. All she could do was send up a cry of outrage that rived the air and drove the mothers back. Still howling, she stooped. Through her blinding tears she searched for the broken half of the glass which the mother had struck from her hand. Finding it, she rose and offered it to her again; and whirled, offering it to Florrie Trotman with a rancorous look. Then she raised it and, with one last shrill cry, smashed it to the floor, and fled.

It was for them to accept her gage . . .

# 2

That slight but intimate pressure of Florrie Trotman's hand remained like an intaglio on Selina's barely formed breast. She
knew, in a remote corner of her mind, that she would carry its
damp warmth and roughness, the feel of it, all her life. It was
the rite which made her one with Florrie's weighty bosom
and Virgie Farnum's perennially burgeoning stomach. It meant
that she would always have vestiges of Iris Hurley's malice and
the mother's gorgeous rage. Although she did not understand
this, she was often seized by a frenzy of rejection and would
rush to the bathroom and there, behind the locked door, rub her
breasts until pain coursed through her body. But no matter
how hard she rubbed, the imprint remained, for it was indelible.

That touch, lingering as the long winter lingered, meant even
more. It made her party to the mother's dark vow. And what
did that vow mean? What would it encompass? Would there
really be candles sputtering in the rooms at night and dark
shapes rushing over the roof? Would there be incantations and
duppy dust and her father weakening until his will was gone and
he wanted only what the mother wanted? Frantically Selina
searched the mother's face for some hint and always found it shut,
inscrutable. Those eyes, when they encountered hers, revealed
nothing. Then the mother got a job in a defense factory and

Selina hardly saw her. Desperately she searched the halls, the cellar, the master bedroom for some sign and, after each futile search, stumbled upstairs to the landing under the skylight and crouched there, the fears festering on her mind like Miss Thompson's life-sore.

And guilt joined her there. For wasn't she betraying her father by her silence? But what would she say?—she almost cried aloud each time. Simply that the mother had vowed? Hadn't she vowed and threatened before? Each day these questions swarmed her mind and she writhed, often moaning, under their attack. Until one afternoon her mind was too bruised to take any more and she crawled up, knowing that she must find help somewhere.

"Miss Mary . . ." She peered through the room's timeless and tarnished yellow fog. "Miss Mary . . ." She groped amid the dusty relics to the bed and the wasted form there.

". . . Aye, it did yuh heart good to see them on a Sunday— the girls in them wide hats with the ribbons flying and the mistress in her lace shawl looking like the fine beauty she was—all going to church . . ." The cracked voice was in full pursuit of the past, the faded eyes blind to all but those scenes.

"Miss Mary . . ." She sat on the low stool beside the bed and touched the hands clasped in painful motionlessness on the blanket.

". . . Faith, it was a fine house. Never a hard word spoken . . . They wus none as happy as them . . ."

"Miss Mary!"

"Tom!" the old woman cried. "Him so tall and strong with a smile for everyone . . . Dead in the war somewheres and me with the child coming and no wedding a-tall . . ."

Miss Mary dreamed loud, Selina called and the afternoon lengthened while time held motionless in the rooms. Finally Selina was too weak with frustration to call. Finally the old woman's rapt voice drove her from the room.

"Miss Suggie, you home?" she called tearfully and pushed Suggie's half-opened door.

Suggie was there, hunched over the bottles of perfume on her vanity, her red chenille robe open around her thick thighs and her hair spread on her shoulders.

"Miss Suggie . . ."

"I quit." Suggie shouted without turning. "That's why you see me home. Yuh think I was gon spend my life cleaning that white woman big house—biting muh tongue when she snot-nose brats insult me? I quit."

"Miss Suggie, listen please . . ."

Suggie turning, her hair whipping black across her face, her eyes straining to see Selina in the failing light. "Selina, mahn, tell muh, you think I could get one these good war jobs . . . ?"

At the sight of her troubled face and the anxious way her arms reached out to her, Selina's own fears abated. Suddenly Suggie seemed more the child than she and more in need of help.

"Yes," she said gently, coming into the room.

"But do you think I could do the work if I put muh mind to it?"

"Yes," she assured her. "My mother's doing it."

Suggie jumped up and strode to the window, the robe flouncing behind her. "I talking 'bout me! Could I do it?" she cried angrily, facing the winter sunset above the park. "Yuh mother and them so can do anything they put their mind to."

At that Selina's fears surged back and the scene in the kitchen was vivid again. "Please, Miss Suggie, listen. My mother's gonna sell . . ."

"Yuh mother! Them so! My people! I's hiding from them with tears in my eyes," she raged, unheeding. "Y'know what they want me to do?" She spun around. "I must put on a piece of black hat pull down over my face and go out here working day in and day out and save every penny. That's what. I mustn't think 'bout spreeing or loving-up or anything so . . ." She swept to the table, poured a long drink of rum and swallowed it in one draught. "But they's sadly mistaken," she shouted defiantly as though the rum had given her courage, "I gon spend my money foolish if I choose." She waved to the perfumes. "And I always gon have some man or the other. When people see me coming they gon know it's Suggie Skeete, even if it's only because I's the biggest whore out. Be-Jees, I ain gon be like them, all cut out of the same piece of cloth . . ."

Selina, weighted down by her own anxiety, her frustration renewed, only half listened. She did not even try to call Suggie again. Then, when Suggie's bitter grievances were over, she noticed Selina's drawn face and cried, "Selina, mahn, what wrong? I talking too much?"

"No, it's my mother. She's gonna sell the land behind his back."

"What you talking?"

"Sell it. Without his knowing."

"She just talking."

"No, she means it this time. She swore."

"She just talking. Neither name of hers down for it."

"She isn't joking. She means it. She's gonna work obeah, I think." Tears stung her eyes.

Suggie's laugh filled the chilly room with its lush summer sound. "Wha'lah, mahn, that obeah foolishness don work in New York. So stop worrying yuhself. She was just trying to frighten you."

"I know she's gonna do something." Her hand struck the air.

"Mahn, she can't do a thing. Not a thing."

Strangely, the resignation she felt was almost soothing. The tears no longer burned her lids and she nodded at Suggie to indicate that she was convinced. For it was not that Suggie had refused to believe, but that she, Selina, had failed in words that would convince her. Selina leaned her forehead on the footboard and said nothing more.

After a time Suggie's worried voice reached down into Selina's numbness. "Selina, mahn, do you really think I could get one these good war jobs—that I could catch on and learn good like yuh mother and them so . . . ?"

"Yes," she murmured, "yes."

Outside in the hall again she pressed her face against the cool paneling to still the voices of Miss Mary and Suggie swirling inside her and to prepare herself for the blaring onslaught of the trumpet. It was her father's trumpet. He was studying the trumpet now that his correspondence course in accounting was finally over. The course had ended, and his ambition to be an accountant had ended the first day he had looked for a job. Trailing slowly downstairs into the trumpet's din, she remembered that day, two weeks ago, and ached for him again.

"Lady-folks, how I look?" he had shouted, entering the kitchen that morning, impeccable in a white shirt, a dark figured tie that blended well with his dark suit, his hair brushed flat and his shoes gleaming in the gray morning light.

Before they could answer, the mother had turned from the sink and said, her voice sharp with reproof yet strangely protective, "But where you going and you only half-studied that course? How you can be putting yourself up in these white people face asking for some big job and yuh's not even a citizen?"

Smiling, he picked up Selina's bread from her plate and Ina's cup of tea and, eating, said, "Don worry 'bout that, Silla. Where it say citizen on the application I gon put yes. They ain gon bother searching up the birth certificate. Besides these white people here does think all colored people is from the South."

"Which places you going?"

"The three places offering the best salary."

With a look both cruel and pitying she said, "You don want no job," and turned to the children. "Instead of him going to some small office where he might have a chance—no, he got to play like he's white."

"Silla, lemma tell you something," he interrupted, his smile gone and annoyance darkening his face, "I ain looking for nothing small. I ain been studying this course off and on for near two years to take no small job. Tha's the trouble with wunna colored people. Wunna is satisfy with next skin to nothing. Please Mr.

White-man, gimma little bit. Please Mr. White-man, le' the boy go to Harrison College so he can be a schoolmaster making $10.00 a month. Please Mr. White-man, lemma buy one these old house you don want no more. No, I ain with wunna. It got to be something big for me 'cause I got big plans or nothing a-tall. That's the way a man does do things!" With that he replaced Ina's cup, handed Selina what was left of the bread and left.

That afternoon, racing through the master bedroom to the sun parlor, Selina saw the tie trailing over the foot of the bed and the jacket thrown carelessly across a chair. Apprehensively she pushed open the door to the sun parlor and saw him—lying there on the cot as though he had been severely beaten and flung there like his jacket. The floor around him was scattered with the accounting manuals.

She waited, as she always did, for him to speak first. Soon the sunset gave way to dusk beyond the glass walls, and shadows invaded the room, overtaking the bare floor, the cot, moving quickly up his limp body. When they slanted across his eyes he whispered, "They's all the same, lady-folks. Here and in Bimshire they's the same. They does scorn yuh 'cause yuh skin black . . ."

Despite his bitterness, there was a nuance, a shading of something else. A frightening acceptance, it seemed to be, which sprang, perhaps, from a conviction hidden deep within him that it was only right that he should be rejected . . . He said nothing more after that, and two weeks later he brought home the trumpet and a beginner's book in music and was soon his affable, teasing self again.

Selina hated it. Its indecent shrieks not only destroyed their intimacy but desecrated the aged silence of the house. Yet she wanted him to play well, for she knew how the mother laughed and said to her friends in the kitchen on Saturdays, "Yes, soul, he call heself playing the trumpet now and can't mark fat with the thing."

She stood in the doorway of the master bedroom now, the

trumpet assaulting her ears, watching him. His body, stretched stiff and tense, looked as though it would vibrate like a struck chord at the slightest touch. The muscles corded thickly in his neck and at his temples; his head leaned back as though bent by a wind. He was all black and gold to her: bright gold trumpet pressed to his dark lips, black fingers faltering on the gold keys. With each uncertain note his head trembled and the perspiration slid in bright tears down his face.

At last he tore the trumpet from his lips and leaned, exhausted, against the stand, shaking the spittle from the valve. "How the lady-folks?" He turned, smiling. "I thought I did hear you sneaking in. Yuh old white friend upstairs complaining 'bout the noise I guess."

"She can't hear anything. It sounds like you'll soon be able to play that song."

"Ah, you heard me then." He smiled widely. "I almost had it down, nuh. I tell you, I must have natural talent for this thing. The book says you must have the scales down pat before you start playing any song. Even the teacher say so. But I ain worrying with all that. I ain got time to be practicing no scales or learning those foolish little pieces the teacher give me. I looking to play real songs—and fast."

"You like this better than the accounting then?" she asked carefully.

"It's a hundred times better," he said with heat, remembering his humiliation. He placed the trumpet to his lips, hesitated and lowered it. His eyes narrowed as his thoughts formed. "You got to get somethin' that you don have to look to nobody. Now take these musicians. They don say cat-dog to a blast. And they does pull down good money—that Louis Armstrong, Erskine Hawkins and the 'mounts of them. People does beg them to play. Besides you does get people respect when you's a musician. You's not just another somebody out here scuffling for a dollar. You's an artist! You can play in any of those big bands . . ."

His eyes on Selina became bright with purpose; he held the

trumpet as if it were the wand which had finally ordered life around him, and without it he would be shunted into the old confusion again.

"Maybe you'll be very famous," she cried, caught by his words.

He pointed the trumpet at her, shouting, "Famous! How you mean, lady-folks? Famous! They does string up yuh name in lights!"

She saw his name in lights in the golden mouth of the trumpet and people crowding around him as he dashed from the theater with a white scarf at his throat and a cape flaring from his shoulders.

He swept on—"Once I get started I gon make 'nough money. Then these Bajan with their few raw-mouth houses will see what real money is! But I wun get like them. Not me! Everybody gon say: 'Deighton Boyce is one man that makes good money and lives good. He wear the best of clothes. He eat the finest. He rides in the swellest cars.' That's the way a man does do things . . ." His eyes flashed and the trumpet flashed as he gestured with it. Seeing that golden streak in the twilit room, Selina imagined that all the things he mentioned would magically appear.

"And when I show these Bajan here, I gon left them to run themself in an early grave in this man New York. I going home and breathe good Bimshire air 'cause a man got a right to take his ease in this life and not always be scuffling."

He raised the trumpet and again lowered it. "Did I tell yuh I gon plant ladies-of-the-night round the house?"

"What're those?" she whispered, remembering with a wrench the mother's vow.

"A flower that does smell only at night. When you in your bed you can smell it and it's like the night-self is the thing smelling so sweet . . . And in the front yard I gon have a flamboyant tree. You ain never seen anything like that tree, lady-folks. The blossom does be a blood red and the branches wide so. And when the blossom fall all the ground does be covered in red like a rug," he said, standing absorbed in the middle of the red-faded Oriental rug.

"Daddy," she whispered, and he waved the trumpet, silencing her.

"And I got the house clear-clear in my mind now. I gon build it out of good Bajan coral stone and paint it white. Everything gon be white! A gallery with tall white columns at the front like some temple or the other. A parlor with 'nough furnitures and a dining room with glasses of every description and flowers from we own garden . . ."

"Daddy." She strained toward him.

"And upstairs 'nough bedrooms with their own bathroom—and every bathroom with a stained-glass window like in a church. People gon come from all over to see those stained-glass windows . . ."

Suddenly Selina leaped up, and as the trumpet made another wide dazzling arc she grabbed it, screaming, "She's gonna sell it. She's gonna sell it all."

"What, lady-folks? Who selling what?"

"Mother. She swore to Iris Hurley and Florrie Trotman that she's gonna sell the land. Your land." The shouted confession took all her strength and, still clinging to the trumpet, she slid to the floor at his feet.

He dropped beside her. "Girl, what you saying? What you saying?" he demanded harshly and, grabbing her chin, forced her head up.

When she saw his eyes and the fear crouched there she knew that she should have said nothing—for it was like shattering his life. A fierce protectiveness welled in her. She knew suddenly that she had to lull him with lies. Slowly she raised her hand to calm him and said softly, "I . . . I'm . . . sorry, Daddy . . . I didn't mean . . . to scare you . . . It was . . . nothing. She was just kinda showing off for them. Y'know how she always fusses about it . . . and talks big about what she's gonna do if you don't sell . . . But it was nothing . . ."

Under her soothing voice, the fear dropped from his eyes and he rose, picking up the trumpet. "She's always talking big," he said with a short empty laugh, "but there's not a thing she can do. Don let she frighten you with her guff, girl."

"But maybe you should write anyway and ask your sister if everything's okay . . ." she pleaded.

"No, I wrote once telling she to look after it for me, but I promise muhself I not gon write again till I make muh first money playing this trumpet. Then I gon write and start making plans. Then I gone." He shouted, "You and me. Ina, if she want to come. Even your mother can come, but she gon have to watch that mouth. I gon be firm with she 'cause it'll be my house and my land and I ain gon stand for no foolishness. And if they don wanna come, I gon make you mistress of the house. The servants gon have to take orders from you. When you want your fancy clothes I gon put you 'pon a plane to New York to do your shopping. And when these Bajan here see you, they gon say, 'Wha'lah, wha'lah, look Deighton Selina! I hear that man living like a lord home.'

"Yes, and it all gon come from this." He gazed fondly at the trumpet, and then at Selina. "But the very first money I make from it gon be ours, lady-folks, yours and mine. And we gon lick it out like sailors . . . Come, what you want? Tell me quick!"

Numbed, beaten, she murmured, "A new coat, I guess."

"A coat! Two coats! And a big doll like you once had."

"Oh, no dolls. Books."

"We gon fill the house with books," he shouted and then paused.

In the silence a child screamed outside and the almost dark sky became suddenly gray with snow. He flicked the trumpet, laughing uneasily. "But g'long, girl, you does start me talking and I don does get my work done."

Out in the hall again, she waited for the trumpet's onslaught, and when it came it was the distraught voice of her failure. She slid face down on the dusty carpet, trying to escape its mocking

87

blast; her legs in the ugly wool stockings struck the carpet once, soundlessly, and she ground the tie of her middy blouse between her teeth to stifle her cries.

Suggie's bell added another shrill note, and she crawled behind the stairs to watch the familiar ritual: Suggie's languorous descent, her perfunctory greeting at the door and the slow climb to the sagging bed. It was a soldier this time, his brass buttons glinting, his cigar glowing red and his eyes, lit by the cigar, following the soft shudder of Suggie's hips under the robe.

For the first time Selina allowed the obscene images to form. She had failed, now she would sin. He's kissing her, she almost shouted, and there're shreds of tobacco on his lips. His black hands are tearing the robe. He's deep between her fleshy legs and the old bed's thumping . . .

"Ina!" she cried, stumbling up and running down the hall to the parlor.

Her sister was at the tall parlor window, partly hidden by the heavy maroon velvet drapes, watching the snow gather over the park while her neglected music book glowed white in the dusk.

Selina, sensing her serenity, quieted a little. She wanted suddenly to stand beside her at the window and wait for the snow, to feel the room behind them with its massive furniture and inviolate calm.

"Ina . . ." she whispered, then added with a nervous laugh, "Suggie's got a new boy friend. A soldier. He looks like a bulldog with a cigar in its mouth. I wonder where she meets all these different guys?"

Ina's only comment was to gather the drapes around her.

In the gray silence Selina searched desperately for words that might bring her from behind the drapes. "I saw that boy who likes you on my way from school today. He asked for you. He said . . ."

"Go away."

"Please, I got something to tell you."

"I don't wanna hear it."

"It's nothing silly this time. Ina? It's very, very important. Ina? You gonna listen?"

"No."

"I'll tell you anyway."

"Don't waste your breath."

But Selina was already confessing. "It's about Daddy's land. Remember that day Florrie Trotman was telling ghost stories and you ran out? Well after you left Mother swore . . ."

"I don't wanna hear it . . ."

". . . to sell it."

"Get out."

A pulse of rage began to throb in Selina's loins. It was as if her heart had been torn from its socket and was lodged there now. She lunged and switched on the chandelier, and yanked open the drapes.

Ina was almost crying as she turned. "Why don't you leave me alone? Why are you always barging in?"

Selina shied from her sister's dark loveliness, muttering, "I just wanted to tell you what she said."

"Don't tell me nothing about that land. D'ya hear! Do you know what all this fuss is about? A patch no bigger than a city block, maybe. That's all. I'm sick of hearing about it. I hate it, d'ya hear. I despise it. Stained-glass windows in every bathroom!"

"You were listening."

"Greek columns around the gallery."

"You were listening."

"Flowers that smell only at night."

"Ya sneak."

"Flamboyant trees."

"Sneak. Listening to run back and tell."

"Listening to what! Nothing but silly dreams."

"He never talks to you, one thing. He doesn't say two words to you."

An unutterable hurt filmed Ina's eyes and her soft mouth quivered. "He doesn't . . . have to . . . say anything to me . . ." she whispered hoarsely.

"Don't worry, he won't."

"I've had better times with him than you'll ever have," she cried.

"You're lying."

"He never takes you anyplace. He shoves a nickel at you and you think he cares. But he always took me out with him . . ." Slowly her voice dropped and she stared with abstracted eyes beyond Selina. "We'd go window-shopping downtown and he'd pick out things he was gonna buy me. It was our game. Every Saturday. He'd pick out crazy things that I wouldn't want . . . lawn mowers and vacuum cleaners and crazy things like that . . . I remember once it was golf clubs . . . I didn't even know what they were for. That was our game . . ." Her voice trailed into a wistful silence and she stood tangled in the memory.

"You're lying," Selina shouted, and Ina said in a voice remote with pain, "Then the other one came and then you. He was always sick and mewling and you're always sweaty and loud. So he talks only to you? Well, you can have him. See if I care. I hate him!"

"I'm gonna tell him what you said." Selina started for the door, but Ina swerved past her and reached there first. "I'll do my own telling," she said fiercely. "I'm gonna tell him that he can't play that awful trumpet and never will play it!" She darted up the hall.

For a moment Selina was too startled to move. When she finally bolted after her, Ina was already at the bedroom door, her fists raised, and whispering tearfully, "You don't have to talk to me any more, d'ya hear . . . I hate . . ."

Selina's fist cut off the next word and smashed Ina up against the wall. Her next blow forced Ina's breath out in a whoozing sound. She pommeled Ina from below, wielding her fists between

90

Ina's raised arms; her fingers dug into the soft places of Ina's body; she clawed at Ina's hair and face, her hands in their eagerness slipping on the tears. She welcomed Ina's efforts to defend herself for they fed her rage and she struck more viciously. After a time Selina wasn't even conscious that she was beating her. She knew only that with each blow the fears that had been clamoring inside her for weeks subsided and the pulse in her loin slowed. Ina, at least, understood her desperation. She had wanted to tell Ina quietly behind the drapes, but she had refused to listen and there was nothing left but violence.

Finally, Ina sagged, yet she still gasped her contempt, "You're . . . you're . . . sweaty and loud like I said . . . Oh, nobody's ever gonna . . . like you . . . or want you around . . . Oh . . . All you'll do the rest of your life is walk . . . the halls and talk to yourself . . . Nobody's ever gonna like you . . ."

With all her strength, Selina brought her knee up under the brim of Ina's pelvis and she screamed. The trumpet shrieked to a stop then, and Deighton flung open the door.

"What wunna two hellions doing? Fighting again?" The horn flashed menacingly, and he caught Selina by the wide collar of her middy blouse and pulled her away. Freed, Ina ran down the hall, her dress flicking away in the dimness.

"You, Miss Ina, come back here," he called, but the parlor door slammed on his voice and the piano erupted into sound as Ina piled loud jarring chords into a wall high enough to shut out the world.

"What happen with wunna now?" He shook Selina.

"She was calling me names."

"Here I trying to learn this thing and wunna got to get outside the door to fight."

"She was calling me names."

"As for you," he shook her again, "you does make me shame sometime—always fighting like some boar-cat. You's yuh mother child, in truth!" He shoved her hard and closed the bedroom door.

91

As she stumbled, crying wildly, the trumpet joined the piano and she was trapped within their dissonance. Then, to complete the assault, Suggie's pagan laugh rang down through the stairwell. The derisive trio lashed her as she had lashed Ina, and she turned, sobbing, and, in the darkness, groped downstairs to the basement and, still sobbing, fumbled into her coat and ran from the house, slamming the heavy gate on them all.

# 3

"I beat up Ina again."

She stood, a penitent, in the narrow smoke-hung booth, which was itself like a confessional, while Miss Thompson, with her penetrating eyes and bruised tragic face, with her attenuated form raised high on the stool, might have been her confessor. The foot with the ulcer was propped on a chair, and she was eating, taking great chunks out of a fried fish sandwich.

She put the sandwich aside and said very gently, "You know what I told you the last time. That you's getting your developments now and it ain't nice for you to be fighting so wild no more . . ."

"I know. I know I'm too old to fight, but I just wanted to tell her something and she ignored me."

"Maybe she didn't feel like talking. Ina's a young lady, honey, and she's got her own troubles."

"I know. I shouldn't have done it. And then my father yelled at me."

"He didn't mean nothing by it."

"I guess not. He was just upset about us fighting. And then I've been thinking all the time . . ."

"You thinks too much."

". . . about my father's land. My mother's gonna sell it. Somehow. And she swore she'd kill me if I told anyone."

Miss Thompson chuckled and took a bite of the sandwich. "Now you know she don't mean that."

"This afternoon I heard like voices trying to warn me."

She laughed lightly. "Now look here, gal, don't be hearing no spirits round here."

"I'm scared."

She lifted her face, and when Miss Thompson saw the eyes wide with tears and the small mouth trembling with the inarticulate fear, her laugh broke off and her smoke-glazed eyes became shrouded with compassion. Quickly she drew Selina between her thin legs; her long worn hands closed in benediction over her head. Softly she said, "What scairt my baby?"

"This feeling I got today." She pressed her face into the warm hollow of Miss Thompson's stomach, her tears dampened Miss Thompson's uniform. "I tried to tell people I was scared and nobody listened. Not one of them—not even my father really."

"Don't nobody listen to nobody much."

"Why?" She brought her head up sharply.

"Why? I don't know why, honey." Miss Thompson tenderly flicked the tears from her face. "Peoples ain't got time, I guess. Or they's just plain too wrapped up in theyself. Look, lemme tell you something, Selina. Don't pay much attention to grown folks, 'cause half the time they don't make no kinda sense. Now you come on with me. Thompson's gonna take off them wet clothes and then fix your hair nice."

She led Selina to the kerosene stove and there, within its radius of heat, took off her coat, dress and the long woolen stockings that were wet with snow. "Lord, honey," she said affectionately, "when is them legs of yours gonna stop growing?"

93

"Never," she said dully, staring at her long loose-jointed legs in the mirror, at the narrow body perched on top of them. Except for the tiny breasts she still belied her sex; she still wore the badge of her frail childhood: the piece of camphor wrapped in cotton and pinned to the inside of her shirt to ward off colds. The bit of camphor intimated another weakness, she thought, staring at it: her inability to convince anyone of her need for help, her failure to abort the mother's plan. Suddenly she ran back into the booth and slammed her body down into the swivel chair and sent the chair hurtling around at a furious spin. Each time she sped past the mirror her face was more blurred until it was only a brown streak. She was blurring into nothingness and she deserved it.

"What's ailing you tonight, Selina Boyce?" Miss Thompson brought the chair to a jarring stop and Selina saw her face again, haggard with fear, and she yelled, "I'm gonna go and tell her to her face that she can't do it!"

"What? What is you talking about?"

"My mother," she cried, kneeling in the chair, her eyes deepening so that you could almost see the plan taking shape in their depths. "I'm . . . I'm gonna go right to where she works—just to show her that I'm not scared of anything—and tell her right to her face that she can't sell it. That I've warned everybody. I'm gonna walk right in there and tell her right to her face!"

"Stop it!" Miss Thompson pushed her down in the chair. "Stop talking outta your head. Lemme tell you something. Even if your momma was doing something it ain't none of your business. You understand that? That's between your momma and daddy. It don't concern you. Stop worrying about big people's problems."

Selina wasn't listening. She settled into the chair and closed her eyes, suddenly calm. The futile search for help that afternoon, the corrosive fear of months was ended by her sudden plan. "All right," she said, "I'll stop worrying."

And her mind did move away from its nest of dark thoughts while Miss Thompson's hands moved in a light sure caress through her hair. She dozed, awakening when Miss Thompson loudly called, "How you like it?" and swung her to the mirror.

She stared, astonished, at the sleek curls framing her face. "You made curls . . ." she cried accusingly.

"What's wrong with that? They looks pretty."

"But I don't wear curls. I don't like them."

"What girl getting her developments goes around with braids?" Miss Thompson fussed and snatched the smock from around her. "Okay, lemme braid it."

"No, wait," Selina said, touching a curl. "They can stay. For tonight anyway."

Later, crossing Fulton Street with the darkened beauty shop behind them, Selina clung to Miss Thompson, using her meager warmth as a shield against the snow and the mixed terror and excitement that flurried inside her. "What time is it?" she asked.

" 'Bout eight."

"How do you get to Berry Street?"

"Where?"

"Berry Street in Williamsburg."

"The Reid Avenue trolley. Why? *Why?*" Miss Thompson swung Selina around to face her.

"I just asked."

"Selina, I'm putting you in that house and you better stay there."

"Oh please, don't you be angry with me too." Selina reached for her.

Miss Thompson struck her hand aside. "Is you gonna stay there?"

She waited for an answer but Selina had not really heard. All her senses were focused inward, shaping her bold plan. Miss Thompson raised her hand once to shake Selina, then let it drop. A look of tragic understanding creased the taut flesh around her eyes, her long lean face sagged with it. "Come on, honey," she said, "lemme put you in your house 'cause I gotta get to my night work."

Selina waited in the vestibule until Miss Thompson disappeared, then put on galoshes, gloves and a hat, carefully tucking in the new curls, and slipped out of the house again. Chauncey Street was deserted. Everyone might have fled indoors as she came out, leaving the night world to her and furtively watching now from behind their closed blinds. She hurried, veiled in snow, wondering how it could fall so gently—like white doves descending—while she was in turmoil and, beyond, the world was in war. The snow should be whipping across the world, castigating it for its wickedness, lashing her for having abused Ina. But instead it was spreading its white and soothing mantle over everything, and even brushing her lips in a cold but gentle kiss. To delight her it was swirling in a golden dust around the street lamps. To guide her it was laying a white path that could lead only to the mother. Waiting for the trolley she was calm, for the snow lighted the vast night and the huddled houses seemed smaller and more frightened than she.

But once she was on the trolley, terror hummed in her chest, growing louder as the car clanged nearer to Williamsburg scattering the traffic out of its narrow track—and the sound of steel grounding on steel penetrated her. The trolley swerved onto Broadway, where the elevator trestle stretched overhead and the ominous rumble of the trains up there in the darkness joined with the trolley's din to make the night more forbidding. Selina felt it pushing against the window and her panic flared higher. She longed to return home, but it was too late, for suddenly the conductor was calling her stop and she was hurrying down the aisle, down the steps into the night.

She had never seen streets like these. The trolley might have taken her to another city, some barren waste land gripped by a cold more intense than winter's and raw with wind, a place where even the falling snow was a soiled brown. Factories stretched unending down the streets, towered blackly into the sky, their countless lighted windows offering no promise of warmth inside. Obscene drawings and words decorated the walls; the war had added its swastika and slogans, lovers their hearts pierced with arrows. Each factory was bedecked with "Help Wanted" signs, making it look like one of the shabby men who walk the city's streets with advertisements strapped to their shoulders.

Selina walked wonderingly through the curtain of brown-sullied snow, and around her the street performed a pantomime. Dark figures hurried past; silent men loaded long trailer trucks, huge tomcats crouched in somnolent wariness in all the shadows and a dog clawed at a box, its stomach sucked in with hunger and frustration. And then a cat, its belly sagging with young, ambled over and brushed her leg with its tail—the one warm gesture in a cold country.

The factory where the mother worked was another bleak building leaning black against the black sky. The hall reminded her of school—the same gray walls and steel stairs, the same damp feel of exhumed places. With unsteady steps she approached the door marked "Office."

The air in the little cramped office was rife with the brassy smell and feel of metal. The walls, the one window, the notices tacked on the bulletin board, the pinup girls on the calendars were streaked with black industrial oil. Only the blond girl at the desk, a yellow pencil stuck in her dyed-yellow hair, had been spared.

Selina paused, staring at the girl's high waved pompadour. It would be warm to the touch, she thought.

"Whaddya want?" The girl put aside the movie magazine she was reading.

"I'm looking for my mother."

"Yeah? What's her name?"

"Silla Boyce. Missus."

The girl took the pencil from her hair, patted the wave back in place and shuffled through a file on the desk. "Yeah, she's here. Her shift'll be through in a little while. Sit down." She waved

Selina to a bench and picked up her magazine, then put it down. "How come a kid like you is out so late?"

"I might look like a kid but I'm not. I'm sixteen," she lied.

"Yeah? It stop snowing yet?"

"No."

"Crummy weather!" A little color slid under the girl's pale skin. "March a'ready and it's still snowing. Every time my boy friend gets a pass it snows. And he don't like to go out in no snow. So we sit home." She rammed the pencil into her hair. "You watch, as soon as he gets sent overseas it'll be spring and I won't have nobody to take me no place."

Selina shook her head sympathetically and looked at the long-limbed women on the calendars and their skimpy fur stoles smeared with oil. "Whadda they make here?"

"Stuff for the war. Shells and cores and crap like that. I never go near the stinking machines and still the stinking oil gets all in my hair and I go home stinking. And the noise! Jees, it's enough to drive ya batty."

"My mother smells of oil when she comes home."

"Ugh." The girl smoothed her pompadour and Selina shifted on the bench.

"Could I peek in where the machines are?" she asked.

"Sure. Nobody'll say anything." She pointed to a door marked "Private" behind her. "Just walk down that long hall to the end."

Cautiously Selina walked down the long corridor, her footsteps accompanying her until they merged with an ominous current of sound. Timidly she pushed open a heavy metal door and almost slammed it back in fright as an enraged bellow tore past her. She was drowned suddenly in a deluge of noise: belts slapping on giant pulleys, long shafts rearing and plunging, whirling parts plying the air, the metal whine of steel being cut, steam hissing from a twisting network of pipes on the ceilings and walls, the nervous, high-strung hum of the smaller machines and finally the relentless frightening stamp of the larger ones, which made the floor shudder. It was a controlled, mechanical hysteria, welling up like a seething volcano to the point of eruption, only to veer off at the climax and start again.

And just as the noise of each machine had been welded into a single howl, so did the machines themselves seem forged into one sprawling, colossal machine. This machine-mass, this machine-force was ugly, yet it had grandeur. It was a new creative force, the heart of another, larger, form of life that had submerged all others, and the roar was its heartbeat—not the ordered systole and diastole of the human heart but a frenetic lifebeat all its own.

The workers, white and colored, clustered and scurried around the machine-mass, trying, it seemed, to stave off the destruction it threatened. They had built it but, ironically, it had overreached them, so that now they were only small insignificant shapes against its overwhelming complexity. Their movements mimicked its mechanical gestures. They pulled levers, turned wheels, scooped up the metal droppings of the machines as if somewhere in that huge building someone controlled their every motion by pushing a button. And no one talked. Like the men loading the trailer trucks in the streets, they performed a pantomime role in a drama in which only the machines had a voice.

Selina's mind spun without control within the noisy vortex. Fleetingly she saw herself in relation to the machine-force: a thin dark girl in galoshes without any power with words, and the boldness that had brought her here collapsed. The machines' howling seemed to announce the futility of her mission. She wanted the streets, as forbidding as they were, and the trolley that would take her back to her world. But even as she turned she saw the mother, and curiosity fixed her there.

Silla worked at an old-fashioned lathe which resembled an oversize cookstove, and her face held the same transient calm which often touched it when she stood at the stove at home. Like the others, her movements were attuned to the mechanical rhythms of the machine-mass. She fitted the lump of metal over the lathe center and, with a deft motion, secured it into the head-stock and moved the tailstock into position. The whine of her lathe lifted thinly above the roar as the metal whirled into shape. Then she released the tailstock and held the shell up for a swift scrutinizing glance before placing it with the other finished shells. Quickly she moved into the first phase of the cycle again.

Watching her, Selina felt the familiar grudging affection seep under her amazement. Only the mother's own formidable force could match that of the machines; only the mother could remain indifferent to the brutal noise. How, then, could Selina hope to intimidate her with a few mild threats? Selina almost laughed at her own effrontery. She thought of escape again, but as she turned, the door opened and the next shift entered, blocking her way. One woman went and stood beside Silla and, as Silla scooped up the finished shell, took her place without interrupting the cycle.

Selina barely had time to dash down to the office before the mother's shift surged out behind her. Their sound—a carousal of laughter and voices—filled the corridor and swirled into the office. Each worker, as she passed that metal door, had regained the power of speech, it seemed, and reveled in it, talking boldly as the machines' roar dimmed in her ears, letting the laughter spill over her parched lips.

They crowded into the office, bringing with them the brassy odor of metal and oil and perspiration. Silla entered with them and, with a vigorous stride, took her place in line. Their teeth and eyes shone with an unnatural brightness in their oil-smudged faces, and as they closed around the desk for their pay, the blond girl's face tightened squeamishly.

She handed Silla her pay envelope and said, "Hey, didja see ya kid over there?"

The mother turned, frowning, and as she saw Selina, her body stiffened with shock, some word of exclamation died on her lips. Cautiously she stepped toward Selina, her hand clutching the pay envelope and raised as though to stave off the bad news.

As the mother bore down on Selina, the room and the pleasant confusion of voices glided into an indistinct backdrop. It was only she and the mother alone together, Selina knew, and cringed in her seat. The mother was standing over her now, a strong angular figure in her somber dress, with her rough-carved features and set mouth, with the dark skin that suggested her mystery.

Selina glanced up and away. A feeling nudged her and fled: the mother was like the machines, some larger form of life with an awesome beauty all her own.

"What happen?" Silla whispered hoarsely.

"Nothing."

"Ina . . ."

"Nothing's wrong. I just came . . ."

"Oh Jesus-God, the piece of old house burn . . ."

"No. It's nothing."

"Something with your father. He got hurt on the job . . ."

"It's nothing, I said. I just came to meet you."

"Just came to meet me!" She shouted and caught herself. Her voice dropped to a menacing whisper. "You mean to say that you came through these dark streets alone, as much murder and rape as goes on in this place?"

"I came when it was still light," she lied. "It was just that I finished my homework and had nothing to do so I decided to come and meet you . . ."

"Oh God, you want licks. How you find this place?"

"I asked Miss Thompson."

"But look at that busy-lickum! Instead of she looking after that life-sore 'pon she foot she sending a child . . ."

"She didn't send me, I came on my own."

The mother staggered back and a silence formed between them that had the quality of sound—it was more charged with sound than the factory and rose swiftly to a point of eruption. As the mother's hand raised high, Selina pulled off her hat and murmured, "See, I've got curls."

The mother's hand dropped, and underneath her stunned rage,

101

there was an odd softness. She muttered in shy anger, "I guess you think you's a full woman now with yuh few curls and can walk streets 'pon a night."

"I came when it was still light," she said, slowly turning her head so that the mother could see the back.

"But look at my crosses! Curls and all now. And taking trolley this time of night by sheself. Oh God, a force-ripe woman!"

On the trolley the mother's rage joined the wheels' clatter and the trains' rumble overhead. "I din want to show my colors in front those white people in the office," she was saying, "that's why I din lick you down right there and then. But I got a mind to do it now. You's too own-way. You's too womanish!" She almost screamed; her hand shot up and Selina shrank against the window. "Patrolling the streets this time of night. Taking trolley out to this hell-hole. Making my heart turn over thinking something happen. I tell yuh, I wun dare strike you now 'cause I'd forget my strength and kill you."

Selina hid her relief behind her glare, and her eyes remained fixed on the mother's face. Silla stirred uncomfortably under the look and finally cried, "But look at you. You like you living your old days first. But where you come outta, nuh?" She bent, questioning. "Yuh's just like my mother. A woman that did think the world put here for she. But the world ain here for a blast!" she whispered, and her eyes moved from Selina's face to the darkness outside the window. "That's the first thing you got to understand. Second, you got to know what you about before putting yourself up in things. Take me on this job, for instance. When I first came they wun put me to work on the lathe. Just because your skin black some these white people does think you can't function like them. But when they finally decide to try me out I had already learn it by watching the others."

"It's so noisy in there . . ."

"Noisy?" The mother started indignantly. "If you let little noise and dirt 'pon your hand keep you from making a dollar you should starve. I tell yuh, to make your way in this world you got

102

to dirty more than yuh hands sometime . . ." She paused, reflecting, "I read someplace that this is the machine age and it's the God truth. You got to learn to run these machine to live. But some these Bajan here still don understand that—that Suggie and yuh father and them so that still ain got a penny to their name . . ." She broke off suddenly, pointing out the window. "Wha'lah, look the beautiful things they does have in this man country!"

The trolley was passing through a shopping area and the dazzling window displays flashed by like stage settings. In one window a manikin bride gazed pietistically into the night, the white gown foaming around her like a white sea.

For a moment Selina saw someone other than the mother she knew leaning over her excitedly—and remembered with a start the photograph on the buffet: the young woman with the soft smile and the pearls draping her breast. Helplessly she loved her for that moment and unnoticed reached up and stroked the bit of fur on her coat collar. Then she remembered her father trembling that afternoon as the dream of the land died in his eyes, and she snatched away her hand.

"You wun think I pass these same stores every night the way I does get on." The mother sat down, the shy delight still in her face. "I see two dresses I want for you and Ina to wear to 'Gatha Steed daughter wedding. I tell you, there's one thing 'bout money. It can buy anything you see there in those store windows." She shook her head, awed, and stared down at her oil-stained hands.

Selina also looked at those strong, square hands and could not remember how they felt or the last time they had touched her. All she knew about them was that they were always dark and determined, that the same deft way they shaped the dough for the coconut bread each Saturday they also scooped up the finished shell from the lathe. They offended her suddenly and she said with quiet venom, "Some people don't care about those things in the store windows."

The mother folded in her hands. "What you saying?"

"I said some people don't care for things in stores."

"But what you talking? What kind of people is they?"

"Ordinary people."

"What they does care 'bout then?"

"Other things."

"Like what?"

"I dunno. Things they don't get in stores. I dunno."

"I bet you don know." The mother turned away, then swung back. "What kind of things is they, Miss Know-it-all?"

"I said I didn't know." Selina tried to avoid the mother's eyes, but there was no place to hide and finally she blurted out, "Well, take 'Gatha Steed. She could buy her daughter that pretty gown in the store window but she can't buy any love there so her daughter would marry the boy from home and stop all the fuss."

"But look at my crosses! Look who talking 'bout love! What you know 'bout it? You might go hide yourself! Love! Curls! Taking trolley by sheself! I tell you, the heat from the hot comb must be sending you off. Love what!"

"Well, that's not in the stores, is it? And some people want it bad . . . Or breath," she said, spreading her hand on her chest and breathing deeply, "that's not in the stores either, and everybody wants that."

They stared at each other, the mother boring into Selina's triumphant face with an equivocal look. Suddenly she drew up, laughing, but it was a frightened empty outburst. "You think you smart, nuh? You think . . ."

"You asked me what I meant."

"Well I asking you to shut your foolish mouth now," she cried and something terrible and inarticulate struggled in her face. Her fingers twisted tight around the straps of her pocketbook. "Love! Give me a dollar in my hand any day!" she cried in a voice that was too loud to be convincing. "Oh, I can see what you gon give, soul. I can see from the way you think now that you ain gon amount to much. Scorning work and money like the father before you."

"I'm not scorning it. I'd just like it for one thing," she said with a meaningful look, "so we could leave soon and go to live on Daddy's land."

Silla's eyes darted away. "What you bringing up that for?"

"I just thought of it."

"Well you can stop thinking 'bout it."

"Why?"

"Who it is you cross-questioning?"

"I'm just asking."

"You does ask too much."

"Daddy was telling me about the house he's building this afternoon . . . It's gonna be white."

Silla's hand flew up. "Stop 'bout the foolish man. He ain the only one got plans."

"I know. You have," she said quietly.

"But . . . but . . ."

"I remember what you said in the kitchen. And you don't have any right to do whatever you're planning . . ."

"You mean to say you been thinking 'bout what I said all this time?" She leaned over, amazed.

"Yes."

"But what is this a-tall?" she drawled in a heavy Barbadian accent and, leaning back, suddenly laughed—a full robust sound that rang through the car, and she did not stop even when the other passengers looked up.

"I've told everybody too what you said . . ." Selina cried in shrill anger against her laughter. "And I don't care if you do kill me. I've told everyone."

"Told them what?" The mother sobered.

"What you said that day in the kitchen about selling Daddy's land."

"Who you was telling?"

105

"Miss Mary . . ."

"Wha'lah, you might as well tell the dead."

"And Miss Suggie and Ina and Miss Thompson. And I told Daddy."

The last shred of Silla's laugh died at that. A portentous silence gathered, and for a time they stared quietly at each other until suddenly Silla grasped Selina's coat collar and brought her close. Silla's breath broke in harsh gusts over her terrified face. "What he said? What they said?"

Caught in the vise of the mother's eyes and breath and the hand tightening the collar around her throat, Selina fumbled. "He . . . he . . . They said . . . they said . . . " She struggled to find the words but fear crowded them out in her mind. Fear that the mother would keep her word and kill her, boldly, right there on the trolley. "Nothing. They said nothing," she cried weakly. "Nobody paid me any attention."

Silla flung her back against the window. "They wus right not to listen. Don't think I din figure you'd be spilling your guts. But what you could tell, first off? And who gon believe a child that does talk to sheself, second? You see, that's what you get for putting yourself up in things before you know what you're up against. I tell you, you's like David without a sling!"

The mother was still laughing to herself as they walked down Chauncey Street from the trolley. It had stopped snowing now and the wind was perched high in the trees. The air had been cleansed by the snowfall so that the winter scene was clearly defined: the bare trees standing like tall lonely men along the white walk, the lamps casting bright circles of cold light. The mother paused under each lamp, lifted her face into the light and, with the wind tugging at her coat, laughed—each derisive outburst echoing down the cavernous street.

Selina, behind the mother, paused each time she paused to laugh and waited for the wind to bring the sound back to her. And when it struck it was more penetrating than the cold and filled her with a dread darker than the night.

# 4

The year passed through its round of spring and summer, a chill mellow autumn, and it was winter again. Along with it, the war swept through its round of death, and Selina, resigned to defeat, moved with them both through her uneventful round of school.

She spent that summer in the library and in Prospect Park with Beryl to avoid the house. At night, her body held the pleasurable feel of their long walks, her mind the image of the green tremulous heat amid the leaves, and Beryl's cool touch as they talked and slept behind the rock. But after each day with Beryl she was glad to be alone in the library. She had found a place behind the stacks on the balcony where she could read undisturbed. The sun always slanted through the high windows, stirring the dust and laying a yellow finger across the page. But she never noticed it. It was as nonexistent as the mother's vow and her own suppressed anxiety during those hours. Only the words and the scenes they shaped existed.

Over the months, the memory of the mother's mocking laugh and the machines' roar dulled and she began telling herself that she might be wrong. Perhaps, as the others had said, there was nothing the mother could do. Certainly there was no sign. The thought was comforting and she had almost come to believe it when she saw the brown envelope protruding from the mailbox one Saturday in March. She glanced at it with a fleeting interest and slammed the gate. Only when she stood on the sidewalk squinting up at the hard sky did something formless and heavy stir inside her. Quickly Chauncey Street and the park dropped away, leaving her alone in a desolate place with the mailbox looming behind her. Slowly she retraced her steps along the slate walk between the stoop and the barren front yard.

She saw it, the large brown envelope, the stamps with the king's profile, the official handwriting. Why hadn't the plane bringing it crashed into the sea? Why didn't she, now, pull it out of the box, tear it up and walk through Fulton Park scattering the pieces behind her?

It was no use. The mother would know. As soon as Selina returned, those eyes would search out the secret; the mother would shout, "Where the letter you just took out the box . . . ?"

"There's a brown envelope from home in the mailbox," Selina announced from the kitchen doorway.

The mother was at the table kneading the dough for the coconut bread as though it was a world without form and she the god shaping it. Over in the corner Ina sat grating coconut. There was a certain peace in the kitchen shaped by the steam from the pots, the humming refrigerator and the remote surge of the March wind outside. The peace crumpled now, and the mother's broad spatulate hands searched for something more substantial than the dough to hold to. Her face took up the confused play of her hands and her mouth opened, shaping a soundless word.

"The key . . ." she managed finally, her hands still ruffling the air. When they were still she looked bewilderedly at them and began rubbing off the dough clogging her fingers. "I got . . . the key . . . someplace 'bout here. Get my pocketbook!" she commanded Selina, and when Selina did not move, she turned to Ina. "Ina, wipe yuh hands and get the key from my pocketbook. This one like she can't hear all of a sudden."

Ina cowered, her stricken eyes expressed her wish to be forgotten in the corner.

"Come," the mother cried, "don sit there with your face like a down-fall. Get the key and bring the envelope."

When Ina left, the kitchen shrank, so that Selina and the mother were brought closer to each other, so close that they saw the thoughts in each other's eyes. Silla flustered, muttering, "I tell you, if looks was to kill, I'd be dead-dead."

When Ina returned with the envelope she sprang for it and then hesitated only inches away. An odd expression tightened her face and shaded her eyes. She almost shied away from it. Ina pushed it into her hand and turned from the room.

"Ina, where you going?" The mother's voice was frightened.

Ina was halfway through the dining room before she answered, "I gotta practice. I finished my share of the grating and I want to practice."

The mother started to call her back, then looked down at the envelope in her hand and was suddenly absorbed in it. She went to the window and there, within a prism of hard sunlight, sat with the envelope lying unopened on her lap and her breathing stilled. Her silence flowed into the larger silence of the kitchen and both washed up against Selina in a chill wave.

"It done now," Silla said, searching the room for her invisible listener. "And it can't be undone." She snatched the letter up then and tore it open. Her nervous fingers clumsily sifted the many papers, and as she read a bitterly triumphant smile slowly formed.

Selina, standing shattered in the doorway, watched those hands, and the night at the factory rushed back, vivid, as though a year had not passed. That night was part of this cold windy day, just as this day had been contained in that night, and they would both reach with long arms into every day to come . . .

The mother's smile had burgeoned into a laugh by now and she sat there holding a slip of paper and laughing with hollow, frightening triumph. But then she must have remembered Selina behind her, for the laugh snapped into silence and she turned.

Her hand lifted in a gesture that pleaded for understanding and even forgiveness. But at Selina's venomous gaze, her hand faltered down and she ordered her sharply, "Go there and tell your father to come here. Tell him it's business." And she turned back to the cold March sunlight, muttering, "Land lying there doing nothing and we here need the money. As God is my witness I did right."

Selina stumbled up into the sound of Ina's piano and for the first time wished that she were Ina and could drown out the noise of life with the piano. As she slid open the bedroom door she wished it, even as she stood there watching her father dress within the orbit of light from the pink-shaded lamp, she wished it.

He saw her in the mirror and winked. "What, lady-folks, you on yuh Sat'day prowl already?"

"Mother wants to see you downstairs."

"What now? Tell she I can't stop. I got my lessons to go to."

"She says it's business."

"Tell she I ain got time." He tugged open his tie and began knotting it again.

"She got a letter from home."

"What that got to do with me?"

"It's about your land."

His hands paused on the tie. "What you talking 'bout?"

Oddly, she felt a sullen satisfaction. She had tried to warn him, to protect him, and he had not wanted it. "I'm talking about your land," she said and walked out of the room.

Quickly he was behind her and she knew that his fingers were still fumbling with the tie. "Wha's this 'bout the piece of ground, lady-folks? What you saying, nuh?"

His bewilderment, the innocence of his question, drained her satisfaction and she wanted only to shield him, to tell him that it was nothing and lead him back into the bedroom. "I dunno," she said brokenly. "She got a letter and told me to call you."

He said nothing more until he reached the kitchen doorway and stood there blinking in its stiff white light. "Silla, what's this 'bout some letter from home?" he asked evenly.

She was at the table again, kneading the dough, her brown arms flecked with flour and her body one taut, inaccessible piece. They waited in a silence filled with dissonance.

"Now, Silla, you know if it's a letter 'bout my land you ain had no right opening it," he said strongly.

Her hands paused on the dough and she slowly lifted her head. Her eyes were calm, her voice soft as she said, "I has made it my business. I has sold the piece of ground."

"You has done what?" He started toward her and she raised a hand stopping him. "I has sold it."

"Silla, this ain no time to joke."

"Joke! Ha! I has sold it, I tell yuh."

Upstairs Ina suddenly began a loud lush piece by Rachmaninoff. At the sound, Deighton's doubt seemed to vanish and he laughed, a high outburst which rose with the music and warmed the kitchen. "Lord-today, you and all making jokes." He fanned her down and smiled at Selina over his shoulder. "Lady-folks, you hear this? Yuh mother and all making jokes. Here it is early Sat'day morning and she making jokes." He turned back to his wife. "What, this is April Fool Day or something so?"

She didn't answer, and his voice trailed into a silence which slowly clenched the air. As the silence held, his jaunty smile waned, then died, and as it died, a faint knowing smile shaped Silla's lips.

At last he whispered, "Woman, don make sport, I say!"

"I ain making sport."

"There's no way in this Christ world . . ."

"Where there's a will there's a way."

"Neither name of yours 'pon a paper . . ."

"I has sold it without muh name being on any paper."

"No . . ." He drew back. "No . . ."

111

"Yes."

"You cun do that," he shouted, and whirled, searching for Selina. "She cun do that, lady-folks."

Silla spun him to her with an exultant laugh. "I not only did it but I'd do it tomorrow-self if I had to."

"There ain no way . . ."

"I gon show you the way just-now," she nodded. Slowly she rubbed the dough from her hands, untied her apron and laid it aside. Then with her mouth fixed in a hard line and her back rigid she strode from the room, past him, past Selina. They heard the cellar door open and the weak wooden steps straining loud under her weight. Then there was only the remote sound of Ina's piano.

The strands of sunlight impaled Deighton in the middle of the bright-patterned linoleum. He passed one hand across his eyes, fending off the glare, while the other still fumbled with his tie. "Selina," he called, without turning to her, "you think she could of done it some kind of way . . . ?"

"I tried to tell you," she said, aching with each word. "I tried to tell you she was gonna do something. Remember that day you were telling me about the house home? I tried then. I tried to tell everybody that day but nobody listened . . ."

"Oh God, I remember," he groaned, covering his face with his hands. Suddenly, standing there with his face hidden behind his hands he was transformed. His body seemed to shrink so that he was merely a stick figure upon which his clothes were draped; his burnished skin became ashen. He staggered to the table and sank down; his head dropped to his arms and he didn't even notice that his sleeves were in the flour.

His anguish was too much for him alone and it reached out, claiming Selina, so that she also stumbled to the table in the corner and sank down.

He did not rouse when Silla returned with a green metal box or even when she shouted, "You wanna know how I did it?

Well, look then," and banged the box on the table. The dust on it sifted down on the mound of dough. Staring at his bowed head she unfastened a small key pinned to her slip. "Come, look," she cried, inserting the key, "I been saving it to show you all this year!"

Slowly, painfully, he lifted his head and stared, dazed, at the box as though he could not quite bring it into focus.

It was filled with letters, all written in the same fine script and all beginning with "My dear brother Deighton." Silla snatched up a letter and held it close to his stunned face. "Yuh see! I has figured for you good. Be-Jees, I figure this thing out day and night. While you was running with your concubine and taking trumpet lessons I was figuring how to do this thing. I say to myself that you don write to the sister so I gon write for you. I sat at this kitchen table late 'pon a night practicing to write your name till I had it down pat. Then I write the first letter. One like a brother would write to a sister—friendly and so and only asking 'bout the land in passing. I take it to a place near my job that does type out letters for people and pay to have it type and then all I had to do was sign yuh name. Yuh even tell she in the first letter that you was taking up typewriting. Ah yes, I figure for you good."

Deighton slowly drifted up into the sound of her voice, and as she saw understanding stir in his eyes, her voice rose, "Yes, I figure for you good. The poor sister was glad enough to hear from you and I begin writing her regular."

She scooped up the letters suddenly and scattered them with a cry over the table, on top of the dough, on the floor, on his limp outstretched arms. "Yes, you tell she some of everything in these letters. 'Bout the children, the job, the war, the trumpet lessons . . . yuh plans 'bout the piece of ground . . . some of everything . . ." She tossed one at him and it struck his face.

"Then three months ago you write and tell she you lose the job and was having it very hard and needed money bad and beg she

113

to sell the land for you. She went to a solicitor and he tell she that you must sign over the power of attorney to she. She send the papers and I sign your name to every last one them. She sell the land and today-self I got over nine hundred odd dollars for it. Yes," she concluded triumphantly, taking the brown envelope from her pocket and slapping the air, "nine hundred odd dollars waiting in a bank in New York and yuh piece of ground that you could throw down anything and it would grow, gone!"

His vacant eyes followed the envelope's flight in her hand. "Silla . . ." his lips fumbled her name. "Silla . . ." he repeated as though struck with amnesia and this was all he could remember out of the obliterated past. "Silla . . ."

"Cry Silla," she said. "Yes, Silla has done it. She has lied and feigned and forged. She has damned her soul but she did it!"

He turned to Selina, reaching out with a helpless gesture, murmuring in a hollow voice, "Look, Selina, how yuh mother has sold the piece of ground behind my back . . ."

But Selina didn't see his hand and hardly heard his voice, for her own tears were too loud inside her.

His hand dropped but he still called to her, "Look, Selina, how she has gone . . . and sold the land . . ."

"Yes, your piece of ground where you was gon build all this fancy house like white people," Silla said.

"But what kind of woman is you?" he whispered and swayed up, staggering toward her as if he could only answer the question by touching her.

Silla retreated in disdainful triumph. Silently they paced each other around the table. Deighton reached for her as though, like Brutus standing in the dead-strewn field with night closing in around him and his defeat certain, he had given Silla a knife to hold, as Brutus had his retainer, so that he might run on it and die. Now that it was time the mother had lost heart and backed away, the unsheathed knife still pointed at him. And he pursued her, pleading, like Brutus, for that agonized embrace, longing to rest his dead dark face on her breast.

It was not a knife but the bank draft which Silla held as she retreated from him.

"Silla," he cried, faltering toward her, reaching, "Silla."

"Yes, Silla. You gon have me arrested? I's a criminal? Go ahead. What jury would say I did wrong? Not even God in his heaven would side with you."

Suddenly he halted. His head dropped and he might have been inspecting his polished shoes, the crease in his trousers or the linoleum's gay pattern. But really he was watching the slow dissolution of his dream: the white house with Grecian columns and stained-glass bathroom windows crumbling before it was even built, the flamboyant tree withering before it could take root. He moaned, breaking inside as the dream broke. Yet, as the moan tapered into a sigh, something else emerged. That sigh expressed a profound relief. It was as though Silla, by selling the land, had unwittingly spared him the terrible onus of wresting a place in life. The pretense was over. He was broken, stripped, but delivered . . .

And something else underlined that sigh: the same unnatural acceptance that had scored his bitter outburst when he was refused the job in accounting. Perhaps he sensed that, like his defeat then, his loss of the land now was simply his due. Moreover, it brought a kind of perverse gratification, a terrifying exultation. There were sins, perhaps, lodged in him and charging the air around him that demanded his perpetual sacrifice.

"Deighton," Silla called softly. She had stopped when he had, her triumph slowly changing to suspicion, to uneasiness and then concern. Her hand lifted now in an almost tender gesture, "Deighton, you can always buy a piece of ground home when we catch our hand here," she reasoned gently. "What was the use of having land there doing nothing?"

She waited for a time and then added with a cautious laugh, "I know you. As soon as you got home you'd be ready to come back. You cun live on no small island after living in New York. But we can still buy land home if you want. Later." She paused,

115

hoping for some response, but he was a hollow man with dead eyes. His still pose suggested that even his heart had stopped and his breath lay trapped in his lungs.

"Deighton." She leaned toward him, frightened. "We'll talk later, nuh?—and then come Monday we'll take the draft to the bank in New York and get the money. You hear? Come Monday."

"Yes," he finally murmured, lifting his empty eyes, "come Monday, please God."

# 5

Monday morning Deighton sauntered into the kitchen, smiling and darkly handsome in a gray suit, dove-gray hat and gray suede shoes. His skin glowed and the rough hair lay smooth over his head. His assured pose matched his dress. The charming smile declared that he knew how well his clothes fitted, how smooth his skin looked, knew the astonished and shy delight he inspired in Selina and Ina at the table. This time he did not pause in the doorway, unnerved by the kitchen's whiteness, but strode in as if it were a drawing room filled with people eagerly awaiting him.

He went up to the mother, who was seated across from the children, and rested his hand familiarly on her shoulder. Strangely she submitted to the caress. A kind of stunned peace draped her figure, shrouded her eyes and lent a softness to her face.

"What!" he cried pleasantly. "I dress and you like you not even wake yet?"

She said nothing and he winked across at the puzzled children. "What wrong with yuh mother, nuh? She like she still sleeping." And his fingers brushed her skin again. "Come, Silla, don let's wait till the subway get crowded and all those people be breathing their germs up in yuh face."

She took a sip of the tea; something in her struggled to shrug off his hand, her lips moved to reply but no sound came.

He bent and said in a loud yet intimate whisper, "You know how sweet you and that subway does hitch up . . ." then flashed the children a wide smile. "Did I ever tell wunna 'bout yuh mother and the subway?" He waited for their reply and finally leaned over and snapped his fingers in their faces. "Lord, wunna like yuh sleeping too . . . Well, lemma tell yuh.

"This was before either of you born. Yuh mother and I was what yuh call courting and I took her to some big movie downtown (I was one man believe in spending money on a woman I like). Well, we sat up like swells in the big movie house and laugh our guts full, and then come back home on the subway. When we come upstairs at yuh mother stop, she took a sudden fright. I ask her what was wrong. And yuh know what—she din know where she was. The head had turn completely from the subway. I had to lead she the way you would lead a child . . ." He waited and then burst out laughing at their uncertain smiles. "The head turn now . . ." he chuckled, going to the window and looking out at the denuded back yard.

"Yuh know, people does say they don like Monday. They does call it blue Monday 'cause another week of work begins. But I did always love a Monday. Like take today. I feel good! I sleep the sleep of the just last night and I ready for the day. I had a sweet sleep—a sleep like I ain had in years!"

He sat down on the window ledge and stretched his legs. With a roguish smile he asked, "Silla, you did sleep good?" not looking at her but at the tips of his shoes. "Silla, I ask if you did sleep good . . ."

"But watch yuh mouth, do . . ." she cried, but without her usual vehemence.

He turned to Selina, laughing. "Yuh see yuh mother there, lady-folks? That's the way she was when we was courting. Never a hard word. A look on her face that did make you think of Jesus meek and mild. Her head always down. I tell yuh, I never even knew what her eyes look like for the longest time. And then one day she raised them. Lord-God, I felt like Paul on the road to Damascus when the light of the Lord struck him and he fell down blind-blind! And lady-folks, I ain recover yet!"

Selina smiled despite her profound puzzlement, and across from her the mother hid her own helpless smile by raising the cup to her lips. Deighton strolled back to her chair and placed his fingers on her neck and said with a sad smile, "And yuh mother had skin like none I ever touch. It was always cool to yuh hand no matter how hot the day. Come," he said tenderly, "let's go to New York and get yuh money."

"Wait, nuh," she pleaded dully, "lemme finish the little tea, and you best eat somethin' too instead of performing like you's on a stage."

He stepped back into a grandiloquent pose. "What I need with food when I has feed on the food of gods last . . ."

"Oh God, yuh don know shame."

"Come then, le's go. I got to work today. You acting all of a sudden like yuh don want the money." He appealed to Selina and Ina. "Lady-folks, yuh see what I got to contend with? Here it is yuh mother done some of everything short of murder to get the money and now she acting like she don want it! Here she think up a plan that would make Al Capone cry shame and now she's hanging back . . ."

Before the silence could form he remarked casually, "All this time I waiting on you I could be halfway to New York." His hand passed in a quick caress over her shoulder. "You might as well give me the piece of paper lemma g'long and bring back the money instead of waiting around on you . . ."

"No," she stammered, "no."

"All right." He shrugged and went back to the window and sat down. His fingers beat a gay staccato on the ledge but his gay smile was gone. "Silla," he called her softly, "what I did tell you Sat'day night when we did talk so long?"

Silla tried to fend off his voice with her hand.

"What I did tell yuh?"

"Oh mahn, stop nuh!" she moaned.

"I did tell you that I was one man never hold a grudge against a soul. And I did tell you something else." He pointed at her back, his eyes narrowed. "I said what's done is done, din I? I said maybe I wasn't meant to have the piece of ground. I even said that what you did made sense. Din I say that?"

When she did not answer, his shout cut the silence. "Din I say that?"

And, helplessly, she nodded.

"And yet yuh acting now like I gon take yuh money and run off someplace . . ."

"I din say that . . ." she protested weakly.

"But yuh acting that way," he declared, half-rising, but checked himself and sprawled on the ledge again. Suddenly he took off his hat and placed it over his face, folded his arms and leaned against the window as though dozing.

Selina's eyes moved in a swift wondering arc from him to the mother while under the table Ina's leg pressed urgently against hers.

After a time he pushed the hat from his face and he was smiling. Walking slowly over to Silla he placed his hand comfortingly on her shoulder and his voice was comforting. "Woman, I been trying to tell yuh for the last two days and nights that it's your money. That I ain quarreling with you no more. Yuh

think I still vex 'bout what yuh did?" He leaned over solicitously and she pulled away a little. "Yes, I still a little vex," he
confessed, "but what I must do, nuh? It gone. And it serve me
right 'cause I's the one marry you knowing full well yuh was
a tearcat . . . The money yours!" He extended his hand gra-
ciously. "You deserve it. You sin enough for it, mahn . . . So
give me the piece of paper lemma g'long and come back . . ."

"No." The mother shook her head as though to clear it. "Take
yuh hand off me . . ."

Deighton sprang back and fleetingly his eyes hardened, then
he was smiling again and making her a low bow. "All right. All
right. But think, Silla-gal." His lips split over his teeth in a grin.
"If I don want to give you this money there's no way on this
Christ earth you can get it. Consider . . . it still got to cross
my hand first. Even if you come up to the bank window with me,
the man still gon put the money in my hand 'cause I's Deighton
Boyce, best-proof. And I know you not gon show your colors
in front those white people by trying to snatch it from me.
Even if yuh did try and the police came, they would see that
the money is rightfully mine. Think! Silla-gal, this is one time
you got to trust me. I got the ace in the hole, mahn . . . But
rest yuhself." He slapped her shoulder jovially. "I coming back
with yuh money . . ."

They waited for all that he had said to penetrate the mother's
lethargy.

"G'long . . ." she murmured finally, and the word seemed
wrenched from her. "But . . . but make haste back here . . ."
She lifted dull eyes to him— "And . . . Oh Christ if yuh was
to . . ." and struggled up, threatening, then lapsed back. "Here's
the key . . ."

All the while Deighton unlocked the green metal box and
gathered the papers together he scolded, "All this time I been
here talking I could of been to New York and back and on muh
way to the job . . ."

He stuffed the papers into the brown envelope and closed the box. As he read the draft, his smile faded, his jaw stiffened, but this was only a moment and he was jovial again. "I tell yuh there ain many men my color ever handle this much money at one time, I bet. I gon get a check and deposit it, Silla," he declared, folding the draft and slipping it in his pocket. Then he carefully arranged his clothes, inspected his shoes, set his hat at a debonair angle and shouted gaily, "I gone!" swirling out of the room.

The air settled slowly after his departure. Now that his blithe voice was gone the silence gradually became as stark-white as the kitchen. For a long time, the children and Silla sat as though he were still there—in a stunned and wondering suspension.

When Selina returned from school that afternoon the mother was still at the table, her hands around the empty teacup and the same numb lassitude in her body. But her face had changed. It was drawn and deeply lined as though she had aged since the morning. At Selina's footstep she raised her haggard eyes, whispering, "He told you something? He told you he wasn't coming back?"

"No."

"Oh God!" she groaned and dropped her head again over the cup. "How I could let a smile . . . ? A smile now and a few words and thing in the night . . ." She struck the table, and the teacup made a fragile exquisite sound in the saucer. She stared deeply into the cup as though she saw her folly in the cold dregs. "Judas smile! Judas words!" She shuddered and pressed her broad hands tightly around it.

"He'll come," Selina said quietly, feeling a twinge of pity for her.

She shook her head. "To let a Judas smile win out . . . To let the man walk out this house with the draft big in his hand and the false smile on his lips and know deep within muh it was wrong and still let he go . . . Oh God, a few words in the night . . . I din know I could still get so foolish . . ."

"He went straight to work since it was late," Selina said impatiently. For how could it be otherwise? What the mother was saying was impossible. Selina's mind refused to admit it. How could he not come back when he knew how she loved him? "Yes, that's what he did," she confirmed loudly. "He took the check to work since it was late."

The mother's dead eyes lifted almost trustingly to hers. For a moment she wanted to be convinced, but the moment passed quickly and doubt scored her face again and her head sank over the cup. She uttered in loud self-condemnation, "I deserve to spend the rest of muh days in sackcloth and ashes—to walk with B.F. mark 'pon muh forehead, Big Fool . . ."

Suddenly she sprang up from the table and the tea things hailed her rising with a tinkling, late-afternoon sound. The wrath was tight in her face and she struck past Selina and began pacing the dining room and hall. Selina watched her form blur into the hall's gloom and then take shape in the dining room— like Proteus rising and returning to a black sea.

Ina came. They heard her oxfords scraping on the slate walk between the stoop and the blown garden and her cautious step in the vestibule. The mother paused, her head raised, her rage leashed for a moment. As Ina came down the hall, she darted out of the shadows. "He told you somethin'?" she cried.

Ina echoed her cry and hugged her books. "Isn't he back yet?" she whispered, apprehension shading her eyes.

"He told you he wasn't coming back?"

"No . . ." she whispered.

Silla waved her aside. "But what he does tell you anyway," and began pacing again.

Ina hurried to Selina in the kitchen doorway. "Didn't he come yet?"

"No."

"Oh no!"

"Oh no, what? He had to go right to work instead of coming home, that's all."

Relief flushed Ina's face. "Yes, that's what he did," she said eagerly. "Remember he kept saying he was gonna be late for work? Yes, that what's happened . . ." But even as she spoke, doubt crept under the words. She broke off and sat at their table in the corner. Nervously she straightened her socks, crossed her slim legs and ran her hand over her neat hair. Under her dress her slight but shapely body looked as if it would always excite passion without returning it, and she touched it now in her nervousness, the small firm breasts, the slim thighs, and all the while her eyes darted longingly toward the door. But she remained. She sensed perhaps that not even the parlor and the piano would offer her a sanctuary this time.

She sat, Selina stood calm in her certainty, and the mother prowled the hall, while outside the March wind blew the sun to the west and brought the early winter dusk surging up in the east. Inside the kitchen the motor on top of the second-hand refrigerator turned over noisily; the door upstairs opened and Maritze's pale footsteps glided up the stairs. Finally all sound dropped away. Even the mother stopped pacing and stood silent and waiting against the wall.

They heard him at the end of another hour. The keys first, and the homey jangle they made as he searched for the right one, then, the rusty protest of the basement gate. They felt the cold blade of wind through the hall.

Then his voice burst in the dark hall—like a light suddenly beamed across a night sky—gay, teasing, ebullient, shouting, "Where's everybody? Where's muh lady-folks? Come, Selina! Come, Ina!" Then the sound of things tumbling and he was gone, to return calling in the same irrepressible gaiety, "Light, light, let there be light, it say in the good book . . ." and he switched on the seldom-used ceiling light, and the rich oak wainscoting, the gilt framed mirror and the red carpet leaped into festive brilliance.

Deighton stood in the arena of light, dapper, resplendent, a new coat draped sportively over his shoulder and the light gray hat at a rakish angle. He might have been posing for a photograph with his wide smile and fixed stance, with the boxes in his arms and piled around his feet—boxes wrapped in gay paper and promising rich, frivolous things.

His eyes roved teasingly to the mother, who stood strangely paralyzed against the wall. "Silla-gal, is that you? What you doing home from work? If yuh know like me, yuh best not lose a day . . ." With that he scooped up more boxes and yelled, his voice muffled by them, "It Christmas, Christmas in the middle of March. I coming through. Out muh way! I coming through!"

He winked over the boxes at the mother as he passed, making a suggestive motion with his palm as though to slap her on the thigh. "Silla-gal, how's tricks? Where muh lady-folks?"

When he saw them he shouted and the boxes tumbled. "Lady-folks, how? There's somethin' fuh everybody today . . . somethin' fuh ev . . . very . . . body," he chanted like a barker, and pranced back past Silla, who stood with the anger trapped and useless inside her.

He returned with more boxes and swooped down on the table, piled the breakfast things in his arms and swept them in a blithe, dangerous whirl to the sink. He whipped off the tablecloth and held it low in front of him, jerking it and stamping his foot. "Wunna know what this is?" he asked gleefully. "A bullfight, nuh! I did see that thing in Cuba once and it near made me puke . . ." He flung aside the cloth and, smiling again, stacked the boxes on the table. As he arranged them in a pyramid he talked headlong, laughing constantly, his hands gesturing. "I had a time today, lady-folks . . . Ha, ha, a time! Lemma tell yuh . . . I went in these fancy stores over there on Fifth Avenuh and din know a thing . . . I din know what size I wanted and I din know what colors wunna would like . . . But I tell yuh what I did and it work . . .

"Lady-folks, money does talk sweet enough in this man country . . . Ha! When I went in these store the first thing I did was to lift muh head and not act like I come asking for a job sweeping the floor or cleaning out their toilet . . . I come in looking like I was somebody big . . . They look at me funny at first . . . But all I did was to start counting muh money . . . and I tell yuh they almost break their neck running to wait 'pon muh . . . Ha! Ha! I was never call so much of 'Sir' in all muh born days . . ."

He had arranged all the boxes by now and stepped back, inspecting them proudly. "Now we ready to work. Come," he beckoned them, and when they did not move he said in mild irritation, "What ailing wunna? You never see presents before? What yuh hanging back for? Come, they's yours!" he shouted and reeled like someone drunk.

Selina gave him a quiet look of disapproval, and as he caught it, the gaiety died in his eyes and he stopped his wild spin. They stood for a moment exchanging a deep and solemn gaze across the room, then he smiled shyly, his hand lifted and fell in a half-formed gesture, his lips parted to say something which remained unsaid. But his eyes were eloquent. They spoke of the hollow places inside him and the grief which underlined his high glee.

"Come sit, lady-folks," he whispered, holding a chair for her.

She came, sat and clasped her hands on the table edge, waiting.

He was laughing again. "Now we gon do this thing up right. You, lady-folks, take off all the ribbons. Miss Ina"—he offered her his hand—"come take off the paper and I'll open them."

When Ina did not move, he started, puzzled, as though there were no justification for her refusal. Then he shrugged and smiled. "All right then, Miss Ina. Selina, it look like you gon have to take off both ribbon and paper 'cause Miss Ina don want no part of the presents."

While Selina undid the wrapping, he gazed at Ina. Something apologetic, penitent, crept into his attitude. For, as always, the image of his mother was imposed on Ina's face. For that moment he was simply the boy submitting to his mother's silent reproach and averting his eyes from the disappointment in her face even as he offered her some childish gift to atone.

"Miss Ina," he began softly, "you remember how we used to walk 'bout downtown looking in the people window when you was small? You remember? No, I guess you wun remember. You was too small. But I used to pick out things for you that no little girl would like—just to be teasing you—but I ain teasing you this time 'cause you's a young lady and must be treated as such." He reached for a box and, noticing the gathering jealousy on Selina's face, said in a kind but firm voice, "Selina, it only right that the first one should be for Miss Ina since she's the oldest."

He half opened the box, peeked in and closed it, rolling his eyes suggestively. "Ah," he exclaimed, "it pretty enough." Then, with an impressive flurry he took out a ruffled pink evening gown. "Yuh see, I ain teasing you this time. I bet I even got the size and all right." He held it out to her. "Come take it. It's yours."

Ina's face reflected her indecision. Her chary glance swept from the gown to his face, to Selina, to the darkened hall where the mother stood, to the dress and back again. Silently she asked their help, but when no one spoke she seemed to give up. A numbness shrouded her eyes and she stared at the gown without interest.

Suddenly, with a grandiose gesture, Deighton threw the gown at her. It exploded like a pink flare and Ina's eyes helplessly followed its dazzling arc. Then, as it curved downward, her arms swept out, her whole body lunged in one live motion and she scooped it up before it reached the floor.

She held it as if it were a child who had fallen. Her face flushed with pensive loveliness as she gazed at it. Tenderly, she straightened one of the ruffles.

He said casually, "I buy that gown special. 'Gatha Steed finally marrying off she daughter this summer and this is for you to wear to the wedding. In that gown you gon put the bride-self to shame."

126

She lifted her face, and the mildness that shaded his eyes was reflected in hers, and they looked very much alike. "Ah," he gave a slight nod and laughed, "you's yuh father child despite everything. Somethin' does happen inside yuh when you see pretty things, nuh?"

She smiled luminously and rose, approaching the table with solemn grace, the pink gown draped over her outstretched arms, and it might have been the symbol of herself which she was offering to him. She sat down opposite Selina and said, "Open the other things."

"Wait, nuh," he said, turning to Selina, "I buy somethin' special for my lady-folks too," and bent the engaging smile on her, seducing her, and her jealousy faded. "Remember once you did tell me you wanted books?" He was struggling in his pocket. "Remember? Books that would be yours, that yuh wun have to take back to these people library? Well, now you got books." He whipped out a slip of paper. "This certificate is good for over a hundred dollars' worth of books in one the biggest bookstore there on Fifth Avenuh. The money pay already. All you got to do is show them this and they gon let you pick out over a hundred dollars' worth of books. Books enough to fill the whole house . . ." he cried, his arms wide, then with a low bow handed her the certificate.

Her shout unleashed a recklessness that infected the other two. Ina excitedly struck the table and Deighton began tearing open the boxes, flinging dresses, skirts, blouses, lace petticoats, shoes at them with a grand gesture, and all the while chanting, "Somethin' fuh everybody. Step right up, ladies and gentlemen, somethin' fuh everybody . . . Everybody win today!"

Each time he opened a box their eager arms shot up, their outbursts matched his exuberance and they transformed the kitchen into a scene of revelry. After a time the mother appeared in the doorway and watched them with lifeless eyes, her rage choking her, and she was nothing in the midst of their gaiety.

"Now hold it there!" he had to admonish them finally, "there's plenty for everybody . . . Behave wunnaself. I don like no bad-behave girls. I want only young ladies in muh house . . . House?" He paused and grinned, suddenly pleased at something. "Yes, house. I said *my house* even though I ain got neither one and never will now!" He turned to the mute, drained figure of the mother. "Come, Silla-gal," he called jovially, "I got somethin' for you and all. Yes, house . . . What I wus saying 'bout house now? Ah, yes. This ain none of mine and it never will be but I want only young ladies in it . . . Now, Miss Ina, come put this coat on . . . It cost a hundred dollars if it cost a penny . . ."

He deftly slipped on her a green coat with a leopard fur collar, leopard cuffs and buttons and a small hat of leopard fur. Wonderingly she stroked the fur, smiling to herself.

"Now come Sunday you put on yuh fancy coat and one these pretty dresses and walk the streets with yuh friends like you's people too . . ."

As she glanced up from admiring the coat, her eyes caught the mother; her smile fled and she looked very vulnerable in the small fur hat. But although fear stained her eyes, she withstood the mother's silent condemnation. "Thanks, Daddy," she declared loudly. "It's just what I've been wanting."

Deighton gave a joyous leap, stripped apart another box and flung Selina a coat trimmed in dark fur. "Feel it, lady-folks! Feel the fur. It soft, soft. Yuh did tell me once yuh wanted coat and yuh see I got yuh coat . . ."

Selina posed in hers also, but when her eyes caught the mother's, her smile disappeared also and she quickly stooped down in her chair.

"I tell yuh, there wun be enough closets in this house to hold wunna clothes . . . Even though it ain none of my house!" He threw his head back, laughing. "Now, a little quiet." He sobered. "Wunna got yours, now I got mine . . ."

A hush fell as he carefully undid the wrappings from an oblong box and lifted the cover. He stepped back so that they could see the golden trumpet resting in its casket of white satin. The flaring bell suggested that every note would be as golden and beautifully shaped as it was.

"It's another trumpet . . ." Selina said uncertainly.

"How yuh mean, girl—another trumpet? This is the trumpet of trumpet. This is trumpet fatha! The best yuh could buy from the best store out there on Fifth Avenuh in New York. It the only one in the world like it. These keys made out of ivory— every last one them! The mouthpiece, lemma tell yuh, belonged to Louis Armstrong-self. The bell plated in gold . . . gold now . . . no brass but gold!" His voice dropped and he whispered reverently, "Yes, it's somethin' to behold, in truth!" He rested his hand on the ivory keys. "It cost me over three hundred dollars but it worth every penny . . . A mouthpiece of Louis Armstrong-self . . ." He continued to stroke it, becoming abstracted.

But when he looked up the roguish glint was still there. "Come," he shouted, "it's time to celebrate this most . . . most splendiferous occasion. I gon play . . . I gon play . . . I don know what, but I gon play somethin' . . ." As he picked up the trumpet the light scattered in bright beads along the tube and around the bell. He pumped the keys and then fitted the mouthpiece to his lips.

The first note was a loud shriek. He frowned, lowered it— "Me and this thing gon have to get acquainted," he said, winking, and tried again. This time it was the fragment of a song, and he strode around the kitchen, blaring it out. As he passed the mother he tore the trumpet from his lips and cried, "Silla! Silla-gal, I almost forgot yuh. I sorry . . ."

The mother's eyes dilated, as did her nostrils. Like someone miraculously roused from death she stirred, and as her torpor lifted her lips formed broken words, "Over nine . . . hundred . . . odd dollars cash . . ."

Deighton laughed and swung the trumpet in a disparaging arc. "Lord-God, woman, nine hundred dollars ain no money out there on Fifth Avenuh in New York . . . But come, don fret, girl.

129

I come back, din I? And I even bring somethin' for you and all. You did think I forget you but I didn't. Now this last box got to be for Silla," and with a flourish he opened a large box and tore aside the tissue paper.

A coat lay in a bed of tissue, a bold red coat with a collar of dark fur. He held it before him as he had the tablecloth and made several passes in front of her, stamping his foot, his lips splitting in a grin. "How's this, Silla-gal? Yuh like it? I did always tell you that red suit your skin. So catch, girl!"

He threw it, and the wide-gored, bold-red coat swooped toward her, but she made no move and it fell like a shot bird at her feet.

"Pick it up, Silla-gal!" he admonished her. "Pick it up and know that they ain penny one left to buy another one. That's it. That's the last of the over nine hundred odd dollars cash lying there!"

Leaning back, he fixed the trumpet to his lips and let out a high screech, sustaining it until the muscles corded under his dark skin. "Ah . . ." he said, smiling ruefully and gasping for breath, "I got to practice this thing long. I ain no Louis Armstrong yet . . . I gone now, lady-folks and Silla, to take muh rest, 'cause I's tired. I did a hard day's work out there on Fifth Avenuh in New York . . ."

He started across the kitchen and then turned sharply. "Wait, lemma ask before I go. Is everybody satisfy? You, lady-folks. You, Miss Ina. Wunna satisfy? You, Silla-gal?" he turned abruptly to her as if to surprise her dissatisfaction. "You satisfy? Good!" he nodded, " 'cause I's well satisfy." Walking close to the mother, he made an elaborate bow.

As though she had been waiting for him to come within range, Silla lunged, the rage, which had been gathering as she huddled over the teacup all day and strode the hall, finally bursting. With a growl she wrenched the trumpet from him and in a powerful downward drop struck it once to the floor. The golden bell crumpled, the loud crash was its expiring note. Her body heaved up, the trumpet rose with it, then crashed again to the floor. This time the ivory keys scattered across the linoleum. One struck Selina's foot, and in her shock she didn't even feel it. Repeatedly Silla's body rose and dropped in a threshing rhythm, the trumpet struck. She might have been a cane-cutter wielding a golden machete through the ripened cane or a piston rising and plunging in its cylinder.

It happened so quickly that for a time Deighton stood dazed, his fingers curved still to fit the trumpet. But his amazement soon changed to amusement, and a high strangled laugh broke. "Woman," he gasped, opening his arms as though to embrace her, "it insured. What you wasting energy for? Another one coming from where that come. I was only joking when I said it's a special Louis Armstrong trumpet. There's plenty more where that come from. It insured!"

Silla paused, her demented eyes on him, the battered trumpet raised to strike him. "I'll get the house despite you!" she cried against his loud laugh. "I'll buy it yet."

"Why not?" He shrugged. "There's plenty of loan sharks out there on Fulton Street waiting for you house-hungry Bajans. Why not? You's a woman with a good war job pulling down this good war money. They be only too glad to make you a loan at six percent and keep yuh in debt the rest of your life. You can buy it tomorrow-self. And Silla-gal, it will be yours. Only your name 'pon the paper, and you wun have to worry 'bout my selling it behind your back."

"I'll get it." Her words stung the air. "And as God is my witness I gon get you too," she added quietly, edging toward him. "And I wun make mistakes this time. I wun let a Judas smile and Judas words in the night and thing so turn me foolish. You could touch me and it would be like touching stone . . . Nothing, nothing gon stop me. I gon steel my heart and bide my time and see you dead-dead at my feet!"

An imperceptible shudder passed over his body, then he shrugged, smiling, "You's God, you must know."

The ruined trumpet clattered to the floor and she slumped

against the wall, lapsing into her dull, disjointed state again, her eyes blank and her lips moving in an endless chant, "Over . . . nine . . . hundred odd . . . dollars cash . . . over . . . nine . . . hundred odd dollars cash throw 'way."

"I satisfy," he cried. "And muh children satisfy. Only you not satisfy, is that it, Silla-gal? I don know what I can do to please this woman." He shook his head in mock bafflement. "Maybe I should of get a black coat instead of the red!" he said brightly, and this caused another spasm of laughter. He snapped his fingers in her numbed face and, still laughing, darted into the passageway, his lithe form quickly blending with the darkness in the dining room.

They heard his laughter resounding through the disapproving silence of the house, rising into a hollow, mirthless hoot. They heard the bedroom door close and the laughter rise one more time, empty now, like an echo scattering over distant hills.

As the last fragment died, Ina lifted her head. Her strength had collapsed with his departure and the familiar apprehension gripped her again. She stroked the leopard fur on her coat as if it was her only comfort. Then, very carefully, she eased back her chair and rose, the clothes piled in her arms, and cautiously edged around the mother and, as soon as she was past her, broke into a run.

Selina remained. Obscurely she knew that this was her place, that for some reason she would always remain behind with the mother. Still kneeling in her chair she gazed around the kitchen . . . It might have been invaded by a band of revelers, she thought. They had dyed its antiseptic air with their laughter and dropped bits of their gaudy costumes as they danced, then rushed out, leaving the trumpet twisted on the floor and the mother's red coat like a raw pool of blood there . . . The day had begun so simply, with tea and the steam rising in a scroll from the cups, promisingly, with her father caressing the mother's shoulder and the soft trust in her eyes.

Her gaze touched the mother and Selina turned away. For it

was like looking at someone insane, who stares at the world without seeing it because of his inner chaos, who wanders blind through the dark labyrinth inside himself.

Silla wandered now to the table and, groping for the chair, sank down and hid her face in her arms. She uttered a sound which beat through the still room—a disembodied wail, a howl of outrage. "Oh, Lord-God . . . I was gon buy them things . . . I was gon buy them as soon as I did catch muh hand . . . I know they's girls and does like pretty things . . ."

At that cry, Selina's sense of retribution for her defeat at the factory turned bitter in her mouth. For there was a part of her that always wanted the mother to win, that loved her dark strength and the tenacious lift of her body. She asked, "You want me to fix some tea?"

But Silla did not hear Selina above her own hollow whisper. "You think I wasn't gon buy them dresses for the wedding? But he always got to be the big sport . . . Always a lot of flash with nothing a-tall, a-tall behind it . . ."

"I'll pick up the paper and boxes and stuff if you want me to . . ." Selina called softly.

The mother heard and lifted her head. A mist covered her eyes, and her lids were puffed as though she were crying without tears. "Yes, nuh," she whispered, "take it all out my sight, do! Over nine . . . hundred odd dollars . . . cash throw . . . 'way . . ."

While she wept without tears, without even a tremor, Selina gathered up the wreckage of the day.

# 6

Months later, on the day of 'Gatha Steed's daughter's wedding, Selina stood in the parlor feeling that she did not quite belong to herself. She was owned by the yellow taffeta gown her father had bought her, her feet imprisoned in the new shoes, her fingers estranged in gloves and her wrists bound by the gold bangles she wore on such occasions. What annoyed her most was a large bow which held up her curls. Whenever she closed her eyes it seemed to grow, crowding the parlor first, bulging then into the halls, the rooms, until it suffocated Miss Mary as she lay rotting amid her gray sheets and bound Suggie and her lover to the noisy bed; it billowed into the streets, into the sky, flaunting its yellow next to the sun's. And as the bow grew she slowly sank under its weight—a frail Atlas buckling under the world.

She opened her eyes, the bow shrank and she turned as the mother entered.

Silla swept into the room and the sunlight leaped toward her, sheening her blue satin gown, and it was like sunlight striking a blue sea. The gown fell to a swirl at her feet and curved low around her full breasts. Blue glass earbobs glinted; blue satin gloves sheathed her oil-stained hands. She paused, calm, almost pensive, buttoning the gloves—framed by the dark oak doors, her reflection held in the tall mirror. But she did not even glance in the mirror. Perhaps she needed no reassurance of her beauty.

For she was handsome, as the women from the hills of Barbados sometimes are, a dark disquieting beauty, which broods in their eyes and flashes in their gestures, which underscores their atonal speech.

Silla had learned its expressions early from her mother and the other women as they paused in the cane fields and lifted their sun-blackened, enigmatic faces to the sea, as they walked down the white marl roads with the heavy baskets poised lightly on their heads and their bodies flowing forward in grace and restraint. They seemed to use this beauty not to attract but to stave off all that might lessen their strength. When a man looked at them he did not immediately feel the stir in his groin, but uneasiness first and then the challenge to prove himself between those thighs, to rise from them when he was spent and see respect and not contempt in their faces. For somehow their respect would mean his mastery of all of life; their contempt his failure . . . Such was Silla's beauty today, heightened by the blue gown.

In contrast, Ina, who slipped in behind her, was like a girl on a cameo brooch—gentle and virginal in the pink gown which billowed to her feet. She wore pink gloves, and a pink hat framed her mild face. She breathed lightly, afraid to upset the delicate balance of her beauty.

"Come, le'we go to the beautiful-ugly wedding if we going," the mother ordered, and they swirled out behind her, the gowns brushing the wainscoting with a rich sound, the mother's perfume pricking the air. They crowded into the vestibule, and the children waited for her to open the last door.

She paused, her hand on the knob, and asked with forced indifference, "Where yuh father?"

Ina's eyes urged Selina to answer.

"Where he is?" Silla asked over her shoulder.

"Dressing," Ina said.

"To go where?"

"He . . . he said he might come to the wedding . . . Later . . . if he felt like it . . ."

Silla swung around, her gown rustling angrily with her sudden movement, and Ina started back while Selina braced herself. "Come to the wedding," she cried incredulously. "Don he know shame? Don he know that every Bajan in Brooklyn know 'bout 'Daffy-Deighton' and his nine hundred odd dollars cash throw 'way and does laugh at he? Be-Jees, let him come!" She shook her head grimly. The door crashed open and she swept down the stoop, one hand holding up the gown, the other hailing a taxi . . .

All three of St. Matthew's tall carved doors welcomed expansively the summer day as well as the wedding guests. Within the dim nave flowers entwined the tall lit candles at each pew; flowers burdened the arched trellis, where the bride and groom would stand, and almost obscured the altar. Their sweetness vied with the women's perfumes and the incense smoldering in the censer, while their gaudy colors seemed too worldly, too hot against the cool marble. Long threads of sunlight reached from the small windows high in the nave, down to the bride's guests and the groom's guests arranged on either side of the center aisle like two warring camps.

Selina sat beside the mother on the bride's side, surrounded by all the faces she saw at every wedding. Always, on these occasions, she loved them. The lavish gowns, the earrings, the small beaded purses made them like ordinary people who loved dressing up and being gay. She saw Iris Hurley, majestic in mauve satin, her wide nose taut with watchfulness, and Florrie Trotman with her abundant breasts constrained in red lace and Virgie Farnum sitting unperturbed amid her restive brood in an off-white satin gown which matched her skin. Their husbands sat with them, and Selina tried to discern in those inscrutable faces some trace of the faults ascribed to them by their wives. She saw nothing. They simply looked solemn and harmless in the tuxedos. Only the mother was without her husband, and even though her head still rose and fell in that proud elaborate bow,

Selina detected a masked but unutterable longing in her glance.

An hour passed. The air became heavy with the flowers' redolence, and the crowd's murmur mounted irritably against the hum of the organ.

"But you know 'Gatha oughta stop! I know a bride should be late but it over two hours now and not bride one!" Ianthe Yearwood, seated beside her husband, Seifert Yearwood, who owned the dry-goods store, turned and whispered this to Silla.

Silla sucked her teeth. "Ianthe, you know 'Gatha got to overdo everything . . ."

An impressive bustle at the rear of the church silenced them. The ushers' hands described a frenzied arabesque now as a small figure draped in white appeared against the sunlight in the doorway. The ushers hurried her and the bridal party behind a screen. Then, in the silence that was as tumid as the heat, they took down the white rope that closed off the middle aisle, and 'Gatha Steed, vivid in green satin, swept, rustling mightily, down the aisle.

The guests strained up in one body to inspect her hat first, a high turban affair of green satin with a plume rising imperially from the front. All over the church, the eyes dropped together from the startling hat to the gown, searching out each detail. All Selina could glimpse among the tall backs in front of her was a dark stain of perspiration spreading under 'Gatha Steed's arm as she passed.

They watched her until she was seated; then, as if controlled by a single muscle, the hundreds of eyes swept back to the bridal procession that seemed never to end—and all Selina could glimpse occasionally was a young dark face amid a froth of colors.

Finally the organ soared into the wedding march and the entire church rose to acknowledge the bride.

She was a small bride. And the heavy virginal white made her appear even smaller. Long-stemmed flowers and a prayer book crowded one arm while she clung to her father's arm with the other. She stepped like someone asleep through the aisle of lit candles and flowers, her face numb, her eyes lowered under the veil. As she passed, black hands reached out to straighten the train which did not need straightening, and curious eyes probed beneath the cloud of veil for her face. But there were only a few murmurs of admiration, for she was a sad bride, who walked toward her bridegroom like Iphigenia to her death at Aulis.

"Dearly beloved . . ." the minister intoned.

At both ends of the bridal table a pair of lovebirds carved out of ice kissed and slowly melted. Atop the six multi-tiered wedding cakes little painted bridal couples kissed under the icing trellis. The fervor of these artificial lovers mocked the real bridal pair. The bride sat in wan resignation before the cakes and lighted candles, barely smiling as the guests kissed her and wished her happiness, while the groom whom her mother had chosen twisted around in his seat to shake each guest's hand, his neck bulging out of his collar as he laughed.

Selina, behind the mother in the receiving line, averted her eyes from the bride, afraid that if she looked at her she would carry the bride's defeat and resignation as a blemish always on her mind. At the end of the bridal table 'Gatha Steed sat with her husband, Reggie. Silla bent and kissed her. "Soully-gal," she said, "everything is lovely. It's a wedding to end all weddings. I tell yuh, it must be like those on Fifth Avenue in New York . . ."

'Gatha Steed, whose smile darted across her face, smiled now and preened like a green bird. "Silla, you know how it tis—I tried to do my best for the girl." 'Gatha's smile snapped on, then off, and she pulled Silla down, whispering, "But hey-hey, Silla, what's this I hear that Deighton lick out a fortune on foolishness in a day?"

"It's true, soul. Close to a thousand dollars gone."

"Oh God-Jesus." 'Gatha clutched her throat. "Soul, you has got your cross to bear in that man. But I hear you still buying the house despite him."

"Yes, soul, I had to go to the loan shark for the money, but at least the piece of old house will be mine someday." Then to mask her pride she added, "Yes, I went looking for trouble and got it. You know what these old house does give . . ."

"Who yuh telling!" 'Gatha laughed and preened and the green plume whipped the air.

They kissed again and Silla moved away. Everywhere they were stopped:

". . . but Silla, how? That wuthless Deighton . . ."

". . . Lord-today! Silla Boyce? How yuh keeping? I hear you buying the house despite that brute . . . But don mind he, he got his coming 'cause God don love ugly . . ."

". . . Wha'lah, is these the children? C'dear, how he could do something like that and got such nice girls . . ."

". . . Silla, is it true? Over two thousand dollars lick out . . ."

Selina listened to the flat-pitched voices abuse her father and praise and console the mother and had to contain her anger. Slowly a thought formed as she watched her. The wedding was really for the mother. In her honor. The flowers and candles, the decorations strung across the ceiling and walls, all the cakes were not there for the broken bride but for the mother. Suddenly she understood that exaggerated bow the mother had given everyone in the church. She too must have sensed that the wedding was really for her.

The voices still clamored around them but Selina noticed that the mother was no longer listening. People still shouted their congratulations about the house but their words seemed to bring no joy now. They cried loud their condemnation of Deighton but strangely she did not join them any more. She did not, even as they called her name, make the elaborate bow. A shadow might have swept the room and crossed her face, for her elation was suddenly gone, and a sad line pulled at her mouth. Glancing up at her, Selina saw the same muted longing she had seen in the church when the mother had watched her friends with their husbands. "Come," she said in a joyless voice, "le'we sit down."

They found Florrie Trotman, Iris Hurley, Virgie Farnum and their children at the table. Their husbands had already left for the bar. Florrie greeted them with a sigh of disgust, "But c'dear, where the food, nuh?"

Silla sat down without commenting, her eyes remote.

"In truth," Virgie Farnum said, her pale skin flushed from the heat, "all these Bajan weddings is nothing but one big to-do-ment. All this silver 'pon the table. Ice birds kissing. Candle and caterers and no food! And did you see the great 'Gatha styling down the aisle?"

"She's something can style so?" Florrie sucked her teeth. "As black as she is in a bright-bright green? And somethin' tie round she head like she's still home selling fish?"

"But Dear-heart, don begrudge the woman she wedding," Iris said. "People home cun afford no big wedding, so when they come to New York and make little money you can't blame them for doing things like the white people."

"What you talking, Iris? I went to a wedding bigger than this home," Florrie said indignantly and waited for their contradiction. "It was when Birdie Worrell marry that old-old man by the name of Gay Lisle Pembroke. You remember old Mr. Gay Lisle?" And again she paused, but still no one spoke. "Well Birdie and old Mr. Gay Lisle had this big wedding. Birdie was in a gown with more lace than the law allow, and old Mr. Gay Lisle did look like he was gon choke up there at the altar in a high collar. Birdie mother spend money she din have hiring fancy cars from town, and the flower girls was hanging out the windows of the cars puking and crying for their foot hurt in the shoe 'cause they wasn't used to either car nor shoe . . . Muh dear, I thought my navel string would burst from laughing that day . . .

"And the reception! Jesus-Mary-and-Joseph! It was a reception to end all reception. After those malicious brutes got through filling their guts and swilling up the rum then they perform. Somebody must of said something to old Mr. Gay Lisle about Birdie looks and he up hand and give the man one! And soon the whole place was like federation. The rum bottles flying. The women and children screeching like bombs was falling. Some treacherous body went and smash the windows of the fancy cars. And the woman that had seven children for old Mr. Gay Lisle tore the gown clean-clean off Birdie . . .

"And what—after all the money spend on the beautiful-ugly wedding it din last. Later that night old Mr. Gay Lisle come flying birdspeed down the road with not a stitch on and Birdie pelting rockstone at he."

"What he was running for?" Virgie Farnum asked.

"How yuh mean! The man was too old to raise up a finger never mind anything else . . ."

Through the laughter, Iris Hurley cried, "But, Florrie, watch that vulgar mouth in front the children."

"Let them close their ears when big people talking." Her slanted eyes swept from her plump daughter to Iris' handsome sons to Virgie Farnum's fractious brood to Selina and Ina.

To Selina, Florrie's glance was as loathsome as her hand had been on her breast. Again Selina felt the sharp sense of alienation. How could she have been born among people like Florrie Trotman with her bawdy stories? She wanted to leave the table. To leave them. But where could she go in the large hall and belong? Perhaps with the men at the bar. She could hear their laughter above the hubbub and there was something warming and friendly about it . . . Perhaps with the young people sitting apart from their parents. Most of them were in college, becoming professionals whether they wanted to be or not. But even as she glanced at the young women, she demurred. The way their gloved hands lay lifelessly in their laps reminded her of the bride. Perhaps—a thought stirred in the darkened recess of her mind for the first time—there was no place for her here . . .

The festive din rose, ruffling the looped streamers and paper wedding bells, buffeting the walls. It subsided only when the food was served. At Selina's table the women were silent as the husbands returned and a white-coated waiter served them. As soon as he left, Florrie Trotman disdainfully inspected the food. "Ham, turkey, potato salad. All this fanciness and not little pudding and souse. Not little peas and rice. Oh 'Gatha is playing white in truth." But despite her sarcasm, she was impressed.

After dinner, after the verbose toasting and the cake cutting, a space was cleared and the toastmaster made the small sad bride dance with her groom. She held away from him, a fragile shape against his big frame. After they had made a few desultory turns other couples joined them.

At Selina's table the husbands had returned to the bar, and the women sat with a bottle of rum on the table.

"Dear-hearts, I don does drink no lot of rum," Iris Hurley said, filling her glass, "'cause it does make my head spin 'round too bad."

"What you talking?" Florrie said. "There's nobody like their rum better than you, Iris, despite all your talk 'bout the church."

"But hey-hey, she like she's trying to make out that I's some notorious drunkard!" Iris' breath came in outraged gusts. "Lemme tell you, Dear-heart, I does only take little rum when I got a cold . . ."

"You must stay full up with cold then."

As Iris bristled, Virgie Farnum said, "Now wunna hard-back women don start fighting please at 'Gatha wedding. Le'we drink to Silla and she house." She lifted her glass and her gray eyes lifted to Silla. "She has persevered and she has won out!"

With the glasses at their lips, they waited for Silla to respond. But her face was still abstracted; her eyes rested on the men at the bar. She searched among them with the wistfulness almost of a young girl, and a look, as brief as her eyelids dropping, mirrored in that fragment of time a deep ache inside her. Suddenly she pushed away her glass and lashed out, "What is the old house for wunna to make such a fuss over it, nuh? Houses! That's all the talk. Houses! When you does have to do some of everything short of murder to get them sometimes. I tell you, I tired enough hearing about them . . ."

They stared unbelieving at her and Florrie leaned over, troubled. "Silla what wrong, soul?"

"She ain been herself since she sat down at this table," Iris said.

"Leave she, nuh," Virgie said. "She taking on 'bout Deighton."

"Silla taking on 'bout Deighton?" Florrie said incredulously.

"Yes, nuh. He's still her husband, ain he. And I know what I talking too. Look, I raise near that man and even though he was never no good, he got a way 'bout him."

Silla groped for words to refute her. "But . . . but what you talking, Virgie? I . . . I don care if the man was to drop . . . dead . . . tonight-self . . . It's just the heat in here and the lot of noise that give me this bad feel. But it gone now. Come"—she managed a smile—"le'we drink."

Still puzzled, they raised the glasses to her and then threw the rum neatly over their tongues.

"Too sweet to muh mout'," Virgie boomed, restoring their gay mood, and filled her glass again.

Florrie nudged Iris, but spoke to Virgie. "C'dear, Virgie, you best watch yourself with that rum 'cause you know you. You'll go home tonight with your grogs in you, and when you hear the shout you'll be tumbling big-big again."

Red mottled Virgie's skin and she shouted proudly, "Not me, soul. I don got that loving-up to study no more. All I studying is the dollar now. I even thinking of joining the Association of Barbadian Homeowners and Businessmen."

"But what is that thing about?" Florrie asked.

"Percy Challenor, Seifert Yearwood and them so is starting it up," Virgie said, "and they want all the Bajan that got property to join. They gon set up some Fund to make loans to the members. You gon join, Florrie?"

"Me join what? You think I would have any Bajan in my busi-

143

ness as deceitful and narrow-minded as they are? Not me. Never no join!" she said with finality and turned to the dancers. "Wha'lah, look at them. Their guts full now and they getting on worse than Trinidadians."

They were not to sit there long, for the husbands returned and, emboldened by the rum, pulled them protesting to the dance floor. As soon as they left, their children scattered.

The mother remained, with Ina and Selina down the table, and together with the sad bride they struck a somber note in the midst of the gaiety. The mother kept turning the small glass of rum pensively between her hands, and when she occasionally looked up, her eyes were screened with the same helpless longing.

Then, a man holding a water glass of rum and swaying to the music glided up behind Silla's chair and, motioning to the children to be quiet, stared down at her bowed head. He was an old man, the last bit of life flickering out in his body, yet he seemed strong. Strength flashed in his taut hands, in his mottled eyes, in his bearing. He had known Silla as a girl, and he kissed her now, shouting, "Come, Silla-mahn, get up."

She turned, a faint smile breaking. "But Seon Braithwaite, you mean to say you ain dead yet?"

He laughed, his teeth very white against his dried, dark skin. "God don want me, mahn. I too black and wuthless." And still laughing, he drank.

"But c'dear, how you can still be swilling rum at your age?"

"Mahn, I preserve in rum. Now come, le'we dance."

"G'long nuh, you know I don does dance."

"I know what?" he cried, angering. "But what wrong with you, Silla, that you change up so since you come to these people New York? You don does dance! You must think I forget how you used to be wucking up yourself every Sat'day night when the Brumlee Band played on the pasture. You must think I forget how I see you dance once till you fall out for dead right there on the grass. You must think I forget, but, girl, I ain forget."

Helplessly she laughed. "But Mr. Braithwaite, how you does remember so good?"

"How you can forget the past, mahn? You does try but it's here today and there waiting for you tomorrow. So come, mahn, don continue sitting here with your face long down. 'Cause you know one thing . . ." He bent low over her. "In the midst of all this"—his gesture took in the bright lights, the gowns, the decorations—"we's in death. So le'we drink our little rum and have our little spree till it come."

Silla's protest was lost and the old man led her triumphantly to the dance floor.

They danced near the edge of the circle, the old man straining the mother close and her blue gown swirling around her feet. All the older people danced with this same graceful restraint— their backs stiff and only a suggestion of movement in their hips and legs. Sometimes as the clarinet pierced the air with a long plaintive note one of the younger women would move away from her partner and dance alone, her arms outstretched and her face rapt as she responded deeply to the music.

Selina's eyes followed the mother while her mind strained to see her as the girl dancing on the pasture. But there was nothing to form the image. She could imagine the pasture. It must have been a wide field with the grass cropped short by the grazing cattle, and scarred by the dancers' bare feet. The world had been when she had not. Time stretched behind and beyond her small life. Years ago, on an island that was only a green node in a vast sea, the mother had been a girl who had danced till she had fainted once, and she, Selina, had been nothing to her. Suddenly she yearned to know the mother then, in her innocence. Above all, she longed to understand the mother, for she knew, obscurely, that she would never really understand anything until she did.

"Isn't it a nice wedding?" Ina was saying. "I wish, though, they'd put out the lights and just leave the candles burning."

Selina noted her sister's faint lipstick and her gloved hands

145

arranged neatly in her lap. She was like the college girls, Selina thought. They all had something she would never have. Grace, quiet poses, and the mildness . . .

A young man came up and, leaning over Ina, asked her to dance in a voice breaking with nervousness. She hesitated a moment, glancing at Selina and then toward the mother on the dance floor; then quickly she placed her hand trustingly in his and rose.

Only Selina and the bride were left now and she felt terribly alone. She traced the brocaded design of the tablecloth to hide her loneliness from the dancers and from the faceless onlookers crowded at the open windows and doors. What must she look like sitting there, she wondered, with the childish bow and the yellow gown that made her skin darker, with her jutting elbows and wrists. She gazed enviously at the children scampering amid the dancers in a game of tag. She was too old for them, yet not old enough for a boy to come, his voice breaking, and ask her to dance . . .

"Guess who?" Damp hands covered her eyes.

"Beryl." She pulled away.

"What's wrong?"

"I hate weddings."

"I don't. They're fun."

Suddenly Selina jumped up. "C'mon, let's dance."

"How can we? We don't have partners."

"I don't care. We'll dance with each other."

"But we're kinda old for that."

"I don't give one damn, d'ya hear? Not one damn in hell about anything."

Beryl started and drew away a little, shaking her head disapprovingly. "Selina, you're mad about something . . ."

"I'm not. Let's just dance."

On the floor they sidled awkwardly amid the other dancers, clutching each other close. Gradually their bodies gave way to the music, their feet caught the rhythm and they were dancing.

The calypso flared in loud lilting rhythms through the hall and reached with fluid arms to the curious crowd at the windows and doors and into the gathering night behind them. Someone sang in the flat but striking accent of Barbadian speech:

*". . . It was the day after Christmas that I went to Barbados,*
*As I walk around in the town I heard a cute little song.*
*The temperature was so damn hot,*
*That I stopped in a rum shop,*
*And before I could open me mout' I heard somebody shout:*
*'Aye, Budda Neffie lock up and he ain do nothing, Pam-palam.*
*He get nine years for he own granddaughter, Pam-palam.*
*Oh, the sweat 'pon he head running off like water, Pam-palam.*
*He swear by Christ he ain done nothing, Pam-palam . . ."*

The dancers overflowed the space and other tables were dismantled. Selina's feet seemed to glance the floor now, for the music had become a high wave lifting her up.

*Now, everybody love their carnival,*
    *Lord, don stop the carnival.*
*Yes, carnival is a decent Bacchanal,*
    *Lord, don stop the carnival.*
*All the West Indian love their carnival,*
    *Lord, don stop the carnival.*
*Ah, gal, it's a Creole Bacchanal,*
    *Oh, Lord, don stop the carnival.*

• • • • • • • • • • • • • •

*I'm a born Creole and about to have me fun,*
    *Lord, don stop the carnival.*
*Especially when you see me drinking rum,*
    *Lord, don stop the carnival.*

• • • • • • • • • • • • • •

*Oh, carnival has come to New York,*
    *Lord, don stop the carnival.*

147

*Everywhere you go you hear the talk,*
*Lord, don stop the carnival.*

. . . . . . . . . . . . . .

*Yeah, Lord we makin' Bacchanal . . .*

The music persisted through the bride and groom's departure; it screeched and thudded late into the evening, binding the dancers together, setting them apart from all other people.

*"Small Island, go back where you come from.*
*Small Island, go back where you come from.*
*You come from Trinidad in a fishing boat,*
*And now you wearing a great big overcoat!*
*Small Island, go back where you really come from.*

*You see them Bajans, they're the worse of them all!*
*You hear them say 'I ain't gwine back at all.'*
*They come by the one and they come by the two,*
*And now you see them all over Lenox Avenue.*
*Small Island, go back where you really come from . . ."*

Selina swayed with the thronged dancers, part of a giant amoeba which changed shape yet always remained of one piece. When she and Beryl danced in the center she felt like the source from which all the movement flowed. When pushed to the periphery, like someone clinging to a spinning wheel. Once, pushed to the outside, she glimpsed a man standing in the doorway. She saw only his legs, but their stillness in the midst of all the movement arrested her, and the stance reminded her vaguely of her father. But then the dancers quickly swept her back to the center and she lost sight of the still legs. When finally she pressed to the edge again she saw that it was her father and his presence drained her happiness.

Deighton stood, uncommitted, between the summer night filled with faces behind him and the brilliant scene in the hall.

He might have been one of the silent surging mob outside who had been shoved by them into the light—or a guest who had purposely arrived late and waited, poised, for his presence to be noted and his name murmured throughout the room. His tuxedo fitted well his lean body. He held white gloves and a top hat. And his face was as carefully arranged as his clothes: the eyes moving casually over the men at the bar, over the deserted bridal table with its burnt candles and melted lovebirds, over the heaving dancers and sweating musicians. His smile was ready.

"My father's here," Selina shouted and tried to pull from Beryl, who was singing loudly with the others, "Small Island, go back where you come from . . ." and did not hear her.

"My father's here. Lemme go." And again she struggled without success. Not only Beryl, but the glaring lights, the loud song and the other dancers seemed to be holding her from him. Frantically she waved until his eyes in their unhurried search finally reached her. He smiled, but at the same time his hand shot up in a forceful signal for her to remain where she was.

His eyes swept on. He saw Ina, her face lifted shyly to the boy's as they danced. Then suddenly he took one short startled step forward, pressing the hat and white gloves hard in his hand. He had glimpsed the mother. Her blue gown amid the other colors and the old man's arm tight around her waist.

He was jealous, unreasonably so, for he knew that the man was old and useless. But he could not help it. At least the old man was holding her and laughing down into her face, while he had not held her since the Sunday night before that Monday of ruin—had not touched her even, or spoken. He slept in the parlor each night now with the tall sliding doors locked between them . . . He followed the line of her body under the blue gown with surprise and guarded desire. Then, as the old man spun her around and he saw her laughing like a girl, saw her breasts rising full at the low neckline, passion thrust him sharp and for a moment he had to close his eyes.

Silla had seen him and, as he opened his eyes, she lifted her head to stun him again with her beauty. Strangely, the same passion lanced her eyes—stronger, more urgent than his even. It reached out across the hall to claim him, to confess that despite what they had both done, despite their silence, they were joined always. Her hand half lifted as though to beckon him close, a gesture that said she would, with her hand in his, declare all this to the others. But even as he took the first tentative step forward, her hand dropped and her derisive laugh drove him back.

The mother laughed, the song soared: "Small Island, go back where you come from . . ." and both sounds tore his thin composure apart. His eyes wheeled over the room in a desperate search for a single welcoming face. To the bar, but the men there had seen him, and as his eyes met theirs, as his hand lifted uncertainly, they turned away with cold nods, and their backs formed a wall against him. His eyes then swung in a wide wild arc back to the dancers; he strained forward as if by sheer will he would force someone there to greet him. But they had seen him by now and they closed protectively around Silla and Ina; someone pulled Selina back. Then, like the men at the bar, the dancers turned in one body and danced with their backs to him.

But still Deighton remained, staring with exquisite pain at their disdaining backs, transfixed by those piercing voices. Until finally his agony was too great and he staggered back. As if choking, he pulled at the stiff collar, his voice struggled up, "Oh God . . . My God . . . why . . ." Before his next word they turned—all, the men at the bar, the musicians, the whirling dancers turned. Even the children crumpled in sleep on the benches against the wall roused and turned their small faces to him. From all over the hall those dark contemptuous faces charged him. Those eyes condemned him and their voices rushed full tilt at him, scourging him and finally driving him from their presence with their song, "Small Island, go back where you really come from!"

# 7

That night and many nights afterward Selina's sleep was marred by the image of her father groping as though blind or drunk from the hall. The image was like an abstract painting, for he was always only an immense hand reaching out and imploring eyes. Each night the calypso song resounded in her sleep, hounding him out into the mob waiting in the dark to claim him.

On her fifteenth birthday she stood in line in the school lunchroom thinking of the dream amid thoughts of the mistake she had made in geometry and the blond boy in Latin whose eyes mirrored her loneliness; she wondered whether her lunch group would give her the customary party. Holding up her tray she shoved and prodded a way through the crowded lunchroom, dodging the sprawled legs and flailing arms that sprang up like traps in her path.

The air was raw with the smell of sweated young bodies, and their shrill voices, strafing the air in almost visible white streaks, spoke of life bursting full yet, at the same time, pleaded for something or someone to give that life form before it destroyed them. The sound always recalled to her the machines at the factory. Its theme was the same one of impending ruin. The machine-force pervaded them, it seemed—was shaping them—and they could not help but echo it.

Nearing her table she saw five cupcakes arranged in a cake with a tiny candle in each, and she hid her happiness by shouting, "I was just standing in line getting good and mad thinking none of you jerks had remembered."

"Make a wish and blow," they yelled, and not knowing what to wish for she sucked in air and let it out and the candles died. They shoved a knife into her ink-stained hands and she cut the small cakes in two. When they had eaten and she had tenderly put away her candles their voices welled up in the usual talk and then suddenly dropped into silence as one girl leaned across the table, whispering, "Remember that cute fella I was telling you all started coming by to see me?"

"Yes," their hushed voices pressed up around her.

"Well, me and him's engaged. Sorta, anyways."

"No."

"Yep."

Their table became the one small center of silence in the lunchroom as they waited, eager for more but afraid. The girl who had spoken was thin, with lipstick blazoned across her mouth and a petulant child's face under a profusion of curls. She had recently been assigned to their table and at first the other girls, all colored and mostly of West Indian parentage, had been distant and disapproving because the girl lived on Fulton Street, played hookey, smoked and talked only of boys. Yet when she talked they listened, helplessly absorbed in all she said.

"How come?" Selina finally asked.

"Where's the ring?" someone added cruelly.

"That's why I said 'sorta,' jerk. Till I get the ring."

"How come?" Selina shouted.

"Well, it was like this," she began, and they hastily formed a tight circle around her while the noise clashed unheeded beyond. "We was in the living room, see. Talking and fooling around. Mostly fooling around. Y'know. Then my aunt had to go to prayer meeting so naturally he had to leave. Soon as he left she started getting on me about the same old crap—going to church and going to school. Y'know. But girl, when she finally cut out to church who should cut back but that cute fool. And there I was in my pajamas . . ."

"Lord," Selina said.

"Girl, I was so embarrassed I almost fell out. But he apologized and said he forgot his cigarettes. So naturally he stayed and naturally we started fooling around again. After a while he turned off them lights and things really got frantic then. So I had to like tell him I didn't mind fooling around if I liked a fella but I didn't go all the way . . ."

Someone snickered and she shrugged. "So he got salty, girl. Said he didn't go out with squares. But he got nice again and said how about us getting engaged. And you know me, I'd do just about anything to get outta going to school. Then he said it was all right to go all the way being as we was practically engaged—and being as all engaged couples do it."

"That's a lie," someone sang out. But no one heard for they were all busy shaping that scene of seduction behind their wide eyes. Beyond their circle a kind of silence also rippled below the noise as if others in the lunchroom listened with drawn breath.

The silence stretched and when it was taut enough to snap the girl said with a proud shrug, "Well naturally, it happened. And to tell the truth I didn't see nothing that great about it at first. But girl, after a while that jive got good to me and lemme tell you, I was moved!"

She sat back, lit a cigarette and the intimate circle fell apart. The others remained leaning on the table, so shaken and spent that it might have been they on the couch in the darkened room. Their shocked eyes fled her face while their hands nervously caught at the bread crumbs and bits of paper on the table. Only Selina gazed wonderingly at the girl. It was wrong, she knew, yet even in the dimness of her thoughts she could not see it as sin; it was sad because it had happened in a tenement on Fulton Street, yet she was envious. For the girl seemed suddenly awakened into life. A woman despite her child's face. Freed of the ferment trapped in all of them in the lunchroom. She had done something else too, Selina sensed, gathering up her books as the bell rang. She had thumbed her nose at them, at her nagging aunt, at everyone . . . Could she, Selina, if given that chance, be that bold?

That evening, waiting for her father in the twilit bedroom, she lit the candle nubs, and with the tiny flames spiraling close to her face she wished for a boy. Not one who would tumble her on a sofa. She was not bold enough for that. But a quiet boy who would read with her in the library, and sometimes kiss her behind the stacks on the balcony. For the first time in her life, her lips formed the wish and she strained in her mind to shape his face.

"Selina? You in here?" the mother's voice intruded. Guiltily she snuffed out the candles and crumbled them, still hot, in her fist.

"What's that you burning? You practicing obeah or something so?" When Selina did not answer she asked, "But why you always draw up in some dark place?"

"I'm waiting for Daddy."

In the room's dim quiescence Selina heard the mother catch her breath as though to speak but she said nothing nor did she leave. Selina waited, puzzled, wondering why her father hadn't come yet. Suddenly she desperately wanted him to come, to see his white shirt hanging disembodied in the dusk as he stood in the doorway, to hear him sigh like a girl as he closed the door on the long day at the mattress factory. For some reason she was anxious and suddenly she jumped up, crying at the mother's silent figure, "Something's happened?"

And the mother's voice came, so gentle that it barely disturbed the silence. "Yes. Yuh father had something happen to his arm today at the factory. Nothing serious but he's in the hospital for a few days . . ."

The strength that had brought her to her feet failed her now and she sank down.

"They start up some new machine and he ask to work on it without knowing what it gave and the arm got caught. The nerve gone, they say. Crush so."

Selina barely heard, for her own blood thudded loud as another voice in her ears. The sound became the machines roaring at the factory, and she saw him, a slim figure with an ascetic's face standing amid that giant complex of pistons and power, shuddering inside each time the steam jettisoned $u_{\downarrow}$ and the machines stamped down.

"They told him not to work the machine till he had learned it good but he wun hear," the mother was saying, her voice dull with sadness. "But that's his way. He does only half-learn a thing. The same with the blasted trumpet and the course he was taking for all those years . . ."

The mother talked and Selina saw the huge hungry maw of the machine opening while her father tended it absently. "Watch," she cried in her thoughts as it clamped down on his arm, sucking it in as it sucked in the metal to be shaped, then spewing it out crushed. Couldn't the machine have seen that he was already crushed inside? Couldn't it have spared him? And thinking of that impersonal brutality, she wept. "When?" she whispered, gagging on the tears. "When did it happen?"

"This noon. They did call me on the job and I went straight to the hospital but . . . but he wun speak to me . . ."

Noon! While she had been listening with almost indecent delight to a sordid story of seduction, while her own wish for a boy was slowly forming, it had happened.

"No tears, I beg you," the mother pleaded, her own voice breaking with them. "I can't bear the tears, you hear! I got enough with your sister crying bucket a drop downstairs and she's a full woman. I can't bear the tears, I say."

But Selina's sobs persisted in the dusk silence, along with the

distant clamor of the streets and Ina's muted wail from below
—until finally darkness spread like a balm through the room.
Then she said, "Where's the hospital?"

In answer the darkness moved as the mother shifted.

"Where is it? I'm going to him."

"No," she said gently.

"No? I say I want to see him and you say no?" She sprang
up, peering through the shadows. "Tell me what hospital."

"I not saying the name."

"You're not saying . . . ?" And she stumbled up and across the
room, feeling her way until she saw the mother's strained face
emerge from the gloom and felt her breath breaking over her
face. "Tell me or I'll phone every hospital in Brooklyn until I
find him."

"They wun say he's there."

"I'll call his job then."

"They wun say either."

"I'll find out, you hear." Selina spat the words in her face.
"You can't stop me from seeing him."

She charged past the mother and was almost out of the room
when the mother called softly, "I ain the one stopping you."

"Who then?"

"Yuh father-self."

She turned, stunned. "You mean he doesn't want to see *me?*"

"He don want you to see him."

"It's not true."

"As God is my witness. That's the only thing he said to me
there in the hospital. 'Don let the children come here.' Those
the only words he had for me and then he turn 'way his face,"
she whispered brokenly, and then suddenly spoke to the presence who always listened and sympathized. "Be-Christ, you does
ask for vengeance and sometime the sight of it when it comes
does make you wish different . . ."

"It's not true," Selina still shouted. "He wants to see me."
Suddenly she remembered the crumpled candles in her fist and

156

flung them down, shouting, "I'm fifteen and I'm going to see him. I'm fifteen and you can't stop me from doing anything now."

The mother's voice drooped tragically; her arms reached out in the darkness. "But look at you. You does get on like you know all but you don know nothing yet. You can't understand that with a man like your father, the last thing he would want would be for wunna to see him when he ain dress back and making like a big sports. Leave him, nuh. He got enough to bear without the look on your face when you see him in that bed . . ." Noiselessly she moved past Selina and at the door added tenderly, "Come down nuh and eat. I made coconut bread for your birthday."

But Selina remained, paralyzed as the blood flowed down, leaving her head and chest chilled. As the tremors began she knew that she also began screaming, yet the screams seemed apart from her, as if someone else in the dark shared her sorrow and impotence and screamed for her. Even when she stopped, the screams continued, refusing to dissolve into silence . . .

It was almost spring when he came home. Already the spring mist hung in a pale gold curtain during the day and in a blue filigree during the evenings. Down the interminable streets, a soft green relieved the bare front yards; the fruit trees in the back yards stirred with new leaves and the ivy flickered green against the worn stone. Selina stood under the leaving tree at the curb watching for the cab while Ina waited in the yard and the mother stood at the parlor-floor window. When the cab came Ina ran out and the mother withdrew.

Except for the bandaged left arm he was no different. The same playful smile, the same mild eyes, and he held his face at the same listening angle. They reached to help him from the cab and he waved them off, leaping out and brushing his lips across their cheeks, "How's the lady-folks? How's tricks?" Without waiting for their reply he strode jauntily across the sidewalk and up the stoop.

They hurried behind him, disturbed because his movements were too swift, his manner too flippant. Noticing a bundle of newspapers under his arm, Selina said, "Lemme carry the papers for you, Daddy."

"No. Leave them, nuh," he said irritably, then seeing her hurt face, he smiled.

It was then that a chill swept her. For his eyes as he glanced down were shrouded by an opaque film. She wondered if he really saw her. She wanted to pass her palm across his eyes and say, "Are you with us?" the way the girls in school did when anyone stared into space. Even his smile was blind. She turned to Ina, whose troubled eyes stared back. Uneasy, they followed him into the house, down the long hall, past the open parlor door, where they knew the mother stood listening to their footsteps.

He waited at the bedroom door for them to open it for him. Selina had lighted his small rose-shaded lamp and drawn the drapes, and the room was as he liked it. He smiled fondly at the frieze of angels and cherubs on the ceiling, at the massive furniture and faded Oriental rug. Then he saw the music stand in the corner and he trembled slightly and the haze quickly closed over his eyes.

"I'll turn down the bed so you can rest," Ina said, hurrying over.

"No." His voice was sharp with alarm. "That's yuh mother bed. Lemma go to the sun parlor, where I can breathe little fresh air."

Again they exchanged a worried look as they unlocked the tall French doors. While he stared down at the blown back yard they made up the cot and gathered up the last autumn's leaves that had lain there all winter.

He lay down fully clothed, the newspapers next to him and the bandaged arm across his chest. His whole body seemed as limp as that arm. All of him might have been sucked into the machine and crushed. And because he was so limp, he seemed quiet inside. A kind of dead peace hovered about him.

"Ah, the air smell too sweet after that hospital," he said. "I tell you, the stench alone in that place was enough to make you sick if you wasn't sick already . . ." Glancing up, he saw their uneasiness and attempted his old playful tone. "Well, come tell me, muh, how my lady-folks?"

"All right." Selina smiled shyly. "How do you feel?"

"How I feel?" He sucked his teeth. "Girl, I feeling fine. Especially now I breathe little fresh air. In fact, I don feel not a thing is wrong with me, except when I go to raise the arm and it wun budge."

"Will it get better?" Ina asked.

"So they say. If I take special exercise and thing so. But it would never be well enough to play no trumpet or work no machine again. So why bother up myself?" Slowly he raised up and gazed down at the limp arm, his head quivering. Slowly the film dropped from his eyes and he half smiled. Bitterly at first. Then a certain joy crept into the smile and into the hollows of his lean face. His good hand groped out to the limp arm and he stroked it almost fondly, as if instead of defeat this was a strange kind of fulfillment—the one thing he had been truly seeking even as he sought the job in accounting and the return home. Still stroking the arm he turned suddenly to Ina and gazed strongly at her. "Y'know, my mother, God rest she in her grave, did always say everything happens for a reason. If a spoon dropped she would say it drop for a reason. I used to laugh at she. But now I come to see what she did mean. After all these years I come to see . . ." His head dropped back on the pillow and he closed his eyes, still smiling, still fondly stroking the arm.

Not understanding, Selina said, "We wanted to come and see you."

He shook his head. "A hospital ain no place for my young ladies. I was up there in a nightgown like some woman, and all around me people hawking and spitting up their insides and crying for pain. And that smell strong enough to choke a horse.

No, that ain no place for young ladies." His voice had dropped to a whisper but suddenly now it surged up. "But everything does happen for a reason and for the best too." He gripped the newspapers beside him.

Selina and Ina turned to each other, baffled again, and in the swift line of their glance, saw the mother behind the door. Her face reflected their bewilderment and she gave them a look that both threatened and pleaded for them not to disclose her.

"Are those old newspapers?" Selina asked.

His hand roved affectionately over them. "Yes, I guess you could call them old. I thought they was old too when I found them in the cabinet next to my bed in the hospital. But when I read them I saw that even though they was old, what they had to say was new. Thank you, Father," he suddenly cried. "Peace, it's wonderful!" he uttered solemnly, then closed his eyes and, smiling, slept.

During those next weeks he read only those newspapers and nothing beyond their pages seemed important. Each was entitled *The New Light*. Each had a large picture of a kindly, round-faced man on the front page, and bold headlines read: "I AM THE FATHER UNIVERSAL," "I AM THE TRUE AND LIVING JEHOVAH," "NEW BIRTH AND REDEMPTION IN GOD . . ."

After the disruptive impact of the trumpet Selina welcomed the stillness as he read *The New Light*. But it was no longer the intimate silence that bound them together. He never paused to talk to her, and when she spoke he started and sometimes stared at her without recognition. He spoke only to himself, murmuring the same puzzling phrases over and over again, "Peace, it's truly wonderful," "Thank you, Father," "Wonderful, wonderful, wonderful . . ."

His life became simple and cloistered. He spent the day in the sun parlor and also slept there. At mealtimes Selina came for him and he silently followed her downstairs and ate with *The New Light* propped against his plate. He no longer went out on

Saturday nights, but early on Sunday afternoons he dressed with Selina's help and went out, returning after midnight. One Sunday he brought home a framed photograph of the kindly man in *The New Light*.

"Who's he?" she asked, although she knew by now.

"It's Father," he said quietly.

"Whose?"

"Father Peace. God Incarnate!" he cried.

She almost laughed. How could a benign little man in a business suit be God? He was not even like the mother's God—that quiet presence who always listened to her, or Maritze's supplicant Lady with her mantle of dust. He was ordinary. She knew that he breathed and smelled like a man. What had her father to do with him? Fear suddenly dropped like a weight inside her and she went and sat down on the floor across from the cot. While she huddled there the sun veered to the west, shattering the bare room with the spring's soft sunset colors. As dusk edged its way in the room Deighton turned on the lamp and continued reading, and Selina waited still, hating the numb peace in his face . . .

During those weeks they all waited. Ina suddenly joined St. Matthew's Episcopal Church and began her preparations for confirmation. Now, at meals, while Deighton read *The New Light* she read the "Articles of Religion." The mother worked overtime at the plant and came home each night, charging with her head like some wary animal, her eyes inflamed with fatigue. Yet no matter how late she came in, the light in the sun parlor was on, and it slanted across her bed and the empty pillow beside her, across her face as Deighton read *The New Light* far into the night.

Upstairs Suggie paced the enameled-blue room, raging as she repeatedly lost the factory jobs, while next door in the dusty rooms, Miss Mary wheezed her memories and hacked away at Maritze with her fretting. And even they seemed to be waiting for Deighton's recovery.

Selina waited, spending most of her time with Miss Thompson in the beauty parlor. She was certain that each morning would bring the end of Father Peace. The obsession would pass like a fever from his body. One day they would hear his teasing voice, "Well, how the lady-folks today? How's tricks?" They would know then that he was restored. Or some Saturday night she would find him at his dresser, caressing a new silk undershirt and humming the tuneless song to proclaim that he was well again. But the weeks passed and the day of his restoration passed with them.

Alone in the sun parlor one day she took up the photograph of Father Peace and gazed at it, wondering at his hold over her father. She became slowly infuriated at the cherubic face smiling back at her and began shaking it, until finally she loosened the glass and it dropped out of the frame, scratching her arm as it fell to the floor and broke.

"What you doing in here?"

Sucking the blood from the scratch, she had not heard her father enter. When she looked up, he was standing over her, repeating irritably, "What you doing in here?"

She was frightened, then angry, and didn't answer.

"What, I asked."

"Nothing."

Then he saw the broken glass on the floor and the photograph in her other hand. He snatched it from her. "What you doing to Father picture?"

"Nothing, I was just looking at it and the glass fell out and cut me."

With his good hand he suddenly yanked her close. An exultant rage shook his voice, "You see? You see? Father struck you down! You interfere with him and he struck you down! Thank you, Father. Go ahead. Go ahead, keep interfering and he gon strike you down each time. Just like he does all them who interfere with him and refuse to believe he's God. Take that big-shot Judge Jones. He put Father in jail. And Father prophesy that he was gon die the next day. And he die!" His voice rose,

162

shrill as a woman's. His breath fanned Selina's face with its heat. He was wholly possessed. "He die, I tell you, that big-shot white judge die . . . and the big-shot white doctors cun tell what he die from. You think Father was frighten for them 'cause they was white? Not Father. He let loose his power and showed them he's God Incarnate. Oh, thank you, Father. Thank you for the sign!" He staggered back, and from the emptiness inside him came a sigh full of relief and trust. "Peace, it's truly wonderful."

Selina slid from his lax hold to the floor and they remained like this for a time: she crouched, sobbing, at his feet, while he swayed above her, murmuring his litany of absolution.

Outside the wind lifted suddenly and swept aside the clouds and the sun splashed in a wave through the glass walls, across the floor, and lay in a soothing hand on them both. The sun, their silence drained her anger and terror, and she was vaguely peaceful. She lifted her head after a time. "Take me . . ." Her hand hesitated near his leg. "Take me to see him."

He roused briefly, then lapsed into his detachment.

"Take me to see him!" She tugged his trouser.

"What . . . ?" He looked down.

"I want to go with you to see him. Please take me. I want to go."

"You want to see Father?"

"Yes."

"Up to Harlem, to the kingdom?"

"Yes."

His eyes suddenly cleared and he peered close at her upturned face. Finally he sighed and with a remote smile said, "All right, come this Sunday I gon take you."

He reached down and tenderly raised her up to the cot. He sat beside her and inspected the scratch and the thin line of dried blood. "It's wonderful, wonderful, wonderful!" he murmured, stroking her arm and lifting his dazed eyes to the sun.

# 8

She had never seen a brownstone house like this one. There was a large flickering neon sign where the cornice should have been, which flashed: "Peace Movement" and at the door another sign: "Peace! Cigars, cigarettes and intoxicating liquors not allowed!" She hurried behind her father out of the pelting rain and the bleak Harlem street into the house. Inside there were no walls but only one long high room, garishly lighted and filled with the festal sound of voices and eating. The crowd blocked their way, but Deighton, Selina clinging to his jacket, wedged his way through until they reached a banquet table which ran the length of the room. Every seat at the table was taken, and the throng behind strained up against the diners, waiting to take their places.

"Is this the kingdom?" she whispered, suppressing a laugh. But he did not hear. His glazed eyes were fixed on the head of the table, which she could not see. She felt deceived. She had expected an altar at least, with a fringed altar cloth and a tall cross as in Ina's church. She had expected flowers, holy statues and stained-glass windows. There was no wine and wafer here. The body of this god was large platters of fricassee chicken, roast duck, spareribs and big bowls of clogged rice; his blood, pitchers of milk and imitation-flavored soft drinks.

It could have been a huge communal wedding with all the

women dressed in white as the brides, or a picnic that had been driven indoors by the rain—except that something somber weighed the air, as dense and palpable as the heat. She saw it in a hardened reflet on the white and colored faces down the table and in the crowd behind. A look of dark and ecstatic love.

As she scanned those faces, a Negro woman suddenly lunged out of the crowd, her work-ruined face convulsed with this agonized love, her big body bucking under the white uniform. "Father, Father, I feel the vibrations!" she screamed and thrashed, sobbing in wild animal grief and ecstasy. A slim girl near the head of the table suddenly dropped her fork and cried in chorus with the woman, "I'm so glad, Father. Thank you, Father. I'm so glad." Her feet beat a rapid staccato under the table, and she dropped her face in her hands.

Through that open space Selina saw the object of their adoration.

He was shorter, browner, stouter and more innocuous than his photograph. The same gentle smile hovered around his full lips, the same calm touched his broad face, and motes of light did a grave dance on his bald head. He wore a double-breasted business suit with a vest and quiet tie. Sitting there, pouring coffee from a silver urn, he might have been the respected head of a large family.

Excitement surged through the room as the adulations increased. Those at the table rose to praise him with food still in their mouths. The muffled cries of love erupted among the standees while others, like Deighton, stood transfixed, their gaze quietly bent on the brown benevolent face of Father Peace. An old woman next to Selina suddenly threw out her arms. "Beautiful, beautiful Father! I knowed he's God. I knowed it," she shrieked above the others. "Listen to me. I was ailing. Father knowed how many years. Them doctors had done given up on me. Then one day *Father* came. There was a gold halo all around his sweet head and he said, 'Rise up and walk, my sweetheart.' And peace, sisters and brothers, I been walking ever since. Thank you, Father! So sweet, Father dear. So sweet!" She gave a sprightly leap, her gray skin flushed with happiness and then she was herself again: an old woman with a caved-in face.

Like a cool wind riving the heat, a young white woman stood up, lifted her face, and the tumult subsided a little. "Father Peace is the perfect expression of God," she said quietly, her face like a Madonna's, her blond hair falling in a golden cowl on her shoulders. "Outside in the world there is immorality, and the things that come of immorality: wars and ambition, hate and carnal lust. The way people live out there is death. Here is only happiness and immortality with Father! Oh, you're so beautiful, Father dear. Your words are beautiful. They are fit company for your beautiful little face and body . . ." She smiled sweetly at him and he gave her a pleased nod, and the others might have vanished and left them alone with their love.

In the frail silence someone sang, "Father Peace is my father . . ." and others took up the song:

*"Father Peace is striding the land,*
*Father Peace is my savior,*
*Got the globe in a jug,*
*And the stopper in his hand . . ."*

Beneath the song, the clapping swelled in a furious accompaniment. While they sang and clapped and the noise thickened the air, the diners and standees exchanged places and the serving women brought food from the kitchen.

Selina was embarrassed for them. She felt suddenly old and terribly wise, while they seemed to her like children being led by the piper into the sea. Impatiently she tugged at her father's sleeve to rouse him, but his eyes were fixed, worshipfully, on Father Peace. Now he stared not at the benign face of Father Peace but at his forefinger. It was crooked invitingly in his direction, beckoning Deighton with a slow hypnotic motion. But only the finger was concerned with Deighton it seemed, for the eyes of Father Peace were moving with gentle interest over the faces of those testifying.

The old woman next to Selina suddenly gasped. Her blurred eyes shuttled back and forth from the beckoning finger to Deighton. Gradually all around the room people paused in their testifying, the singing lost its jubilance as other eyes traced that finger to him. They stared curiously at him, and a great envious sigh ruffled the air. Suddenly the old woman shoved past Selina and grabbed Deighton's sleeve. "Brother, Father's recognizing you!" she shrieked in a brittle breaking voice. "Go on, Brother, Father's recognizing you tonight. He's chosen to recognize *you* tonight! Go on!" She gave him a little push.

Deighton pitched forward, trembling, and Father Peace suddenly turned his head Deighton's way and smiled and pointed casually to a vacant chair at his right side. Groping his way with his good hand, Deighton stumbled forward amid the heat and crush of bodies, through the suddenly tumid silence, drawn it seemed by an invisible thread pulled by Father's finger. At each step the crowd parted deferentially and then quickly fused behind him. Everywhere eyes followed him with wondering envy.

"Daddy!" Selina called softly, immobilized by shock. "Daddy," she cried in a sharp warning as he sank in complete surrender into the chair close to Father Peace. As she started after him, the old woman grasped her shoulder. "Father hasn't recognized you," she hissed. "And there ain't no daddy in the kingdom but Father Peace."

Selina struggled, crying, but the old woman held her back and the fused bodies blocked her way. All over the room the silence erupted into shouts of "wonderful, wonderful," and the renewed singing stifled her cries.

The singing, clapping, testifying and eating continued. The walls, hung with huge portraits of Father Peace, expanded at each crescendo of sound and shrank whenever the tumult

167

dropped. And then suddenly it ceased, as if a huge hand had pressed it into silence, and Father Peace rose in the heat and glare in the room.

"Peace, everybody."

"Peace, Father, peace!" They shouted the answer.

"Peace, everyone, righteousness, justice and truth be with you tonight and always. Your hearts are filled with merriment, your bodies exude enthusiasms for you are the chosen! You have recognized and realized that God's presence is a living reality. Because of this I came!"

"So true, Father dear," a man shouted and shook his body as though to free it of his clothes.

"The cosmic forces of the world obey me and work in harmony for all who are aware of my vital presence on the earth, and work destructively against those who choose to dismiss my presence and lightly value me . . ."

For a long time he tossed the meaningless words into the rapt silence, all the while smiling genially. Then suddenly his plump hands gripped the table and he shouted, "God flows through my personal body. Don't ever have limitations in your awarenesses. If you live after the things of the flesh you shall perish but if you do condemn the deeds of the body you shall have eternal life . . ." The short arms described eloquent arcs; he strode up and down in a kind of dance.

And the call came, "So true, Father. So true, sweet Father."

"Individual freedom is something glorious to attain for only then can you be truly one with God. Be wholly independent. God's conception and nobody else's."

"I love you, Father!" A young woman stretched her white arms to him. "I love you."

"God is your father, your mother, your sister, your brother, your wife, your child, and you will never have another! The mother of creation is the mother of defilement. The word *mother* is a filthy word. When a person reaches God he cannot permit an earthly wife or so-called children to lead him away. God is all!"

Deighton leaped up from his seat of recognition, trembling, the perspiration coursing past his blind eyes. "So true!" he cried. "So true. I am nothing!" And his arms flew out in a gesture that did, indeed, cancel his entire self. "God is everything. Need you, Father, need you."

And others leaped up, shouting their happiness and their need; their feet pounded out their joy.

Selina's head ached and she felt the tears rising. She did not understand. She was no longer wise or old, but confounded by life still. She thought suddenly of Percy Challenor presiding like a threatening god at the head of his table on Sundays. They were alike, he and Father Peace. They ruled. What was it that made her father unfit to do the same? Why was he the seduced follower and not the god . . . ?

At last the frenzy of Father Peace subsided and he was the smiling patriarch again. He ended with a resigned sigh, his arms open. "So here I stand with everybody adoring, adoring me. So much adoration is worth more than two hundred million dollars. So much adoration you cannot put a price on it." He sketched a vague benediction, "Father is always here, always there and everywhere. Universally!" He left the room.

A song followed him.

*"Father is on the hilltop; Father is walking the sea;*
*Father is working in the valley, redeeming humanity.*
*Father is always present; Father is all divine;*
*Father is God Eternal, Father-mother sublime.*
*Praise be, Father!"*

When the song died there were only the anguished cries of love and the heat and a certain calm. Reluctantly the followers began to file out, and Selina made her way to her father.

Standing behind his chair she gazed at his bowed head, at the limp hand hanging at his side. Fleetingly she wanted to leave him—to deny him. For his crushed pose somehow offended her. "Let's go home," she cried. She shook him hard, realizing as she did the weakness of her arms and voice against his inertia. But still she shouted and struck until there was no more strength in her arms and she sank, exhausted, in a chair beside him.

They sat together, yet apart, and gradually the noise moved further away, leaving only the small sounds of the women gathering up the dishes. Soon even this ceased, and when she lifted her tear-streaked face the hall was empty, the lights dimmed, and the cleared table was like a huge altar upon which some monstrous sacrifice had taken place. She looked again at her father and this time she was filled with a sad acceptance. She would have nothing now but his shadow. His substance was irretrievably lost . . . Gently she touched his sleeve. "Daddy, wake up," she whispered. "It's over. He's gone. Everybody's gone. C'mon, let's go home . . ."

This time he raised his head and turned his dulled eyes to her.

"C'mon, let's go. It's late and I've got to go to school tomorrow."

He rose painfully, pulling himself up by the table edge. She slipped her arm through his, and as Antigone led her blind father into Colonus, Selina led Deighton from the kingdom into Harlem.

# 9

They ate breakfast together on Sundays now that Deighton had found God. In the dining room with the second best china on the oak table. And only the soft scrape and tap of their forks on the plates—a sound of triangles struck and quickly held—tempered the harsh chord of silence. Deighton read *The New Light*, Ina hid behind the fashion page of the Sunday paper, eager to leave for church; Silla held her set brooding face low to her plate, and Selina sat tense and vigilant beside her father, nudging him when he forgot to eat but eating little herself.

This morning the silence was somewhat pleasant, for a shaft of sunlight from the kitchen roved amid the crystal in the china closet, lit the stained-glass wisteria lamp over the table and evoked the faces in the brown-faded family photograph on the buffet. Deceived by this false ease, Selina gaily waved a biscuit at her father and said, "Pass the butter, Daddy."

He absently reached for it, and then jerked back, bursting out petulantly, "You musn't call me 'Daddy.' Din you hear Father-self say there ain no father or mother in the kingdom? I'm Brother Boyce. Wunna must call me that!"

In the clenched silence his words circled the room, touching Ina, whose eyes flitted fearfully to the mother and then dropped behind the paper, sweeping across Selina so that the biscuit shook in her hand and her sudden dread was like a piece of it lodged in her throat. They pressed around Silla and her head drooped under their crush. Her hand twitched and the angry outburst leaped to her lips but she restrained it. She seemed unwilling to speak, almost afraid to break the long months' wary silence—but when the words persisted, she reluctantly laid aside her fork.

She gave him a quiet look and her voice held no anger as she asked, "Who should they call 'Daddy' then?"

Out of his emptiness a hollow voice spoke. "Father says there's no marrying. No children. He is the only Father and we's all his children and brothers and sisters to one another. Father says . . ."

Silla gazed with an angry pity and bewilderment at him, and strangely her love—that web of passions that both claimed and disclaimed him—crept beneath her perplexity and her hand began to shape some tender comforting sign. But it faltered down without hope as she saw his limp arm on the table. For the first time since his accident she looked openly at it. A tremor struck her shoulders and, like someone dying, her eyes set with horror, as if she had been presented with the condemning evidence of a crime she alone had committed. Suddenly she had to know if she was really guilty, and she sought the answer in the children's faces. But Ina raised her paper, shutting the mother out, and Selina, understanding that mute question, withheld her answer by turning aside. Desperately Silla leaned toward Deighton, who chanted still: "There's rebirth in Father . . ." and whispered, "Deighton, who put you so?"

". . . and freedom . . ."

"Who put you so, I ask."

"Life in Father!"

"Life . . ." she said cautiously as though testing a new word. "Life? Lemme tell you, life ain up in no Father Peace kingdom," she said gently. "It out here scuffling to get by. And having little something so you can keep your head up and not have these white people push you 'bout like you's cattle. That's what it tis . . ." Her open hands offered him the meaning.

"Peace in Father . . ."

"Peace . . ." She smiled wistfully and shook her head. "It ain that easy to come by, mahn."

But he nodded firmly, confident that he had found it.

His certainty made Silla doubt. Perhaps he had found peace. An unreasonable envy seized her—for did she not yearn for peace lying alone in the wide bed each night?—peace with him sleeping beyond her locked door, peace from the ache in her loins . . . ? And a new fear welled, for his bland peace might become a wall which she could never hope to penetrate. This dread suddenly swept aside her tenderness and twisted her love into wrath. She leaped up, the chair tumbling behind her, and hurled at him across the table, "But be-damn you, don you know you's flying in the face of God with this foolishness?"

At her shout the shaft of sunlight thinned and fled and the shadows resumed their old places. She strained toward him, her splayed fingers pushing the tablecloth into ridges. "But where you come outta, nuh? You ain no real-real Bajan man. What Bajan man would have his head turn by some bogus god? Tell me!" For a time she pressed him for an answer but Deighton only shied from her loudness and stared emptily at her from behind the protective film over his eyes. Finally in disgust she turned and addressed her silent listener. "No . . . he ain no Bajan. Look Percy Challenor who was working the said-same job as him is a real estate broker now and just open a big office on Fulton Street. More Bajan than you can shake a stick at opening stores or starting up some little business. They got this Business Association going good now and 'nough people joining. Even I gon join. Every West Indian out here taking a lesson from the Jew landlord and converting these old houses into rooming houses—making the closets-self into rooms some them! —and pulling down plenty-plenty money by the week. And now that the place is near overrun with roomers the Bajans getting out. They going! Every jack-man buying a swell house in dichty Crown Heights. Percy Challenor and them so gone! Iris

Hurley in a house with more wall-to-wall carpeting than the law allow. Even Virgie, with that regiment of children, gone!"

The weight of their successes weakened her and she fumbled blindly for the overturned chair and sat down with her head bowed and the lines of her face down-curved in a bitter design. "It's not that I's avaricious, or money-mad," she whispered to herself, her thick child's fingers tracing the pattern of her fork. "Or that I's a follow-pattern so that everything they do I must do. But c'dear, if you got a piece of man you want to see him make out like the rest. You want to see yourself improve. Isn't that why people does come to this place?" She put the question to his blank stare. When he said nothing, she stated simply, "You don belong here, mahn. Oh, it's not this Father Peace." She dismissed him with a contemptuous wave. "It's that you was always looking for something big and praying hard not to find it."

Her knowing look pierced him until *The New Light* gradually slipped from his hand and the shielding veil slid from his eyes. Selina saw that veil rising, felt him stirring into awareness against his will and quickly slid forward in her seat, blocking his view of the mother. Very gently he drew her back. "It's all right, lady-folks," he said. "Let she say what she must . . ."

Suddenly, with his fingers lingering reassuringly on her arm, Selina wanted to leave. To rush out and lock them in that forbidding Victorian room. To find some quiet place out of reach of their voices and there read until she forgot them. She didn't care what they did! And the biscuit she was holding dropped with a soft thud. The mother could hold the knife and he could run on it and die and she didn't care. But then, in the tense wait, he sighed like a girl and she loved him, and the mother lifted her fine dark eyes to him again and she both loved and hated her . . .

"All that studying!" Silla's arms rose and fell tragically. "And your heart in none of it. You din really learn that course in radio repairing. You was glad enough when you din get the job in accounting. You din really want to play no trumpet. Always half-

studying something. It's like"—she searched for the thought—
"like you knew before you began that you wasn't really smart
enough to learn it good—or like you did say deep to yourself
that you din want to make good at anything. A show! All of it
nothing but . . ."

He motioned her to stop. It was a selfless gesture which said
that he did not wish to spare himself, but only to spare her the
pain of saying it and the anguish streaking her face like tears.
"Silla . . . Silla," he murmured. Closing his eyes he called her
within the dim confusion of his mind. Perhaps, for him, she was
nothing more than his own inner voice, publishing at last the long
catalog of his failures . . .

"What you got now for the over nine hundred odd dollars
cash throw 'way?" She thrust her chin toward him for an answer
and he simply shook his head. "What it mean now—all those
fancy silk undershirt? Where's your jokes and the change jingling
in your pocket to make like a big sports in front the children?
And above all"—her voice dropped but her bitter gaze held his—
"where's the concubine you had all these years whose sweet
sickening smell you brought home every Sunday morning?"

"I know, Silla, I tell you I know. Stop, nuh!" And again his concern was for her, not himself.

She could not stop. The wall she had built against the thoughts
during their long silence had cracked, the words streaming
through, and she was powerless to stop them. Then, too, she did
not want to stop. For his humility galled her. His quick assent
to all she said goaded her on. Why didn't he leap up and shout
her down, or lean across the table and smash the words from
her mouth? But no, instead he exulted in the pain each word
brought and repaid her abuse with compassion. It was his wish
to suffer that suddenly spurred in her the need to make that
suffering full. She rose, her eyes groping through the shadows to
the family photograph. Gazing at it, she said with dread emphasis, "Then years back, it was the car. The piece of old car you
had to have even though it was depression, just to make like a

175

big sports in front the boy. That piece of old junk that made his heart worse and killed him before his time."

Finally he responded, leaping up and leaning across the table, his dark taut face quivering. His whisper held the dark and arid joy of relief. "Silla, is that what you did always think? All this time?"

Her head snapped his way but her eyes were crowded with another face. "Yes, all this time. I can still see that wreck of a car going birdspeed down the road, lurching like somebody drunk and the boy lurching in it and laughing."

And slowly Deighton also saw that scene rise in the room's shadows and it absorbed him entirely. For moments there was no sign of his breathing even. Selina and Ina were crouched fearfully in their seats, their eyes closed and their heads bowed. Gradually Silla grew uneasy at his stillness. Regret tinged her eyes and her hands made to pull the accusation from the air. Then he smiled. This one, sad and apologetic, told her that he understood all now, that he knew how that memory must have underscored each harsh word and prompted every unkind act. How, at night, it must have sometimes caused her body to turn cold under his. It was a smile of gratitude. For she had unwittingly probed deep into that shadowy turn of his mind and found the doubt hidden there. She was the one who had driven it out, unmasked it and shaped it into words. Now there would be no need to question that uneasy guilt. He could embrace it.

"Who . . . what . . . put you so?"

He almost laughed at the innocence of Silla's question. In answer his hand traced some airy abstract figure above his plate and then dropped to *The New Light*. He stared at the bold headline: FATHER IS THE ONLY FATHER, and as he read, the dark balm settled once again over his mind; his eyes misted over with peace; his body began to sag with it. He was safe. That was when he said in a vague monotone, "I going, Silla. Father asked me to work and live in the kingdom here in Brooklyn. I

176

was gon say no, but I going now. It's for the best," he said gently, gazing around at them. "I going. Thank you, Father."

Silla's protest was only a faint incredulous cry, and her hands had to convey in jerky scattered motions the upheaval inside her. Only Selina's scream, splitting the already troubled air, spoke for her and the stunned Ina. She whirled to her father, ready to win him with her tears and if this failed to strike him until he roused and denied what he had said. But she shrank back, terrified suddenly at that empty but determined face, not recognizing his blind eyes. Her loud lament filled the room.

"Selina, what it tis? What he saying?" Silla called. "Ina, tell me, nuh!" But neither could answer. "What it tis you saying?" she begged Deighton.

"I going, Silla."

But his answer was not enough, and she swung away, seeking in desperation her invisible listener. "What he saying?"

This time she must have received the full answer, for slowly, as though she were being bled, the dark strength drained from her face and it became flaccid and gray with defeat. The inner stay that gave her body its bold lift snapped and she slumped in her chair. "Is that what he want? To leave?" she whispered wonderingly, shaking her head in disbelief. Then she suddenly cried, "Then let him. Let him!" But her loud assent was thin and false on the air. Quickly her lips sought to retract it, but she was committed. When she realized this, she plunged ahead, shouting to convince herself, "Yes . . . yes, let him g'long. Watch, he'll be back here before the cat lick it ear. Let him go. And I gon see that he go today-self. But he'll provide for these two or . . ."

"Father will provide," he said calmly.

She was too bruised inside, too spent for anger, and she said dully, "Father provide? What? Peace? I can take peace to the store? I can fill their stomachs with it?" Her shattered eyes sought Selina across the plates of uneaten biscuits and cold eggs, and she murmured with sad vindication, "Look, look how you did waste love! Now go out someplace. Both of you. I don't want no more tears 'bout here today!"

Silently Selina filed out behind Ina and accompanied her to church, but she did not stay there long, for she did not know how, nor did she want, to pray. Besides, the nave was cold. The same numbing cold that circled her heart. She left Ina praying with a passion she had never suspected in her and wandered, blind, through the streets, past the despoiled brownstones that had been converted into rooming houses, glancing at the roomers who stared like prisoners from the windows of their cubicles while their children chalked their names on the stoops. When dusk fell she watched a group of them at their last game of potsie under a street lamp, and their lusty shouts seemed to usurp the air . . .

When she finally returned home, exhausted from her wandering, she knew from the unnatural stillness that he was gone. Even though, when she looked, his shoes were still in the closet and his silk underwear piled neatly in the dresser.

# 10

She went to see him every Saturday at the peace restaurant on Fulton Street which he managed and where he lived. Usually she went alone for Ina always made some pained excuse, alone up Fulton Street, where every bedizened store window hawked the Saturday sales, a Fulton Street already odorous with barbecue and port wine, where, even at noon, there was a hint of the night's certain violence. She passed the queues of children outside the movie houses, the soldiers on leave outside the bars, Percy Challenor's real estate office and glimpsed him towering like a behemoth amid his clients.

The peace restaurant was a block from Percy Challenor's office, just where the elevated train curved onto Fulton Street, and the trestle's shadow lay across the restaurant's tiled floor and marble tables, it reached to Deighton standing at the cash register, his left arm dangling and his face cavernous with peace. Each Saturday he said in the same gentle but remote voice, "Peace, how's the lady-folks? How's Miss Ina? And Silla?" and led her to a table out of the sun. She sat there content all afternoon watching him ring up the checks. At sunset he would come over and with his good hand touch her face. "It getting late. Make haste and get home safe."

At home Selina invariably found the mother waiting for her under the stoop, her face disguised by shadows but her voice, and her hand grasping Selina's arm, betraying her anxiety. "Well, what he had to say for himself this time?"

"Nothing."

"How you mean, nothing? He ain talking nothing yet 'bout coming back or so?"

"No." Selina would pull away her arm and leave the mother standing there in the gloom.

Once, when Selina and Ina returned from the restaurant, the mother met them with the usual question, and Ina suddenly cried, her eyes dark with tears and hopelessness. "Why do you ask the same thing all the time? Can't you see he's not coming back? Can't either of you understand that after all these months? He's happy. I looked at him good today and saw how happy he is. And I'm not going back there again, it's no use. He doesn't want or need us any more!"

After this the mother seldom asked for him, but her face became more drawn each time Selina returned from the restaurant, her eyes more haggard, and she began working longer hours at the plant.

During that summer, the last summer of the war, Deighton often allowed Selina to sit in his room in back. It was a small cool room which the flies had not found—chaste white and furnished with a cot, a dresser, one chair, a washbasin marred with rust and a photograph of Father Peace. It could have been a monk's cell, a place for meditation and penance. Sometimes he came in and lay on the cot reading *The New Light* while she stared out the barred window at the children from the tenement upstairs playing in the back yard. Over the weeks their silent afternoons took on a certain intimacy. She often washed his socks now and spread them in the sun on the window sill to dry.

She was washing his socks the day the mother came into the restaurant—rubbing them between her fists while gazing out at the children, thinking how their piercing shouts suggested the intense sun, the tall singed weeds and the dust. Hearing the mother's voice she thought that it was the mother of the children—some heavy harassed woman calling down through the fire escapes.

Then, suddenly, all other sound dropped away, leaving only that voice. It was as if the entire tumultuous sweep of life had stopped: the children fixed in the hurtling attitudes of their play, the traffic on Fulton Street grounded to a halt. All over the world time and motion had a stop. In that pause her own heart ceased, and she knew then that it was the mother. Clutching the wet socks in her fists she charged down the passageway, ready to drive her out. But as she burst into the restaurant she halted and her arms dropped uselessly at her side at the sight of the policeman. The authority of his white face and uniform, of his big hand on her father's arm, choked her cry. The sight of the mother in the doorway trapped the breath in her lungs.

Silla, in a dark dress that denied the summer, her eyes aggrieved and bitter, was shouting in a voice shrill with rage,

"That's he, officer. That's he, I say. His own don't count since he take up with this bogus god, so let him go back where he come from! He don need nobody now but Father? He's happy? Well, le's see how happy he gon be back home!"

"All right, all right, lady. I'm asking the questions, not you," the policeman called and turned again to Deighton. "C'mon, mister, is ya name Deighton Boyce?"

Deighton said nothing, but his vacant eyes reached over the policeman's shoulder to the mother and he gave her an understanding smile. They ranged over the customers with the same gentleness. Looking over his shoulder he saw Selina and the smile became almost radiant. He sketched a vague sign that said she must not mind, that he welcomed this final humiliation, for not only had he sinned, but they also: the customers, the policeman, the mother, the waiters, all—even she—and his penance was for them also.

But Selina did not see him. In her jarred mind the room suddenly canted to one side, then spun in a wash of sunlight. As quickly it returned, sharp, in focus, and she made to answer his gesture and smile, to plead with the policeman for him. But even as she fought to speak, the restaurant wavered again and his figure dissolved. Because she said nothing, she was forgotten. Her body—less raw and shapeless now under her summer dress —fell heavily against the counter; her eyes—immense and old in her thin face—saw nothing but dark streaks in the eddying sunlight. She heard nothing more. All she knew was that the socks were cold and dripping and somehow confused in her mind with blood.

She did not see the policeman grab Deighton's injured arm and, as he felt its limpness, drop it; nor did she hear him say, not unkindly, "I'm asking ya one more time if ya name's Deighton Boyce, mister. This woman's sworn out a warrant for your arrest and deportation for illegal entry into the United States. Ya hear that?"

Deighton wet his lips but said nothing.

"Look, mister, this is a serious charge. You understand? Is it you?"

"It tis," the mother cried, her voice sagging with pity now. "That's he. That's his name. His head turn, officer, and he don even know himself anymore . . ."

The policeman shook him roughly and this time something touched Deighton's face. He suddenly became curious. His eyes flitted wonderingly over the customers, asking, it seemed, how they had managed life, envying them their work-scarred hands and dull faces. He studied the policeman's face and in his shattered mind it became the white faces in the stores of Bridgetown long ago. Those faces, stippled red by the tropic sun, that had always refused his request for a clerk's job and thus turned the years at school, and his attempts to be like them in his dark wool English-cut suits (even in that sodden heat!), and his face—clean though black—into nothing; that had utterly unmanned him before he was yet a man; that had stripped him of any possibility of self and then hustled him out . . . Suddenly he laid his hand in resignation on the policeman's shoulder and said, "Yes, officer, they did call me Deighton Boyce."

"Okay, let's go." Quickly the officer guided him through the maze of tables to the door. There Deighton paused and gently freed his arm and went up to Silla. The cast lifted from his eyes and at the same moment Silla's rage fell away and they searched each other's faces.

They might have been alone with the world around them stilled and the years rubbed away like smoke from a glass. For the look they shared must have been the same as when they first met: shy yet curious and at its core the stir of love. Silently they asked each other what had gone wrong, what it was that had ruined them for each other, and their mutual bewilderment confessed they did not know.

It was only a moment. The policeman's hand was on his arm again, the world intruding. Deighton's eyes clouded over; he gave Silla that blind pietistic smile and glided past her, murmuring his chant of absolution, "Father will provide. Peace, it's truly wonderful."

As he moved away, with the shadow of the el rippling over his bowed head, Silla's eyes followed him with enraged pity. Weeping, reaching for him, she shouted, "Let him go back where he come from if he don't count his own. Let him go back!" Even when the Saturday crowd had engulfed him and strangers paused, puzzled, in front of the restaurant, she still cried, "Let him go back where he come from!" and a passing train lent the words a thunderous emphasis.

"Hitler," Selina murmured and drew the sheet up to her chin. A car sped by and fleetingly threw its yellow light into the dark bedroom and across her rigid face.

"Hitler."

Ina stirred beside her and whispered, "What're you saying?"

"Hitler."

"Hitler? Who're you calling Hitler?"

"Hitler."

"Selina, who're you calling that? You're calling mother that?" and the bedsprings strained loud as she sprang up.

"Hitler."

"She's gonna hear you!" Ina warned, her eyes luminous with dread in the light of another passing car. "She's still sitting out there in the dining room. Why start something else now? Just leave bad enough alone. There's nothing we can do . . ."

"Hitler."

"Look, he'll be better off home. Believe me! We'll go see him. When I start working next year I'll save the passage money for both of us and we'll go see him. Please," she pleaded, shaking Selina. "Please don't start anything this hour of the night. Just leave things alone."

"Hitler," Selina suddenly shouted and sat up.

Ina shrank from the cold implacable venom in Selina's face. In the jarred silence Ina seemed to retreat from the bed, from the

183

room. "What is it with you two?" she cried. "Why're you always at each other's throats? You're alike, you know that! The same."

"Hitler."

"Oh stop!" She collapsed, murmuring brokenly, "Stop, she's gonna hear you . . ."

"Hitler."

The name struck with the regularity of a metronome in the dark room, until finally Silla softly opened the door and switched on the light. For a long time she stood blinking curiously at the faded wallpaper and prints, Ina's cosmetics on the vanity and the furniture as if they, not Selina, were hurling the name at her. "Who you calling Hitler, Selina?" she whispered finally, a profound hurt darkening her already numbed eyes.

"Hitler."

"You's saying I's the worse person in the world? You think I did want to do it? It was the man made me—the foolish half-crazy man . . ."

"Hitler!" The scream severed her voice.

Helplessly Silla stumbled across the room like someone old and infirm, drawn, by Selina's envenomed eyes and her frenzied shout, into the dangerous orbit around the bed. As she reached the bed, as her hands hesitantly sought the footboard, Selina sprang. It was a sure deft charge that sent the sheet billowing and whacking the air like a sail. She tottered up, her nightgown and the sheet twisted around her quivering body, her thin arms reaching out to grasp the mother's dress. "Hitler." She spat the name in the mother's face and brought her small fist down on Silla's shoulder. "Hitler," she cried and struck again. This time her bangles glanced sharply across the mother's chin.

After the first shocked cry, Silla did not utter another sound. She could have easily tumbled Selina back on the bed with a blow, but she did not even ward off the fist flailing her shoulders. Nor did she move away. Her only gesture of protection was to lift her grieved face out of the way.

For a long time there was only the sodden sound of struck flesh and the shouted name. At each blow Ina quivered under the sheet as though she were being beaten and outside the cars hurtled through the silent night streets. Selina struck until her arms were too heavy to lift. Her shout tapered to a moan then, and she sagged helplessly against the mother. Her rage died reluctantly. Her loose fists still made little angry motions even as she clung for support to the mother's neck; her lips still shaped the name even as her eyes glazed with sleep and her face sank into the curve of Silla's neck. Clinging to the mother, she slept.

Slowly Silla lowered her face and gingerly touched the sore places on her shoulders and arms. She stared down, with a strange awe and respect, at the limp figure huddled against her and the thin arms wound loosely around her neck. Carefully she lifted Selina's legs over the footboard, and with the sheet trailing behind them she carried her out of the room, up through the dim hall to the parlor, and turned on the chandelier. For a long while she sat quietly holding her on the sofa under the brilliant light. Then, almost reverently, she touched the tears that had dried white on her dark skin, traced with her finger the fragile outline of her face and rested her hand soothingly on her brow. She smoothed her snarled hair. Yet, despite the tenderness and wonder and admiration of her touch, there was a frightening possessiveness. Each caress declared that she was touching something which was finally hers alone.

On the day the war ended, a cable arrived saying that Deighton Boyce had either jumped or fallen overboard and drowned at a point within sight of the Barbados coast and that a posthumous burial service had been read at sea.

While Silla read them the cable, the radio announced the war's end, and all down the sun-swept streets windows were raised and the news was shouted. Strangers embraced on Chauncey Street. And the dark soldiers whiling away their leaves in the bars on Fulton Street grabbed the whores and spun them in a wild dance out into the street and kissed their laughing mouths; one shouted, "C'mon, baby, this is *one* time I'll buy you a drink. The goddamn war's over."

# BOOK

## 4

*Selina*

# 1

Selina carried what seemed the weight of winter in her body, which felt sear, numb and as though laid in some chill place until spring would come. But she knew that the inert heaviness inside her had nothing to do with winter, nor would the spring deliver her. It was simply the burden of her year-long grief. That was what had thinned her face and, like a cancer, fed on her breasts (which, in that last year before her father's death, had suddenly burgeoned) and on the flesh that had begun to soften her frame.

But it was not the same neuter body of years ago. For often at night it sent up an importunate plea for a boy, and his face, whose every feature she had shaped and reshaped endlessly, would sweep across her mind, stronger than her grief sometimes, until she could almost see him in the darkness beyond her bed. She would ease up so as not to frighten him away and, hugging her cold shoulders, her eyes vast and disembodied in the dark, she would search for him, just as, she believed, he was searching for her. But even as she thought she spied him, her father would intervene, his face wavering with reproach behind its watery veil, and the scene she had fashioned from the cable's cryptic message would rise, luminous:

*Dawn at sea with a tropic mist moiling over the ship in smoky gusts and her father alone at the rail, the salt mist on his sunken face and soaking his shirt until it was like silk on his skin. The dawn hour was all peace, his peace merged with that of the sea,*

*his body sharing the rhythm of the ship's meditative rise and
fall. Gradually the mist thickened until his body seemed to
buckle under its weight. But oddly, as his body drooped, his
mind soared, roaming free in a vast emptiness. For a long time
there was only this nothingness, this pure peace, until a light
burst in the void and bizarre shapes spiraled up. It was the sun
rising in a brilliant coin behind the pale form of a distant island.
When he saw the island, he emitted a low frightened cry, his
hand rose to blot it out. For that low mound, resting on the sea
like a woman's breast when she is supine, was Barbados. Time
fled as the mist fled and he was a boy again, diving for the coins
the tourists tossed into the sea, and he saw the one he wanted
most in the bright disk of the sun . . .*

It would never have happened if she had loved him more.

Standing now, a year later, in the bedroom, with a brilliant
but cold winter sun gilding the walls, she believed this and
slipped on the black dress, which fell to the black stockings at
her knees. The black was not parading her grief as Ina called it,
but simply, for her, the outward and visible sign of her inward
and spiritual desolation. If there had been stigmata which she
could have had incised on her hands or forehead to mark her
loss, she would have had them done, and not cared what the
world said.

"You can't go to a party in black."

"It's not a party." She snatched up Beryl Challenor's fussily
printed invitation and read aloud, " *'Please come to a pre-evening
soiree and housewarming of my new room,'* whatever that is!"
She tossed it back on the dresser.

"You still can't go in that black."

"There won't be any boys."

"You still . . ."

"All right, I heard you," she cried and swung to her sister
standing disapprovingly in the doorway. "Do you think I want to
go to the damn silly pre-evening whatever it is? It's just that she

called and insisted I come. Besides, I won't be there long, since it ends at four and it's almost that now."

Turning back, she regretted having yelled, for the quick hurt had brushed Ina's eyes. Glancing up at her sister's blurred reflection behind hers in the mirror, she was truly sorry, for Ina also had been drained by the year's mourning. Her tall, graceful form under the trim suits she wore now that she was working for the telephone company was almost thin, her face, with the delicate sweep of bone under the smooth dark skin, was drawn. Selina sometimes saw her start and scan the room for their father's spectral presence. She had brought down his rose-shaded lamp and kept it lighted on her dresser. This evening, as on every Saturday evening, she would pensively dress by the lamp and Edgar Innis would come, the boy who had danced with her at 'Gatha Steed's daughter's wedding and who was as mild-mannered as she. They would talk softly in the parlor with the doors open, and Ina would sometimes play the piano for him, while the mother sat in the next room breathing her distrust through the wall.

"But where you find him, nuh?" Silla would start as soon as he left. "He does give me a bad feel, he's so softy-soft. But you still best watch yourself with him, because I ain having no concubines round here and I ain supporting no wild-dog puppies. Out you'll go!"

But Edgar Innis was only a spoke in the small wheel that was Ina's life, while its hub was the church. Each Sunday at dawn she and the other choristers glided behind the dull glittering gold cross, through the chill marble gloom of St. Matthew's Episcopal Church, singing—their voices as ephemeral as the strands of incense in the air.

*"Oh Lamb of God,*
*Oh Lamb of God,*
*That takest away the sins of the world,*
*Grant us thy peace . . ."*

Ina would sing, her mild eyes fixed on a stained-glass window of Christ holding three lambs. When the sacring bell rang and the priest elevated the Host Ina would raise her soft face to the mosaic of Christ with an expression at once trusting as a child's and ardent as a woman's. When the priest placed the wafer on her tongue and the chalice of wine to her lips her eyes would seek the Christ over his shoulder.

"But who put you so that you must sit up in a church morning, noon and night, nuh?" the mother would rave. Ina never answered, and her silence became like a deep moat, beyond which she remained cowed but inaccessible . . .

Selina turned now and, pulling on her coat, murmured, "I'm sorry I yelled, Ina," and passing her at the door, she wished that she could summon more eloquent words to ask forgiveness for all her abuse.

The sun had gone, leaving the sky like a sullen gray wash strung above the roofs. A wind, equally as sullen, snarled the shorn branches of the trees, and the city's snow—begrimed, stained tobacco color in places with dog urine—stretched in a hard crust along the curbs.

The snow in front of the Challenor house in Crown Heights had been cleared to make room for a patrician-black Packard car. The car was consonant with the house, a regal brownstone with arched windows and elaborate stonework. Only Gert Challenor, who opened the door for Selina, seemed alien to the setting. She was as disheveled and flustered as ever, and still unsure of what to do with her hands.

"Is this Selina? Wha'lah, wha'lah, look how the lot of grief has drag down this girl!" She drew Selina into the paneled hall, her plump face squeezed tight with sympathy and making soft clicking noises with her tongue. "Percy, come. Deighton Selina here!"

He appeared like a genie conjured up by his wife's shout. His dark three-piece suit, the gold watch chain draped across his corpulent middle, his shrewd eye declared that he moved now in a world of business.

"Selina girl, how? You been through more than some grown people."

"And look, Percy, she wearing black and all like some woman."

The powerful head nodded. "It only right a child should mourn it father, no matter how he die . . ."

Selina tensed and Gert Challenor quickly shouted in the lovely hall that had been meant for quiet voices, "Beryl, come down, nuh. Selina here."

A door slammed upstairs and they heard quick muffled steps; then, in a flurry of petticoats, Beryl descended, shouting Selina's name. Confronted by those full legs and Beryl's fully developed, almost plump body, by the breasts jogging slightly under her sweater as she ran down, Selina saw herself with sudden and painful clarity. She was nothing—a mere stick that could barely support the black clothes or Gert Challenor's comforting arm on her shoulder—while Beryl was a bright burst of health in the dim hall. She might have spent all her seventeen years curled and cushioned in a warm nest and now, for the first time, taken flight down those stairs. Caught in her rushing embrace, Selina smelled health like a sweet musk on Beryl's flesh; her breath as she kissed Selina was redolent with it.

"Selina, the invitation said pre-evening, not five o'clock. Nearly everybody's gone. You did it on purpose."

"Yes," she said, returning the kiss. "I didn't want to spoil the fun."

"You wouldn't have spoiled anything. Everybody understands. And why wouldn't you let me come and see you? For a whole year! Why're you like that?" and chiding Selina, Beryl led her upstairs.

The room was as Selina had pictured it from the invitation, all pale pink and frilled virginal white, with Beryl's old dolls arrayed on the bed. Four girls were there: Florrie Trotman's thin diffident daughter, Una; one of Virgie Farnum's gray-eyed daughters and Seifert Yearwood's two dark tense girls.

"Look who finally got here." Beryl presented her.

Their eyes converged on her, encountered the black clothes and her wasted face, and fled. She took a rancorous delight in their discomfort, yet she was also sorry for them, and said, too loudly perhaps, "Well hello. Isn't anybody gonna speak to me because I'm late?" Then handing her coat to Beryl, she added pleasantly, "Una, you're putting on some weight. You look good."

"You think so, Selina?" Una said, pleased.

"Uh-huh."

Una's helpless smile brought tentative smiles to the other faces and then, relieved, they rushed Selina with a loud and clamorous greeting. When she was finally seated with a slice of cake and a glass of soda, Virgie Farnum's daughter Rita said, "I asked everybody else, Selina, so it's your turn. Do you have your own room?"

"No, I'm still cooped up with Ina," she said. Then, "No, wait. In the summers now I do. I move into the sun parlor."

"You see." Rita's skin, paler than her mother's, flushed angrily. "Out of everybody I know, I'm the only one still without my own room."

"Well you know what I had to do to get this, doncha?" Beryl said, lying carefully on her bed, with her skirt tucked neatly under her. "I had to get an eighty average for a term. My father's orders. Did I work! Studying every night because that school is so hard. Selina, you should have gone to Bergen High, not me. It's full of Jewish kids and every one of them is a brain. One girl writes love letters all during geometry class and still gets a hundred on every exam."

Amid their laughter, she added, "When I graduate this summer I'm going to demand a Lady Elgin watch as a present. I'll have deserved it. And hey," she whispered, "my father says I might get a car . . ."

Their astonished gasps tugged at the air. "Oh, not for years yet," she said, "when I finish college."

"You know what's a good graduating present from college," Una said, "going to Europe the summer you graduate, just like the rich white girls. Or Mexico."

"We're getting a trip to Barbados if we finish college," one of the Yearwood girls said.

Beryl sat up, waving all this aside. "No trips. Not me. I'll take the car. When the trip's over you've got nothing to show for it."

For a long time they argued this, then Beryl said, "Which would you prefer, Selina?"

She started, for sitting there with the untouched cake and soda in her hands, she had, in her mind, withdrawn from them to stand—invisible and critical—in a shadowy area outside their warm pink circle. For some reason she wanted only to be an onlooker.

"Come on, Selina. I'll go along with whatever you say."

"Both."

"Both then! The trip right after graduation and then, when I go to med school, or, if I'm not smart enough to get in, to law school, I'll ask for the car. Please, dear Lord, let these next four and a half years fly!"

"Which one do you want to be?" Selina quietly asked.

Beryl shifted uneasily on the bed. "Either, I guess. My father says both are the oldest and most respected professions in the world, and since I'm the oldest . . ."

"I thought of medicine too," Una said as Beryl's voice trailed into uncertainty, "but all that blood, ugh! So I'm gonna be a social worker. What're you gonna take up, Selina?"

"I don't have the vaguest idea."

Beryl suddenly laughed and leaned over the bed to her. "Remember when you wanted to be a poetess?"

"Yes and would recite those crummy poems to you." But although she laughed and felt the old intimacy spark between them she was troubled by Beryl. Beryl's face had somehow lost its individual mold, that soft pleasing form that she used to gaze at, rapt, as they lay together in the grass of Prospect Park. Now, some trace of Gert Challenor's evasiveness and docility lay aslant it.

"No more school for me after this," Rita Farnum was saying. "I want a job so I can start making money right away and get whatever I want."

Beryl, her eyes abstracted, said suddenly, "I think I prefer law, Selina. Because my father says then I could help him in the business and with the rooming houses we have over your way. He says he's getting tired of yelling at the roomers for the rent. And he says maybe I could even be the attorney for the Association some day."

"What Association?" Selina asked scathingly, overcome by sadness and envy. Sadness for Beryl, whose father, like a priest at confirmation, had placed his huge, pink-palmed hands on her head and transferred his acquisitive spirit to her. Envy, because all that Beryl said would come true. Beryl's life was planned, ordered, while hers was as vague and formless as mist. "What Association?" she repeated brutally.

Beryl drew back a little. "The Association of Barbadian Home-owners and Businessmen. Haven't you heard about it? Your mother belongs. My father says it's going to be the biggest thing since Marcus Garvey. He says they're even starting up a young people's division. It's gonna be called the Young Associates and we'll be eligible when we're in college."

Slowly Selina put aside the cake and soda and stood up, a drawn figure in black amid the room's flushed pink. She felt their sudden uneasiness. "What do you say, Beryl?" Her voice, though low, cut the silence.

"What d'ya mean? I say the same thing. We need something like the Association."

Selina went and knelt on the edge of the bed, her face as close to Beryl's as when they had lain in each other's arms behind the black rock—and the pain of those lost days and of those lost

196

selves fired her cruelty. "I mean what do you say about anything? You begin everything with 'My father says this or that' or 'My father's gonna give me this or that'—but what do *you* say, what do *you* want?"

"I don't understand," Beryl began and turned to the others, then swung back to Selina. "I say the same thing he says." Her voice was sharp but unsure.

Again she appealed to the others, and when their eyes darted away she searched Selina's for the meaning of her question and at the same time strained in her mind to understand. But her eyes remained baffled and slowly tears of frustration and doubt gathered. "Why would you ask something like that?" she whispered and then suddenly cried, grabbing Selina's arm, "What's wrong with what he says, or what he's gonna give me? What's your father gonna give you?"

Her hand reached her mouth too late. Her eyes dilated and a small choking sound came from her throat. "Selina . . . Oh Lord, I'm sorry. I forgot. I didn't mean that. I forgot. You made me so mad I forgot . . . I swear I forgot . . ."

Selina did not hear, for the familiar upheaval had started. The cold and powerful wave drowning out her mind, the same one, she imagined, that had borne her father down to the sea's floor. She was hardly aware of picking up her coat or of leaving the room. Only when Beryl caught and clasped her from behind on the stairs did she slowly rouse.

"Selina, please, I didn't mean anything. I just forgot."

Selina would have turned then and told her that it was all right but for the tears. She could not bear for Beryl to see them. But she would have liked to turn and tell Beryl, very quietly, there in the dim hall with the others gathered apprehensively on the landing above, what he had given her. How one cold March afternoon long ago she had found him stretched on the cot in the sun parlor in his shirt sleeves, his head cradled in his arms and humming. "Is it spring?" she had asked, her breath coming in cold wisps. He had drawn her down beside him, loosened her

197

arms and said, "Yes." And suddenly she had sensed spring in the air, seen it forming beyond the glass walls and had not been cold any more.

How could Beryl understand that this was what he had given her? and its worth? But oh, Christ, she raged, perhaps it was not enough. For hadn't envy pricked her at the solid sure things Beryl would have? Things that had not been part of his legacy since he could not, like Percy Challenor, stand in the halls and yell at the roomers for the rent money to buy them. What, then, had been his way?—and since he had made her like him, what was to be hers? Before she could grasp them the thoughts flickered out—tiny flames snatched by the wind of her mind.

"Selina, tell me, please, what was so wrong with what I was saying?" Beryl whispered against her ear. Selina turned in her tight hold and through her own tears she saw Beryl's tears of confusion and doubt. Beryl's face was no longer tranquil and smooth from her seventeen-year stay in the warm nest, but worried. Selina remembered how she had always thought of Beryl's mind as a neat well-lighted room—and suddenly she wanted to restore Beryl's calm. For if Beryl was always sure and untroubled, it would somehow mean that their years together and those other selves were not utterly lost. Whenever she saw Beryl, she would glimpse them.

"What was so wrong with it, Selina?" Beryl pleaded for an answer.

"Nothing. It's just me," Selina said softly and watched the doubt slowly shift and break, like ice in a spring thaw, and Beryl's eyes emerge, dark but clear and tranquil, like lake water.

"Why're you like this?" Beryl whispered, and Selina heard a rustle on the landing above as the others strained to hear her answer. But she made none. Very gently she pushed away Beryl's arms and hastened downstairs. Once outside she lifted her face full to the wind, welcoming its brutal but cleansing lash.

# 2

"I tell yuh, you like you ain one-two particular about college.
Here it tis . . ."

"Oh please, not again this morning." Selina got up from the
table and, taking her cup, went out to the back yard and stood
amid the broken flower pots, rusted toys and tools, the last autumn's leaves, drinking the hot tea quickly against the chill and
watching the steam twist into the morning haze.

It was a spring haze and soft. At noon it would turn gold in
the sun and in the evening hang in a blue wistful blur against the
darkening sky. Gulping the tea and shivering, she sensed the
earth swollen with life and heaving in its blind act; she smelled
the sad, sweet, fecund musk of birth. All over the ruined yard
green tufts nudged toward the sun and their own brief life. New
leaves craned in the wind. Aching, she thought of the lovers tonight in the pavilion and the silence that would seem loud with
the sound of their mouths and hands.

Her irritation gone, she turned and stared at the mother
through the kitchen window. Every morning she found the
mother at the table, sometimes asleep or simply staring down
into a cup that had long since been emptied. For days the bed
upstairs remained untouched, dust sown like fine seeds on the
rose satin bedspread. Instead of sleeping she cleaned at night—
Selina would hear the vacuum cleaner's whine in her sleep—
and studied a course in practical nursing, since she worked in a

199

hospital now that the war plant had closed. She would be studying in the kitchen, yet the lights in all the rooms, the halls, even
the chandelier in the parlor would be burning, giving the high-
ceilinged rooms with their gilt and rich wood a festive air. Often
she fell asleep amid the books on the table or stumbled with exhaustion into the dining room and slept, fully clothed, in one of
the stiff-back chairs, her body braced.

Yet, on Saturdays, with her friends in the kitchen and the window sweating from the cooking, it was as though nothing had
happened. The old formidable strength flashed in her hands as
she kneaded the dough. The probing eyes that gave no hint of
what lay behind them still set off her angular handsomeness.
There was the familiar determined thrust to her back. And her
voice still soared with theirs as, together, they inveighed against
a world they did not trust.

"I tell yuh, Silla," Florrie Trotman said once, shaking her head,
"you's a real-real Bajan woman. You can bear up under I don
know what."

No, they did not know about the nights, Selina thought grimly,
reëntering the kitchen.

"Here it tis near time for you to graduate and nobody can't
even mention college or so before you ain ready to fly off," the
mother said and she might not even have left the room.

She turned to make some sharp answer, but paused, unsettled
by something in the mother's voice. The usual harsh imperative
note was missing. Ever since the night Selina had struck her, she
had often surprised a veiled assuagement in the mother's glance,
a guarded respect in her voice. Frowning down into her empty
cup, Selina tried to remember that night, but it was only a
blurred memory of striking and shouting the name, and then
climbing out of a black depth to find herself in bed with the
sheet in place. It could have been a dream, since the mother
never mentioned it—except for her strange apologetic air and
her hesitant attempts at reconciliation.

Under this covert gaze, Selina experienced tangled emotions:

bewilderment as to its real meaning; disconcertion at the love and admiration it masked; a dark satisfaction at its mute plea for forgiveness when she knew she would never forgive; and fear at the possessiveness lurking behind its softness.

Caught in this mesh of feeling now she said carefully, "Oh all right, I'll go at night and work during the day like Ina."

"No, you'll go during the day along with Beryl and them so. The college is free so I can manage. Besides, Ina is different. She ain interested in nothing but clothes and the church . . . but the teachers did always say you had a good mind, so it got to be train right. You made up your mind what you gon study?"

"No."

"Well, there's always teaching or so. Some profession that's practical. Percy Challenor once said you might even make a good doctor . . . Yes . . ." She suddenly became absorbed in this thought and her voice lapsed, then surged back strongly. "Yes, maybe I could even see my way for that." A small wistful smile softened her face and, still absorbed, she did not even hear Selina's loud protest. "If I could only make upstairs into smaller rooms and charge little more . . . But that old woman wun dead and the free-bee ain thinking about moving." She sucked her teeth in disgust. And then her old indomitable temper flared; her head snapped up menacingly. "But I gon start thinking hard for both of them and we gon see."

Selina realized the seriousness of that threat one afternoon weeks later, sitting beside Miss Mary's bed, watching the old woman's face, more wizened and fey now, screw in her painful effort to speak. Selina knew what she was trying to say. It was the old ream of memories which she could have said for her.

"Tom . . ." It was a dry rasp after a long struggle.

"Him so tall and strong with a smile for everyone," Selina said.

"Aye."

All afternoon they whispered together, the old woman's eyes, buried in a web of wrinkles but still alert, urging her on, and Selina filling in the words and feeling vaguely happy. For the room with its musty smell of the past and stale light was comforting. Its timelessness meant there was neither time nor change and she could imagine, sitting there in her black clothes, that when she went downstairs she would find him. Suddenly she saw the old eyes grope toward the door and she heard a step behind her. Thinking it was the daughter, Maritze, she reluctantly started to rise, but the old woman snatched her dress and she saw terror, like a thick mucus, drown out her eyes.

"What?" She turned, peering through the tarnished light.

The mother stood in the doorway, an ominous figure broken off from the hall's gloom with her face lost in shadow.

"You want me?" Selina asked and, as in the restaurant, felt the world ground to a halt and her heart pause.

A bewildered whisper came from out the shadows. "But girl, what you does find in sitting up here with this rank, half-dead old woman, nuh? Or with that whore next door? Why you would rather visit Thompson with that smelly life-sore on her leg than Beryl and them so? Why?" The question impelled her into the room. "Why?" Her perplexed face emerged from the dimness.

"What do you want up here?" Selina asked coldly.

"I can't fathom you a-tall, a-tall."

"Don't come in here. She's scared and she can't talk."

"What it tis you does find here?" Silla suddenly shouted, and the dust, motionless for years, moiled as in a wind. When Selina offered no answer, she strode up to the foot of the bed and, thrusting out her face, stared with bitter curiosity at Miss Mary. "But why you wun dead, nuh?" she whispered.

The wasted arms began beating the covers in panic, the sunken mouth gaped wide in a mute scream as though Silla, lowering darkly at her from the footboard, were the embodiment of all she had ever feared and the image of her imminent death.

"What it tis you waiting on? Tell me. You can't take this old house with you. It belong to me now. You don understand that yet?"

A choked protest came from Miss Mary's ruined cords.

"Yes, it belong to me!" Silla cried and gestured widely and then glared down at her again, adding, "And I gon get you out yet. Yuh hear that? I gon call in the Board of Health to see all this dirt and get you out that way. Yes, and your long-face daughter too that never once count me to speak because my skin black . . ."

With this her full rage suddenly broke. "All this dirt!" she shouted and bounded across the room with a lithe animal lunge and scooped up the cracked oil paintings and slammed them down, breaking the frames and plunging her foot through the canvas. "All these old junks!" She tore open the boxes of rotted clothes and smashed the piles of delft across the floor. "All this dirt!" She ripped the gray sheets on the furniture and then came wheeling out of the wreckage and the spiraling dust to the footboard of the bed again. Her arms reached out pleadingly. "Why you wun dead?"

For a time they struggled silently, Silla's curved fingers drawing the life from Miss Mary, while Miss Mary strained to hold it. The old head with the skull transparent under the wisps of hair quivered up, the wasted body writhed out of Silla's reach. But as Silla leaned forward, her fingers tightening and her face becoming more menacing, Miss Mary slowly dropped back, weakening, until finally she lay still. Through the maze of wrinkles a profound disappointment emerged, and defeat. It was as if Silla had proved to her at last the futility of her long wait.

"Oh God, how could you do something like this?" Selina whispered, too stunned and shamed to move or even speak before.

Silla's arms dropped and with them, her high anger. She gave Selina that assuaging, apologetic look; her hand sketched a plea for forbearance. But at Selina's cold condemning stare, the gesture died and, giving the old woman a final bitter glance, she left.

Miss Mary died a few months later. Entering the room, Selina saw the wizened form contorted in the last throes, the pinched mouth open as if to speak and the quiet stare. She was not afraid, for there was no difference between this and Miss Mary's living death in the dust-yellow tomb. A thought sparked and died as she stood there beside the bed. Perhaps everyone had his tomb: the mother hunched over the table all night might be locked in hers, her father, stretched on the cot, might have been sealed in his, just as she was shut within the lonely region of herself. She might never find a way out, but like Miss Mary, move from one death to another. Suddenly she resented the old woman for having lured her as a child into her tomb with her crooning memories. For the first time her resentment reached out to her father for having died and left her always to mourn. She wanted something else. She sought it in the old woman's set eyes, which were startlingly blue now and clear, as though life was simply an impurity which death washed away. The air in the room seemed washed also. The tarnished dust was gone and the silence no longer hummed of the past. She heard noises from the street, the brash, surging, alive sound of children playing. It rushed in to fill the emptiness, and caught between that clamorous call and Miss Mary's fixed silence, she knew what she wanted. It was not so much a thought as something deeply felt. To flow out of herself into life, to touch and know it fully and, in turn, to be touched by it. And then, sometimes, to withdraw and be quiet within herself . . . But how? How even to begin? She did not know.

## 3

"Lord-God, death been busy enough 'bout here! Come, mahn, le's wash the taste of it out we mouth," Suggie hooted and tossed the rum neatly over her tongue. "The old woman in she grave! The long-face daughter move away from all you colored people! Yuh mother overcharging the new roomers something unmerciful, so le'we toast till we's tottering!"

Selina smiled thinly and raised her glass. While she sipped Suggie spun across the room, her black hair whipping and the red chenille robe flaring high, and put a record on the phonograph. A loud lilting calypso exploded in the room and she danced, subdued at first. Then slowly she lifted her head, her arms, her eyes half-closed, and her full hips swayed in wide emphatic motion that swung the robe softly around them. She sang:

> *Saga-boy, come in muh bed,*
> *I got a fine brush to tease yuh head.*
> *Saga-boy, don 'cause me cry*
> *Yuh know I want you, stop acting shy."*

She lured the invisible lover with somnolent eyes and lush arms, with each thrust of her hips. She danced over to Selina. "Come, mahn, the music too sweet to waste."

Protesting, Selina sidled along with her, a slight, somber figure in her black clothes next to Suggie. Selina glanced up at her as they danced. With all the different mouths and hands and bodies that had touched her Suggie seemed untouched, still innocent. Yet Selina had just passed the newest lover on the stairs and saw the signs of their love-making: the tossed bed, the bottle of rum and Suggie's bare body under the robe. His smell should be still on her, yet she smelled only the subtle fragrance of Suggie's body. Could what they had done be so sinful and yet smell so sweet?

Her mind began to reel from the rum and Suggie's fragrance as her feet reeled in the dance. The room joined the dance and soon Selina felt that the walls and furniture were spinning while she stood still. This made her laugh suddenly. The records dropped on the spindle, the room spun, Suggie sang and she laughed.

Soon her laughter became confused with tears. Until laughing and sobbing all at once, she was too weak to dance. Dragging Suggie with her, she stumbled across the room and they fell, amid wild shouts and laughter, onto the bed.

The last record dropped, the last loud rhythms spun the room, and then there was only the soft whir of the turntable and the laughter and sobs catching in Selina's throat as they died. Suggie got up, turned off the machine and returned. They lay in a pure silence, gazing out the window at the twilit sky and the pale stars embedded there, at the dark fringe of trees in Fulton Park and above them the bright smolder of Fulton Street's lights.

The sky was completely dark, the stars full, when Selina said, "Miss Suggie, do you think I'll ever meet anybody—a boy, I mean."

The small bed light went on, revealing Suggie propped on her elbow and her eyes, still wanton and warm from the dance and her afternoon pleasures, suddenly tender. Caught in the snatch of light she reminded Selina of a painting she had once seen on a museum trip from school. The figure of a woman in a gay-figured cloth seated against a torturous mass of foliage with sunlight scattered in bright flakes on her bronze flesh which, like Suggie's, absorbed the light, with the same ripe, gently sloping breasts and liquid languid form. The woman's expression had made Selina pause, and then followed her as she trooped behind the others. It had been serene despite the green violence of the background, wise yet artless, voluptuous, and above all secretive—as if she held what all men truly sought, and was proud yet fated to suffer in the knowledge and possession of it.

This was Suggie's look now and Selina, helplessly envious, said almost harshly, "Well, do you?"

Suggie shook her head, amazed, her full laugh starting low in her throat. "Jesus-God, it about time, soul. I was beginning to think that nature had by-passed you. Lemme look good now." Squinting, she examined Selina's face: the full mouth always parted, it seemed, for some impulsive word, the abrupt nose the graceful upward slant of her bones under the dark brown tight skin, and finally the eyes, wide and willful under straight down-swept lashes which seemed to have ensnared all that they had ever encountered in their depth. Suggie lay back and turned off the light. "Yes, somebody someplace gon look at you twice. But you best stop looking like you spending your old-days first."

Offended, Selina said, "Well, I won't go to bed with him the way you do or that girl in school did."

Suggie snorted. "Mark my words, soul, a time gon come when the body is willing and the mind is weak and before the cat lick it ear your legs gon be cock high."

Their laughter struck the air like a bold wind and died slowly like a wind and the silence flowed back. After a time Suggie said, "I bet you thinking hard 'bout the boy."

"Yes, but about whether I'll ever be anything or do anything too." She turned and felt Suggie's breath like a warm soothing gust on her face.

"How you mean—be anything, do anything, when you's go-ing to all this college and thing this fall? You got to be something after all that hard learning. But lemme tell you one thing." Her hand groped for Selina's and pressed it warningly. "Watch out for this so-called Barbadian Association. They gon want wunna kind that gon be professional and so. They'll down hand on you, mahn, and when you hear the shout you wun be able to call your soul your own."

"I'd never go there."

"The Association. That's all the talk now. The beautiful-ugly Association! What it tis anyway? Nothing but a bunch of Bajan running their clapper-mouth!" Yet beneath Suggie's sarcasm there was longing and a tinge of envy.

She fell silent, and Selina, detecting that envy and longing, turned away, puzzled. Soon Suggie touched her and said won-deringly, "You know something, mahn, when I was a girl coming up I never once did think about what I was gon do or be or any-thing so. All I ever thought about was spreeing. That's a funny thing, nuh?" As her voice fell her laughter suddenly struck the darkness in a bright spark. "Lord-God, how I did love a spree! Did I ever tell you 'bout the time I spree so much I lost my panties?"

"No."

"'Deed I did, faith. A pretty new pair of pink panties. I wore them to this bus excursion. Mahn, I spree so that day I near drop. Dancing—the music licking sweet—and sea-bathing and eating muh guts full. But as soon as night fall there was my downfall, some boy ask me out for a walk and licking 'bout with that wuthless brute in the sand I lost the pretty new pair of pink panties. The sea carry them off."

"What kind of licking about?"

"Loving-up, nuh."

"How old were you?" Selina sat up, staring down at Suggie in the dark.

"Twelve or so. You think everybody is as slow as you?" Her laugh was a murmurous summer sound. "After that I said I was gon behave. But I cun stop. I did like the boys too bad . . ."

She bounded up and Selina heard her pouring rum. "Come, mahn," she cried, turning on the lights, "le's drink to Suggie Skeete. She was born in wickedness and gon dead so." She tossed her head proudly and drank.

Selina took the glass but did not drink. "Miss Suggie," she said as Suggie came and lay across the bed this time, her head against Selina's thigh, "would you go back?"

"Go back? Where? Home, you mean?" The sagging bed thumped the floor as she sprang up, her incredulous eyes boring into Selina. "Me go back there? You think I looking to dead before my time? Do you know how bad those malicious brutes would lick their mouth on me if I went back the same way I left? Tell muh, why you think your father is at the bottom of the sea tonight?"

And then Selina realized that she had not thought of him for the afternoon. That she had been dancing and drinking and laughing while dressed in the black. Guilt rapped her sharply and she deflected it onto Suggie. What right had she with her wild sinfulness to speak of him? She started up but Suggie held her.

"All right, I sorry. Don swell up. Nobody's to call his name, I know. All I meant was that he cun face those people tongue and neither could I. Besides, the bloody place wun be the way I does remember it anyway." She sucked her teeth, dismissing it, and drank again.

"I'm going down."

"You's offended 'cause I call his name, I know . . ." Suddenly she leaped up and knelt in the middle of the bed, her hair tumbled wildly about her face and her arms extended as she pleaded, "Oh God, Selina-mahn, stop thinking 'bout death. Take off the blasted black clothes!" Her hands swept out as if to divest her of them. "Life is too strong out here, mahn. You think your father would want you walking 'bout like this? Not him. Not the way he did dress. Not the way he did love his sport! Take them off. You wun forget him if you do. Beside, you got to do the living for him. So c'dear, put on something bright and find yuhself some boy or the other out there and get little loving-up and thing."

Selina laughed helplessly, disarmed by her violent earnestness. "I'll think about it," she said.

Suggie sat back on her heels, suspicious yet pleased. "Well, that's something at least." She rose and stood shyly against the unused bottles of perfume on her vanity with her robe in a motionless swirl at her feet and her glass raised.

"I propose a toast to Miss Selina Boyce." She bowed to Selina. "May she grow to a fine-looking woman. May she find somebody decent to marry she and treat she right. May she have plenty money and houses but not have it turn she foolish. May she have 'nough friends . . ." Her voice dropped. " 'Cause she's the only one I can call friend in this man New York. She don know what it tis to have she come and sit with me 'pon an afternoon, to have

209

she listen. It ain no joke having things burning inside you and not a soul to say 'yuh-cat, yuh-dog.' So the best to Miss Selina, the only one in this New York that ever treat me like I was people too."

The rum flashed, her body lifted in a lovely feline pose and she drank. "Come, girl, have the rest." She tipped the glass to Selina's lips.

The liquor traced a stinging line down Selina's throat, and closing her eyes she imagined it lighting up inside her, so that she could see her heart leaping in its socket and the blood coupling with the air in her lungs and all the intricate workings of her body. For the first time she was vividly aware of the small but sturdy life she contained. She rose, reaching for Suggie, and felt the same life pulsing there. "I think I'm a little drunk," she said, clinging to her.

"Drunk what! Yuh's just beginning to feel like yourself again, that's all."

"Maybe I could take off some of the black now, y'know?"

"Now yuh talking, mahn." Suggie embraced her, and then slapped her lightly on the behind. Together, laughing, their arms circling each other's waists, they crossed the room and opened the door. A wide bar of light from the hall made a path for them and the rich colors of their laughter painted the darkness.

4

The month Selina started college the mother evicted Suggie as an undesirable tenant, without once breaking the disdainful silence she had always maintained with her. She did it by securing affidavits from the new roomers, in which they swore that they saw men visiting Suggie all day and night. Thus, the petition asserted, Suggie was obviously a prostitute since she did not work. It claimed that she was giving the house an unsavory reputation and thus lowering its property value. It cited the harmful influence of a person of such low morals on the landlady's two daughters . . .

The petition was granted and the date set for Suggie's removal.

On that day, with her trunk packed and the vanity cleared of her perfumes, Suggie strode the room, her hair waving in a black plume and her red chenille robe—faded now and the tufts gone—snapping angrily around her feet.

"Oh the bitches! The malicious bitches! I's a prostitute? Is that what the bad-minded bitches swear to? Is that what they put in the bloody affidavit? That I's a harmful influence. Tell me how I harm you?" She suddenly whirled angrily to Selina, who was lying face down on the stripped bed, her long, thin form inert. "Tell me! All I ever did was to give you little rum and make little joke about loving-up and so. That's all. How's that a harmful influence? Is you a drunkard now? Is you a whore? Tell me?" she demanded, her eyes almost demented and her hand lifted threateningly.

Painfully Selina raised up, her eyes dry in her drawn face, as though the source of her tears was exhausted. She leaned toward Suggie's raised hand, willing to accept the blow, and said in a broken whisper, "No, I'm not a whore and I'm not a drunkard and neither are you. It's not you, Miss Suggie. It's just that I'm to have no one, that's all. Look how she practically frightened the old lady to death . . . And now she's got this crazy idea about filling the house with roomers to make more money for me to be something I don't want to be. But you just wait"—a dry malevolent light splintered her eyes—"I'm going to show her."

Suggie's hand dropped and she sat heavily beside Selina. "Don mind me, mahn, I know that's what it tis. She did stay downstairs and hear we laughing up here 'pon an afternoon and it did cut she to the quick."

"Yes, but she won't stop me from seeing you. Tell me where you'll be."

Suggie swung away, suddenly angry. "No, I ain able for she to find out and come and kill me too . . . Oh, it's not that, Selina-mahn." Her anger fell away. "It's that where I'm going ain gon be much. No place for you to come. So don ask. Come help me dress before the piece of man come."

Later, waiting in the vestibule while the man with whom Suggie would live brought down her trunk, Selina still pressed her for the address and Suggie still refused it. When they heard him coming, she forced a bottle of perfume into Selina's hand.

"I don't want perfume, just tell me were you'll be!"

"Take it." Suggie closed her fingers around it. "You don even have to use it. Just open it sometimes and pass it across your face. It does smell too sweet."

The chill feel of utter desertion she had watching Suggie leave persisted through her first year of college. This was real while everything that happened at school had the unreality of a play viewed from a high balcony. She sensed being surrounded by white faces but few ever came into focus. She sat in class, mechanically taking notes, and all the voices—the professors, students, even her own when she recited—seemed like distant echoes. She crowded into the high-speed elevators that soared and plunged through the towering steel structure of the city college and was only vaguely aware of the bodies crushing hers and their odd milk smell. In the huge stainless-steel lunchroom, she avoided Beryl Challenor and the others, and, eating quickly, fled the unremitting shrill of female voices, the dense cigarette fog, the clatter of dishes and the strident bridge games, for the library.

Every afternoon she walked from the college to the center of the city, and only during these long reckless walks did she rouse a little. Holding her books like a shield, she weaved down through the East Side, past the sedate brownstones and the tall apartment houses thrusting into the sky, glancing, in her swift walk, into the richly appointed lobbies. At Fifth Avenue she walked almost cautiously past the luxurious displays in the tall windows and covertly watched those to whom the street belonged: the meticulously groomed, mink-draped women, who tapped out their right of possession with their high heels, who moved secure in an aura of wealth, with ennui like a subtle blue shading under their cold eyes and a faint famished touch to their pallid cheeks. They made her rage inside, for she knew, walking amid them in her worn coat and tam, that she was non-existent—a dark intruder in their glittering inaccessible world.

Evenings always found her striding, head up, tam askew, through Times Square, that bejeweled navel in the city's long sinuous form. To Selina it was a new constellation, the myriad lights hot stars bursting from chaos into their own vivid life, shooting, streaking, wheeling in the night void, then expiring, but only to burst again—and the concatenation of traffic and voices like the roar from the depth of a maelstrom—an irresistible call to destruction.

She loved it, for its chaos echoed her inner chaos; each bedizened window, each gaudy empty display evoked something in her that loved and understood the gaudy, the emptiness defined her own emptiness and that in the faces flitting past her. She walked with a swagger here, gazing boldly into those faces, always hoping to happen upon some violence, or to be involved in some spectacular brawl. For hours she stood outside the Metropole, listening to the jazz that poured through the open doors in a thick guttural flow that churned the air into a pulsating mass; sometimes the music was thin and reedy, sometimes brassy and jarring, yet often soulful, and always expressing the chaos in the street. She would shift amid the crowd for a glimpse of the sailors strung along the bar, the brilliant streak of a woman's blond hair in the dimness and smoke, a gleam of silver on the drums, the pomaded head of a Negro musician. Standing there with her books stacked on the ground between her legs, her fists plunged in her pockets and her lean body absorbing each note, she would feel sucked into that roaring center, the lights exploding inside her, and she would be free of the numbness.

"Fulton Street is nothing compared to Times Square. Nothing!"

"'Course it ain't." Miss Thompson agreed and drew the hot comb through her thick hair. They were alone in the booth with the one dangling light staving off the darkness. Miss Thompson's thin haunches rested on the high stool with a kind of permanence, her fleshless thighs held Selina's chair steady between them, and the foot with the ulcer gave off its faint but unmistakable odor of putrefaction. "Ain't nothing but bars and storefront churches—poor colored peoples losing religion and getting religion. That's all it is. But there's one place that's got all of 'em beat. One Hundred and Twenty-Fifth Street on Saturday night! Lord, all them colored peoples dressed back, honey, and falling in and out of the Apollo Theater. Colored peoples sitting up in Frank's Restaurant being served by white waiters! All them good-timing niggers riding in Cadillacs . . . Honey, I seen it just once and I got all choked up inside I was so proud to see my peoples living so swell!"

"It can't compare to Times Square. And Crown Heights is certainly nothing compared to those apartment houses on the East Side. Perhaps if my mother and them could see them they'd stop taking on so about a few old musty brownstones."

"They seen 'em," Miss Thompson said sharply, "because they worked in 'em, and lemme tell you something, Crown Heights still looks just as good. Seems to me that anybody going to college could understand that."

"I'm sorry." Selina patted Miss Thompson's leg. "I do understand that. What it is, I guess, is that I'll never understand how

214

anything is worth what my mother has done to get that house. You know," she said, shame gathering in her eyes, "now that the house is crawling with roomers she's taken to hiding in the hall to watch them. If they ring the bell too loud, or run down the stairs, she springs out of the dark and shouts, 'Don ring down the bell!' or 'What, you gon break down my stairs!' or 'Turn down the blasted radio, this ain Fulton Street!' "

They shared a helpless laugh and she said, "It is kind of funny to hear her, but it's terrible too. I shudder each time she does it. Oh, she's not the only one. And what right have they? And over what? A few moth-eaten houses!"

Miss Thompson cupped her hands gently over Selina's bowed head. "Honey, I know. West Indian peoples are sure peculiar, but you got to hand it to them, they knows how to get ahead. I don't know, maybe someday you'll understand your momma and then you'll see why she does some of these things."

"I never want to understand her, Miss Thompson." Her voice was hard.

They were silent. Soon Miss Thompson was finished, and while she gave herself a manicure, Selina cleaned the booth. Then Miss Thompson reached for a cane and, leaning on it, eased down from the stool.

"How come you're using a cane now?" Selina asked, coming over to her. "Is the foot worse?"

"Now don't start fussing." She waved Selina off with the cane. "Peoples see you with a cane and right away you's about to step down into the grave. I'm just taking some weight off this old foot."

"Why is it you never told me how you got that sore?" Selina helped her change into the shapeless black dress.

" 'Cause it ain't nothing for a child to hear."

"I'm not a child any more, Miss Thompson," she said quietly. "Can't even you see that?"

Miss Thompson gave her a quick, penetrating look, then sat down abruptly. With her fine long hands on the cane handle and the black dress falling to her feet, she lifted her aged sunken face into the harsh light and began talking, quickly, in a voice without emotion.

"All right, I'll tell you. Went down home one summer to visit my folks. I was a little older than you maybe and had done been up North a couple of years so I had me a little New York style. Well, I guess I had too much style for them crackers down home. Every time I went to the store them mens sitting outside would come looking at me kinda funny, especially one big red cracker with a shovel. One time he come saying: 'Lord, this here is one of them uppity niggers. Done been up North and got herself a white boy friend.' They just whooped and hollered at that. But they laughing was ugly. I knew what crackers give so I went on in that store quick, got what I wanted and then lit through the back. But that cracker with the shovel must of been thinking for me 'cause there he was up the road apiece, smiling and making dirty signs . . ." She paused and looked meditatively at Selina, then shifted, sighed and said flatly, "He didn't get to do nothing with me wrassling and hollering, but he did take a piece clean outta my foot with that rusty shovel." She tapped the foot lightly with her cane, her gaunt face impassive. "For years it wouldn't give me no trouble. Then it would act up, like now. So I figure I'll use this here cane awhile." She rose with a final movement that precluded all comment.

Selina sensed this but still pressed forward to speak, the deep well of her eyes mirroring that scene and her horror. Through her shock she divined something: that sore, in a way, was the thing that had really yellowed Miss Thompson's eyes, grayed her skin and given her face its tragic mien . . . Suddenly she ached for violence, as she did plunging along Times Square. It came on her like a thirst. In a wild pulse beating at the pit of her body. To grab the cane and rush into some store on Fulton Street and avenge that wrong by bringing it smashing across the white face behind the counter. Her breathing was a loud râle in the stillness. "Miss Thompson . . ."

"Don't ask no fool questions! You don't know nothing about the South so just don't ask no questions!" she said harshly and pulled the light chain.

"I declare," she said pleasantly when they were walking down Fulton Street, "you's my baby, always been my baby but you's too serious. Sitting around with folks like me that's done through with life. Worrying yourself. Missing folks. When I was your age, honey, I was having me some good times. Yes indeed. Don't think I was always old and hard and rusty. And don't think there wasn't plenty mens wanted to marry me neither! Somebody was always in love with me and I was always in love!" Her words slowly dissolved in the night air. Around them the traffic hurled, laughter and music spewed from the bars, and next door to the bars, from the store-front churches came ecstatic singing, the ringing clash of tambourines and the moans and shouts of the saved.

"Yes, honey, start having you some good times."

"How?" she said bitterly. "You're always telling me that but how, where?"

Miss Thompson swerved sharply her way and stopped her with the cane. "I'll tell you how and where. Right down there at this here Association your people have. That's where. Your momma was telling me all about the dances and nice social things they has for the young people. You might meet some nice boy down there and . . ."

"Are you serious?" Selina drew back in aversion. "I wouldn't be caught dead there. With those money-changers!"

"They's your people," Miss Thompson said casually and resumed walking. "But you won't go. And I knows why." She gave Selina a piercing and disdainful glance. "You's afraid. Scairt. Frightened."

"It's not a matter of being afraid."

"That's all it is a matter of," she said knowingly and hobbled on, her eyes fixed indifferently ahead. "Scairt that if you went you'd begin to understand your momma and them a little better.

Scairt that then you wouldn't be so hard on them all the time . . ." She rapped the cane in emphasis. "Scairt that you'd have to change some of your ideas. Just plain disgraceful scairt."

"Change my ideas! It would just convince me that I'm right."

"Then I dares you to go!" Miss Thompson struck the cane triumphantly, her eyes turned gleaming to Selina. "I dare you. Just once!"

"Why?"

"I double-dares you."

"But why? Why would you want me to go there?"

"To understand, that's why. So when you start talking so big and smart against people, you'll be talking from understanding. That's the only time you have the right to say whether you like them or not, or whether what they done was right or not. But you got to understand *why* first. So I dares you to go. Just once."

"All right," Selina cried irritably, "I'll go. But just once. Just to show you I know what I'm talking about."

"You promise?"

"I promise."

"I know you's not a person to go back on a promise."

"No."

"All right then. Now leave me," Miss Thompson said with sudden weariness and stopped Selina with the cane. "Leave me. You done walked far enough. Go on back."

Selina was puzzled and hurt. "Don't you want me to walk you home?"

"No."

"Are you angry? Did I say something disrespectful?"

Miss Thompson smiled, her face cavernous and old. "No, it ain't you, honey. I just wants to walk quiet and think about my bed, that's all." She gave her a gentle but probing look in farewell. Selina had on a bright chiffon scarf instead of her tam, and this, blowing around her face, made her eyes bright and blown somehow, and accented the faint reddish cast to her dark skin.

She had on a pair of medium-heeled shoes, and her body under the coat was slight but softly molded now, as were her legs.

"You was right, honey. You ain't no more child," Miss Thompson said softly and walked away, looking oddly indestructible despite the cane and her swathing black dress.

"I'll see you," Selina called, and the cane lifted.

# 5

Selina kept her promise to visit the Association, announcing her decision just as the mother—handsome in a black coat with a high silver fox collar—was preparing to leave for the meeting. There was a careful silence, during which she felt the mother's innate mistrust seethe beneath her astonishment, saw it twitch in her face and in the sudden confused play of her hands. She submitted to her scrutiny. It was a long wait before the distrust ebbed and the mother said with uncertain relief, "Well, it about time you got some sense in that head. Come along then."

The meetings were held in the basement of a small, formerly condemned factory building on Fulton Street, which the Association had bought cheaply and was slowly renovating. Light bulbs hung from the network of pipes and vivid yellow and red banners hid the damp stone walls. The banners showed two black hands in a firm handclasp against a yellow background, with the Association's full name at top, and below on the banner was embroidered the Association's motto:

A banner and the American flag draped the platform where the officials sat, their dark, sharply planed faces set with an almost funereal seriousness, their watchful eyes fixed on the audience. And the audience of perhaps three or four hundred reflected the officials' gravity and subjected them to the same rigid surveillance. Their watchfulness was like a chill current of air to Selina, who sat beside the mother, Florrie Trotman and Iris Hurley. Their silence was a deep wide bowl into which the speaker poured his words.

The speaker was Cecil Osborne, a small fierce man with work-ruined hands, gold-edged teeth and a high, finely molded nose rising out of his thin face. He held the nose always at a high scornful angle, using it, it seemed, to judge the world.

It was an installation meeting for new members and he was telling of the Association's accomplishments and aspirations, his voice rising and falling in the rich cadence of Barbadian speech. He spoke with fervor of the "Fund," to which all members contributed and which in turn made small loans to members. ". . . But we got bigger plans," he shouted, and the high nose caught the light, "we looking now to set up our credit system under government protection. When you hear the shout we'll have our own little bank. Then watch us move . . ."

He told of the political ambitions of Percy Challenor and other members and the Association's potential influence in local politics and community affairs. Leaning over the lectern, a small finger wagging, he warned them of the city's plans to replace the brownstones around Fulton Park eventually with housing projects. "Gone!" His short arm cut the air. "All those houses we sweat so to buy and now, at last, making little money from gon be soon gone! That's why we got to have a voice at City Hall to see that they go slow. And if we have enough pull and enough money behind us, they gon have to listen . . . !"

After going on for some time, he bared the gold-etched teeth in a smile, "C'dear, we ain all business. I know they does say a Bajan don know how to enjoy himself. But we does break down sometime and play little bridge maybe on a Sat'day night. Oh, nothing like how those big-shot white executives does play in their exclusive clubs—all the while drinking the best of scotch and smoking the finest of cigars. No, we don have none of that. We ain white yet. We's small-timers!" he cried in sudden fury. "But we got our eye on the big time . . ."

Then, suddenly, he became pensive. "But tell me why we start this Association now when most of us gon soon be giving business to the undertaker? I gon tell you. It's because of the young people! Most of us did come to this man country with only the strength in we hand and a little learning in we head and had to make our way, but the young people have the opportunity to be professional and get out there and give these people big word for big word. Thus, they are our hope. They make all the sacrifice, all the struggle worth while." Then, very proudly, he announced that in another year or two the Association would be offering a scholarship to one of its deserving young members.

Finally the nose dipped and the small wiry arms reached out in conclusion, "This then is the Barbadian Association. Still in its infancy. Still a little fish in a big white sea. But a sign. A sign that a people are banded together in a spirit of self-help. A sign that we are destroying that picture of the poor colored man with his hand always long out to the rich white one, begging: 'Please, mister, can you spare a dime?' It's a sign that we has a *business* mind! I thank you!"

There was something frightening in the way they applauded, without the slightest change in their sober watchful faces, and the ejaculations of "Hear! Hear!" like gunshots punctuating the din.

"The man is an orator!" Florrie Trotman declared.

Selina's hands started up and as quickly dropped. She stared wonderingly at the small figure stiffly bowing the way a boy would. All the years she had seen him and never suspected the power and passion in his voice, in his ruined hands. Slowly she gazed around at the faces that had moved in an endless parade through her childhood, at the blurred hands pouring that crescendo of sound into the air. They were no longer individuals suddenly, but a single puissant force, sure of its goal and driving hard toward it. Their surety of purpose frightened her. It was enviable. She felt some conviction that had held firm in her suddenly jar and tilt dangerously. She could not suppress a spurt of disappointment that it was not her father standing there receiving their acclaim. Oh God, she pressed her hands into the rough wool of her skirt. Oh hell, she wanted to leave!

The applause had ceased and the insatiable silence returned. Another speaker, Claremont Sealy, was on the platform—a large solemn man with slow hands and discolored teeth. She forced herself not to listen, until after a time she felt an uneasy stir in the silence and saw the man's face working and his finger stabbing out at the banners on the walls. "They need changing," he was shouting. "You need to strike out that word *Barbadian* and put *Negro*. That's my proposal. We got to stop thinking about just Bajan. We ain't home no more. It don matter if we don know a person mother or his mother mother. Our doors got to be open to every colored person that qualify . . ." He paused and shook his head tiredly. "I know it gon take time. Wunna gon have to ruminate long, but I ain gon return till I see that word *Barbadian* strike out and *Negro* put in its place. I thank you!"

The silence swept up to him in a cold wind and trailed him out of the room. Then, as rain comes in the West Indies—without warning, to lash the earth in a helpless hysterical deluge—their indignation broke with the same fury. The meeting was at an end. Their set faces were contorted, alive now, with wrath. The women's arms, which had been folded judicially on their high bosoms, now punctured the air with outraged gestures. The dank basement was hot with their anger.

The furor was to Selina but another dimension of their force, which would sweep aside all like Claremont Sealy from their sure way. For a long time, while the debate raged around her, she sat with her slim neck bowed, her slight body tensed under her sweater and skirt, feeling somehow devitalized, without purpose, a nonentity in the midst of their formidable force. The understanding that Miss Thompson had spoken of seemed even more remote . . .

"Oh Jesus-God, I can't get over how your own can turn against you." The loud condemnation of Claremont Sealy was almost over but Florrie Trotman still raved, her massive bosom bubbling up. "Look how that man want us to let in the Sammy-cow-and-Duppy for them to take over. But look at him—with his teeth yellow-yellow like he bite the Virgin Mary!"

"He's nothing but a *commonist*," Iris Hurley said flatly.

"But what you know 'bout communist?" Silla said irritably.

"How you mean, Dear-heart? They's a contentious, discontent bunch just like Claremont, looking to overthrow the government by force. Look how that Russia is looking to make war in Korea and we just come out of war . . . You think we could own house in Russia? Or have this Association or talk 'bout the government the way we do? You think Claremont could of get up in Russia and say what he said tonight? Never happen! They'd cart his tail off to Siberia to freeze!"

"You best hush," Florrie warned, "and know that you can't talk about such things nowadays 'cause the authorities will take away house and all and ship you back to Bimshire."

"I tell yuh, I wun mind if they did take the blasted house, I'm so sick of aggravating myself with roomers," Silla said with disgust.

A troubled frown suddenly touched Iris Hurley's usually unperturbed face. "Yes, the roomers is a nuisance but . . . but . . ." She glanced hesitantly at Florrie. "I does still feel sorry enough for them sometime, y'know . . . Even though they ain Bajans they's still our color . . ."

"Sorry!" Florrie's enraged whisper cleaved Iris' voice. "Sorry for roomers? Sorry? But Gor-blind yuh, Iris, who did sorry for you? I ain sorry for a blast. I had to get mine too hard. Let the roomers get out and struggle like I did. I sorry for all the long years I din have nothing and my children din have and now I got little something I too fat and old to enjoy it and my only son dead in these people bloody war and he can't enjoy it. That's what I sorry for!" Tears stung her small slanted eyes and she pulled her Persian lamb coat angrily around her and swung away her face.

Their small uncomfortable silence held in the midst of the hubbub until Silla said in a very low, pained voice, "The terrible thing is that Florrie make sense. People got to make their own way. And nearly always to make your way in this Christ world you got to be hard and sometimes misuse others, even your own. Oh, nobody wun admit it. We don talk about it, but we does live by it—each in his own way. C'dear, Iris, I know you feel sorry for the roomers. Even Florrie does, despite her talk. You think I like myself when I'm in the hall getting on like a black-guard with them? But Iris, if it wasn't for them you wun be in Crown Heights today . . ." Her voice suddenly lapsed, her thick hands lay open and tragic on her lap, her face sank deep into the fur collar. Then she said, very simply, "We would like to do different. That's what does hurt and shame us so. But the way things arrange we can't, if not we lose out. And another thing, Iris. It's true the roomers is our own color. But if they was white or yellow and ｃun do better we'd still be overcharging them. Take when we had to scrub the Jew floor. He wasn't misusing us so much because our skin was black but because we cun do better. And I din hate him. All the time I was down on his floor I was saying to myself: 'Lord, lemme do better than this. Lemme rise!' No, power is a thing that don really have nothing to do with color. Look how white people had little children their own color working in coal mines and sweatshops years back. Look how those whelps in Africa sold us for next skin to nothing . . ." Again there was the flat drop in her voice and the silence like a fragile bubble in the uproar around them. Then she said—and each word seemed to wrench her deeply, "No, nobody wun admit it, but people got a right to claw their way to the top and those on top got a right to scuffle to stay there. Take this world. It wun always be white. No, mahn. It gon be somebody else turn soon— maybe even people looking near like us. But plenty gon have to suffer to bring it about. And when they get up top they might not be so nice either, 'cause power is a thing that don make you nice. But it's the way of this Christ world best-proof!" A tragic acceptance lined her face and the bowed chastened faces of Florrie Trotman and Iris Hurley. "What's that saying 'bout the race is not to the swift?" Silla sucked her teeth cynically. "I tell yuh, you *best be* swift, if not somebody come and trample you quick enough."

The silence echoed and reëchoed with each word, and Selina again felt that certainty within her threaten to topple and break on the floor of her mind. Sitting there, with her underlip clenched childishly between her teeth to stave it off, she tried to define it. It was her own small truth that dimly envisioned a different world and a different way; a small belief—illusory and undefined still—which was slowly forming out of all she had lived. This was what teetered now before the mother's carefully wrought testimony and her voice—that well-tempered instrument which she used with infinite skill. Then, too, the mother might be right. That thought made Selina suddenly bear down on her lip until the skin almost broke, it fanned her rage and dread into a fierce heat. If only she could turn and give the lie to that argument and shout her truth to them all! If only there was a way to prove to them and herself how totally she disavowed their way! But how, when her own truth was so uncertain and untried? How, when she knew nothing of the world or its ways? This was the gall and the humiliation. She turned, some angry word springing to her lips, only to die there as she found the

225

mother's eyes fixed on her with their mute plea for understanding and tolerance—not only for what she had just said but for all she had ever said or done.

"Girl, don sit up here listening to me," she said gently. "G'long over with the young people."

Selina leaped up, intending to rush from the room, yet impelled by the mother's strong gaze on her back toward the large group of young people. Their faces came into her angry focus, in a scale of colors first, from the smooth black of Iris Hurley's two handsome flaccid sons to the pallor of Virgie Farnum's sons and daughters; then their features, the harsh, sharp-boned beauty of their parents tempered by their youth and easy childhoods. She gave them an abrupt wave, avoided Beryl Challenor's surprised, pleased and apprehensive smile, and sat a little apart. They were excitedly discussing the scholarship award that Cecil Osborne had announced and Claremont Sealy's condemned proposal, and hardly noticed her. She was left alone with her confusion, despair and savage thoughts.

Prim, pious, pretentious pack! She noted the girls' tightly closed legs, the skirts dropping well over their knees, the hands folded decorously in their laps. No boy's hand had ever gained access to those breasts or succeeded in prying apart those clenched knees. Her cold glance swept the young men: Queers!

". . . the older people will naturally resist it, but what Mr. Sealy proposed is inevitable . . ." Dudley Risbrook, the president of the Young Associates, was saying. He had already graduated from college and worked as a probation officer and took business courses at night. He had neat hands and eyes that had never lost the shocked and shattered look of some terrifying experience of his childhood. ". . . The board will just have to work out some scheme whereby real control remains in their hands . . ."

Their voices crisscrossed around her like wires, but somehow held no meaning. What was it that made them so unreal? Why should she feel such loneliness and alienation among them when, after all, they were her people? Where was her place if not with them? The question clung like a lesion to her mind and a dull throbbing began behind her eyes, nausea churned her stomach and threatened to erupt as she suddenly heard her name and saw Julian Hurley's sly eye on her.

"Selina!" he was saying, his effeminate hand hailing her. "You haven't contributed a syllable to the discussion. At least tell us your impression of our Association."

All around, the eyes reached, as if they were strong arms, to hold her there until she answered. She barely noticed them—only Julian held her eye and mind: his handsome face and sardonic smile. She was glad suddenly that he had called her, grateful for his small viciousness, for the evening's ferment now coalesced into a single loathing. She almost smiled at him.

Then, with her hands relaxed on her crossed knees and her eyes like deep pits which hid her venom, she said very quietly, "I think it stinks," and exulted at Julian's congealing smile and the others' stricken eyes. She wished that her father could witness it. And Suggie. "And why does it stink? Because it's the result of living by the most shameful codes possible—dog eat dog, exploitation, the strong over the weak, the end justifies the means—the whole kit and caboodle. Your Association? It's a band of small frightened people. Clannish. Narrow-minded. Selfish . . ." With each word she slid forward until her small folding chair tilted precariously. Her hands, her hissing voice beckoned them closer—and as though robbed of their will, hypnotized, they leaned closer. "Prejudiced. Pitiful—because who out there in that white world you're so feverishly courting gives one damn whether you change the word *Barbadian* to *Negro?* Provincial! That's your Association."

As she jumped up, the chair tipped forward, fell and folded with a crash. Their eyes, still glazed hypnotically, stared at it and did not even see her rush from the room.

In her flight through the dim-lit lobby outside she passed a figure in the shadows, glimpsing only the metal clasps on his galoshes. Then, at the door she hesitated, suddenly afraid to leave the lighted warmth of the meeting room for the cold night and the stale glitter of Fulton Street. Her trembling fingers could not turn the doorknob. She rested her face against the cold glass panel in the door and that cold sting on her face was less cold than the self-loathing that gripped her. For they had done nothing to deserve her insults, nor had she come any closer to her own truth by maligning theirs. Why had she promised to come? Confused, aching, she rubbed her forehead on the glass, sucking back her tears, then remembering the shadowy figure behind her, she asked softly, "Would you mind opening the door for me?"

She started to find his hand almost immediately on the doorknob, a long loose hand, very dark in the dim light, which somehow gave the impression he was long and loose all over.

"What is it? Are you feeling sick?" His voice was kind but flat.

Oh, he's young, she thought, and for no reason was disappointed. She had thought he was an old man standing very still and patient in the shadows. "No, it's the doorknob," she said, "I can't turn it."

"Look, if you're sick I'll get someone inside to take you home."

"I'm not sick and I don't need anyone in there to take me home," she said petulantly and, looking up, was trapped in a pair of somber, somnolent eyes gashed deep under the man's brow. They revealed an unnerving detachment and disdainful amusement beneath their heavy lids, a weariness and withdrawal. His tall slack body, under a worn bulky coat, gave the impression that it had once been full-fleshed and powerful—and this, along with his hooded eyes, made him somehow like an athlete who had been permanently injured in the heat of a rough game and now sat watching it without enthusiasm from the side lines. His gaze, distant yet piercing, transfixed Selina now, baring her every defect, it seemed, but offering no comment, passing no judgment. She chafed under the look, knowing how exposed she was with her tears and distraught hands, with the wildness and anger still in her face. She wanted to ask him savagely what he was looking at, to shout at him to open the door, but then she saw that, unlike his eyes, his full mouth was expressive—as if there lay the true index of his feelings—and that his flared nose and high facial bones had been sensitively molded. His body—long bones strung loosely within the integument of skin—seemed to jar easily. She thought of how his skin resembled a rich dark-brown cut of silk and forgave him. She looked away.

His dry laugh was knowing. "Suddenly you look better. You can probably open the door yourself now. Or are you going back inside?"

"I'm not going back in there." She gripped the knob but did not turn it.

"Did something happen?"

She paused suspiciously. "Are you a member?"

"No, aren't you though?"

"Me? Never. I only came tonight because I foolishly promised . . ." She forgot him as her anger stirred again and her self-disgust and anguish.

"I could tell something had happened from the way you came flying out of in there," he was saying, a speculative eye on her. "Tell me."

"I blew up!" she finally cried under his insistent look. "Told off the young people. I was just gonna sit there and not say a word and leave quietly as soon as my mother took her eye off me—but then that Julian Hurley, that fairy . . ."

His laugh was weightless and she wondered fleetingly what had drained his strength. At her inquiring glance he said, "I've always thought so myself."

His laugh and conspiratorial whisper, their breath falling together in a white mist on the glass panel created an intimacy that both warmed and disturbed her. "Go on, tell me what you said," he urged, regarding her with a detached amusement.

Again his stare drew the words from her and she talked easily, forgetting that he was a stranger. Her hands, which had the mother's same strong gestures, struck out now in emphasis, then dropped as she finished, and added sadly, "I was cruel and childish and cowardly—and I don't even know what I was trying to prove."

"Perhaps that you're not a joiner."

She uttered a small laugh and murmured vaguely, "I don't know what I am."

He bent swiftly, startling her, and she felt his eyes moving in a slow and shrouded dance over her face. "What do you do that you like?" And there was an imperative note in his voice.

She could give no answer and suddenly wanted to leave, sensing some inexplicable danger in his question and annoyed with herself for talking so openly with a stranger. She drew on her worn tam, pulling it low on her brow, reached for the doorknob and found his hand there.

"What do you do that you like?"

There was no evading him. Her hands finally shaped a negative sign; her eyes, swiftly crossing his, confessed her emptiness. "Nothing," she said softly. "Not a thing, which, I suppose, makes me nothing."

She wondered at his sudden relieved sigh as he raised up, and at the interest darting briefly across his eyes. Puzzled, she asked, "What're you doing here if you're not a member?"

"My mother," he said casually, his indifference restored. "She's not well and she wheedled me into picking her up in the car. I looked in but she's not there. She must have gotten a lift home. God." He shuddered, even though he laughed. "In there looked like the GOP convention. All they needed was some cigar smoke."

"Well, they're pretty worked up. Claremont Sealy harangued them about excluding other West Indians and American Negroes and then flounced out."

"Heresy!"

"Worse than that. They're calling him a communist."

He laughed. "Lord, between you and Claremont they got their licks tonight."

"My mother's going to be furious," she whispered with sudden dread.

"Are you going to wait for her now?"

"No, I'm going home and to bed. I can always take her lectures better lying down."

"Then come, I'll drive you."

"Oh, no thanks."

He tapped her hand, smiling with surprising gentleness. "You've been well trained, I see. I mean I'll walk you home by way of a bright busy street. How's that?"

She withdrew her hand, but his touch echoed over her skin, releasing something exquisitely pleasurable inside her.

"I'll keep my distance, I promise." He raised his hand. "I'm harmless. Here, I'll prove it." He started for the meeting room. "I'll get a character witness . . ."

Laughing, she caught his sleeve. "Okay, I'll go with you."

All of Fulton Street was fleeing the wind, the refuse of overturned garbage cans joining the driven snow and scudding pellmell down the street, the few people hurrying close to the buildings, their bowed heads butting the wind. The only sanctuaries were the bars with their light falling in bright squares on the sidewalk and the music and laughter drowning the wind's roar whenever the doors opened.

The man kept his distance as he had promised, striding unconcernedly a little ahead of her, his shabby coat open and billowing up in the wind and his coarse hair covering his head like a warm cap. She studied his long unstrung steps, suppressing a laugh at his looseness. It was all-pervading, it seemed, affecting his speech and gestures; his thoughts, even, must be loose.

"We could have avoided all this cold in the car," he said, slowing down and taking her arm.

"I wasn't afraid of going in the car. I just wanted to walk," she said and steeled herself against a stinging onslaught of snow and an inner eruption at his touch. She knew that she should politely draw away her arm, but she didn't want to. His hand was warming, a buffer against the impetuous wind. Then, he might be offended if she did and simply walk away from her, returning to his shadows and leaving her alone on this violent street. Rather than pull away, she would have liked to return his touch. To confess that something inside her which had always been closed was slowly opening like a fan, shimmering with color, and that his touch was the long-awaited signal.

She pointed to the neon drake projecting over the White Drake Bar. "Even the drake's floating tonight!" she cried. Indeed, as the wind swung the huge sign, the white drake did seem to be floating on the night sky. "Come"—she led him—"let's look inside. Just for a minute."

They stood in the doorway of the bar, out of the wind's hurtling path, and while she peered in, he stood to one side, smoking, his heavy gaze wandering with guarded interest over her clumsy overshoes, her slender form under the fitted coat, up to the tam pulled defiantly low on her forehead. Snow rimed her lashes, so that it seemed she couldn't see, but the eyes beneath were clear, swept clean by the wind, it seemed. They reflected her excitement and the rose-lighted scene in the bar; a mote of snow was magnified in their black depths—the entire crystal filigree displayed there like a jewel.

"All of Fulton Street must be inside . . ." she whispered to herself, watching the men brawling and drinking at the bar and the rose light scattered like bright mica over their whiskey glasses and over their teeth as they laughed. The way they were laughing it could have been summer with the leaves in Fulton Park and the lovers murmuring in the pavilion. The whores were there, perched like painted birds on the high stools, their paste jewels glinting rose in the rose light, and the men in their brutal innocence lurched around them and, for the price of a drink, laid bold hands on their ravaged bodies.

"Y'know," she said, awed, "after school I go hang around outside the Metropole near the Roxy in New York." She heard him suppress a little surprised laugh and was pleased. "But it's not as good as the White Drake. Here, everybody is *really* having a good time. Lord, look." She reached out to him as a spotlight suddenly singled out a short rotund man—his hair meticulously marcelled—lounging against the bar. She saw him suddenly stiffen, heard his abrupt anguished shout,

*"Got up early this morning*
*But didn't have no place to go . . ."*

and his hoarse voice rising, wailing in the blues. His round face and stout body slowly became transformed by its sad passion. His eyes squeezed shut as he sought the words in the darkness and pain of himself and then opened; his dark distorted face lifted, quivering, into the downpouring light and his plump hands, studded with rings, now opened, now closed in ecstasy, as he lamented to the gods for them all . . .

His lament ended and Selina turned away, her arms falling limp at her side and the excitement dying in her eyes as an ineffable sadness welled. Greater than the singer's. For he, at least, was part of that rough carousal in the bar, drinking and jiving the hostile night into oblivion with them. She remembered how remote the dark wind, the cold streets had seemed at the Association and how afraid she had been to leave once at the door . . . She turned, wanting to tell the man how it was to be outside peering in at that intense life, but, for the first time, his eyes fled hers. He had been regarding her with a benign amusement, but now his eyes shifted and his big loose body, propped against the door, flinched as though he knew what she would say and felt the pain of it already. She sensed this and was not hurt.

For a long time they walked apart and in silence, their boots slurring the snow, until finally he paused and laughed. "I'm very disappointed in myself. I was so sure standing behind you in the lobby that I could guess everything about you . . ."

"Such as what?" Smiling, she turned to him.

He took her arm. "Such as you went to one of these factories called city colleges, desperately trying to be the dark counterpart of the American coed and studying to be a teacher or social worker—or if your parents were more ambitious, a doctor or lawyer. If you were the oldest you played the piano badly, the second-born, the violin worse. Worn those ugly silver bangles since you were born practically. Religiously went to the hairdresser every two weeks. Belonged to the Episcopal Church, a Negro sorority and of course the Association. That you were already looking around for a nice, ambitious West Indian boy, lighter than you preferably, whose life you could order. Dreaming already of the wedding that would end all weddings and settling down to the house, the car, the two clean well-behaved children. And, of course, you were still a virgin."

The wind, bursting over the roofs, stripped their laughter apart. "Isn't it grim?" she said. "How do you know so well?"

"I've made an exhaustive and exhausting study of my subject." He pressed her arm. "You must fit some of the categories."

"Only one or two, thank God. Hey, we go through the park. I live on Chauncey."

"Oh?"

"Yes, no Crown Heights yet. We're always a little behind. But my mother's working on it."

"What does your father say? I know as a rule they don't have much to say but . . ."

"He's dead," she said and tumbled from her high excitement. A memory sloughed off and she freed her arm. She saw her father suddenly striding with his taut slim grace through the park, headed for Fulton Street and his women. What had Suggie said kneeling in the rumpled bed—that she must live for him . . . ? Well then, let it be summer and Saturday night and she some bold woman with a warm laugh and the man her father!

Giving her a sharp look, the man said, pointing to the statue of Robert Fulton, "I used to pride myself on being able to run around the ledge without falling as a boy."

"Me too, and I never met you here?"

"You were far too young."

"How old are you?"

"Twenty-nine."

"Were you in the war?"

"In a way. I never killed anyone, that is. My outfit always managed to get there when all the gore was over and everybody blown to bits. We just picked up the pieces, shoveled them out of sight and pushed on. We called ourselves the clean-up detail." His voice was light, almost gay, and as he lit a cigarette his eyes in the small flame were expressionless. "The only thing that bothered me was the setting. If it had been Europe I wouldn't have minded. The snow can cover a lot and then you don't get the smell. But where I was, in the Pacific, you'd see the goddamn bodies strewn all over the place and everything blooming. That used to get me. Birds singing and some bastard's smashed face staring up at you out of the grass. No, I didn't like the setting . . ." His voice dropped and his eyes narrowed to mere crescents, smarting from the smoke of his cigarette and the wind.

She said cautiously, "Well, at least you didn't have to kill anybody."

"I'm not sure whether that wouldn't have been easier than what I was doing. Besides, killing is supposed to have a very therapeutic effect. It might have been a good purgative to have plunged my bayonet into somebody's gut . . ." and suddenly laughing, he lunged, charging with his cigarette. His slack body became fused, powerful, lithe with grace; there was an almost lurid brightness in his hooded eyes.

His flapping coat struck her on the chin and she said, "Were you shell-shocked?"

His hollow laugh rose higher and he clasped her shoulder for a moment. "Shell-shocked is World War I vintage. They had other names this time. No"—he sobered, his hand fell away—"you can't blame the war. That would be much too simple. Come, let's sit in the pavilion for a minute. I don't go for all this walking."

235

With a slight misgiving she followed him up the wide stone steps and amid the tall fluted columns and stone benches. "Come, let's sit in the caretaker's place. In these last dark days of neighborhood decline it's probably open. We might have to clean out a few winos though."

But the small dark room with its warm smell of leaves was deserted. While she stood in the doorway he found a bench, then called, laughing, "You can come in, I promise not to talk about the war."

They sat close on the bench but not touching and the echo of his laugh was the only sound. He had forgotten her. Whenever he drew on the cigarette and the bud of light illumined his face, she saw that his eyes were abstracted, almost closed, and that he was absently wiping his long spatulate fingers on his knee. Gradually she picked out gray patches of light in the room. Ghosts of the summer lovers, she thought, and knew that she should leave. The same cautioning voice that had urged her to withdraw her arm before warned her now. He might not even hear her good-by or notice her leaving. She would be quickly home, finding Ina just returned from some meeting at the church and undressing by her rose-shaded lamp. She would submit to the mother's tirade on her behavior at the Association, then go to bed—frighteningly alone with her rage and desolation until sleep came. Or she could remain and hope that he would, in talking, touch her again, causing that warm, almost painful, burst of pleasure.

"Y'know," she said very gently, not wanting to startle him, "I could never guess anything about you."

His fingers paused on his knee and she sensed him slowly relinquishing his thoughts. "What?"

"I could never guess a thing about you even though you're a Bajan."

She discerned his wry smile.

"Why not? All you have to do is look in my palm. It's all there." He placed his hand in her lap.

"I can't see it in the dark." She pushed it off, laughing.

"You don't have to see it. Just feel the lines. They tell all."

"Impossible."

"Try it." He replaced his hand. "See if it doesn't work."

Finally, because his hand remained insistently on her lap, she took off her glove and with her forefinger traced his smooth dry palm.

"What do you find?"

"You work," she said.

"I do not."

"You're looking for work."

"I am not."

"You go to school."

"I do not."

Remembering his fingers on his knee, she said, "You give piano lessons."

"Hell no, the piano teacher I had saw to it that I hated the piano at an early age."

"I give up." She pushed his hand away. "You have no fortune."

"Ah, you finally read the lines right. You're very good." He lit a cigarette and the struck match threw his suddenly pensive face into relief. It was then that she saw why his mouth appeared so expressive. There was a small muscle just below his lip which pulled almost imperceptibly now at his skin. Only when he clenched the cigarette between his lips was it still.

"You musn't get frightened if I talk oddly at times," he said softly.

"It doesn't frighten me. It just makes me think you're shell-shocked."

His laughter and the smoke came in a warm gust against her cheek. "I love your simple, to-the-point diagnosis," he said and rested his forehead on her shoulder.

It was such an innocent, tired and impersonal act that for a moment she did not move. Then she said, "I'd better be going. My mother might be home wondering what's happened to me."

"Yes, and thinking the worst too." He raised his face and rested his lips lightly against her cheek. For a time she permitted this with the same startled passivity, then turned away, but his mouth caught hers as she turned, and the hand with the cigarette held her firm. She did not protest, but stiffly accepted his light kiss. Only when his mouth pressed harder and the little center of heat they created between their mouths flowed inward did she respond.

Her mouth opened to his and her arms opened and lifted slightly in a lovely pose that described her wonder. Her arms remained like this as his hands and warm mouth explored her face, as he laughingly pushed back her tam and kissed the line it had left on her brow. His lips brushed her closed eyes and he said, "Your snow's all gone," and at her questioning glance, added, "You were carrying your weight in snow on your eyelashes back there at the White Drake."

She laughed—a low sound that was caught and held between them. It was a little like drinking rum with Suggie, she thought —the same airy sensation in her head, the same feeling that she was suddenly luminous inside and festal. Now her arms dropped and her faltering hands caressed his rough hair, her fingers lightly traced his features as they had the palm of his hand before. And her touch confirmed what she had seen in the lobby: the passionate line of bone that belied his eyes' indifference, the silken texture of his skin, the full expressive mouth. She whispered quickly, "What do *you* do that you like?"

His mouth paused on her cheek and his fingers reached thoughtfully for his knee. Then his laugh shook them both. "All right, you win. I'm like you. Nothing. Only this perhaps." His hand brushed her breast. While he gently unbuttoned her coat and sweater, while his hands and mouth discovered her slight breasts and the tiny nipples formed under his lips, one part of Selina thought of the mother. She might be awaiting her in the kitchen, the angry words building up inside her. Or still at the

Association, in the lobby perhaps, performing the long ritual of saying good night, or Beryl and the others might be clustered, outraged, around her. If only the wind would rise strong enough to sweep them all like scraps of paper down Fulton Street, past the White Drake, through the park to the pavilion—so that they might witness how utterly she renounced their way, and have the full proof that she was indeed Deighton's Selina!

At her small vengeful laugh, the man's body fused into one long insistent piece. His eyes lifted to hers with an impassioned question, his lips formed some amazed apologetic word. Clumsily, she touched his hair to quiet him and pressed him to her with a permissive murmur. Then, deftly, he swung her around so that she lay on the wide bench with her coat under her.

It was as if the night had mounted her, as if that was the thing intruding between her slim legs and bringing the first bright pain and then slowly, steadily, rhythmically piercing her. The night, not the man, had the feel of wool and warm flesh and the smell of old cigarettes. She lay open to the night and it came rushing in like the sweet dark burst of life itself, and behind the broad slant of its shoulder the world dropped away and time and the long hurting memories, the dead faces.

Then, slowly, images, long imbedded in her mind, rose and died with each intrusive thrust: that Sunday long ago in Prospect Park—the lovers on the slope, the sense of being free of herself on the ridge above the ball field, then Beryl's secret and her despair . . . Suggie languorous and laughing amid her tumbled sheets . . . the girl proudly whispering of her seduction in the lunchroom . . . it was like being sick and having her father carry her up to the high bed and sinking, feverish, into its soft depth . . .

Words from the mother's daily lectures (wild-dog puppies, concubines) were vivid with meaning. A concubine was some-one who lay impaled by a stranger's body, open to his dark intrusion, and who felt only innocent and created. She was some-one who knew that it was a sin without propitiation yet gladly committed it . . .

After the long final shudder they lay like lovers in a summer field, sharing an immense peace and exhaustion. Slowly the world filtered back and time and the small room that had been filled with the rustling of their bodies. As the mist over her eyes cleared, she saw the man peering down at her, his eyes like gashes in the blackness of his face and the amazed apologetic word still on his lips. He sat up, fumbling for a cigarette, and smoked quickly, his face averted. She sensed him returning to his detachment and was suddently cold.

Finally he turned and leaned urgently over her, the smoke screening his face, and said in a tense whisper, "Look, I'm not just some low bastard who goes around deflowering young girls."

"I know that," she said tenderly, putting her hand over his mouth. "Besides, it was not your fault."

"How old are you?"

"Eighteen."

He bowed over her in an odd gesture of obeisance, his face touching her shoulder, his body spreading its warmth over her again. "Oh, Christ, how I know what it is at eighteen . . . all that goddamn pain and waste . . ." Suddenly he raised up, the lurid brightness in his eyes. "Look, how would you like to take lessons from me—so that when you're my age you won't be like me. Shell-shocked, as you so succinctly put it. Oh, I love your style, you know." He kissed her. "Your swinging *nothing* style."

"I don't know," she said warily. "What are you like now?"

"You'll see," he said gravely and drew her coat around her.

# 6

It was a season of forgetting, the remainder of that winter and the oncoming spring, for her body, joined with his, drove the past deep into the obscured reaches of her mind. At first, she went to him nearly every day after school. He lived apart from his parents in a brownstone rooming house they owned, in the large basement kitchen which he had converted into a kind of studio. A closed grand piano, scarred by cigarette burns, was near an old-fashioned coal stove; an easel with an unfinished painting stood beside the sink under the window, with the palette, brushes and oils on the drainboard. There were books instead of dishes in the closets, and an old oversized Victorian sofa sagged against a wall, a telephone concealed under its collapsed belly. The room was barren of color except for a few oil paintings scattered around. They were mostly of human figures—broken distorted shapes in a violent setting of primary colors—done in impasto, so that the colors rose in clamorous relief from each canvas, dazzling, almost assaulting, the eye. Beyond the room was a wind-trodden garden.

"I once had plans for in here," Clive told Selina a few days after their first night, his somber eyes moving absently over the room. "Take down the front wall and put in glass so the place wouldn't be so gloomy and moribund, fix up the garden, get some decent furniture . . . But since I'll be splitting soon . . ."

At her frightened start, he smiled. "Oh, not until I get enough money to go far enough this time." After a long pause, he added, chuckling, "My mother cries whenever she comes here."

They were lying at either end of the long sofa, facing each other, their legs entwined. His lax form was strewn amid the cushions as if carelessly thrown there, his eyes overcast and distant and the cigarette held tightly between his expressive lips as if to control them. When the ashes fell he carelessly rubbed them into the sofa. Selina's eyes, unlike his, roamed the room. To her, the few objects there and their simple arrangement formed a still-life of their afternoons together. The feeling it evoked reached back in time. She and Clive were joined, just as she and her father had been, in an intimate circle, with the world driven off. She leaned up, laughing down at him. "She probably cries at the thought of your living in a kitchen. Hasn't she ever said anything?"

"No, I cured her of commenting on my life when I was living in the Village. Oh, don't get wide-eyed." He waved her down, laughing. "It was more the lower East Side than the Village, it wasn't romantic and I failed miserably. I lacked real dedication. When I was broke I saw no point in going without a meal or scrounging one off someone when I could be home in forty minutes eating good Bajan peas and rice . . . Anyway, about my mother." He paused, the smoke twisting up. "Well, I had just come through my baptism of fire in the army. Therefore I was a man. As a man I was entitled to my own place. Sic, the Village. It was faulty reasoning but, after all, I was only twenty-four." He gave her a sad fleeting smile. "So I had my cold-water flat where the light was bad, my weird friends and an income from Uncle Sam. I went back to college, but just to get the money and keep peace with my mother. I was even painting . . . but talking mostly, endlessly, philosophically—invoking the name of Bergson and never having heard of *élan vital*—that kind of thing. Our presumption was appalling. It was at one of those intellectual Bacchanalias—with everybody on the floor talking at once, shoes off, the Chianti flowing—that my mother dropped by. God only knows how she found the place! But there she was, in the doorway." His hooded eyes shifted suddenly from her rapt face to the doorway but mirrored nothing. Only his mouth tightened around the cigarette. ". . . All unstrung from the subway ride and awed by those white weird faces. But not awed enough not to say in raw-raw Bajan: 'But c'dear, Clive, where this bunch come outta, nuh?' I got to the door fast and said something which I've very conveniently forgotten, but to the effect of 'get the hell out.' " He broke off, his eyes sweeping back to Selina, alive now with pain. "Try to see her," he said urgently, his body tense. "She's the small hard dry type of West Indian who lives endlessly and endures all. And she endured that. For a moment anyway, and then left."

Selina averted her face, shaken by the same paroxysm of anguish that seized him, cowering helplessly for a moment as he cowered as though about to be struck. Gradually he fell back limp amid the cushions, his eyes emptying, but the small muscle at his mouth still pulsed.

He said casually, "As you can imagine my days there were numbered. The disgrace of one's mother stalking one down! But what the hell, I had been planning to leave anyway."

"Why?"

"Those damn dirty feet. Everywhere I went people were always shedding their shoes and displaying their grimy feet. Now I have the sensibilities, if not the soul, of the artist, and those feet offended me to the core . . ." At her uncertain smile, he laughed—a full boyish sound—and pressed her legs between his. "Oh God, I love to shock you. You so want to be shocked. No, it wasn't the feet or my mother even." He sobered quickly. "The whole pathetic Village scene got to me after a while. All that passion and poverty. That horde of colored cats in hot pursuit of a few mangy white chicks—desperate for a sponsor and a taste of the forbidden. The few sad colored chicks enacting their historic role with the whites. And those others of confused gen-

243

der: *he-whores* and *bullers* as the Bajans would aptly call them. All mixed together in one desperate potpourri . . . Sweet Selina, beware Bohemia!"

"Weren't you in on the chase?" she said coldly.

He irritably spat out shreds of tobacco. "Look, I told you I was only twenty-four, and even though I had been to war and buried the dead I was much less of a man then than you are a woman at eighteen. Of course I chased, but again my sensibilities defeated me after a time. The ones I knew were so sorry-looking and used . . . I couldn't bear being the instrument of their vengeance or using them as mine. Besides, I passed through Korea on my way home and the Korean women spoil you—it's an art with them . . . So home to Brooklyn!" he cried, pointing wildly. "Wolfe was wrong. You *can* go home again. But it costs. And he was right. Only the dead *do* know Brooklyn! So here I lie, surrounded by certain remnants: this sofa, which was so damn sacrosanct when I was a boy that I could never sit on it. That piano, which you know about already. Those chefs-d'oeuvre"—he fanned down the paintings—"which you don't know about. Let's just say they're the painful attempts of one little colored boy to make it on the strength of a nonexistent talent . . ."

His eyes closed wearily. "Selina, you make me talk too much. I had taken a vow of silence after that session of verbal diarrhea in the Village, and now you come with your wild hungry eyes and I gladly start talking away what little substance I have left. I don't want to talk!" he suddenly shouted so that she started. Laughing, he leaned over and pulled her down on him. "I don't want to talk. I just want to forget inside you," he said softly against her mouth. "When we wake it'll be evening and we can take a drive before you go home."

"I'm afraid it won't be Korean art," she said, smiling as he undressed her.

He kissed her breast. "Forgive me for that. It was a cheap attempt to impress you. Anyway, you're far more original than your lost sisters in Bohemia. There, they run to type. Either so frantic that before you can say hello you're hauled off to bed and the whole thing is like giving an injection that means the difference between life and death, or the analytical type, where you have to be a past master at *coitus reservatus* in order to discuss your souls' sicknesses midway. No, I like nice healthy girls who get in and out of bed with style and the least amount of fuss." He bowed to her.

Even though she laughed with him, she said, "I do feel badly in the mornings though, Clive," and stiffened, thinking of how the ashen light filtering through the bedroom each dawn became the specter of her guilt. How regret pricked her, looking at her sister's smooth innocent face. How her body—still loose from his and warm from her brief sleep—would chill at the thought of the mother unsuspectingly awaiting her with breakfast and that apologetic look . . .

"I know you do," he said softly. "And I love you for not giving way to it. This damn puritan morality decrees that we pay for the night's pleasures with the morning's remorse. But we're getting around it. The guilt is fast becoming our real pleasure. Think of your Catholic sinning, his exquisite guilt on his way to the confessional—only to rush from there to sin again and suffer. Oh Christ, I want to stop talking, Selina. Please. Stop me . . ."

But even as her body arched to meet his that afternoon and on all the other afternoons, she could sense the detachment which his eyes and his bland voice reflected. Even as his body, taut and graceful then, moved above her like a sea in which she drowned, she could sense the thoughts crowding her out in his mind. He accepted her high and eager passion as casually, it seemed, as he did her invasion of his life. But sometimes, in the calm after the crest, while their bodies were still joined, his eyes would move in a grave and wondering perusal over her face, piercing her skin, it seemed, to seek out her mystery and the wellspring of her passion, and his frown then would betray a certain helplessness and wonder. At those moments, as transitory

245

as they were, a dim thought would stir amid her pleasure: in some way she was stronger than he, she possessed a hard center he would never have. Had Suggie ever felt this profound woman's strength? Or the girls romping with their lovers on the slopes . . . ? But the moments would pass and he would withdraw, his detachment restored.

Occasionally she found him seated before the half-finished painting on the easel. "Don't look so surprised. I still like to go through the motions once in a while," he had said the first time she had found him there. One hand was always thoughtfully caressing his knee while his hooded eyes seemed to avoid the unfinished painting as though it jeered him, and the smoke from his cigarette screened it from him. Then, sometimes, after a tense wait, he would stab up paint on his knife, touch his face, leaving a smear there, and stealthily approach the canvas.

To Selina, he was the painting. With the sunlight slanting across his rough hair, the smoke wreathing his head and the colors streaking his dark skin, he was a warrior reclaimed from the past—the tribal symbols of war on his face.

When dusk, moving as stealthily as his hand, crept down the ruined garden to crowd the room, he would remain at the easel, staring openly then at the painting and smiling softly, as though his eyes projected the finished perfect image in his mind onto the obscured canvas. Only when she turned on the lamp would he rouse and smile abstractly across at her. Even then, she knew, he did not really see her . . .

"It doesn't matter to you whether I come around or not," she said one night, wandering with him through the blocks of brownstone rooming houses near her house. The few lighted windows were bright studs in the setting of dark unrelieved stone, their light dying as the ravaged houses seemed to pull the night quickly down around them, like old women drawing heavy veils over their ruined faces.

She waited, her eyes narrowing with annoyance. "I said it doesn't matter . . ."

"I heard you," he said and strode on, his long legs striking out in their loose careless way and his full lips folded around his cigarette. "I guess I've gone so long without wanting anyone around—not even a woman—that I'm in-grown. What you need is some nice, clean-living West Indian boy whose intentions are wholly . . ."

"You're insulting me and evading my point."

"All right, I'm evading it." He shrugged. "Look, things just happen. The way you came. The way you'll stop. Yes, you will, so don't protest." He placed his hand playfully over her mouth. "You will, because people like you who seize hold don't need my type, not for long. Take that first night when you seized me in all my innocence," and laughing suddenly, he kissed her. "For a while there I flattered myself that retirement had increased my charm and I would never want for women again. Egotist! Sap! Finessed by a virgin! It wasn't even me you were seizing. You might have been grabbing life itself by the throat, throttling it, cursing it, 'Look here, you dirty bastard, you got me into this mess, now do something about it! And take this while I'm at it.'" His fist smashed into the air. "'And that!'" It hooked powerfully. His knee shot up. "'And there's one in the groin for good measure!'"

He released her with a wild boyish laugh, which the wind caught and carried across the street, and which the shut houses there hurled back.

She hardly heard the laugh or its wild echo. Her shocked senses were fixed on the picture he had drawn of her—as someone ruthlessly seizing a way and using, then thrusting aside, others. It recalled the mother's argument at the Association. This was the mother's way!—which had seemed so opposed to her own small yet undefined truth, which had so infuriated her. A heavy dread made her pause. Her face became drained suddenly, her eyes dazed with the horror of that possibility. She turned to tell him that he was wrong, then faltered, remembering how his eyes sometimes pierced her as they lay on the

247

sofa. Perhaps he *had* discovered this self crouched in the dim rear of her mind and had led it shivering, naked, despicable into the light to confront her.

His laugh failed at the fear her eyes reflected. "What's wrong?" He bent anxiously. "It's a compliment. I'm envious. When I was eighteen I was too damn cowed and callow to try or do anything . . . And, I suppose—though I don't know for certain—it's only when you do something, commit yourself in some way, that you begin to feel around for what you are and what you want . . ." His eyes were weary suddenly and the smooth muscle at his mouth gave a sad tug. "Yes . . . even if nothing makes sense you still have to be doing something. That's a bitch, isn't it?" Laughing softly, he bent closer to her. "Forgive me, I mangled what I was saying before by trying to be funny but it was a compliment."

His hand reached for her, but she held it off, whispering incredulously, "But is that the way you see me? That's the way my mother is, not me!"

"Then I guess it proves that you are truly your mother's child."

She struck him on the chest and the hollow thud resounded in the night stillness. Her voice was sibilant with rage. "Do you know what my mother is like? The things she's done? What she did to my father?" Pushing angrily past him, she began walking.

He joined her and said quietly, "No, I don't know."

"Then don't be so free with your analysis."

"All right, but tell me anyway."

When they had walked some distance and she had calmed a little, she told him—dredging up the memories and then fumbling for the words to shape them, her hesitant whisper sometimes lost in the mild spring wind which swept her face and lifted the coat around her slender body. After a time she forgot him as her eyes, huge in the narrow darkness of her face, saw those scenes and those dead lost faces projected vividly on each darkened house they passed. When the pain became too great her loafer shoes scraped angrily on the pavement and her hand flew up. Gradually these small fierce gestures ceased and her words came easier as the leaden weight of the memories lessened. Finally she paused and, leaning tiredly against an iron fence and smiling wistfully, she added, "It's childish, I know, but sometimes I think that he outwitted us all and really swam ashore, and is home now living like a lord and glad to be rid of this place and of us."

She was unaware of Clive until his head dropped lightly to her shoulder in the same odd gesture of obeisance as on their first night. They remained like this for some time, his head bowed to her shoulder and her remote eyes reaching beyond him. Around them the dark houses lowered down in disapproval and the spaced lamps defined the long reach of the street.

"Forget what I said and come back with me."

"Now? I can't." And suddenly she laughed, a clear burst that seemed to dispel the night. She held him tightly around the waist. "I want to but it's too late. You see, my mother thinks I'm in school all these nights—studying in the library—and she knows that closes at ten o'clock."

"Please, it will prove you've forgotten what I said. Come on."

Later, stretched luxuriously beside him within the bright circle of the lamp they always kept burning, she said, "This was all one elaborate ruse to evade my point."

Laughing, he rubbed his face between her breasts. "What was it now? If it mattered to me whether you came around or not?"

"Yes."

"Oh Christ, Selina, don't reduce me to the banal! I'm glad to see you when you come. How's that? Is that enough?"

It was enough! she told herself each night, lying alone with the loud sounding of her heart and her body still holding the warm impress of his. If he would not give, she would! and she used her allowance to buy him paints, a new easel and a silk shirt, which he never wore. Alone at night with her heart's sound she knew that in his own way he gave her much. For wasn't life tolerable because of him? School had even moved into focus, and her mind, freed of those hollowed faces and dark thoughts, eagerly swept in all she heard and read.

In the spring term her program adviser suggested that she take a course in the modern dance. She did, found that she liked it and was good, and met Rachel Fine.

She came over to Selina in the school cafeteria one day late in the semester—a small-boned girl with wiry legs, moving with jaunty grace in her careless attire; dead-black hair piled in hacked swatches above a small tense face which was unnaturally pale because of the black weight of hair, blue eyes set elusively behind surprisingly tawny lashes and a small adamant mouth.

"Hello, can I sit here? I'm Rachel Fine. I'm in your dance class."

"I know. You're very good," Selina said, shifting her books to make room for her.

"Thanks. I should really be in the advance class since I've been studying the dance for years on my own, but these rigid jackasses here insist that I take all the prerequisite courses first . . ." While she talked her hands were busy preparing her coffee, wielding a cigarette and plowing through her hair.

Selina suppressed a smile at her flurried motions, intrigued by the small white fingers constantly plunging into that forest of hair. "Why don't you talk to your program adviser about it?" she said.

"That's the jackass I'm referring to."

Their laughter created a sudden bond and the girl said, "What I really want to say is that I've been watching you all term and you're very good and I wondered if you might like to join the Modern Dance Club. You see I'm president and I'm trying to put the damn club on its feet. Right now it's just a bunch of dead beats who can't dance and we desperately need some talent and I was hoping maybe you . . ."

Selina's smile stanched the flood of words. "Well, I'm not much of a joiner but I'd like to try. Just so long as I can get away by six o'clock."

Bounding up, the girl executed a graceful turn in the narrow space between the crowded tables, then held out her hand to Selina. "Everybody calls me Fine."

"You can call me Boyce," she said, taking the small warm hand in hers.

That next week Selina went with her to the club and became so absorbed that she forgot the time and had to rush to the subway wearing the long black tights under her clothes. When she reached Clive's it was nearly dark. He was sitting thoughtfully at the easel, the fading light picking out the white crescents of his eyes and the canvas. For a time he peered at her in the black tights, then throwing back his head, he laughed; his long arms lifted dramatically. "All is lost!" he intoned. "She's gone arty."

She started to laugh with him but became annoyed and, throwing her books on the sofa, began taking off the tights. "I haven't gone anything. I told you this girl asked me to join the dance club."

"And I told you beware Bohemia. She's probably some Prog from the Village hootenanny set who just loves Negroes."

"She lives in Flatbush." Laughing now, she threw the tights at him.

He wound them around his neck. "I guess they welcomed you with open arms."

"Well . . ." She hesitated and sat down, her taut brown hands falling limp in her lap.

"Well, what?" He leaned forward insistently.

"Well, there was a funny silence when Rachel first introduced me. You know the kind I mean . . ." She stopped, unable to describe the abrupt drop in their animated talk when she entered, the subtle disturbance in their eyes before they said hello. Nor could she describe her own feelings standing there:

251

the sudden awareness of danger that made her hastily scan the room, a momentary desire to leave and thus spare them her unsettling dark presence; then, just as strong, the determination to remain . . .

Her hand struck out and she shouted at him across the room, "What am I supposed to do—curl up and die because I'm colored? Do nothing, try nothing because of it?"

Her question was an angry spark in the darkening room. She heard his light step, and when he sat beside her, she moved away, hating him suddenly and herself and the afternoon which he had ruined. "I'm not going to do that!" she cried, her eyes cutting across his.

In the glow of his cigarette she caught his tired expression and the small muscle pulling at his mouth and turned back, her anger gone, and whispered, "I don't want to do that, Clive."

He stretched out on the sofa and drew her down so that she lay in the warm valley between his bent legs, her face on his chest.

"No," he said gently, "you can't do that because then you admit what some white people would have you admit and what some Negroes do admit—that you are only Negro, some flat, one-dimensional, bas-relief figure which is supposed to explain everything about you. You commit an injustice against yourself by admitting that, because, first, you rule out your humanity, and second, your complexity as a human being. Oh hell, I'm not saying that being black in this goddamn white world isn't crucial. No one but us knows how corrosive it is, how it maims us all, how it rings our lives. But at some point you have to break through to the larger ring which encompasses us all—our humanity. To understand that much about us can be simply explained by the fact that we're men, caught with all men within the common ring."

He paused, seeking words in the dark air and in her barely visible face, then he relinquished the search and burst out irritably, "Look, I don't want to get started on this tired race theme."

But Selina was eager to define her first uneasiness at the club and, struggling for each word, said, "The funny feeling you get is that they don't really see you. It's very eerie and infuriating. For a moment there until everybody suddenly got friendly I felt like I didn't exist but was only the projection of someone or something else in their mind's eye. Oh, maybe I was just being oversensitive, I dunno . . ."

"I don't either, dear Selina." He reached up and stroked her troubled face. "Who knows what they see looking at us? The whole damn thing is so twisted now, so deep-seated; the color black is such a hell of a powerful symbol, who can tell." His voice, though still flat, had a bitter edge to it now. "Some of them probably still see in each of us the black moor tupping their white ewe, or some legendary beast coming out of the night and the fens to maraud and rape. Caliban. Hester's Black Man in the woods. The Devil. Evil. Sin. The whole long list of their race's fears . . ."

He gave a short laugh that was hollow at its center. "Maybe our dark faces remind them of all that is dark and unknown and terrifying within themselves and, as Jimmy Baldwin says, they're seeking absolution through poor us, either in their beneficence or in their cruelty. I don't know"—his limp voice trailed into a disgusted silence, then—"But I'm afraid we have to disappoint them by confronting them always with the full and awesome weight of our humanity, until they begin to see us and not some unreal image they've super-imposed . . . This is the unpleasant and perhaps impossible job and this is where I bow out, leaving the field to you, my dear sweet odd puritan Selina" —he prodded her playfully—"and to the more robust among us. Me, I can't be so bothered. To hell with them. I'm assured of my humanity lying here alone in this goddamn room each day seeing things in my mind that I can't get down right on canvas."

His voice dropped, and the silence, crouched like some hungry animal in the darkness, snapped it up. She sensed him drifting away, his body as well as his thoughts this time, even though his breath was on her face and his long loose form under hers. But then his hands were groping for her face again and he was saying softly, "You see I tried once. You want to hear, or am I talking too much?" He leaned up solicitously.

"No," she said, kissing his hand. "I love you."

"I know, but you'll still leave me." He gave an abrupt laugh. "Anyway, I had this friend, some poor sick cat with a blond beard and a gutful of trouble who used to come around and drink up my whiskey and keep me up until dawn talking—but he was my friend. The only thing wrong was that he was always asking me how it felt to be colored. I just used to shrug it off, until once he told me about awakening from a nightmare with the feeling that he had suffered some irrecoverable loss, and that then he knew how I must feel all the time . . . We were both high that night but I realized finally that I had never really proved to him that I was anything other than a Negro. I told him off, I'm afraid. We even exchanged a few drunken blows before he got the hell out . . ." His body shook with a sad soundless laugh and he caught her face and pressed it into the curve of his shoulder as though fearful she could see him despite the darkness.

"I sat there for a long time after he left, I remember. No longer high. The slime of everything I had said to him on my tongue. Cursing myself now! For why lash out at him? Poor bastard with his fat beard and scared eyes who paints worse than I do. He was *trying*. And why hurt people when they're so damn fragile inside . . . ?"

As his words dissolved around them, he eased his hold on her. When she raised up to speak, he gently placed his finger on her mouth. "Don't make me go on ad nauseam, please." He kissed her. "And forgive me for maligning your friend. It's just that you rushed in here so wide-eyed with trust, having forgotten what they can't ever seem to forget, and I started remembering."

Silent, holding each other, they watched the lighted windows in the houses beyond his wasted garden. Families were sitting down to dinner, she knew, the children playfully kicking each other under the table as they waited, their small stomachs weak and warm with expectancy as the steam flew up from the pots. Watching those bright windows, she feared for the children and wished suddenly that time would drop away, now, and leave them safe in those warm rooms, with the eager smiles fixed on their dark faces.

Clive touched her. "Tell me about the club. Are you any good?"

She raised up, laughing suddenly. "I'm very good. For a beginner."

His astonished laugh joined hers. "Arrogance! Oh Christ, that's their undoing. It'll be smoking next. Drinking soon. Pot finally!" Laughing, he swung her deftly under him. "Come, then, let's celebrate your advent into the arts. Our way." He turned on the lamp.

Minutes later, holding him in the slow warm dark heave of their passion she dimly heard the telephone, its ring muffled under the sofa, but persisting until Clive, cursing it, lifted the receiver. She heard a querulous rasp, felt him stiffen and knew that it was his mother. His only answer was a listless "yes," yet Selina detected a faint and puzzling Barbadian intonation in his voice. She slid from under him, cold suddenly, and began to dress. When he finished she was seated in the far corner of the sofa, fully dressed, her questioning eyes fixed on his worried face.

"What's wrong?"

"My mother's down at the Association and doesn't feel well and wants me to pick her up in the car." He began dressing hastily, the muscle visibly tugging at his mouth. "I'm afraid she has developed the most esoteric of the white man's afflictions: acute anxiety to the point where she thinks she's getting a heart attack. Jesus, the ingenuity of that woman is fantastic. I wonder what she'll do when I get enough money to split for good? Wait," he called, hurrying out, "I'll be back."

She waited, her legs drawn up under her skirt, her bewildered eyes reflecting the lighted room in their deep centers. She was still unnerved by his mother's call; and his slight accent, his abrupt departure sketched another dimension of him, a new facet which troubled her. Suddenly, huddled there in the corner of the sofa, longing for him to return, she felt as abandoned as the unfinished painting on the easel.

# 7

Spring had ended. Coming up the subway stairs onto Fulton Street Selina saw the sun lingering late above the roofs and smelled a summer redolence in the air. A sinuous breeze wound her bare legs and, laughing, she gave a small joyous leap, her body still fluid and toned from the long afternoon rehearsal with the dance group. She was on her way home to eat before going to Clive's and she moved swiftly through the crowd—a slender dark girl with supple legs, a strong graceful lift to her head and back, and an almost irrepressible vitality in her stride, in each cutting swing of her arms. She might at any moment, it seemed, burst into a wild spin or execute another exuberant leap there on the street.

At the beauty parlor Miss Thompson beckoned her through the

smoke-hazed window, and she thought with a secret smile of Miss Thompson's recent suspicious looks. "I can't stop now," she called from the doorway and then added impulsively, "I've got a wild date tonight," and darted away as Miss Thompson shouted, "You-Selina, come on back here . . ." Waving to Miss Thompson over her head she hastened across the street and through the park, where the flush green hid the subtle neglect.

As she unlocked the tall iron-grille basement gate, her sister's tall slim figure and anxious face suddenly appeared behind the openwork of the gate and held it shut against her. "Florrie Trotman . . . Florrie Trotman . . ." Ina's whisper was no louder than silence.

"What about her?" Selina asked impatiently, shaking the knob.

"She was . . here . . . just now . . . and she said . . . Oh, she told mother that she saw you . . ." Ina shook her head in disbelief. "She . . . told her . . she saw you and Clive Springer going into his place together! And that you stayed there . . . for hours! Is that true? Selina, is that true?" she demanded, staring hard at Selina's expressionless face. As the silence grew, Ina's mild eyes darkened with horror and she slowly recoiled. "What were you doing there, Selina . . . ? Oh Lord, how could you . . . ?" Her weak hands slid from the gate and she fell back.

As Selina pushed past her shaken sister and down the hall, she was strangely relieved that the deception was over and even aware of a vague fulfillment. Somehow it was complete now that the mother knew, and Selina was almost calm. She wanted to smile entering the kitchen. For here was the mother she knew and loved despite everything. No longer penitent and subdued, but restored, resplendent in anger, her handsome angular face alive with rage, her strong body swooping down on Selina now like some giant bird.

Silla struck and the books Selina held crashed to the floor and the white room leaped into violence. Her hand flew up and Selina raised her face to receive that first full blow. In the pause before the hand descended she gave the mother a soft and solemn nod to confirm all that Florrie Trotman had said, to inform her also that the old threatening talk of concubines and wild-dog puppies and expulsion would be of no use. But even as she held the mother immobile with her clear hard gaze, her voice issued smooth with the lie. "It's not what either you or Florrie Trotman think. It's perfectly respectable. I met him at the Association. The only reason he hasn't come by to meet you is that he knows you disapprove of him . . ." The hand quivered menacingly nearer. "I tell you he's not even interested in me that way! He considers me a child. I just go around and sit with him and talk while he paints. Why do you always want to cut me off from everybody? Why can't I have a friend . . . ?"

The tearful question hung, unanswered, and the mother's inbred distrust flared up. But something tempered it suddenly: another self—small and long suppressed—emerged, some part of the mother that yearned, indeed, needed, to believe her. Selina caught that momentary hesitation and added in an even voice, "Mother, I'm not going to spend all day in the school library or lunchroom being dull with those other West Indian girls. I'm taking these boring science courses to please you. I'm even willing to study medicine to please you, but I've got to have someone to talk to and be with once in a while. Please don't order me to stop seeing him. I'm doing nothing wrong and I'll never disgrace you!"

The upraised hand wavered, then slowly dropped. The wrath that held off the world slowly shifted to bewilderment. "But where you come outta, nuh?" the mother whispered, peering dazed into the pleading yet adamant eyes as if Selina were a stranger. "Oh God, look how trouble does come!" Her sudden cry seared the silence and she turned from Selina, searching for her silent inquisitor, summoning him to witness this new outrage. And he came, gliding out of obscurity, mute, diaphanous, yet felt in the room. Once again they complemented each other: the mother with her voluble urgency and he with his inviolate calm.

"Look how this deceitful girl went down to the Association only to get on like a black-hat in front the young people and to pick up with a piece of man. Oh God, I did see she coming in here all hours of the night from the so-called library, so secretive all the time but I din think. A man now! A man that wun work! That does call heself painting pictures. That's something too? His own mother say that you would run from the beautiful-ugly pictures—that they's like somebody pick up a can of paint and slash it so!" Her arm slashed out; her voice dropped tragically. "That's somebody for this one to be associating with . . .

"People say the army turn him so, but he was always wuthless. Years back he wanted to go to some art school, but I know the mother burn every last one of the so-called pictures and dash his tail in college. But then what?—he jump up and join the army . . . The only child now! And with a good mind! He could of been some big professional. I tell yuh, his own father wun speak to him. After Levis Springer pulled down two jobs for years to make a head-way! Look the poor mother! Every morning Clytie carried that boy for somebody to keep so she could do day's work. Clytie wore one coat for years so the Great Master Clive could take piano lesson . . . And what she get for it? I know every hair 'pon she head is white-white and she does walk the streets talking to sheself, swearing somebody begrudge she the houses and work obeah on the boy."

She paused, her head bowed in intimate communion with the suffering of Clytie Springer. Finally she turned her pained eyes to Selina, who stood unyielding amid her scattered books with the frightened Ina behind her in the doorway, and she reasoned softly, "Girl, that ain nobody for you to be associating with. A man that's hiding from work with tears in his eyes! You's only spiting yourself. Here it tis the Association is raising the money now for the scholarship fund and if you did belong you could win it. I know you would win it. If you would only join . . ." At Selina's disdain she broke off and something of her old fine scorn scored her voice. "But she ain interested. She got a piece of man now and the head turn. But look at them! They just suit each other. Two missing links!"

"How's your mother taking it these days?"

"Not a word. She's trying to believe me, but yet she's still waiting for the worst to happen. My stomach to start bulging or morning sickness . . ." she said with a joyless laugh and kicked the sand.

It was the last warm Sunday of the summer and they had spent it at the beach. Now, as the bright verve of the day calmed into evening, they were walking along the beach to Sheepshead Bay to watch the boats come in. The air was laden with the sea's smell and struck through with mutable sunset colors. Flushed rose, rich golds and mauve hung in a filigree across the sky, trailed behind the sun like a resplendent robe and gilded the sea with iridescence.

Absorbed in the day's final radiance Selina fell behind Clive and then stopped. Her slim arm, burned a deep mahogany, lifted in wonder; her body, which held the sea's rhythm after her long day in the water, struck a still, lovely pose. Clive turned and she motioned him to be silent as she sensed the immense pause around her: the small stirrings in the air had ceased, the gulls had dropped to their black pilings, the wine-dark sea lay still and her own heart paused—and together they marked the day's passing with a frail fleeting silence.

"The day's gone," she called softly and he nodded.

By the time they reached the roadway that ran parallel to Sheepshead Bay dusk had closed over the land and the street was prepared for night. Colored lights hung in spangled loops from the clam bars to the hot dog stands to the fashionable restaurants and exclusive yachting clubs that lined the street, making a festive glow against the quickly darkening sky. The street was crowded as though everyone had hurried there to escape the encroaching night and, safe now under the canopy of lights, they strolled with bare arms swinging, the girls' hair blowing in bright cowls, or milled around the various stands, their voices as gay and their laughter as high as the strung lights. In the exclusive clubs the yachting set danced on platforms cantilevered above the beach, their sunburned faces cooled by the breeze off the bay.

Selina and Clive passed through the crowd—dark forms amid the white faces. They quickly turned off and headed down to the bay, across a barren tract of sand and rough grass which lay between the street and the bay, moving amid the beached boats to the pile of rocks at the water's edge. Taking her hand, Clive led her down almost to where the rocks slid under the water, and they sat there, facing the mouth of the bay, where the sea spread in an ominous invitation. The water lisped in an incessant caress against the rocks at their feet, and behind them the dark sandy tract lay like a no man's land, separating them from the gay street.

" 'Come in under the shadow of this red rock,' " he said and drew her close beside him. As they sat in silence, the last boats came in, sculling noiselessly up the channel, their lights like struck matches in the sultry night. A big yacht strode the middle and its wake slapped the moored boats into fitful motion and washed up to Selina's bare feet the flotsam of the bay—a sluggish oily muck of garbage, beer cans and condoms floating like dead amoeboid fish. The wind brought slanting across their faces the faint smell of the city's incinerators near by. After the droppings of the city were burned they would be used to fill in the marshes, making land where there had been only brackish water and tall weeds. The furnaces rose stark out of the flat land, their chimneys silhouetted in phallic grandeur against the sky.

Clive gently cupped her small breast and said jokingly, "You know, your mother should appreciate how you've bloomed a little under my hand."

She laughed absently, watching the foam charge and hiss amid the rocks. "I'm afraid she only appreciates the fact that I'm going to hell with myself. She came across my leotards the other day and received another shock. And she's never recovered from the shock that all you do is 'paint pictures' as she puts it."

"She should have capped it by saying bad pictures."

She turned, suddenly serious and annoyed with him. "Why are you so sure they're bad?"

His hand dropped and a wan yellow light slowly filmed his heavy eyes. There was a long thoughtful pause before he answered. "Because I think there's a kind of wonder you have to have (among other things) to be really good. To see things the way a child does almost—with freshness and excitement. Without it you can be facile, competent, but not really good. I'm very short on any kind of wonder." He smiled ruefully. "I was probably better at nineteen than at any time since."

"I never told you," she said carefully, "but I heard how your mother burned your paintings once."

He was silent for a time and then his laugh struck, loud but empty. "She used them to start the fire. Did you hear that too? That was when she was in her violent period. Poor thing"—he sobered—"she was so desperate, I remember. She just couldn't understand how I could want to go to some art school even if they had given me a scholarship instead of to Columbia to study law. Well, one thing, they made a damn good fire."

Tears dimmed her eyes and she stared at the black wavering void of the sea, shaking her head. "How could she have done that? Why didn't she just disown you and throw you out?"

"Mothers? Hell, they seldom say die! Fathers perhaps. Like my poor father. He just acts like I don't exist. But not mothers. They form you in that dark place inside them and you're theirs. For giving life they exact life. The cord remains uncut, the blood joined, and all that that implies. They hold you by their weakness, their whining, their sickness, their long-suffering, their tears and their money . . . We're all caught within a circle of women, I'm afraid, and we move from one to the next in a kind of blind dance."

His words swirled like blown sand around them, stinging her, and she wondered briefly if he had included her in that ruinous circle. She said, "I guess your mother considers it a crime to paint."

"Amen!" he said. "To her, to your sainted mother, to the whole damn country, as a matter of fact, people who paint pictures are criminals. We don't rob banks or commit murders but we do something worse. We get in the way, we confuse things and we make them uncomfortable. Take the Barbadian Association. They've got plans, haven't they? Good, sound plans. They're going to have their own little credit system and bank. They're going to play the white man's game in their small way. Now tell me, what can they do with aesthetes with paintbrushes in this kind of plan? They simply cannot afford us."

"Why, then, don't they just leave you alone?"

For a time he did not answer, and when he did speak his voice was low-pitched with understanding, and the small muscle pulsed with compassion. "Because it's a long haul and they need all of us. Because there are so few of us and so many of the whites, and they are so strong and contemptuous . . ."

He lit a cigarette and the match spun in a tiny red hoop into the water. "And then there's something else," he added in the same quiet tone, "something more frightening. When we snub their way they begin to ask themselves: 'Can we possibly be wrong and they right?—those fools with brushes?' Oh, it's never conscious, but they've still got to get rid of that hidden doubt. And the way they do it is to make you embrace their way. So they hound the frisky sheep back into the fold, and lure the foot-loose son back into his father's house with feasts."

His voice dropped into the immense silence and the cigarette burned unheeded between his fingers. Out in the bay a motor sputtered and a boat slipped among the others on its way to spend the night or the time needed to make love in some se-cluded inlet. It glided past their silent forms, and gay voices reached across the water to them.

"They've no right to stifle you," Selina shouted and she might have been shouting at the gay party aboard the cruiser. "Do you know my mother is still, almost blindly, going ahead with her plans, even though she knows about us, still saving feverishly so I can study medicine when I want none of it!"

He stirred uneasily, his gashed eyes shifting over the sky, as if he saw there a vision of Silla and his own mother with disillusionment seeping into their strong-visaged faces even as their voices soared with their ambitious plans. Suddenly he cried savagely, "Christ, we are what they call us—ungrateful whelps! They break their balls buying those gloomy barns to make it easier for us and we throw it back in their teeth. Who are we to scorn them?"

"I don't care, I won't be like them!" she replied as savagely, and angrily struck the water with her foot so that the spray burst in a white design before them and then dropped. "I won't be cut out of the same piece of cloth."

"And most people want just that," he offered, his eyes shrouded and aloof again, his voice bland. "Because who wants to be out here alone? Who can take it? Most people want to be one with the lowing herd, to be told, to be led. They gladly hand over themselves to something . . ."

"Like Father Peace," she whispered, remembering with the old ache her father's head bent in ecstasy and immolation on the huge banquet table.

"Yes, anything, nearly, will do because the dumbest slob back there on that roadway realizes one thing if nothing else: that he comes alone from birth and goes alone to death. So while he's around he wants his share of the bread and circuses, and above all he wants something to hide under. He says to hell with autonomy. He says take that crap about individuality and shove it!"

"But there are some who don't say that," she protested loudly.

"A few," he shrugged and flung the cigarette butt amid the rocks, where it lay smoldering. "There had to be, if not man would have been the biggest dud of creation—maybe he is any-

264

way—and on top of this small select heap sit the few truly great artists like little gods. And how they pay for that high seat! The world takes more than its pound of flesh sometimes. It's devised all kinds of torture, the most exquisite being a colossal indifference. Yet despite all that he creates . . ." He gave her a wry bitter smile, his eyes sought the sky to the west, where the lights of Coney Island glowed in a permanent sunset. "Despite all that!"

He stretched, yawning, and when his arms dropped he said casually, "Oh, and then there's my unhappy breed. Far below the gods and a little above the slobs and worse off than either. We languish in our own special kind of limbo, gaining for ourselves the slob's ridicule and the artist's contempt. We're the men of minor talents. The Pretenders. What's wrong with us?" He glanced at her intent face as though she had asked the question. "Any number of things. We're not bold enough. We think and talk too much, and don't really feel. We were born the wrong color. We despaired before our time. We have the forms, the techniques, but no substance. We're not really driven . . . Oh, there are any number of things upon which we can very conveniently hang the blame. Christ, my kind knows what they should do—call it quits and high-tail it back to the herd. But we hold out. Hoping. Hoping for what?" He bent his harsh gaze on her and then muttered, "We're the least among the apostles."

His words sank into the vast silence of the sea and the night. This final utterance had consumed him and his eyes closed in a profound weariness and his face became like a mask—very still, with his high-molded bones composed in a taut design under his smooth black skin, his lips pressed in a sad line. He might have fallen asleep, but for the hand gripping his knee and the muscle twitching at his mouth.

Selina was shaken by the massive despair his still pose suggested. "Clive," she called softly and touched his hand. "Doesn't it help at all when you know all this?"

His eyes did not open, but his lips slowly shaped that amused tolerant smile he always gave her. "My sweet naïve Selina, if only the diagnosis was the cure!" Suddenly with a hoarse broken cry he pitched forward as though shoved from behind by some powerful invisible assailant. His body began a swift drop, and it was only his long arms reaching out and his hands frantically grasping hold of the jutting portions of the rock that saved him from striking his head and somersaulting into the water. The fall broken, he crouched on the last narrow ledge at the water's edge, his hands desperately gripping into the rock, his big loose body bent almost double and his head bowed between his knees as though he were retching.

Selina had leaped up with a warning cry, her arms darting out but missing him as he had plunged forward. Now that he was safe she stood on the shelf of rock above him, her arms still outstretched, and gazed with mute terror down at his quivering shoulders. For a moment she wanted to close her eyes or run across the barren tract to the roadway, to flee—before his suffering ruined her too. Then, as quickly, she loved him and knelt beside him, wishing that she could absorb all that he suffered and leave him free.

As she huddled there, trembling with him, afraid to speak, another scene swiftly rose from the sea into the night mist and she saw her father crouched in dread before her on the red-faded Oriental rug in the master bedroom, his dream of escape dying in his mild eyes as she started telling him of the mother's vow to sell his land . . . In her stunned mind the scene was related to something the mother had recently said about the Association. She tensed as a thought gripped her. As it slowly formed her eyes became fierce with determination and her breathing quickened.

"Clive, let's go away," she said firmly, her hard eyes fixed on the wraithlike boats. "Please. You know how you're always talking about getting far enough away. Well, let's do it. I know a way to get the money!" He stirred, puzzled, and she added with a tinge of excitement, "Yes, I know a way. Remember I told you about this scholarship the Association will be awarding soon?

Well, I'm going to win it. It'll be enough money for both of us to go someplace far, out of the country. I'm going to join the Association and win it. I know I can do it! I swear I'll do it!" In a sudden resolve she slapped the rock and cried out at the pain. She stared at her stinging hand, intensely aware that this was her hand, as were the long bare legs in the shorts and the heart pushing excitedly against the wall of her chest, her mind— she was all of one piece suddenly, all fused with purpose . . .

"Clive!" she cried, and the wind carried her exultant cry across the bay.

He lifted his face and he had recovered by now; his eyes were hooded again, his face withdrawn.

"I'm going to do it." She knelt before him, and caught his face between her hands. "Staying around here isn't good. We'll go someplace where you can work. Please. I'll get the money. It'll take some doing but I'll get it . . ."

Shaking his head, he gave her a wan incredulous smile.

"Oh yes, I will," she said fiercely. "I'll apologize, and watch, they'll welcome me back. It's what you were saying before. How they want you to come back to prove that they're right. That's how it'll be. I'll be contrite, dedicated, the most willing worker they've ever had—and I'll win it!"

The night and the sea both refused to absorb her words. It was as if they had entered into the pact with her, and until the act was accomplished the words would hang there. Suddenly tired, she leaned against him, her legs trailing down into the chilly water, her excited eyes shaping her plan out of the black void while he gazed wonderingly down at her. Overhead a gull wheeled in the darkness, on the bright roadway the speeding cars sprayed gravel behind them, on a cabin cruiser anchored in the bay a man and woman held each other in the cramp of love—and the woman's cry of pleasure was echoed by the blaring horns and the gull's sharp, lonely complaint.

# 8

Again she and the mother took the walk through Fulton Park, passing the empty pavilion, down Fulton Street to the Association. This time it was not winter but the beginning of autumn, with a wind that still held the summer's warmth at its core and the first leaves falling and forming little nervous whorls on the stone path. This time the mother was not relieved but worried, her suspicious gaze shifting over the dark gathering of trees, her plunging stride scattering and crumbling the leaves.

"I tell yuh, she don't know she own mind." Her thoughts, flurrying inside her like the leaves at her feet, erupted into a fitful mutter. "All of a sudden now she want to go back to the Association. Why all of a sudden? After she perform so down there the last time . . . Why?"

Selina flinched at each menacing move of the mother's head. Only the image of Clive crouched at the water's edge, his shoulders quivering in despair, sustained her. Only the memory of her father stumbling in defeat down Fulton Street—the Saturday crowd engulfing him as the sea did later—kept her resolve intact. So that she turned with an ingenuous gaze that seemed to bare her whole self and pleaded, "Mother, I just want to apologize. It's been on my mind all this time but I've been so ashamed I couldn't get up enough nerve to do or say anything. But I want to apologize now . . . Please."

The mother struggled with her indecision, her gaze darting toward Selina and quickly away, as though she did not want to risk finding the deception behind those widely innocent eyes. "And what about the piece of man you been licking about with?" she cried, and the enraged question desecrated the night silence. Selina hunched her shoulders penitently; her voice faltered with shame. "I told you I've stopped seeing him. We never did anything wrong, still I guess it didn't look right—my going there like that—so I've stopped."

The mother slowly succumbed. The part of her that wanted, indeed, needed, to be persuaded of this won out, and when she finally spoke, the words were uttered with veiled relief by this self. "I tried to tell you that he wasn't nobody for you to be associating with, but you wun hear. You was always famous for putting yourself up in things before your time. You did always think the world was put here for you one . . . Well, come 'long then!"

In the basement lobby of the Association building, in that atmosphere of solidarity and purpose, she made a chastened figure behind the mother, her head bowed from those dark taut faces and skeptical eyes, cowering inside as the voices beat through the air in their dissonant chant. Florrie Trotman's restive yellow eyes and face emerged from the crowd and Selina forced a courteous smile.

"Wha'lah, look Selina! Silla, din I tell you the girl would come to she senses?" Florrie cried triumphantly.

Percy Challenor bore down on them and she heard her own hurried respectful whisper, "Hello, Mr. Challenor. I thought I'd come back . . . if it's all right . . ."

The entire lobby seemed to pause while his officious eyes probed deep, while that speculative frown gathered. Then his hand rose, pink-palmed, and the stentorian voice spoke for them all, "Girl, how yuh mean? We's glad to see yuh back."

Inside the meeting room she left the mother with a reassuring glance and hastened toward the young people. Most of them were already there in their own large grouping to the side. She saw Julian Hurley's dark sardonic profile, Beryl Challenor's complacent face and Dudley Risbrook seated importantly among them all. Her resolve wavered and she fought to restore it as they looked up and their suddenly chary eyes fended her off. For a moment it was as if they would rise in one body and chase her from the room. And in that same moment Selina asked herself what was there for her to fear when she was all of one piece. Nearing them, she bowed her head to show how willing she was to accept their censure. Her arms hung defenselessly at her sides and she begged softly, "Don't say anything yet please . . ."

The air stiffened and she smiled. It was her father's smile, the one he would use when even his charm failed him—a thin, resigned, and disarming smile that had always won him forgiveness long ago. "Please . . . just hear me out. I know I behaved inexcusably the last time I was here. I said some very stupid and childish and cowardly things which I didn't even mean. I don't know why I said them. All these months I've been asking myself why . . . and I still don't really know. I'm . . . I'm always doing crazy things like that. Just to disrupt and make a scene, I guess. You know that, Beryl." Her eyes pressed Beryl to intercede for her, reminding her that they had often lain in each other's arms behind the high rock in Prospect Park.

"I should have come before, I know. But I've been so ashamed. I couldn't even look any of you in the face when I met you on the streets. You know that, Una," and she noted that Una Trotman's hands twitched indecisively. "Perhaps it's too late but I had to come anyway . . . to beg your forgiveness . . . to apologize."

Her words hung unresolved, and she stood unforgiven before them. She heard Julian Hurley's fingers drumming a derisive staccato on his chair leg, and caught his cold smile; and with a contemptuous glance she told him that she knew why his eyes darted to each man that passed. Then, her gaze fixed Beryl again.

"Oh Selina . . . why . . . ?" Beryl whispered after a long unyielding silence. "Why're you like this . . . ?" and they might have been on the dim staircase in her house again, the others listening above as Beryl whispered the same question. She turned to the group now, her smooth face troubled. "I don't know what to say . . . Maybe we could forgive her just this time. She's always been like that, flying off, getting mad for no reason. I know. And I think she's really sorry and since she's apologized, I guess . . ."

"Oh, it's all right," Dudley Risbrook declared with a pompous gesture. "After all, a little criticism is healthy. Besides, if your own can't criticize you, who can?"

"C'mon, Selina." Una Trotman offered her a chair. "Maybe you can think up a good gimmick for our fall dance. Nobody else has yet!"

As she accepted the chair with a grateful smile to all, she was almost disappointed it had been so easy . . .

From then on, she went to every biweekly meeting of the Young Associates and spent all day Saturday there. For the first two months she seldom spoke, and when she did, her voice was low, her manner unassuming. But gradually she became a little assertive, until after a time, there was a stir of interest when she raised her hand and an attentive silence as she spoke. Nor did she volunteer in the beginning, but when the Association started its own small banking and loan company she quietly volunteered to work as a clerk there on Saturday mornings. When the Young Associates organized a membership drive she wrote most of the circular, and a copy of it, with her name, was put on the bulletin board. As the building was renovated she helped decorate, and on the Association's eighth anniversary she planned and danced in a program given at the local YMCA, which netted six hundred dollars for the scholarship fund.

"How is it you're in everything so tight?" Clive asked her one evening in spring as they lay on the sofa.

She lifted her head from his chest, laughing, her black, fine-textured eyes glowing in the fading light. "Well, I found out something that's probably true of most organizations: Nobody wants to do the hard work. Dudley expends all his energy being pompous, Julian is clever but lazy, Beryl was never very bright and the rest of them don't have any ideas. So there's me. The older people are beginning to notice how busy and dedicated I am too. In fact"—she winked at him—"somebody mentioned the scholarship the other day with an eye on me. And now that my mother's in the inner circle she's got her own undercover campaign going. And me, I'm mum."

"You really intend doing it, don't you?" he said, and a certain astonishment underscored his amusement.

"I mean to get it!" She jumped up. "It's almost too easy in a way. I want to do more. Can you understand that? I want more intrigue, more deception, more duplicity! I want to work harder! Take this bazaar we're planning. I want to do everything. I get impatient with the others muddling . . ." She broke off, dropping back down, pensive suddenly. "Perhaps that way I'll feel less guilty when it's all over. But it's not that so much. I just want to prove how I can do anything for you." She bent and kissed him, her tongue and her mouth crushing into his, and then lay down on him again, saying with a small laugh, "I think I'm a little crazy."

He made no comment, but through the cigarette smoke his shrouded eyes appraised her intense face, and for a moment something akin to admiration and envy belied his aloofness. He started up as though he would ask her, outright, what was the source of her strength? whence did she get her daring?

"Clive," she said, her voice and face soft with trust, "where will we go? Where will you take me?"

His body involuntarily recoiled, the heavy lids closed, and he made a noncommittal gesture.

"I wish you would decide," she said, and then laughed. "Oh, don't tell me. Let it be a surprise. I don't care where it is, just so it's far away." Her arms closed around him. "Just so it's someplace warm too. Please, I hate winter."

All during her first year at the Association, she paid him these brief clandestine visits, appearing in the doorway with a sly roguish smile and a finger on her lips. She always found him sprawled on the sofa now, for he suddenly had stopped painting altogether. The unfinished canvas remained on the easel near the sink with its back to the room. The paint on his ivory-handled knife, on the brushes he occasionally used, on the palette had dried. He never mentioned it, and Selina, although she was troubled, said nothing.

Sometimes she found him reading, but usually just lying there, his body utterly drained, his dark face unnaturally still, except for the faint twitch at his mouth. For minutes she might stand above him, unnoticed, her books cradled loosely in her arms and the expectancy dying slowly in her eyes. Other times he would fix her with a critical look that sought to define her to himself. Once, as she rushed in late with her tights on under her clothes, he said, almost accusingly, "Why is it you've never danced for me?"

"I would but I need music. You'll have to play."

With sudden compliance he got up, opened the scarred and dusty piano and began playing a soft melodic piece, which he started over again when she was ready.

She danced nervously at first because of his hard gaze, but gradually she forgot him as her mind and body, drawn to the music, became coördinated: her mind translating the sound into movement and her body shaping it with restraint, a certain skill and grace. Her movements were simple, yet each lift of her arm and subtle motion of her head, each fluent turn and leap attested to her control and her sure conception of the piece. It ended and she came to a finished stop, her arms dropping lightly to her side. "Am I any good, you think?"

273

At his equivocal silence she tensed, feeling that if he condemned this part of her, it would be as if she had been utterly condemned.

"You've been working very hard, haven't you?" he said.

"Yes . . . You know I took lessons all last summer on my own . . . Look, it's hard to dance to something right off . . ."

He closed the piano. "You're very good. You have soul." And his casual tone did not completely mask his own wistfulness . . .

Often they lay in silence for her entire visit, Selina watching the sky change over his shoulder and listening to the sounds of the house: water gushing through the pipes in the walls and the roomers' footsteps above. Sometimes though, despite his frown, she would talk excitedly of all she was doing, sitting on the floor before the sofa with her smooth-fleshed legs bared and her strong hands sketching the words as she talked . . . During that year, whenever he wanted her, she offered herself with the same full passion.

Those brief visits linked her days and gave them meaning. They kept her purpose clear—to free them both. The vitality hinted in her stride, in the cutting swing of her arms suddenly burst at the full to sustain her, and she was happy that for the first time she was living at a pitch and for a purpose. Alone at night she visualized her mind as a faceted crystal or gem mounted on a pivot. Each facet was a single aspect of herself, each one suited to a different role. Thus, for the Association, there was, surprisingly, a part of her that enjoyed the sense of importance and power, that could speak persuasively and subtly impose her will, that could dissemble . . .

At school, another facet appeared and she was absorbed in her work. On Sundays she studied in the school library until the city's lights showered the sky like diamond chips flung by some profligate hand; then she would leave, hurrying through the deserted library and halls to the subway and Brooklyn and Clive.

Each day after her classes she practiced with the dance group or alone in their studio off the gym, and another facet spun into focus then, excluding all her other selves; her sole concern became to mold her body into an expressive whole.

That summer, caught in the momentum, she could not stop, and worked in an office, saving her salary for when they went away, took lessons in the dance and gave her week ends to the Association and Clive. They spent Sundays at the beach, walking over to the bay at dusk to sit on the rocks—and the sea, the heavy night air, the distant clangor of the buoys seemed to echo her last summer's pledge.

Quickly it was fall again—the sere leaves falling in the park— and she was elected vice-president of the Young Associates a week before it was announced that the first scholarship would be awarded that coming spring. With a final surge she flung herself into the last round of school, the Association and her dance group.

"Clive, yours truly is to make her debut!" she announced one day near the end of winter, rushing in hatless and disheveled, with a long streamer of the wind in tow.

"Oh God, in what now?" he laughed.

She swept down on him with a wild shout. "In the dance, of course. I'm going to do the birth-to-death cycle—something the mimes do, but Rachel and the teacher adapted it. It's to be the feature of the recital!" She leaped up and bowed, then waited for his comment, her small breasts braced under her sweater, her immense eyes overwhelming her face. When he said nothing, she cried, "Just think, I'll be on stage alone. Me, following in the footsteps of Isadora Duncan! Watch, I'll do it. It begins with birth naturally." She sat on the floor in the pose of a fetus: her legs drawn to her chest, her slim arms around them and her supple back bent until her forehead rested on her knees.

"Get up!"

His harshness stunned her and for a time she could not get up. Paralyzed there, she remembered a game called statues, which she and Beryl used to play as children. Beryl would spin her

275

around, then release her abruptly, and she would assume some grotesque pose. She felt like that now—like a child being scolded for playing statues. What was it in her that displeased him? Her loudness for one, she knew, and the way she rushed at things. Her roughness. How could she expect love when she was like this? Hadn't Ina predicted it that day long ago in the hall?

Her limp arms slipped down her legs. Forcing a light laugh, she said, "I'm sorry. I'll spare you my cavorting."

His eyes avoided her hurt eyes and his slack body contracted with sudden self-disgust. "Christ, Selina, forgive me. I don't mean to hurt you. It's just that your enthusiasm is a little hard on my inertia at times. Please . . ." He extended his hand.

Taking it, she pulled herself up and sat beside him. "I will grow out of this giddiness," she said softly and then cried, "Oh, I'll be so glad when it's all over and we'll be gone!"

He said with an indulgent smile, "You are shamelessly romantic, you know."

"I know." She laughed. "It's my father's doing. Look, are you coming to the recital?"

"You know how I hate that goddamn city . . ."

"All right." She kissed him. "You'd probably make me nervous anyway."

"You nervous? Impossible."

"I used to be . . ." Suddenly her eyes glazed over with a memory and she smiled to herself. "Once, long ago, I had to recite in the Sunday School Mother's Day program. Well, I promptly wet through to my new dress, just before my turn, I was so nervous. My mother was in tears, I remember, and they had to skip me until I dried out." As he laughed and pulled her close, she added anxiously, "I just hope I don't revert to that opening night."

She repeated this to Rachel Fine at the dress rehearsal, and Rachel, with her quick savage little laugh, said, "Go ahead. It'll give an authentic touch to the childhood sequence . . ."

Selina's laugh joined hers and scattered in a gay fugue across the stage. They were resting behind the high wall of scenery, all the way at the back of the stage. Selina was stretched flat on the floor, her body light and finely tuned from the long rehearsal while Rachel reclined against the wall beside her, her small dead-white face disembodied in the shadows, her hands describing their usual nervous arabesque with her cigarette, her wild hair, her quick gestures. The chorus, hidden from them by the scenery, was rehearsing before the deserted theater.

"Besides," Rachel added, spouting smoke, "why be nervous in front of a bunch of giddy girls? What'd those lumpen know about the dance? Just finish with a flourish and they'll think you're the greatest. Is your mother coming?"

"My mother!" Her laugh flared in the dimness. "Are you kidding? Do you want her to take apart this building barehanded? She caught me practicing once and wanted to know what kinds of foolishness they were teaching at these so-called colleges."

"Well, my mother doesn't mind, just so long as it doesn't lessen my chances of making a good marriage. Speaking of that—Bobby might be here if he comes down from school tomorrow."

Selina turned, surprised. "Bobby? You took him back?"

Rachel shrugged; the pale hand plunged deep into her hair and something genuinely tragic crept into her eyes. "Yes, we're at it again. What was I going to do, Boyce?" The same tragic note lined her voice. "Every guy I went out with after him had, what I call, the stench of the tit about him . . ." Despite Selina's laugh Rachel remained serious. "I mean it and it's not funny. There wasn't a real man among them. Bobby at least comes close, so I chucked my pride and got on the damn phone one night and begged him to let's try again. He said he didn't mind, so we're trying."

"Why didn't you ever tell me why you broke up?"

A shy silence held until Rachel slid down beside Selina and said softly, "I was afraid you might not understand. You see it

277

was over the stupid engagement ring. Remember I told you how my family and his kept pressuring us to get engaged . . . ? Well, finally they arranged that his father's uncle who's in the jewelry business should get this ring for us. God, how I wanted that ring, Boyce. The diamond was so big and it sat up high on the setting like it said 'Here I am—all four carats of me!' I thought of how the kids in school would be turning all shades of envy . . . Yet, when he started putting it on my finger, I felt like puking. I swear! I told him I didn't want his father's uncle's damn diamond and that I didn't want him either if he couldn't understand why . . ."

After a pause she added with a grim little laugh, "All hell broke out of course. My mother took to her bed. Told me I was killing her. First the hair, she said, and now the ring."

"What about the hair?" Selina bent over her, feeling a sudden kinship and bond.

"I chopped and dyed it," she said flippantly. "It used to be very blond and long, and everybody was always saying I was like a little *goye* with my blond hair and blue eyes. Except, of course, the little *goyim* brats in school. Then, when it started turning dark, everybody started commiserating—like it was a tragedy. So I got fed up and on my fifteenth birthday I cut it myself and drowned it in black dye . . ." Suddenly she gave the hacked hair a fierce tug and cried despairingly, "Oh, I know it makes me look like a bomb. My boy friend's always pestering me about it. Men! Boyce, you should be glad you can do without them!"

Selina gave her a meaningful look which was lost in the darkness, but a charged silence settled between them. Rachel stirred, curious, her white hands plucking at the air. Suddenly she struck a match and held it close to Selina's face, and her own small puzzled face dropped close.

"My dear Fine," Selina began, blowing out the match, "I've had a lover all this time."

Rachel's shock, her momentary disbelief, was a jarring chord which was finally broken by her dazed whisper. "You dog." Then with her harsh sputtering laugh she cried, "You dog! Why haven't you ever . . . ?"

"Because you were always so damn busy talking about Bobby or somebody else, I never got a chance." Laughing, she sat up, leaned her head against the wall and said quietly, "He's an artist. He paints. We're going away soon and live together—openly—and to hell with marriage!"

Rachel clutched her shaggy hair, one hand pressed her tiny breasts, her thin voice beat up ecstatically, "Oh, we artists! Where're you going? When?"

Very calmly, her eyes reflecting the scant light and Rachel kneeling before her, with the darkness like a high tent around them, Selina told of her plan and of Clive, her voice falling below the sound of the piano and the muffled slur of the dancers' feet.

When she finished Rachel fell back on her heels, struck silent for a time before she gasped, "Jesus Christ, you're an operator."

Strangely, instead of laughing also, Selina's head suddenly dropped, as if one of the overhead curtain weights had fallen and struck her. "Fine, I'm going to feel like hell taking their money. But what can I do? If we don't get away, he'll go to waste in that room and I'll rot down in Howard's med school."

"But where're you going?"

"We don't know yet. Anyplace, it doesn't matter."

"You could go to the Caribbean," she said, and Selina, still depressed, hardly heard her. "Especially since your family's from there. Besides, it's very cheap living on some of the islands, and if you really intend to dance you could learn a lot down there. I know because my aunt is a wheel in this cruise agency. She arranges the entertainment. Look, maybe I could swing jobs for both of you. You could skip out at one of the islands on the ship's return run . . . They might not even miss you, and so what if they did."

"No, Clive wouldn't go for it," she said.

"Oh, that's too bad because it would save fare," and then she added brightly, "I met Bobby on a week's cruise to Jamaica and Haiti one spring. Late at night, when all the peasants were tucked in, that tub became our private yacht. It was our honeymoon . . ." Wistful suddenly, her restless hands stilled for a moment, she added, "I didn't care if we never saw land again . . . Hey," she said, turning toward the stage. "They're calling you. It must be your turn again. Come on."

But they both lingered, reluctant to leave the dark tent, knowing perhaps that their intimacy would end once they left, that the world would separate and drive each into herself again. Rachel caught Selina's arm, "Hey Boyce, let me dance your solo with you."

"All right." Selina took her hand and, laughing suddenly, pulled her up. "Just go easy so you don't show how shaky my technique really is."

"I promise," Rachel said, and as they leaped together into the arena of light, their heads poised, their slim arms hailing the nonexistent audience, she added, "Let's show these elephants in the chorus that dancing is an art, not just a course in calisthenics!"

# 9

The following night at the recital, fear eddied, then heaved in a wave inside her as she waited—kneeling alone on the stage—for the lights and heard the restless, ominously breathing audience waiting for her in the darkness. She knew how exposed she would be despite the heavy stage make-up and the black leotard, how utterly dependent she would be upon her body. It must speak for her and, crouched there, she feared that it would not prove eloquent enough.

But as the light cascaded down and formed a protective ring around her, as the piano sounded and her body instinctively responded, she thought of Clive first, and then of Rachel—how she and Rachel had danced the night before as if guided by a single will, as if, indeed, they were simply reflections of each other. At this, her nervousness subsided, and she rose—sure, lithe, controlled; her head with its coarse hair lifting gracefully; the huge eyes in her dark face absorbed yet passionate, old as they had been old even when she was a child, suggesting always that she had lived before and had retained, deep within her, the memory and scar of that other life. Her slender arm boldly hailed the audience now, and their hushed suspense, palpable on the air, made them suddenly harmless.

And she danced well, expressing with deft movements the life cycle, capturing its beauty and exceeding sadness. The music bore her up at each exuberant leap, spun her at each turn so that a wind sang past her ear; it responded softly whenever the sadness underscored her gestures—until at the climax, she was dancing, she imagined, in the audience, through the rows of seats, and giving each one there something of herself, just as the priest in Ina's church, she remembered, passed along the row of communicants, giving them the wafer and the transmuted blood . . .

The brief cycle was ending and she was old. Death tapping at her skull and seeping chill through the blood. She recalled Miss Mary's shriveled form on the high bed, and slowly sank down, borne down by the piano's dying chords, prostrate finally in death.

In the moment's stillness she knew that she had been good. And when the applause rushed her like a high wind, it was as if the audience was offering her something of itself in exchange for what she had given it. She bowed to that thunderous sound, exultant but a little shaken, and as she turned and leaped off-stage it was as if she was bearing something of them all away with her.

The other dancers awaited her in the wings and their extravagant praise was louder, headier, than the applause. They swarmed her and she lost all awareness of herself. The raw milk smell of their heated bodies and breath, the odor of grease paint and powder drowned out her mind like an intoxicant. Her happiness erupted in a wild hoot that cut through the din—and suddenly she wanted to remain with them always in the crowded wing, to shout and never get weary.

A heavy-set blond girl with fine white down on her flushed cheeks laced her arms around Selina and said in a hot whisper, "Selina, I had a catharsis. I swear. All term in Greek drama I've been trying to figure out what it was and now I know. I had one! When you started dying I felt I was dying. I'm drained. Purged. Oh, you were so Greek!"

Selina laughed into the girl's hot distended eyes. The girl was in the chorus, and Rachel, who described her as having her legs screwed on the wrong way, always positioned her in the rear line. Now, before Selina could reply, the girl was swept away, and other voices vied for her ears and other eager arms reached out until they all became fused into a white shifting welter of faces. Rachel emerged after a time, wearing her gaudy costume, her face still bedaubed with the heavy make-up. This, along with her hacked hair, made her like some other-world creature who had come to make sport among men. She caught Selina's arm, and despite the throng, they were suddenly alone.

"You were so good, Boyce, it was frightening."

Selina nodded gently, understanding. "I felt the same way watching you," she whispered. "It is frightening. Because you know that if you go on you'll almost fly out of yourself. That's what you want but still, in a way, it scares you."

The noise snatched her voice. The thick-set blond girl was

shouting from atop a chair, "Hey kids, let's celebrate at my house. I called and my mother says it's all right since my father's out. Come on, I live near here. I'll make some punch and we'll spike it with some of his you know what . . ."

Their shrill acceptance echoed high in the wings and they lunged, one huge body with many legs and flailing arms, into the dressing rooms and there pulled on their coats over the costumes and then charged through the halls into the street.

The night was not vast enough, nor the towering college and the imposing apartment buildings around it substantial enough to withstand their brash voices. The buildings slid back, it seemed, to give them room. The evening sky with its noxious pall of smog lifted higher above the coldly glittering city. And even the city's pulse—that low, tremulous hum of chaos—was stilled.

They trooped in bold formation down the street, spanning the entire sidewalk and spilling into the gutter. The wind snatched at the frothy costumes under their open coats and then scooted ahead, carrying their exhilaration in a warning to the other pedestrians. Selina, Rachel and the blond girl, Margaret Benton, were in the vanguard, and they made a startling trio—Selina, in the black leotard, her coat flaring wide, resembling somewhat a cavalier; Rachel a fabulous sprite and Margaret, her hair catching each passing light, a full-blown Wagnerian heroine.

They advanced through the East Side, bearing toward the river until Margaret led them into an old and ponderous greystone apartment house, whose grandeur had been eclipsed by a modern apartment house that was all lightness and glass beside it, and whose future was hinted in the decrepit row of tenements on its other side. They followed her through a tarnished gilt and marble lobby into the elevator cage, and when they spilled into the hall, Selina hardly noticed the smiling woman at the door, or how the smile stiffened as she entered. All she felt was a passing dismay at the artificial opulence of the furnishings, which obscured the room's high-ceilinged beauty.

The woman quickly disappeared, and they sprawled on the living-room rug, laughing and talking at a high pitch. They danced, Selina and Rachel doing a reckless lindy in their stockinged feet. Later, they flowed out into the kitchen to watch Margaret pour a long amber stream of bourbon into the punch. "Libations to the gods!" Selina shouted and, swooping down, touched her forehead to the floor. The others knelt around her and then jumped up, clamoring for a drink. After their second glass she and Rachel did a pantomime of two drunks while the others shrieked and scrambled out of their way.

Gradually the noise died and they lay in an exhausted circle on the rug, talking softly and drinking. Selina and Rachel sat together, Rachel smoking and talking of Bobby and Selina half listening and thinking of Clive. Later tonight, alone with him on the sofa under the bright lamp, the day would reach its fitting end. A rush of desire warmed her as she thought of his face at the height of their passion. It held then a lovely expression of almost unbearable pain and ecstasy. He would grasp her roughly and thrust deep, seeking to discover her even as he sought to rid himself of his pain in her—and as her hand caressed his tense back, his hair, as her luminous eyes assured him that she did not mind his roughness, he would gather her up, laughing as they plunged together in that last joyous burst . . .

They were all dancing again—Selina and Rachel twirling each other dangerously—when Margaret hurried over and, taking Selina's arm, tried to pull her away. "Hey, come with me for a minute," she said, "my mother wants to meet you . . ."

Selina shrugged her off, protesting, "But we're dancing. Anyway, why does she want to meet only me?"

"Because I just told her how good you were and how I had a catharsis watching you. Please." Her eyes, lost in her plump face, pleaded.

"Oh, all right," Selina said. "But wait till we finish our dance." After the dance she and Rachel drained their punch glasses, touching them first, and then she left her with a grandiloquent gesture. "My public calls."

"You ham," Rachel laughingly called, as Selina, bobbing to the music, and waving her empty punch glass above her head, followed Margaret.

"Hello," she said and swung into the small sitting room behind Margaret.

The woman there must have carefully arranged her smile before Selina had entered. While she had been dancing down the hall perhaps or finishing her punch with Rachel, the woman's mouth, eyes, the muscles under her pale powdered skin must have been shaping that courteous, curious and appraising smile. Months, years later, Selina was to remember it, since it became the one vivid memory of the evening, and to wonder why it had not unsettled her even then. Whenever she remembered it —all down the long years to her death—she was to start helplessly, and every white face would be suspect for that moment. But now, with her mind reeling from the dance and slightly blurred from the punch she did not even notice it.

"This is Selina, Mother," Margaret said and the woman rose from a wing chair under a tall lamp and briskly crossed the room, her pale hand extended. Her figure in a modish dress was still shapely, her carefully applied make-up disguised her worn skin and the pull of the years at her nose and mouth. Under her graying blond hair her features were pure, her lackluster blue eyes almost colorless. Something fretful, disturbed, lay behind their surface and rove in a restless shadow over her face.

She took Selina's hand between hers, patting it, and Selina could *feel* her whiteness—it was in the very texture of her skin. A faint uneasiness stirred and was forgotten as the woman led her to the wing chair and said effusively, "Well, my dear, how does it feel to be the star of the show?"

Selina fell back in the chair and, laughing, gestured upward. "A little like the real ones. Very high up. Out of this world almost."

The woman's laugh joined hers. "What was it you danced again?"

Margaret called from the doorway, "The birth-to-death cycle, Mother, and I had . . ."

"I know, dear. A catharsis." Irritation flitted across her pale exterior, but when she turned back to Selina she was smiling. "I should think you're much too young to know anything about birth or death."

"I don't. I had to rely on my imagination."

The smile stiffened and the woman studied her openly, sharply, then asked, "And how was my Margaret?"

Thinking of Rachel's description of Margaret she said, too enthusiastically, "Very good. The entire chorus was good."

"Yes . . . I keep telling her she'll never get out of the chorus if she doesn't lose some weight." She touched her own narrow hips. "But still it's good for her. All girls want to dance or act or write at some stage. I fancied myself a great tragedienne after I played Lady Macbeth my freshman year . . ."

For a long time she talked of this, perched on the edge of a chair near Selina, her white textured hands meshed on her lap, her pale eyes under the finely arched eyebrows bright with a smile. Selina turned the empty punch glass in her hands, listening politely but impatient to leave, while Margaret stood near the door, outside their circle.

Still the woman talked, but after a while the brightness left her eyes and from behind their pale screen she regarded Selina with an intense interest and irritation. Her lively voice became preoccupied. Other words loomed behind it and finally she could no longer resist them and asked abruptly, "Where do you live, dear, uptown?"

"No, Brooklyn."

"Oh? Have you lived there long?"

"I was born there."

"How nice," and her hair gleamed palely as she nodded. "Not your parents, I don't suppose."

"No." Despite the encouraging smile, Selina added nothing more. She was vaguely annoyed. It was all like an inquisition somehow, where she was the accused, imprisoned in the wing chair under the glaring lamp, the woman the inquisitor and Margaret the heavy, dull-faced guard at the door.

Suddenly the woman leaned forward and rested her hand on Selina's knee. "Are they from the South, dear?"

It was not the question which offended her, but the woman's manner—pleasant, interested, yet charged with exasperation. It was her warm smile, which was cold at its source—above all, the consoling hand on her knee, which was indecent. Selina sensed being pitted against her in a contest of strength. If she answered unwisely the woman would gain the advantage.

She muttered evasively, "No, they're not."

The woman bent close, surprised, and the dry sting of her perfume was another indignity. "No . . . ? Where then?"

"The West Indies."

The woman sat back, triumphant. "Ah, I thought so. We once had a girl who did our cleaning who was from there . . ." She caught herself and smiled apologetically. "Oh, she wasn't a girl, of course. We just call them that. It's a terrible habit . . . Anyway, I always told my husband there was something different about her—about Negroes from the West Indies in general . . . I don't know what, but I can always spot it. When you came in tonight, for instance . . ."

Her voice might have been a draft which had seeped under the closed windows and chilled the room. Frightened now, as well as annoyed, Selina gazed across to Margaret, who stood in a stolid heap at the door, her eyes lowered.

The woman's eyes followed Selina's and she called, "Can you remember Ettie, dear? She used to call you Princess Margaret because you looked so much like the real princess then."

287

"A little," the girl murmured. "She was very nice, Selina." Margaret gave Selina a fleeting glance.

"She was wonderful," her mother cried effusively, "I've never been able to get another girl as efficient or as reliable as Ettie. When she cleaned, the house was spotless. Margaret, remember what your father used to do when she cleaned?"

"Yes . . ." It was a strained whisper after a long pause. "He'd . . . he'd take off his shoes in the doorway—just like in a Japanese house . . ." Her pained glance fled Selina's. "She was just like one of the family, Selina."

"She was!" Her mother carried this to a higher pitch. "We were all crazy about her. Margaret was always giving her things for her little girl. She was so ambitious for her son, I remember. She wanted him to be a dentist. He was very bright, it seems."

Her voice, flurrying like a cold wind, snuffed out the last small flame of Selina's happiness. She started to rise, and the woman's hand, like a swift, deadly, little animal, pounced on her knee, restraining her, and the brisk voice raced on, "We were heartbroken when she took ill. I even went to the hospital to see her. She was so honest too. I could leave my purse—anything —lying around and never worry. She was just that kind of person. You don't find help like that every day, you know. Some of them are . . . well . . ." And here she brought her powdered face with its aging skin close to Selina's, the hand fluttered apologetically, ". . . just impossible!" It was a confidential whisper. "Oh, it's not their fault, of course, poor things! You can't help your color. It's just a lack of the proper training and education. I have to keep telling some of my friends that. Oh, I'm a real fighter when I get started! I wish they were here tonight to meet you. You . . . well, dear . . . you don't even act colored. I mean, you speak so well and have such poise. And it's just wonderful how you've taken your race's natural talent for dancing and music and developed it. Your race needs more smart young people like you. Ettie used to say the same thing. We used to have these long discussions on the race problem and she always agreed with me. It was so amusing to hear her say things in that delightful West Indian accent . . ."

Held down by her hand, drowning in the deluge of her voice, Selina felt a coldness ring her heart. She tried to signal the woman that she had had enough, but her hand failed her. Why couldn't the woman *see*, she wondered—even as she drowned—that she was simply a girl of twenty with a slender body and slight breasts and no power with words, who loved spring and then the sere leaves falling and dim, old houses, who had tried, foolishly perhaps, to reach beyond herself? But when she looked up and saw her reflection in those pale eyes, she knew that the woman saw one thing above all else. Those eyes were a well-lighted mirror in which, for the first time, Selina truly saw—with a sharp and shattering clarity—the full meaning of her black skin.

And knowing was like dying—like being poised on the rim of time when the heart's simple rhythm is syncopated and then silenced and the blood chills and congeals, when a pall passes in a dark wind over the eyes. In that instant of death, false and fleeting though it was, she was beyond hurt. And then, as swiftly, terror flared behind her eyes, terror that somehow, in some way, this woman, the frightened girl at the door, those others dancing down the hall, even Rachel, all, everywhere, sought to rob her of her substance and her self. The thrust of hate at that moment was strong enough to sweep the world and consume them. What had brought her to this place? to this shattering knowledge? And obscurely she knew: the part of her which had long hated her for her blackness and thus begrudged her each small success like the one tonight . . .

"Oh, please say something in that delightful West Indian accent for us!" The woman was standing over her now, brightly smiling, insistent. As she gave Selina a playful shake the punch glass slid from her limp hands to the floor and broke, splintering the woman's brittle voice and its hold on Selina. Leaping up Selina savagely flung off the woman's hand; the woman fell back, her startled eyes arcing past Selina's, and struck the lamp, which teetered and then crashed to the floor. Just before the darkness exploded in the room, Selina was at the door, viciously shoving aside the dazed Margaret, then rushing out, down the hall, veering sharply into the living room. The others converged on her with gay shouts, Rachel shouting among them, "What kept you? Come on, let's dance . . . Hey, Boyce, what's wrong . . . ?"

In her distraught eyes, through her welling tears, they were all —even Rachel—sinister figures who would cage her in their arms until the woman came and she was utterly destroyed.

"Get out of my way!" She struck brutally at the soft white arms reaching for her. "Get out of my way!" She charged their circle, scattering them, and snatching up her coat, hurled from the apartment, down the long flights of echoing marble stairs, through the seedy lobby out of the building.

The woman's face, voice, touch, fragrance, pursued her as she careened through the maze of traffic and blurred white faces, past spiraling buildings ablaze with light. Car horns bayed behind her, the city's tumid voice mocked her flight. She ran until a stitch pierced her side and her leg cramped. Clutching her leg she limped—like an animal broken by a long hunt—into the deep entranceway of a vacant store and collapsed in the cold shadows there. And like an animal she was conscious only of pain. Long shafts of pain struck true and quivered in each muscle, her lungs wrenched from their socket with each breath, her heart battered the wall of her chest as if, understanding the truth, it rejected her and wanted to escape.

Still groggy with pain, she raised her head after a time. The meager glow of a distant street light fell aslant the window and, suddenly curious, she held her face to the light. With trembling fingers she found her handkerchief and, wetting it, wiped off the stage make-up and then rubbed the dirt from the window. She peered shyly at her reflection—the way a child looks at himself in the mirror. And, in a sense, it was a discovery for her also. She was seeing, clearly for the first time, the image which the woman—and the ones like the woman—saw when they looked at her. What Clive had said must be true. Her dark face must be confused in their minds with what they feared most: with the night, symbol of their ancient fears, which seethed with sin and harbored violence, which spawned the beast in its fen; with the heart of darkness within them and all its horror and fascination. The woman, confronted by her brash face, had sensed the arid place within herself and had sought absolution in cruelty. Like the night, she was to be feared, spurned, purified —and always reminded of her darkness . . .

Above all, the horror was that she saw in that image—which had the shape and form of her face but was not really her face —her own dark depth. Her sins rose like a miasma from its fetid bottom: the furtive pleasures with Clive on the sofa, her planned betrayal of the Association, the mosaic of deceit and lies she had built to delude the mother. They took form in the shadows around her—small hideous shapes jeering her and touching her with cold and viscid hands. They were unbearable suddenly, monstrous. With a choked cry of disgust, her arm slashed out, her fist smashed that mouth, those eyes; her flat hand tried to blot it out. She struck the reflection until the entire glass wall trembled—and still it remained, gazing at her with her own enraged and tearful aspect.

It was no use. Exhausted, she fell against the glass, her feverish face striking the cold one there, crying suddenly because their idea of her was only an illusion, yet so powerful that it would stalk her down the years, confront her in each mirror and from the safe circle of their eyes, surprise her even in the gleaming surface of a table. It would intrude in every corner of her life, tainting her small triumphs—as it had tonight—and exulting at her defeats. She cried because, like all her kinsmen, she must somehow prevent it from destroying her inside and find a way for her real face to emerge. Rubbing her face against the ravaged image in the glass, she cried in outrage: that along with the fierce struggle of her humanity she must also battle illusions!

Her angry lament filled the entrance, reached the street, and the few passers-by glanced nervously toward the source of the sound and hurried on.

# 10

It was eleven o'clock when she took the subway to Brooklyn. As the lights along the tunnel wall stabbed into her vacant eyes, she thought of Miss Thompson—the long black dress almost hiding her wound and her long thin hands on the cane handle— recounting, dispassionately, her story of violation. In each light she saw the shovel cutting like a scythe in the sunlight and, in a way, it was no different from the woman's voice falling brutally in the glare of the lamp.

She was one with Miss Thompson, she knew, as she pulled herself up the subway steps to Fulton Street and saw the closed beauty shop. One with the whores, the flashy men, and the blues rising sacredly above the plain of neon lights and ruined houses, she knew, as she stumbled past the White Drake Bar. She paused across from the darkened Association building, where the draped American and Association flags billowed from the cornice. And she was one with them: the mother and the Bajan women, who had lived each day what she had come to know. How had the mother endured, she who had not chosen death by water? She remembered the mother striding home through Fulton Park each late afternoon, bearing the throw-offs under her arm as she must have borne the day's humiliations inside. How had the mother contained her swift rage?—and then she remembered those sudden, uncalled-for outbursts that would so stun them and split the serenity of the house.

The mother might have killed them. For they were the ones who drove her to that abuse each day, whose small faces reflected her own despised color. She might have come home some day, the bitterness rankling deep, and seeing them there—Selina with her insolence and uncombed hair and Ina feigning some illness— she might have smashed out and killed them . . .

Who are we to scorn them? Clive's cry on the summer night a year ago resounded through her numb mind and she turned and walked the lonely blocks to his house.

"Clive," she called as she unlocked the gate. "Clive," she said, blinking in his lighted room.

He turned an anxious face to her, one hand cupping the telephone and motioning her to be quiet with the other, then he quickly bent to the phone again and said with an irritable resignation, "Yes, yes, all right, I'll be over . . ."

The rest of what he said was blurred in Selina's mind. Only the slight Barbadian accent emerged distinct, and was frightening. The small hope that had nudged a way through her despair fell back. She knew that it was his mother, so that when he finished and said wearily, "She's at it again. Even had the doctor this time," she added bitterly, "She's not sick. It's like all the other times. An excuse to get you there."

He might not have heard her. He stretched out on the sofa, and the disquieting stillness settled over his dark smooth-planed face, and spread the length of his big slack body. His hooded eyes closed. The only small proof of life, and of the turbulence beneath, was the tiny muscle pulling faintly at his lip. Then, as if impelled up by his thoughts, he got up and began changing his shirt, his back to her.

"She's not sick!"

This time he turned and looked at her, and started, his fingers pausing on a button. "What happened?" he said and came toward her, then paused apprehensively a few steps away.

The upheaval she had undergone was all there. In her consumed face that was streaked with traces of the heavy make-up and her tears. In her eyes that were like huge lamps whose light had been overturned and extinguished by her weeping. In her drooping figure in the black leotard which was an attenuated shadow of her self.

"What's wrong, Selina?" he said gently. "What happened? You weren't any good?"

"It wasn't that."

"What was it?"

Not knowing how to tell him, she tried to dismiss it with a weak shrug.

His eyes narrowed shrewdly. "What is it—somebody said something?" he asked sharply. "One of those white people insulted you?"

"This woman," she said finally in a voice drained of all weight and color. "This girl's mother . . . She . . . she . . . well, she just put me in my place, I guess you might say . . . Reminded me that I was only a nigger after all . . ." Her tears started up and she forced them back with an angry blink. "And I didn't say a word. That's what gets me now. I just sat there and took it and then ran like a scared rabbit. I feel like I've been running all night . . . Oh, it's not that I didn't know it would happen someday. I even had a little speech I used to rehearse that would cut down the first person who said anything . . . You know how you do . . ." Her dulled eyes lifted to his, and he nodded, his face, his long loose body constricting with each word.

"And I couldn't remember a word of it. I just sat like a dolt and took it. You see, she kept smiling all the time. If she'd been openly nasty or crude with it I could have . . . I would have . . ."

He motioned her to stop, to spare herself—as if he knew the rest: her blind flight through the city, the hour huddled in the doorway, and her near delirium there. When he spoke his voice was low-pitched with her suffering.

"Christ, Selina, it happens. I took that same crap all through the army . . . And every time I tried to sell a painting or get a showing somebody slapped me down with a smile . . . It happens, and whether it's a rope or a kick in the butt, a word that slipped out or a phony smile, it's the same damn thing. I guess when you're in the pit you've got to expect a stone up side the head once in a while or a well-aimed spit in the eye. Maybe it's about time it happened . . ." He suddenly slashed out with his hand and the lurid brightness filled his eyes. "Maybe you've lived in this goddamn cocoon too long anyway. Now you know that man's greatest genius is for inflicting pain . . ." His voice receded into thoughts that excluded her, and he absently began buttoning on the clean shirt.

"Look, don't go this time, Clive," she said. "I don't want to be alone any more tonight. Besides, I've got to tell you . . . You see, a lot more happened. After I ran away from there I hid out, thinking—things tumbling over each other in my mind— and I don't know any more if when we go away I can live the way we planned—or, if I can even get the money the way . . . Oh, I can't tell you like this, standing here . . . Lay with me, please, so I can tell you. Just stay this one time. You know it's nothing again—that she's not really sick . . ."

As she pleaded, his eyes eased away from her face, he stepped back and his arm slowly lifted—like a wall rising between them to shut her out, high enough, indeed, to shut out the world. "I've got to go!" he said irritably.

And suddenly her resentment exploded in her eyes in a bright flare, her body stiffened with anger. "You'll always be saying

295

that," she shouted up at his hidden face, "always be running there every time she cries wolf. It's terrible what you two do to each other. Do you know that?" She bounded close and struck down his arm. "It would hurt her less, it would be far kinder of you if you did go away. Far away, and send her a postcard every once in a while telling how nice the weather is! That would be better than staying here—reminding her of what she's done to you, and with her reminding you of what you've done to her . . ."

"Don't get analytical!" he said impatiently. "Besides, I know all . . ."

She swept him into silence with a look. "I don't think you even mean to go away with me," she said. "You can't."

He winced but said with an attempt at lightness, "Perhaps, dear Selina, I'm simply a lost cause."

At the sadness beneath his flippancy, her anger dissolved. She turned a little away, defeat pulling down her thin shoulders. Her eyes slowly filled up with a wistful thought. "Maybe if I had been older and knew more," she murmured, "you could have loved me . . ."

"Oh, Christ!" His arm shot up again and, after a strained moment, dropped to reveal a rueful half-smile and a pained light seeping under his shrouded eyes. "I do," he said, very soberly, "in my own messed-up way I do, believe me—but it isn't what you need or would want after living with it for a time. But I do."

"Then stay with me. Just this one time. Because I need you more than she does tonight. Stay, and no matter how often the phone rings don't answer it."

For a moment she thought he hesitated, she thought she even glimpsed his hand start toward her, but the effort died in his eyes and a cry—wrested from the hollow of his despair, rising up the wall encrusted with his defeats and fear—beat through the room, driving her back, "What in the hell am I supposed to do? I'm the one who has her walking the streets talking to herself and people laughing at her!"

She said nothing more after this, and above the slight prom-
ontory of her nose, her eyes became very dry, black, knowing
and resigned. Nor did she respond in any way when he paused
on his way out and bent over her with a wry smile. "I guess
you know we've been quarreling like two winos on Fulton
Street. Anyway, wait for me. I'll be right back if it's nothing
again. And we'll be together, inside each other, quietly, and
that will help." He kissed her parched lips. "Wait."

But this time she did not wait. When the gate swung shut
behind him she detached his key from her key-ring—fumbling
like someone blind—and placed it beside the telephone; then
turning off the lamp near the sofa, she left. At home she slipped
in unnoticed through the parlor floor and, later that night, the
mother and Ina found her on the cot in the sun parlor, still
dressed in the black leotard and her coat, her body shaken by
sobs even though she slept.

# 11

A week later the Barbadian Association presented its first scholarship award, and up until then Selina did not leave the house.
She lay during the day on the cot in the sun parlor watching—
with numb eyes—the sun wheel slowly across the sky, while the
same numbness moiled like smoke around her bruised mind.
Rachel Fine telephoned every day, but Selina could not talk to
her. When Ina, in her tweed suit and her hair rolled neatly on

her neck, came in to ask what was wrong, she murmured, "I'm tired, that's all." She gave the mother the same explanation—and Silla, to hide her anxiety, shouted, "It's the lot of running, that's what. All the lot of studying and breaking your neck down to the Association all the time and coming in here all hours. You does have to overdo everything . . ." Then, at Selina's drawn face, she added gently, "What it tis troubling yuh, nuh?" And when Selina did not reply, she withdrew.

Every night that week Selina had the same dream. It awaited her near the end of her sleep and ushered her into a parlor where she wandered familiarly amid the ornate Victorian furnishings until footsteps sounded outside. Terror seized her then, for she realized that she was only an intruder. Frantically, she searched for a window, but found none; nor was there a second door or a closet. In desperation she plunged into the open grand piano, tearing a way through the wires until she reached the street.

But at the piano's jangling alarm, the others followed, pursuing her through narrow streets where huge factories eclipsed the stars, and filling the low-humming night silence with their execrations. Finally, they gave over the chase to a beast—and he came, huge, silent, swift—a low-slung, dark-furred animal with eyes as innocent as a child's. She could hear his deep growl and feel his breath on her legs. And there was something appealing in that warm breath. Some perverse part of her suddenly wanted surrender more than escape, and thought with pleasure of the claws ripping the last breath from her throat . . .

She had almost stopped and turned, almost surrendered, when an empty bus loomed in front of her. The folding doors opened. She stumbled in—just as the beast caught her leg, slashing a deep furrow in the calf. The bus door closed on his bloody paw, and sent him tumbling—howling and snapping—into the gutter.

The pain in her leg was real as she drifted, moaning and exhausted, away from the dream, and discerned through its shifting haze, the illusory shapes of the bedroom furniture. And she moaned again, hating the dawn sitting palely at the foot of her bed, for it brought only the memory of disaster, a dulling anguish and desolation.

"Selina." Her name came faintly to her across the valley between the beds which Ina had bought after finding out about Clive. "You're having a bad dream."

To Selina, her sister embodied the dawn with her blurred face and filmy nightgown—an ephemeral figure that would vanish with the sun.

"You've been moaning in your sleep all week," Ina said. "Look, did something happen that night we found you sleeping in your clothes?"

"No," she said.

"I thought maybe something had happened. You're probably just nervous about the presentation tonight, though."

"Yes, that must be it," she said, and dread, like the dawn chill, suffused her. For a moment she wanted to retreat into sleep, and then remembered what awaited her there. There was no retreat. The only brief sanctuary was here, she realized, lying in the dawn lull with her sister, and she turned and said kindly, "Did I wake you with my moaning?"

"No, I wasn't sleeping. I've been so nervous all night. You see, I'm getting married."

"Oh . . ." and the shock fully awakened her. Somehow she had thought that Ina's life was permanently fixed in its quiet round of the telephone company, night school, the Saturday visits from Edgar Innis and church. "Edgar's very nice," she said lamely.

"Yes." Ina's slim brown hands absently smoothed her covers.

Selina wondered at her flat tone and her abstraction. "Have you told Mother?"

"Last night."

"What did she say?"

"She didn't know what to say so she said the usual." Ina smiled thinly. " 'Be-Jesus-Christ, you make up wunna bed hard yuh lie 'pon it hard . . .' et cetera."

299

"You'll have to have a blowout of a wedding."

"I know. I don't want to but I've decided to let her go ahead." Suddenly Ina's face strained toward Selina in the amorphous light. "You see, I want to do something she'd like," she said with sudden intensity. "I mean I've never done anything to please her. I've been thinking about that all night. At least you joined the Association . . . but I've never done one thing really. So I'll let her give me the wedding. Oh, and Edgar's joining the Association. She'll like that. He's been thinking about it ever since he read that membership circular you wrote, and now that they're more liberal and admitting other colored people he decided . . ."

Remembering the circular, Selina wanted to draw the covers tight around her head, as her sins, in all their hideous forms, gathered at the bedside.

"You see, we might buy a house later on," Ina was saying and she might have been talking about strangers whose lives did not concern her, "and we might need a second mortgage from the Association. Oh, not a brownstone. I couldn't take this whole business of renting rooms and gouging people. Just a small place on Long Island. That's enough for us . . ."

Why her disinterest, Selina puzzled, her joylessness? Wasn't Edgar Innis what she wanted: neat, cautious, Barbadian, light-skinned, so that the women at the wedding couldn't accuse her of not trying to lighten up the family? Why this apathy, when marrying Edgar would mean a mild happiness and a retreat? Did Ina glimpse the sad tinge to that happiness—in the sanctioned embrace two nights a week, the burgeoning stomach, the neat dark children, the modest home on Long Island, the piano lessons to the neighbors' children and church each Sunday—the slow blurring of the self, the steady attrition of the soul over all those long complacent years?

Was life, no matter what, tinged with this sadness? And if Ina sensed it—she whose happiness was assured—what of Selina, who had no one now and no idea of what the years held? Oh, Christ, she swore angrily, to be a child again running in a blur under the trees to meet her father on a summer Saturday night!

"I guess you won't be getting married for a while yet," Ina said.

"No." She turned, wondering suddenly as she gazed at her sister's graceful form and the soft eyes which expressed her immanent mildness if she was still a virgin.

"For a time there I thought you might run away and marry Clive Springer."

She started. "No." And her body, her mind ached at the thought of him sleeping now on the broken sofa.

"I'm glad. He's so odd, he always frightens me."

Yes, she's a virgin, Selina thought.

That was the last they said for a time. They lay in the small beds, separated by a valley, and it was as if they had always held these muted talks in the dawn and known this lovely silence. As the sun invaded the room, Ina mused aloud, "I want Miss Thompson to do my hair for the wedding."

"She's gone South, y'know," Selina said. "To take a rest from the shop."

"Won't she be back?"

"I don't know. She said so, but I don't know." For hadn't she seen death stalking Miss Thompson down Fulton Street each time they parted, and smelled it in the life-sore?

"Well I hope so. Oh, not because of my hair, but because you two are such good friends," Ina said and suddenly came and sat hesitantly at the foot of Selina's bed. Her cologne was a spring morning smell as she bent toward Selina and paused, her arms a little outstretched as if to embrace her; just as Selina, turning shyly away, longed to tell her that she too sensed the subtle sadness in all of life and was also afraid. But they did not touch or speak, and after a time Ina said, "Think you'll win the scholarship tonight?"

And numb with dread, she could only shrug.

301

The presentation was held in the Association's impressive new hall, which was filled tonight. All across its wide sweep the watchful eyes converged on the speaker, and now, after a long evening of speakers, their anticipation weighed ominously on the air.

Selina sat among the Young Associates at the back, her body clenched under her evening gown and her breathing constricted by an order of the Association pinned across her chest. Cecil Osborne was making the presentation speech, and his bruised hands and slight body, the gold-etched teeth and incongruous high nose made her love him. He was almost finished now. She saw him fit the glasses on his high nose, saw the black hands fumbling with an envelope. During this pause, the silence surged angrily through the hall, as though their patience had been finally outraged and they would rush en masse onto the platform and snatch the envelope from him. He lifted his face, the glasses sparked, the gold teeth glinted and he spoke Selina's name.

It was a clear sound across the distance and she steeled herself as the faces swung round. Above the sudden applause she heard the loud dissonance of her heart and, amid those smiling faces, saw the mother, who was not smiling, whose blunt hands lay quietly on her lap, whose face was that of the mother in the photograph at home who gazed with shy love at the child on her lap.

Selina moved, unaware that she moved, down the aisle, scanning those myriad reflections and variations of her own dark face. And suddenly she admired their mystery. No, not mystery—she lifted the gown to mount the platform—but the mysterious source of endurance in them, and it was not only admiration but love she felt. A thought glanced her mind as Cecil Osborne held her face between his ruined hands and kissed her: love was the greater burden than hate.

The applause burst afresh and she gazed wonderingly over the smiling faces, which resembled a dark sea—alive under the sun with endless mutations of the one color. They no longer puzzled or offended her. Instead, their purposefulness—charging the air like a strong current—suddenly charged her strength and underpinned her purpose. The lightness in her chest eased and her heart calmed.

She picked up the check and, without glancing at it, said, "In one way I wish I could accept the award and use it as you would like. Because I know that's how I could best express my respect and affection. But I can't accept it—which means probably that I'll never be able to convince you of how I feel now . . ." She laid down the check and a bewildered silence surged up. She stiffened as the mother's face congested with fear. "I can't accept it," she said intimately to her, "because I don't deserve it. And the reasons are despicable . . ." She paused, then added with a futile gesture, "but no longer even important enough to mention. Let's just say that my dedication was false and the outstanding contributions Mr. Osborne spoke of were all pretenses . . .

"Even my apology was phony." Her pained eyes met Beryl Challenor's. "But I offer it again, for the last, and mean it. Forgive me. My trouble maybe was that I wanted everything to be simple—the good clearly separated from the bad—the way a child sees things. But it's not simple or separate and children can't understand it. Now that I'm less of a child I'm beginning to understand . . . But still I can't accept the award," she cried across those rigid faces to the mother. "Oh, not only because I don't deserve it, but because it also means something I don't want for myself . . ."

The words rang hollow throughout the hall as she hurried down the platform and through the perplexed and unforgiving silence. The loud rustle of her gown, the staccato tap of her heels in the stiff silence bespoke her final alienation. And as the familiar faces fell away behind her, she was aware of the loneliness coiled fast around her freedom.

"Yuh lie!"

Selina unpinned the order of the Association, placed it on a shelf and said evenly, her back to the mother, "I was not lying."

"Yuh lie!" Silla slammed the door of the coatroom underneath the main hall and the explosion, reverberating through the cavernous silence, gave violent emphasis to her accusation.

Selina turned, and her body instinctively braced. She was confronting, she felt, not only the mother but all the others. They had charged downstairs to crowd the room behind her; she sensed them wedged into the corners and secreted among the coats on the racks. Not only the mother's pitched anger, but their collective abuse, swelled the air.

"Lies! Getting up in front people talking a lot of who-struck-John about how much you like them and then throwing their money back at them. Talking in parables! Using a lot of big words and still not saying why you refuse good money. Disgracing me before the world! Oh Jesus-God, an ungrateful, conniving, wuthless whelp! If I had the will of you . . ."

Silla's rage lit the air like a dazzling pyrotechnic display, and heightened the dark handsomeness of her face, and her fine eyes. Selina felt the old admiration, but none of the old weakening— she was no longer the child who used to succumb, without will, to that powerful onslaught.

"Poor-great!" Silla hurled at her. "Poor-great—that's why you refused the money. Poor-great like the father before you."

Finally, breathing the angered air which sparked her anger, Selina silenced her with a single vehement gesture. "All right, Mother, I'll tell you even though I shouldn't." Her voice was in sober counterpoint to Silla's. "Last week I intended to take the money. But not for what you thought. Not to save for any exalted plan you had for me. I wanted it for one reason: to go away with Clive. Yes," she nodded as the mother lurched back as though shoved. "I never stopped seeing him even though I promised. That's why I became so devoted to the Associa-

tion . . . Why did I change my mind? I just couldn't . .
Something happened and I couldn't any more . . ."

Silla stared at her as she would at a stranger who had ac-
costed her on the street with some improbable story. Once, her
hand tried to fend her off, to make her vanish. Once, she glanced
at the coats as if seeking their help. Her incredulity, her helplessness was that of a child almost and, as the light ebbed in
her eyes and the strong dark flush drained from her skin, she
seemed to be quietly dying inside.

"Oh Christ-God," she cried weakly, and a dull light stirred in
her eyes like the last vestige of life. "All along I did feel something was wrong. All of a sudden acting so interested in everything . . . But I din think. I din think . . ." A strangled word
stained the air. "Spitework! Spitework, that's what it tis. Because
of what I did to yuh father. All these years you been waiting to
get at me. Ever since the night you did call me Hitler you
been waiting. You did always think I killed him. Yes. But I din
do it out of hate . . ."

For a time she pursued her tortured thoughts, unable to stop,
or to wake into the world again until she had confessed. "I . . .
I din mean to send him to his death—it's just that I cun bear to
see him suffering . . ."

Remembering his ignominious death, an uncontrollable cruelty
seized Selina. "You did it because you knew he was never coming back to you."

Silla's eyes passed over her face to search the room, as though
this were her invisible presence speaking and not Selina. After a
silence filled with her guilt, she whispered, "Yes—and that's why
you did all this—lying so and licking 'bout with the crazy boy,
disgracing me tonight. Spitework, 'cause you never had no uses
for me, but did think the sun rose and set 'pon yuh father alone."

"Yes, I blamed you," Selina said quietly. "Maybe you're even
right about why I did all this. I don't know . . . But it's no use
talking or thinking about him any more."

The mother sprang forward at her irreverence. "Not think about him? How, when he was like Christ to you?"

"He's dead!" The piercing cry was an admission long withheld and now finally wrenched from its secret place. "And I want to forget him, so that when I go away . . ."

"Going 'way?" And before Silla could recover Selina added with finality, "Yes, even though I didn't take the money. I'll find a way. And I'll be going alone."

Silla—her body thrust forward as though it, as well as her mind, sought to understand this—stared at Selina's set face. Then, groping past her, Silla found a chair, and sat numb, silent, the life shattered in her eyes and the hanging coats gathered behind her like sympathetic spectators. Finally she said, but her eyes did not clear, "Going 'way. One call sheself getting married and the other going 'way. Gone so! They ain got no more uses for me and they gone. Oh God, is this what you does get for the nine months and the pain and the long years putting bread in their mouth . . . ?"

And although Selina listened and felt all the mother's anguish she remained sure.

Silla was saying numbly, "Here it tis just when I start making plans to buy a house in Crown Heights she . . ."

"I'm not interested in houses!" Her scream burst the room and soared up to the main hall.

The mother nodded bitterly. "Yes, you did always scorn me for trying to get little property."

"I don't scorn you. Oh, I used to. But not any more. That's what I tried to say tonight. It's just not what I want."

"What it tis you want?"

"I don't know." Her reply was a frail lost sound and, strangely, it seemed to assuage Silla. She scrutinized Selina's pensive face, beginning dimly, it appeared, to understand. Her arms half lifted in a protective gesture, and her warning sounded. "Girl, do you know what it tis out there? How those white people does do yuh?"

306

At her solemn nod, at the sad knowing in her eyes, Silla's head slowly bowed.

Quickly Selina found her coat and, putting it on, stared at the mother's bowed face, seeing there the finely creased flesh around her eyes, the hair graying at her temples and, on her brow, the final frightening loneliness that was to be her penance. "Mother," she said gently, "I have to disappoint you. Maybe it's as you once said: that in making your way you always hurt someone. I don't know . . ." Then remembering something Clive had said, she added with a thin smile, "Everybody used to call me Deighton's Selina but they were wrong. Because you see I'm truly your child. Remember how you used to talk about how you left home and came here alone as a girl of eighteen and was your own woman? I used to love hearing that. And that's what I want. I want it!"

Silla's pained eyes searched her adamant face, and after a long time a wistfulness softened her mouth. It was as if she somehow glimpsed in Selina the girl she had once been. For that moment, as the softness pervaded her and her hands lay open like a girl's on her lap, she became the girl who had stood, alone and innocent, at the ship's rail, watching the city rise glittering with promise from the sea.

"G'long," she said finally with a brusque motion. "G'long! You was always too much woman for me anyway, soul. And my own mother did say two head-bulls can't reign in a flock. G'long!" Her hand sketched a sign that was both a dismissal and a benediction. "If I din dead yet, you and your foolishness can't kill muh now!"

Faces hung like portraits in her mind as she walked down Fulton Street: Suggie and her violated body, Miss Mary living posthumously amid her soiled sheets, Miss Thompson bearing the life-sore and enduring, Clive and his benign despair, her father beguiled by dreams even as he drowned in them, the mother hacking a way through life like a man lost in the bush.

307

Those faces, those voices, those lives touching hers had ruined her, yet, she sensed—letting her gown trail on the sidewalk—they had bequeathed her a small strength. She had only this to sustain her all the years. And it did not seem enough. It might be quickly spent and she might fall, broken before her time and still far from the center of life. For that was the quest. And a question flickered in her mind like a reflection of the lights flickering along the street: What was at the center?—the neon drake over the White Drake Bar floated, glittering, and went out ——Peace, perhaps, as fleeting as that was, and the things that shaped it: love, a clearer vision, a place . . . The expectation made her shiver in the early spring night, and the nipples rose on her breasts as she emerged out of the dim thought into the Saturday-night hoot and call of the bars, into the dark faces and voices swirling through her: "Hey baby, where you going all dressed back?" a man called from the doorway of the White Drake, and suddenly remembering, she stopped in a candy store and called Rachel. As soon as she reached her Rachel said, her voice thin and a little aggrieved over the distance, "I've been calling you all week."

"I know. I just couldn't talk to anybody."

"What happened in there that night?"

"Let's just say for now that Margaret's mother was unpleasant."

"The bitch. I thought it was something like that. The bitch—spoiling everything. I ran after you but you were too fast for me."

"Fine, you've got to do something for me. Remember telling me how I could get down to the islands? Well, you've got to fix it for me."

"Just you?"

"Yes."

"Okay, I won't ask questions. We'll go see my aunt tomorrow. Once she sees you dance you'll get it And I'll buy the champagne. Pink."

"What for?"

"That's what you're supposed to drink before you sail. To wash the bad taste of everything out of your mouth, and to give you strength."

"Give us strength in our time, oh Lord," she said, laughing sadly.

"Amen," Rachel said. "Amen."

She walked through Fulton Park. Before, on a spring night, the mothers would have been sitting there, their ample thighs spread easy under their housedresses, gossiping, while around them spring rose from the pyre of winter. Tonight the moon discovered a ruined park which belonged to the winos who sat red-eyed and bickering all day, to the dope addicts huddled in their safe worlds and to the young bops clashing under the trees and warming the cold ground with their blood. But despite the ruin, spring stirred and, undaunted, arrayed the trees, hung its mist curtain high and, despite the wine-stench, sweetened the air. Selina strolled, unafraid, through the mist and lamplight, pausing at the pavilion to listen, with a dull desolation—to the lovers murmuring in the shadows.

Spread wide beyond were the ravaged brownstones, and she wandered there, remembering how, in the past, those houses would have been drawn within the darkness of themselves by this time, and the streets empty and echoing like streets at dawn. Now, the roomers' tangled lives spilled out the open windows, and the staccato beat of Spanish voices, the frenzied sensuous music joined the warm canorous Negro sounds to glut the air. As she passed, a man—silhouetted against a room where everything seemed poised for flight—burst into a fiercely sad song in Spanish.

The song led her to a vast waste—an area where blocks of brownstones had been blasted to make way for a city project. A solitary wall stood perversely amid the rubble, a stoop still imposed its massive grandeur, a carved oak staircase led only to the night sky. The spring wind, moaning over the emptiness, shifted the dust and bore up the odor of crushed brick and plaster, the dank exhalations from the cellars, while the moonlight played over the heaped rubble in a fretwork of light and shadow, and glinted with cold iridescence on the splintered glass.

On the far perimeter of the plain, the new city houses were already up and occupied. As Selina stared at those monolithic shapes they seemed to draw near, the lighted windows spangling the sky like a new constellation. She imagined she heard footsteps ringing hollow in the concrete halls, the garbled symphony of radios and televisions, children crying in close rooms: life moving in an oppressive round within those uniformly painted walls.

The project receded and she was again the sole survivor amid the wreckage. And suddenly she turned away, unable to look any longer. For it was like seeing the bodies of all the people she had ever known broken, all the familiar voices that had ever sounded in those high-ceilinged rooms shattered—and the pieces piled into this giant cairn of stone and silence. She wanted, suddenly, to leave something with them. But she had nothing. She had left the mother and the meeting hall wearing only the gown and her spring coat. Then she remembered the two silver bangles she had always worn. She pushed up her coat sleeve and stretched one until it passed over her wrist, and, without turning, hurled it high over her shoulder. The bangle rose behind her, a bit of silver against the moon, then curved swiftly downward and struck a stone. A frail sound in that utter silence.

# Afterword

## Mary Helen Washington

The small fierce band of Barbadians who emigrated to the United States between 1900 and 1940 came to escape the brutal colonial exploitation of blacks in the West Indies. Given only the most menial jobs, deprived of advanced schooling, their racial and cultural inferiority assumed, disenfranchised (in 1930 only 6000 Barbadians out of 188,000 could vote), these landless people—plantation workers, cane cutters, peasant farmers—left the land they rightfully owned whenever the opportunity to come to America presented itself. (A large West Indian migration to England occurred after World War II.) "Like a dark sea nudging its way into a white beach and staining the sand," they flooded into America, but especially into New York City, the place they called "The City of the Almighty Dollar," a place where any smart, hard-working Bajan could make enough money to "buy house." The extraordinary pull of New York was its image as a place of immense wealth and unlimited opportunity availble to anyone with a business mind and an unshakable determination to "study the dollar" and imitate the whites.

"'Lord, lemme do better than this. Lemme rise!'" Silla cries when she is down on her knees scrubbing "'the Jew floor,'" and she feels it is the inevitable nature of power to give way to the next group forceful enough to seize it. Like the other Barbadians in her community she has staked out a claim to power with this carefully conceived plan: work night and day to buy house; rent out every room,

311

overcharge if necessary; sacrifice every penny to maintain property; keep strict vigilance on the children so they will enter high-paying professions; stick close to other Bajans, and exclude American blacks who are only a "keepback"; as soon as one house is paid for, move to the next desirable location—preferably Crown Heights; imitate the Jew. In spite of all evidence to the contrary, Silla persists in this belief that the magic uplift will occur in her life if she adheres religiously to the formula:

> "More Bajan than you can shake a stick at opening stores or starting up some little business.... Every West Indian out here taking a lesson from the Jew landlord and converting these old houses into rooming houses—making the closets-self into rooms some them!—and pulling down plenty-plenty money by the week. And now the place is near overrun with roomers the Bajans getting out. Every jack-man buying a swell house in dichty Crown Heights."

By skin color, by African origin, by their colonized status, the West Indians of Paule Marshall's novel are inexorably connected to all black Americans, but it is their distinctiveness that yields the peculiar themes and images of this novel. The Boyce family does not belong to the tradition that created such American novels as Richard Wright's *Black Boy* or Gwendolyn Brooks' *Maud Martha* or Toni Morrison's *The Bluest Eye*. These transplanted Barbadians are an employed, literate, ambitious, property-owning, upwardly mobile, tough community of first-generation immigrants. Not one person in this novel is unemployed. These people came to "'this man country,'" as they call it, *on purpose*, as willfully as many white immigrants; and they exercise their collective force to get what they need and want. Their power and literacy and community strength are essential to the tragic vision of *Brown Girl, Brownstones;* for, like the brownstones they inhabit, they are a formidable army— huge, somber, watchful, ancient and beautiful—but "doomed by the confusion in their design." At the end of the novel, the father, Deighton Boyce, is dead by suicide; the oldest daughter, Ina, is withdrawn into the church and a safe, dull marriage; Silla is alone, and Selina is left wandering, trying to make sense out of her world and her history. Like all tragedies, the events in *Brown Girl* seem inevitable, as though the characters are unknowingly wedded to the destructive forces within and committed to some conjugal ritual from which they cannot be released. Only Selina, the old child, the observer, the figure of redemption, the Ishmael left alone at the end to tell the story, is able to break the bond.

But the monumental tragic figure at the heart of *Brown Girl* is the mother, Silla Boyce. This large and brooding figure strides through the novel as she does through Fulton Park on her way home from work, so powerful that Selina imagines the sun itself giving way to her force. Selina calls her "'the mother,'" not "'my mother,'" reinforcing this sense of Silla's dominance and power. Silla is *the* mother much as someone might be called *the* president. This angular woman in somber dress, with rough carved features and dark skin that suggests her mystery, is not only the mainstay of the Boyce family, but she is preeminent in the Bajan community. She is the pioneer, forging a path through unfamiliar territory, cutting the bush for those behind her, crushing whatever is in her way. With her powerful gift of words she expresses, in the accents and idioms of the Bajan community, its fears and aspirations. She is the avatar of the community's deepest values and needs.

Paule Marshall tells us that her own mother had this skill with words, and, like Selina, she became immersed in the oral traditions, sitting in the kitchen listening to her mother and her friends engaging in a high order of oral art. In the kitchen, where Silla makes Barbadian delicacies to sell, her friends, Florrie and Iris and Virgie, are spectators, silent and awed by Silla's immense power. Rapt and respectful, they acknowledge Silla's leadership, for don't they all know that "'in this white-man world you got to take yuh mouth and make a gun.'" On every issue confronting their lives, Silla imposes her own meaning, affirming for herself and the others the role of language in the survival of oppressed people. With Silla the language becomes an art form, giving expression to the tremendous vitality and creativity she has no other way to express:

*On the church:*

"Lemme tell you, Iris, you don see God any better by being sanctified and climbing the walls of a church and tearing off your clothes when you's in the spirit.... Not everyone who cry 'Lord, Lord' gon enter in...."

*On the causes of World War II:*

"It's these politicians. They's the ones always starting up this lot of war. And what they care? It's the poor people got to suffer and mothers with their sons."

*On Barbadians' allegiance to England:*

"You think 'cause they does call Barbados 'Little England' that you is somebody? What the king know 'bout you—or care?"

*On the political exploitation of Barbadians:*

"The rum shop and the church join together to keep we pacify and in ignorance."

*On poverty:*

"It's a terrible thing to know that you gon be poor all yuh life, no matter how hard you work. You does stop trying after a time. People does see you so and call you lazy. But it ain laziness. It just that you does give up. You does kind of die inside...."

Here is a woman who understands poverty and political demagoguery and the harassment of the downtrodden and can express that understanding in haunting poetic words; but with all that understanding, that clear knowledge of "the way things arrange" to destroy her people, she still chooses to imitate the swift and the powerful, for if not, she says, "'somebody come and trample you quick enough.'" She plots for months to sell Deighton's land, his life-long dream, declaring in front of her friends that she is prepared to damn her soul to get the down payment for that brownstone:

"Be–Jesus–Christ, I gon do that for him then. Even if I got to see my soul fall howling into hell I gon do it.... I gon fix he and fix he good. I gon show the world that Silla ain nice!"

314

She evicts her boarder and kinswoman, Suggie Skeete, for being an "undesirable" tenant; she terrifies one daughter, the lovely Ina, into meek submission, and she tries to force Selina into medical school. She betrays Deighton to the immigration authorities for abandoning the family and has him deported. When Selina counters Silla's materialism with the scornful remark that money cannot buy love, Silla cries out in a loud though unconvincing voice, "'Lord! Give me a dollar in my hand any day!'"

But Silla is not a monster. She reflects more clearly and more intensely our own struggles between innocence and guilt, our own contradictions and failures. This same bitter, enraged woman is the mother whom Selina says is the only prop, the emotional mainstay of their family. With her mouth fixed and her back rigid, Silla, the figure forging the way through the bush, is also the young girl coming alone to a new country, the young mother taking the train every morning to Flatbush and Sheepshead Bay to scrub floors for a few "'raw-mout'" pennies; the woman in the factory pitting her life and strength against the machines because "'You got to learn to run these machines to live.'" Silla becomes comprehensible to us as Selina, the witness and record keeper, passes from childhood innocence into maturity and experiences the adult pain —the grown-up black pain—of Silla's life. When Selina comes to the full knowledge of Silla, she sees not just *the mother* but the wild teenager dancing herself into a frenzy, longing for a better life, the passionate and mysterious lover, the scorned wife, the community leader, and above all, that ancient African woman whom the entire western world has humiliated and despised. And she, Selina, becomes one with the mother and the other Bajan women "who had lived each day what she had come to know." How, she wonders, had the mother endured, "she who had not chosen death by water?"

Silla's life is a paradigm of the Barbadian community. She is the touchstone, for she proclaims aloud the chaotic trouble deep in the core of the community. Her endurance, her rage, her devotion to the dollar and property, her determination to survive in "this man country" is theirs. Her lights and shadows are theirs. Her tragedy is theirs. That is why Silla is never seen alone in this novel and why

Selina can never think of her alone: "It was always the mother and the others, for they were alike—those watchful, wrathful women whose eyes seared and searched and laid bare, whose tongue lashed the world in unremitting distrust." The bowed figure of Silla, exhausted and weary as she studies or cleans all night to avoid the dreams she must encounter in sleep, stirs both pity and awe because she is the community. She symbolizes its power, she reflects its values, she embodies its history. Her sorrow is the sorrow of the race.

While Silla is exposed throughout the entire novel—she is prepared to show the whole world that " 'Silla ain nice' "—Deighton always remains hidden, his face "a closed blind over the man beneath." His dark body is often described as limp and sensual; whereas Silla's body is nearly always in the position of reprimand: stiff, towering, and unbending. Silla is associated with wintery images, cold, white, stark, and unfeeling, while Deighton's warm sensuality and carefree demeanor are like the summer sun. Despite the fixed hardness between them, they both yearn for their former passionate life together, and one of the important tasks of the novel is to explain this irreconcilable split between Deighton and Silla and to relate it to the character of the community.

That pivotal communal ritual, the wedding of 'Gatha Steed's daughter, a huge and elaborate extravaganza of satin dresses, imperial plumes, and endless bridesmaids—but hardly a trace of traditional Bajan life—is a profound testimony to the community's successful imitation of white America. It is a suitable ritual ground to announce the divorce of Silla and Deighton. Silla moves through the ceremony alone, expressing the weariness and sadness of heart that both she and the forced bride feel. Once again Silla is the touchstone, for only she will admit aloud that she has done everything short of murder to attain her ends and that the accomplishment has brought her no peace. But what Silla says aloud the others disguise. The entire wedding is like perfume misting over a deep and pervasive odor. The unhappy little bride is being forced to marry a proper Barbadian and to abandon her lover, a black southerner. 'Gatha Steed's friends pretend to be impressed with her ostentatious display, but their response to her is full of jealous venom:

"As black as she is in a bright-bright green? And somethin' tie round she head like she's home selling fish?...Oh 'Gatha is playing white in truth."

The men and the women sit separately for most of the wedding as is customary, their physical separation pantomiming the deep antagonisms between Silla and Deighton. When Deighton appears at the door and hesitantly proceeds toward the circle of dancers, Silla pronounces the rejection of the entire community, "'Small Island, go back where you come from,'" declaring him outcast because he will not live by their standards. They need to anchor their lives in material security and so they struggle for their little credit unions, their small banks, their business associations, and what little land they can accumulate. In this desperate fight to beat the white man at his game, they cannot afford aesthetes with paint brushes, or lovers like Suggie Skeete, or failed men like Deighton Boyce.

The second great communal scene in *Brown Girl* is Selina's first visit to a meeting of the Association of Barbadian Homeowners and Businessmen, a ritual dominated by men just as the wedding was by the women. There, joined together like the brownstones they inhabit, the Bajan community seems to become a single force, "sure of its goal and driving hard toward it." With power and passion they declare their ambition to have a voice at City Hall, to build a credit union and a bank, to give these people "big word for big word," to puncture that implacable wall of white so that their presence will be heard and acknowledged. The main speaker of the meeting sums up their ambitions with this terrible admission of their own sense of invisibility and fear of blackness:

"We ain white yet. We's small-timers!...But we got our eye on the big time...."

The passionate fury which the Association arouses is reflected in their bodily gestures when they denounce Claremont Sealy for suggesting they include black Americans in their organization. Faces are contorted with wrath, arms punctuate the air with outrage, the basement is hot with their anger.

This passion for money and property and status contrasts ironically with the passionless generation of children they beget. Except for Selina, they are orderly, docile, and homogenous, each like a still–life painting, compliant to the brush strokes their parents impose, awaiting without question the codified life:

> the sanctioned embrace two nights a week, the burgeoning stomach, the neat dark children, the modest home on Long Island, the piano lessons to the neighbor's children and church each Sunday.

They will reconstruct the dreams of the parents, dreams of acquisition, binding themselves fast to a crumbling community where chaos and uncertainty are controlled by group force, with the final inevitable result: "the slow blurring of the self, the steady attrition of the soul over all those long complacent years."

The small, willful, quiet Selina, always listening unnoticed in the corners of rooms, absorbing culture and tradition, is the griot of this community, the preserver of its near and ancient past. Caught between the rigid codes of the Barbadian community, her mother's need for security, and her father's definition of a proud manhood that supersedes everyone's concerns, Selina is the one who must interpret and make sense of all these conflicting pressures. Just as she stands outside of the early family photograph, merely the swelling in her mother's belly, she remains throughout the novel somewhat of an outsider, drawn irresistibly to Fulton Street and jazz rhythms and blues music, to everything that admits to the chaos, uncertainty, and mystery of life. Paradoxically she must disrupt the destructive circle of the community's boundaries at the same time that she must preserve the power of its rugged endurance in a hostile white world. She remains always on the edge, a marginal woman, reaching for a life not bound by their comfortable, grim illusions: "Knowing, she still longed to leave this safe, sunlit place at the top of the house for the challenge there."

The questions Paule Marshall sets before her major characters are always the same: how do we remember the past so as to transform it and make it usable? How do we preserve those qualities of survival and endurance that are at the deepest emotional core of one's black identity? How do an oppressed people survive spiritually, and on what grounds can they construct a future in a world in which the "soul-beauty of a race" is despised, a world which yields no true self-consciousness but only lets one see the self through the revelation of the other world. This peculiar sensation, this double-consciousness, as DuBois called it, this sense of measuring one's soul by the tape of a world that looks on in contempt and pity, is the problem at the heart of *Brown Girl.*

The spiritual dilemma of the black woman has never been acknowledged or recognized or understood. Paule Marshall says that until Gwendolyn Brooks' novel *Maud Martha,* it was rare to see a black woman in literature with a conscious, interior life. We have seldom seen black women characters struggling over such questions as suicide, or racial violence as a means to freedom, or feminism in conflict with racism, or their call to public ministry, or their need to transform their lives into art, and that is because the women who raised these issues have been silenced, omitted, patronized, made invisible. It is with these historical and literary omissions in mind that we must view Selina's movement toward wholeness, for she proceeds to this task with little precedence in literature.

Selina is given several guides, each of whom connects her with her culture in vital ways and provides important messages about the uniqueness of Selina's own identity. First there is Suggie Skeete, an upstairs roomer whose pleasure-loving, old-world ways are remnants of the past in Barbados, where people "does take a drink while the sun hot-hot and yuh wun know whether it was the sun or the rum or both that had yuh feeling so sweet." Suggie, with her weekly lovers, her codfish smells, and her inability to hold a job, is someone for the respectable Bajan community to "lick their mouth on," and indeed Silla evicts Suggie as a prostitute. Suggie gives Selina crucial lessons of love and passion to thwart the puritanical codes of the Bajans. In contrast to Silla warning Selina about "'licking about with some piece of man,' " Suggie urges her to take off the clothes of mourning and embrace life like a lover.

Selina's second guide is the black American hairdresser, Miss Thompson, whose beauty shop on Fulton Street is like a way station from which she oversees the comings and goings of all who pass. Miss Thompson's face is described as "an African wood carving: mysterious, omniscient, the features elongated by compassion, the eyes shrouded with a profound sadness." It is her priestly function to listen, comfort, direct. She presides over Selina's elevation to womanhood, giving her her first curls, pronouncing that she ain't no more child, and finally telling Selina the story of her own resistance to the brutality of racism. She is the link to Selina's larger community—to black Americans, whom the Bajans despise, to the Barbadians with whom she encourages Selina's reconciliation, and to her half-forgotten African past. Selina realizes the full effect of Miss Thompson's ministry when she has her first real encounter with racism and, though she is stunned and humiliated, ultimately reacts with outrage and affirmation of her oneness with her own people:

> She was one with Miss Thompson... one with the whores, the flashy men, and the blues rising sacredly above the plain of neon lights and ruined houses.... She was one with them: the mother and the Bajan women, who had lived each day what she had come to know.

A long line of characters before Selina discovered that they belonged to those armies of darkness and had to share that suffering in order to discover identity and integrity. John Grimes in Baldwin's *Go Tell It On The Mountain* struggles to free himself from this dark, despised, and rejected people, but he finally understands in a vision that "the body in the water, the body in the fire, the body on the tree" have claimed him. The Invisible Man awakes into darkness, and it is in the embrace of darkness that he, like Selina, finds illumination.

But the most powerful guide given to Selina is *the* mother, Silla Boyce. For all of her worship of Deighton, Selina experiences the most profound connection to her mother. So complex is her feeling

320

for Silla that she constantly vacillates between a loving awe and a violent angry distrust for Silla. Literature has rarely revealed so passionate a relationship between mother and daughter as we see in *Brown Girl.* In that tender scene after Deighton is deported, when Selina calls her mother Hitler and blames Silla for destroying the father, there is as much passion between them as there is anger. Selina strikes her mother's flesh until she falls exhausted and helpless against her mother's neck and then, reverently, Silla touches the tears, traces the outline of her face and smoothes her snarled hair, "Each caress declared that she was touching something which was finally hers alone."

In spite of this possessiveness, Silla never teaches Selina the ways of compromise nor female self-abnegation. In fact, she teaches her almost nothing of the "female" arts. She tolerates Selina's adventurous spirit with a grudging respect and in subtle ways encourages it. When Selina, at 13, begs to be allowed to go to Prospect Park without her older sister, Silla says with some annoyance: "What you need Ina for any more? You's more woman now than she'll ever be, soul. G'long." And her parting words when Selina is just seventeen years old reveal this same respect for her daughter's independent spirit:

G'long! You was always too much woman for me anyway, soul. And my own mother did say two head-bulls can't reign in a flock.

When Alice Walker says of her mother that she "handed down respect for the possibilities—and the will to grasp them," I am reminded of Silla Boyce and the legacy she passes to Selina. In all of her tirades and machinations, she never once tells Selina that she is less for being a woman, and in fact, with her own life she shows Selina that a woman is the central figure in her own life. The romantic side of Selina may very well be her father's doing, but that assertive, willful, forthright girl, taking her life into her own hands, managing city college and a full-time love affair at eighteen, is Silla Boyce's daughter.

At the end of the novel Selina makes the conscious, political choice to return to Barbados, to search out the lost meaning of her homeland, to discover what went wrong for her people in "this man country." She will not complete college as her mother has planned, nor will she, like Ina, fit into a neat Barbadian life, nor will she, like Clive, withdraw into self-pity. In making the choice to return to Barbados, to begin again, Selina symbolizes the community's need to reorder itself, to recognize the destruction of human values in a community devoted to money, ownership and power. *Brown Girl, Brownstones* is thus one of the most optimistic texts in Afro-American literature, for it assigns even to an oppressed people the power of conscious political choice: they are not victims.

When Selina dances at the end of the novel, we see her way of being in the world. Utterly dependent on her own body (as we all are), its huge old eyes, coarse hair, dark skin, she captures in womanly movements both the pain and beauty of life and embraces them both. She dances memory and passion, expressing her own individuality, her reflections of other people, and the needs of us all caught in this cycle of life and death. At the end of the dance she goes through the night towards the river and up to the East Side into marble and gilt halls where her new identity will be tested. There, with the strength of community, the power of the mother, she confronts truly her own dark depth and finds in that upheaval not Deighton's, not Silla's, not the Bajan community's—but her own Selina.

Like Selina, Paule Marshall, whose parents emigrated from Barbados during World War I, grew up in Brooklyn, New York; and like another one of her characters, Reena, she went to college there, graduating Phi Beta Kappa from Brooklyn College in 1953. After college she worked as a magazine researcher and eventually a writer for *Our World Magazine*. Gradually developing a sense of herself as a creative writer, Marshall began working at night on *Brown Girl, Brownstones;* in 1959, at age 30, she published that novel, which explores her own girlhood through the character of Selina Boyce. It is the novel that "paid homage" to the women who first instilled in her the gift of oral art. Two years later, in 1961, Marshall dealt with the problems of aging in her collection of short stories, *Soul Clap Hands and Sing.* In 1969 she published her most ambitious novel, *The Chosen Place, The Timeless People,* the story of a black woman, Merle Kibona, who emigrates to England, where she plans to go to school. But in London she is caught up in a vicious net, "taken in, like so many of us poor colonials come to big England to study, by the so-called glamor of the West." Merle's affair with a wealthy Englishwoman, the idleness and self-indulgence of a life without work, are part of the profound confusion in her past. Merle Kibona, the link to all black people in the Diaspora, carries Selina's quest to another level, for Merle wrestles with the corruption of history to find her place in the hemisphere, not just within the family. In 1982, Paule Marshall plans to publish her third novel, *Praisesong for the Widow,* continuing her obsession with history, with the need for black people to make the psychological and spiritual journey back through their past. The protagonist of this novel, Vernell Johnson, jumps a cruise ship in the West Indies and finds her way back to her ancestral home in the Sea Islands of South Carolina.

It is startling to realize that although Marshall has published three major books and numerous short stories and articles, she is just now—in the 1980s—being "discovered." During the 1960s she was a founding member of the Association of Artists for Freedom, a protest organization formed after the bombing of a Birmingham church in which four little black girls were killed. Along with James Baldwin and Amiri Baraka, Marshall was considered one of the aspiring young black writers in the 1960s; yet when Baldwin published *The Fire Next Time* in 1964, ushering in an era of popularity for black writers, Marshall's work remained unknown. With the exception of Lorraine Hansberry, black women writers remained obscure and unread during the decades dominated by civil rights and black nationalism. It was the decade of feminism that brought Paule Marshall to our attention. In 1970, the turning-point year for women writers (Kate Millett's *Sexual Politics,* Robin Morgan's *Sisterhood is Powerful,* and Shulamith Firestone's *The*

*Dialectic of Sex* all appeared then), her story "Reena" was republished in Toni Cade Bambara's anthology *The Black Woman,* and the literary presence and power of Paule Marshall were finally established.

It is fitting that Marshall should have been rediscovered through "Reena" because this story sounds all of Marshall's themes. Like most of her work, "Reena" is woman-centered, a very deliberate choice. In an interview in *Essence* magazine (May 1979) Marshall says that women figure prominently in her writing because their power shapes her work:

> I'm concerned about letting them speak their piece, letting them be central figures, actors, *activists* in fiction rather than just backdrop or background figures. I want them to be central characters. Women in fiction seldom are. Traditionally in most fiction men are the wheelers and dealers. They are the ones in whom power is invested. I wanted to turn that around. I wanted women to be the centers of power. My feminism takes its expression through my work. Women are central for me. They can as easily embody the power principles as a man.

Reena and her friend, Paulie, meet again as adults at the wake of Reena's Aunt Vi, a domestic whose life was spent sleeping in at the homes of wealthy white employers. Reena and Paulie, as representatives of the next generation, review Aunt Vi's past and their own, not for nostalgia, but to collect the strength and vision in that life: they must go back before they can go forward. Collect all of Marshall's characters—Selina Boyce, Merle Kibona, Miss Thompson, Reena, Vernell Johnson—and their journeys form a kind of reverse Middle Passage, taking them, and us, from the United States to the West Indies, to Africa, and back to the States again. These women, whose lives and traditions were forever changed by the Middle Passage, emerge under the pen of Paule Marshall as central figures in that history, determined to order the meaning of their past and to find in their spiritual strivings the means to construct a future.

*The Feminist Press at The City University of New York* offers alternatives in education and in literature. Founded in 1970, this nonprofit, tax-exempt educational and publishing organization works to eliminate stereotypes in books and schools and to provide literature with a broad vision of human potential. The publishing program includes reprints of important works by women, feminist biographies of women, multicultural anthologies, a cross-cultural memoir series, and nonsexist children's books. Curricular materials, bibliographies, directories, and a quarterly journal provide information and support for students and teachers of women's studies. Through publications and projects, The Feminist Press contributes to the rediscovery of the history of women and the emergence of a more humane society.

## NEW AND FORTHCOMING BOOKS

*The Answer/La Respuesta (Including a Selection of Poems),* by Sor Juana Inés de la Cruz. Critical edition and translation by Electa Arenal and Amanda Powell. $12.95 paper, $35.00 cloth.

*Australia for Women: Travel and Culture,* edited by Susan Hawthorne and Renate Klein. $17.95 paper.

*The Castle of Pictures and Other Stories: A Grandmother's Tales, Volume One,* by George Sand. Edited and translated by Holly Erskine Hirko. Illustrated by Mary Warshaw. $9.95 paper, $19.95 cloth.

*Challenging Racism and Sexism: Alternative to Genetic Explanations* (Genes & Gender VII), edited by Ethel Tobach and Betty Rosoff. $14.95 paper, $35.00 cloth.

*Folly,* a novel by Maureen Brady. Afterword by Bonnie Zimmerman. $12.95 paper, $35.00 cloth.

*Japanese Women: New Feminist Perspectives on the Past, Present, and Future,* edited by Kumiko Fujimura-Fanselow and Atsuko Kameda. $15.95 paper, $35.00 cloth.

*Shedding and Literally Dreaming,* by Verena Stefan. Afterword by Tobe Levin. $14.95 paper, $35.00 cloth.

*The Slate of Life: More Contemporary Stories by Women Writers of India,* edited by Kali for Women. Introduction by Chandra Talpade Mohanty and Satya P. Mohanty. $12.95 paper, $35.00 cloth.

*Songs My Mother Taught Me: Stories, Plays, and Memoir,* by Wakako Yamauchi. Edited and with an introduction by Garrett Hongo. Afterword by Valerie Miner. $14.95 paper, $35.00 cloth.

*Women of Color and the Multicultural Curriculum: Transforming the College Classroom,* edited by Liza Fiol-Matta and Mariam K. Chamberlain. $18.95 paper, $35.00 cloth.

Prices subject to change. *Individuals:* Send check or money order (in U.S. dollars drawn on a U.S. bank) to The Feminist Press at The City University of New York, 311 East 94th Street, New York, NY 10128-5684. Please include $3.00 postage/handling for one book, $.75 for each additional book. For VISA/MasterCard orders call (212) 360-5790. *Bookstores, libraries, wholesalers:* Feminist Press titles are distributed to the trade by Consortium Book Sales & Distribution, (800) 283-3572.